One More Night

NEW YORK TIMES BESTSELLING AUTHOR

BRENDA JACKSON

Previously published as *One Night with the Wealthy Rancher* and *Full Court Seduction*

Recycling programs for this product may not exist in your area.

ISBN-13: 978-1-335-40639-2

One More Night
First published as One Night with the Wealthy Rancher in 2009.
This edition published in 2021.
Copyright © 2009 by Harlequin Books S.A.

Special thanks and acknowledgment are given to
Brenda Jackson for her contribution to the
Texas Cattleman's Club: Maverick County Millionaires miniseries.

Full Court Seduction
First published in 2017. This edition published in 2021.
Copyright © 2017 by Synithia R. Williams

This edition published by arrangement with Harlequin Books S.A.

For questions and comments about the quality of this book, please contact us at CustomerService@Harlequin.com.

Harlequin Enterprises ULC
22 Adelaide St. West, 40th Floor
Toronto, Ontario M5H 4E3, Canada
www.Harlequin.com

Printed in U.S.A.

CONTENTS

ONE NIGHT WITH THE WEALTHY RANCHER   7
Brenda Jackson

FULL COURT SEDUCTION   163
Synithia Williams

Brenda Jackson is a *New York Times* bestselling author of more than one hundred romance titles. Brenda lives in Jacksonville, Florida, and divides her time between family, writing and traveling. Email Brenda at authorbrendajackson@gmail.com or visit her on her website at brendajackson.net.

Books by Brenda Jackson

Harlequin Desire

The Westmoreland Legacy

The Rancher Returns
His Secret Son
An Honorable Seduction
His to Claim
Duty or Desire

Forged of Steele

Seduced by a Steele
Claimed by a Steele

Visit the Author Profile page at
Harlequin.com for more titles.

ONE NIGHT WITH THE WEALTHY RANCHER

Brenda Jackson

To the love of my life, Gerald Jackson Sr.

To everyone who joined me on the Madaris/Westmoreland Family Reunion 2009 Cruise to Canada. This one is for you!

Provide things honest in the sight of all men.
—*Romans* 12:17

Chapter 1

"What are you doing here, Summer?"

Summer Martindale's eyes froze on the document in front of her at the sound of the husky voice. It was a voice she hadn't heard in almost seven years, yet she distinctively remembered the sensuous timbre and how every audible vibration could stir her senses in a way that even today she could not explain.

In a way she wished she could forget.

She inhaled deeply and after a moment, she lifted her eyes and stared into Darius Franklin's dark and intense gaze. It was a gaze that was emitting a chilling glare.

Summer could just as easily glare back but refused to let him know how disturbing it was to see him again. What had once been between them was over and done with. He had made sure of that in the worst possible way, which she could never forgive him for. His actions had caused her pain—a degree of pain she vowed never to experience again.

"I could ask you the same thing, Darius," she finally responded. Her tone was just as sharp as his had been.

He stood tall, all six foot one inches of him, as he leaned in the doorway with his arms crossed over his chest and his gaze fixed directly on her. She thought at that moment the very same thing she'd thought when she'd first laid eyes on him. Darius Franklin, with his pecan tan complexion, close-cut black hair, charcoal gray eyes and neat pencil-thin mustache, was an extremely handsome man. But there were other noticeable changes. His cheekbones appeared more pronounced and his lips seemed firmer.

His dark stare, as well as the way a muscle seemed to twitch in his jaw, were all the evidence she needed that he wasn't happy to see her and if truth be told, she wasn't happy to see him, either. It would be a lie to claim she hadn't thought about him over the years, because she had. Yet at the same time, the memory of what he'd put her through—the humiliation, heartbreak and pain—made her regret ever lowering her guard and letting him into her life.

He stepped away from the door and she watched his every move, wishing she weren't drawn to how fit his body was, and wishing a tug of desire had not invaded her stomach. Although he wasn't as lean as he used to be, he wore his masculinity well. Well-toned muscles outlined his chest and shoulders—muscles she could easily see through the material of his chambray shirt. And then there were jeans that hugged his firm hips and strong thighs. They were thighs that could keep a tight hold on hers as he thrust deeper and deeper inside of her.

She forced the turbulent memories away. Her gaze moved back up to his eyes and she tried not to flinch at the cold look in them. Something inside her shivered and she wondered how a man she had once fallen in love with so deeply could end up treating her so shabbily.

"I live here in Somerset."

His voice cut through Summer's thoughts. *He lived here in Somerset? Maverick County?* That information immediately filled her with apprehension and dread, as well as curiosity. *When had he left the Houston Police Department and why?*

"I live in Somerset, as well," she heard herself say. "I moved to town last month to work here at Helping Hands as a social worker."

Surprise lit his eyes. "A social worker?"

"Yes."

She understood his surprise. When he'd last seen her seven years ago, he'd been twenty-four years old and a detective with the Houston Police Department. And she'd been a nineteen-year-old trying to escape the clutches of an abusive fiancé by the name of Tyrone Whitman. After she had broken off their engagement, Tyrone had refused to get out of her life, to leave her alone. He had stalked her for months before he'd finally caught her alone in her apartment, and for three hours he had held a gun to her head, threatening to blow her brains out.

While the SWAT team had been trying to talk Tyrone into surrendering, Darius had broken into the apartment by coming through a bathroom window. He'd apprehended Tyrone and saved her. That night, Darius Franklin had become her knight in shining armor.

He was the same man who had stopped by her apartment the next day to repair the window, and the same man who, after learning that a not-too-smart judge had posted bail for Tyrone, made it his business to become her protector until the trial. After that, he was the same man who she began seeing on a daily basis, who would drop by when his shift changed to spend time with her, to show her how special he thought she was.

The same man who during that time, for one night, had been her lover.

"So, you went to college and got your degree?" he asked, and for a split second she could have sworn she detected a degree of admiration in his voice, but the look in his hard gaze told her she'd been wrong.

"Yes, I got my degree," she responded, proud of her accomplishment and quickly remembering he was one of the few people who'd encouraged her to do so, and convinced her that she could. He had made her believe in herself. And a part of her had believed in them, in a future together. He had proven her wrong.

"Congratulations."

"Thank you," she said briskly, putting aside the document she had been reading. "So, why are you here, Darius? Although we've established the fact that we're both living in Somerset, I'm sure this town is big enough for the both of us. What brings you to Helping Hands?"

"I'm here to install the security system as well as the billing account for the shelter," he said, as if that explained everything.

She nodded. "I was told the Texas Cattleman's Club would be sending someone over to do those things," she said, finding it hard to concentrate.

She had heard a lot about the Texas Cattleman's Club, a group of men who considered themselves the protectors of Texas and whose members consisted of the wealthiest men in Texas, mostly from old money. The TCC was known to help a number of worthy causes in the community and Helping Hands, a newly opened women's shelter located in the small, impoverished section of wealthy Maverick County, was one of them. They provided all the shelter's funding.

Summer had interviewed for the position at the shelter and once she had been offered the job, had decided it would be a good way to have a fresh start. She had made the move from Austin, where she had been living for the past six years.

"How did you get the job?" She couldn't help but ask.

He shrugged. "I own a security company."

She raised a brow, surprised he had gotten out of law enforcement. He'd made a good police detective and she'd figured it would be his career. "How long have you been living in Somerset?" she asked.

"Around six years."

It was the same amount of time she had lived in Austin. He had moved here a year after they had broken up. She quickly recalled that they really hadn't broken up since they had never truly been together…at least not like she'd assumed they had.

"If you're through with your interrogation, I'd like to get to work," he said.

"Fine. I'll get out of your way if you need to work in here for a while," she said, getting up from her desk. Seeing him again after all this time was just a bit too much. Bittersweet memories were trying to invade her brain and she was determined to fight them back.

"If you need anything, just let the shelter's secretary, Marcy Dillard, know. I'll use this time to go to lunch."

She grabbed her purse out of her desk drawer and quickly moved past him toward the door.

"Summer?"

She paused just before reaching the door and turned around. "Yes?"

He still had a hard look in his eyes. "I would say welcome to town, but I wouldn't mean it."

She narrowed her gaze. "Then I guess that means we'll have to learn to tolerate each other, doesn't it?"

Without waiting for him to respond, she turned and continued walking out the door.

Darius leaned back against the desk and watched Summer until she was no longer in sight. It was only then that he made an attempt to begin breathing normally again. But it was hard because although he couldn't see her, he still managed to feel her presence.

Seven years was a long time, yet today when a startled Summer had looked up at him and met his gaze, he'd felt a sensation that was like a swift kick in the gut. Potent memories had flooded his mind, forcing him to recall what she had come to mean to him in such a short period of time, and just how deep her betrayal had cut.

He hit his fist on the desk, angry and frustrated. How could he still find her so desirable after all this time? After all she'd done? Why had seeing her sent sensuous shivers down his spine? She was seven years older, no longer a mere nineteen-year-old who hadn't decided what she wanted out of life other than to be free of an obsessive ex-fiancé. She was just as stunning as he remembered. Even more so.

She had matured beautifully. She was about five-eight, tall and slim with shoulder-length straight brown hair and hazel eyes he could always drown in. Her skin tone, the color of café au lait, had always tempted him to lick her all over.

Darius bowed his head momentarily as even more memories he had tried so hard to forget resurfaced.

After college, he'd gotten a job with the Houston Police Department as a detective with aspirations of moving up the ranks. Authorities had been called to the scene regarding a domestic dispute, and Darius and his partner, Walt Stewart, had been the first to arrive.

A young woman who had obtained a restraining order against her ex-fiancé was in danger. The man, named Tyrone Whitman, had broken into her apartment and was holding a gun to her head, threatening to kill her unless she took him back.

While Walt tried talking him into surrendering, Darius was able to get into the apartment through a rear bathroom window, overtake Whitman and free Summer.

Concern for her safety when Whitman was released on bond allowed Darius to convince himself that it was important to keep checking on her. But then it became obvious it was a lot more than that. Point-blank, he had been attracted to her and thought she was a special woman who'd gotten mixed up with the wrong guy, and was trying to get her life together. Against his better judgment, although he'd been warned by Walt that Summer wasn't really what she seemed, he had fallen for her, and fallen hard.

He'd assumed he had gotten to know her, and thought she felt the same way after a night they had spent together filled with so much sexual chemistry that it could only end one way: they had made love. Deep, passionate love. Shudders passed through him just remembering that night and the effect it had on him. It was a night he could never forget, although over the past seven years he had tried like hell to do so.

And it was a night that apparently had meant more to him than it had to her.

The following day he had left town when he received word of his brother Ethan's near-fatal car accident. He'd had to leave immediately for Charleston and when he couldn't reach Summer, and had been unable to leave her a message because her voice-mail box was full, he'd left word with his partner to let her know what happened. When he had returned to Houston a week later, he discovered that Summer had packed up and left town without leaving word as to where she'd gone. She'd told Walt to tell him that she wanted to build a new life for herself and was leaving town with an older man. A very wealthy one—something Darius was not.

After nearly losing his brother, it had almost destroyed him to find out that he had lost her, that she had turned her back on what could have been between them to take up with a man with money.

A hard smile formed on his lips and he wondered what she would think to discover that he was now a wealthy man, thanks to smart investments and the success of his security firm. She thought he'd been hired as a laborer for the TCC—he could just imagine her reaction when she discovered he was a member of the Texas Cattleman's Club. The same club that was funding the shelter, including her salary.

Another thought crept into his mind, one that made his skin crawl. What if she knew already? What if the reason she was in Somerset was because she'd heard about his success and assumed after all this time she could ease her way back in his good graces? A woman looking for a wealthy husband would do just about anything. He'd been gullible before and wondered if she thought he would be gullible again. Considering her actions seven years ago, he wouldn't put anything past her.

He leaned against her desk as those thoughts filled his mind. She wasn't wearing a ring on her finger, which was a good indication that she wasn't married. And she *had* acted surprised to see him. But then it could have very well been an act. He had found out the hard way just what a good actress she was. One thing was for certain: he wouldn't be letting his guard down. She had taken advantage of his heart before but she wouldn't be doing so again.

He was about to begin the work he'd come to do when his cell phone went off. Recognizing the special ringtone, he pulled it off his belt and clicked it on. "Yes, Lance?"

"Hey, man, sorry I missed your call earlier."

"No problem. I just wanted you to know that I heard from Fire Chief Ingle. I'm meeting with him tomorrow evening to go over some things. He indicated that he'll have the official report ready in a week and that it contains proof that the fire was deliberately set."

Lance Brody was Darius's best friend from college at the University of Texas, where the two of them, along with another good friend, Kevin Novak, had been roommates. The three had forged a bond that would last a lifetime. There was nothing one wouldn't do for the other and Darius could rightly say that he could give his two friends credit for his financial success.

Lance, along with his younger brother Mitch, had come from old money and together they owned Brody

Oil and Gas Company. The two had included Darius in a number of successful investment opportunities. So had Kevin, who'd made his fortune in real estate development.

Lance and Kevin had grown up in Somerset and had tried convincing Darius to move there after college but he had opted for the job in Houston instead. Then, shortly after that incident with Summer, he'd decided he would move to Somerset to start a new career and a new life.

He worked closely with his friends, and Lance had hired him to investigate a fire at the Brody Oil and Gas refinery a few weeks ago. Although there was significant damage, no one had gotten seriously hurt. Darius had no doubt the fire had been the work of an arsonist, and now Chief Ingle had confirmed his suspicions.

"I can't wait until we nail Alex. I intend to make sure that he rots in jail," Lance was saying.

Lance and Mitch were certain they knew the identity of the arsonist. He was the longtime hated rival of the Brodys, a man by the name of Alejandro "Alex" Montoya.

"Calm down, Lance. The man is innocent until proven guilty," Darius said.

"Wait until the report comes out. Mark my word, Alex Montoya is the person behind that fire."

"That may very well be the case," Darius said, knowing just how convinced Lance was of Alex's guilt. "But it has to be proven. How's Kate?" Darius asked, trying to change the subject. Lance and Kate had eloped to Vegas a few weeks ago.

"Kate's fine and I know what you're trying to do, Darius."

Darius couldn't help but chuckle. "If you know, then humor me. I need like hell to laugh about now."

"Sounds like it's been one of those days for you," Lance said.

"You don't know the half of it. Summer is here."

There was a pause. "Summer? *Your* Summer?"

Darius could have really laughed out loud at that one, since Summer had never truly been his. But at one time he'd thought she was, and he had told Lance all about her. "Yes, Summer Martindale."

"What's she doing in Somerset?"

Darius sighed deeply. "She's a social worker at Helping Hands. I showed up to set up security and work on the billing system for the place, and walked right into her office."

"Must have been one hell of a reunion."

"Hey, what can I say?"

Lance chuckled. "You can say you need a drink. Sounds like it, anyway. Meet me at the TCC Café when you're ready to take a break for lunch."

Moments later, Darius hung up the phone thinking Lance was right. He needed a drink.

Summer settled into the booth at the Red Sky Café three blocks from the shelter. It was the first week of August and such a beautiful day that she had enjoyed the walk. It had given her a chance to compose herself after seeing Darius again.

She glanced around the café. The Red Sky was a place she had been frequenting for lunch since working at Helping Hands and she had become friendly with the owners. The Timmons had grown up in this section of Maverick County and had been instrumental in approaching members of the TCC about the need for a shelter in the community.

The shelter was a full-service center that provided a safe place for women who'd experienced all types of violence to heal and plan for their future. Helping Hands had opened their doors a few months ago and she'd been hired as part of its counseling team. Summer couldn't help but appreciate the members of the Texas Cattleman's Club for funding the shelter. She of all people knew how important such a facility was.

She had dated Tyrone for a few months, but it was only after they'd gotten engaged that she'd discovered his mean-spirited, possessive nature that on occasion would become abusive, both mentally and physically. She had sought the help of a shelter in Houston and there had found the strength to break things off with him. The social worker at the shelter had helped her to see that although she couldn't control Tyrone's behavior toward her, she could control how she responded to it and remove herself from the situation.

Her choice to end things was something Tyrone couldn't accept and he had begun stalking her, which was the reason she'd put the restraining order in place. Months had gone by when he'd appeared at her apartment one night, and forced his way inside, threatening her life. Chills went up her spine as she remembered that time.

After her own horrible experience with Tyrone, not to mention her heartbreak with Darius, she didn't trust her instincts where men were concerned so she just left them alone. Over the years she had buried herself in her books, getting her degree. After college she had concentrated on her work as an advocate for battered women.

"What are you going to have today, Miss Martindale?"

Summer smiled as she glanced up into the face of Tina Kay, one of the waitresses. Tina had been one of her first clients at Helping Hands and at seventeen, one of her youngest. A runaway after being shifted from foster home to foster home, Tina had become the victim of physical abuse at the hands of her boyfriend, a guy who had convinced her she deserved the beatings he'd been giving her.

Summer couldn't help but recall her own story. After high school, she had wanted to see the world. Aunt Joanne, who had raised her after her parents had been killed in a car accident when she was thirteen, tried to get her to remain in Birmingham. But she'd left Alabama to work her way to California. Along the way, she ended up in Houston where she found a job as a waitress at a chain restaurant. That's where she'd met Tyrone. The company he worked for frequently made deliveries to the restaurant. Something told her he was bad news, but she had wanted to believe there was some good in him. Boy, had she been wrong.

"Just the usual," Summer finally said, relaxing in her seat, looking forward to her grilled chicken salad.

She took a moment to study Tina, who looked so different than the young woman who'd come to the shelter with a swollen eye, cuts around her mouth and bruises on various parts of her body. "And how have you been doing, Tina?" she asked.

Tina's smile widened. "I've been doing fine. The Timmons are letting me use the apartment above their garage. I've enrolled to take classes at the local community college next month and thought I'd brush up on my math.

That's always been my weakest subject. I ordered one of those do-it-yourself math books online."

"And how are those self-defense classes going?" The shelter offered the classes weekly and attendance was always at capacity.

"They've been great. The instructor is just awesome. I've learned a number of techniques to protect myself."

She could hear the excitement in Tina's voice and felt good about it. The man who had roughed Tina up had left town but there was a warrant out for his arrest. Summer's thoughts shifted to Tyrone, who'd gotten a twenty-year sentence. It would have been less if he hadn't told the judge just where he could shove it. She shook her head, wondering how she could have ever thought that she loved the man. She could now admit that at eighteen she had been young and rather foolish.

"I'll be back with your order in a second," Tina said.

When Tina walked off, Summer settled back in her seat, allowing herself to think about the man she'd left at the shelter. The one man she had tried so hard to forget. She'd thought moving to Somerset would be a fresh start. A new town. New people. A new job. She hadn't figured on being confronted with a blast from her past.

One thing she told the women she counseled at the shelter was that they could confront and conquer any challenge they were presented with, and she knew she needed to take that same advice. Fate was playing a cruel trick by putting her and Darius in the same town. But she would handle it. And she would handle him.

An irritated and frustrated Darius walked into the TCC Café and glanced around at his surroundings. What used to be a twenty-six-room mansion had been converted into a place where the TCC members could unwind and relax, which was just what he needed.

In addition to the café, the TCC also included a golf course, a state-of-the-art spa, riding stables and an air-conditioned pool house with a retractable roof as well as numerous meeting rooms, game rooms, a well-stocked library and a formal dining room.

Darius, Lance and Kevin, along with Mitch and another friend of the Brodys named Justin Dupree, spent a lot of time shooting pool in the game room. Last fall they were practically glued to the club's projection television screen during football season.

He saw Lance sitting at a table in the back. The café served both lunch and dinner and it wasn't uncommon for Lance to meet him here for lunch. However, nowadays Lance was quick to rush back to the office since his new wife Kate had decided to remain at Brody Oil and Gas as Lance's administrative assistant.

Darius shook his head. Knowing Lance the way he did, he doubted his best friend let Kate get much work done. Hell, he wouldn't either if he had the woman he loved pretty much underfoot all day.

The woman he loved.

Something twisted in his gut at the thought. Thanks to Summer, he doubted he would ever be able to love another woman again.

"I need a beer," he said, frowning, sliding into the booth across from Lance.

"I've already ordered you one. I was looking out the window when you drove up," Lance said, studying Darius carefully.

"Thanks. I had hoped to at least get the security analysis completed on most of the computers today so I can decide what software will work best," Darius said, smiling a thanks to the waitress who placed a mug of beer in front of him.

"So, you're going to do it instead of one of your men?"

Darius nodded. "Heath left yesterday for Los Angeles to guard some actress who's been getting death threats, and Milt is still in Dallas," he said of two of the six men who worked for him. "The others have been assigned to various other projects around town. That means I'll have to go back over to the shelter when I leave here."

Lance nodded as he took a plug from his own beer. "It also means you'll be seeing Summer again."

Darius didn't say anything. Yes, that meant he would probably see Summer again today. No telling how many more times he'd see her before he finished up what needed to be done at the shelter.

Because of the nature of what went on at women's shelters, Helping Hands needed top security twenty-four hours a day, seven days a week. The TCC had decided to upgrade all the computers to eliminate the risk of getting hacked. The majority of the women seeking refuge at the shelter were the victims of domestic violence, women whose lives could be placed in danger if their batterers discovered their whereabouts.

"Tell me about her, Darius."

Darius met Lance's gaze. "I've practically told you everything about how we met and how things ended. She went to college and got a degree, and now works for the shelter."

"Did you mention anything to her about being a member of TCC?"

"No. She thinks my company was hired to handle security at the shelter."

Lance smiled. "In a way, that's true."

"Yes, which is why she doesn't need to know any different." Darius felt his face harden when he said, "There can never be anything between me and Summer again."

Yet he knew making sure of that wouldn't be easy. Summer was the type of woman who easily got under a man's skin. Just the memory of walking into that office and finding her sitting behind the desk had the power to make him feel weak and vulnerable.

And that was the one thing he could not let happen. He did not have a special woman in his life and preferred keeping it that way. Desire for anything more had died seven years ago with Summer's betrayal.

Chapter 2

"Mr. Franklin wanted me to let you know he left for lunch but will be coming back, Ms. Martindale."

"Oh. Thanks, Marcy," Summer said, trying to keep her voice as normal as she could. After taking a file off Marcy's top tray, she went into her office and closed the door behind her.

Today she had taken an extra-long lunch, hoping by the time she returned Darius would have finished what he'd come to do. But it seemed that would not be the case. Summer bit her lip, deciding she would be professional as well as mature about the matter. He had a job to do and so did she, and as long as they each knew where the other stood, there was no reason they couldn't at least be decent to each other. But then what right did he have to be upset with her since she was the injured party? He was the one who'd left town after discussing their night together with his partner. He probably didn't know Walt had told her the truth, and he was upset because she had left town when he'd returned. It was crazy how men thought sometimes, but it didn't matter now. He had made it quite clear what he thought of her and she hoped she'd left no doubt in his mind just what she thought of him. So there. That was that.

She dropped down in her chair thinking, no, that wasn't that at all. Not as long as the sight of him could send sensations oozing up her spine. Whenever he looked at her, even with anger flaring in the dark depths of his eyes, she felt stirrings in places she didn't want to think about. He'd always had that effect on her. In the past she'd welcomed it, but now she despised it.

She drew in a deep breath and for the first time in years, she felt like the world was closing in on her. It had taken her a while after leaving Houston to pull herself together and decide that no man—Tyrone or Darius— was worth that much pain. But she had moved on with her life. She was proud of her accomplishment and intended to obtain her doctorate after working in her field a few years.

"Don't you have anything to do?"

Summer blinked and saw Darius standing in her doorway. She glared at him—so much for thinking they could be decent to each other. "You should have knocked before entering my office."

He shrugged. "The door was open."

"And that gives you the right to just walk in? I could have been with a client."

"In that case, I would hope you'd be professional enough to shut the door for privacy. But you aren't with a client *and* you knew I was coming back, so stop making a big deal out of it," he said, stepping into her office and closing the door behind him.

Summer just stared at him for a moment, wondering how on earth the two of them were supposed to get along. Of course, whoever hired him had no idea they knew each other, and there was no way she could go to anyone at the TCC and request that they swap security companies without a valid reason.

"Look, Darius. You have a job to do and so do I. Evidently, I'm the last person you expected to see today. However, we're professionals and are mature enough to make the best of it. It shouldn't take you more than a day at the most to finish up here and—"

"Wrong."

She lifted her brow. "Excuse me?"

He crossed his arms over his chest. "I said you're wrong. Finishing up things here will take me every bit of a week. Possibly two."

His words hit her like a ton of bricks. "You've got to be kidding."

"I don't kid."

She pressed her lips together to keep from saying, *No, but you do kiss and tell.* Instead, she asked, "Why will it take *that* long to install a security system?"

There was a pause. A long pause. And for a moment, she wasn't sure he was going to answer her.

"The reason it will take so long is because in addition to installing a new security system on all the computers in this building, I'll be setting up a billing system for the Texas Cattleman's Club. I'm getting paid well to do a good job and I don't intend to do otherwise by rushing through things just to make your life less miserable."

"My life isn't miserable," she all but snapped.

"Sorry. It was foolish of me to assume that it was. And I see you're not wearing a ring so I guess you didn't get a rich husband after all."

Summer wondered what he was talking about and decided she really didn't want to know. "Look, Darius—"

He moved to her desk so quickly she jerked back in her chair. He placed his palms down on her desk and leaned over, his face within inches of hers. "No, you look, Summer. You're right, we are two professionals. Two adults who just happened to have had an affair that led to nowhere. I'm over it and so are you. So let's move on."

"Fine," she snapped.

"Great." He straightened his tall form, moved away from her desk and looked at a closet door across the room. "Unfortunately, the mainframe is in this office so I'll be spending more time in here than any other place. You might be inconvenienced a few times."

"If I'm scheduled to meet with clients, I'll use one of the vacant conference rooms," she said, trying to keep her voice civil.

He nodded. "And if you're not scheduled to meet with a client?"

"I have the ability to work through distractions."

He lifted a brow and held her gaze for a moment. "Do you?"

"Yes."

"Then we don't have anything to worry about," he said, looking at his watch. "Are you meeting with a client sometime today?"

"No, I just have paperwork to do. Will you be shutting down my computer?" She could tell they were both trying to be courteous and hold a decent conversation in less-than-biting tones. But in spite of everything, she couldn't stop the sensations that stirred inside of her every time she looked into his eyes.

"No, but if that changes I'll give you advanced warning."

"Thank you."

He moved to the other side of the room. "Right now I need to get into this closet."

She swallowed as she stared at him under her lashes. His hands were on his hips, unconsciously drawing emphasis to his jean-clad hips and thighs. Tapered. Perfectly honed.

Deciding she had seen enough—probably too much—she picked up a file off her desk, leaned back in her chair and began reading. She tried like heck to concentrate on the document in front of her, but every so often she would look up and glance over at Darius. He was standing in front of a huge unit that had a bunch of wires running from it. He was concentrating on the computer's mainframe but her eyes were concentrated on him, drinking him in with feminine appreciation. He might be an arrogant ass but he was a good-looking one.

And as if he could feel her eyes on him, he looked up and met her gaze. Their eyes held for a moment longer than necessary before she dropped hers back to the document in front of her, thinking, *so much for working through distractions.*

Darius stared at Summer. Although he wished he were anyplace else other than here, he couldn't stop looking at her and remembering. She had gone back to reading, so he let his gaze travel over her, noticing the way her shoulder-length hair had fallen in her face. She absently brushed it back, giving him a view of her face once again. It was a face that had been his downfall the first time he'd seen it.

He could vividly recall just when that had been. After crawling through her bathroom window, she had seen him before Whitman had known he was in the house. With eye contact, Darius had encouraged her to stay calm and not give him away. Using the training he'd acquired, it had taken only a couple of quick kicks to bring Whitman down. He hit the ground before he'd realized what had happened to him.

It was then that a nearly traumatized Summer had rushed into his arms, holding on to him as if her life depended on it. Even after the police officers had rushed in and handcuffed Whitman, she had still held on to him, like she was too shaken to let him out of her sight. Since it had been almost quitting time, he had followed the squad car that had taken her to the hospital to get checked out. He'd also dropped by her place the next day to repair her broken window.

During the weeks that followed, he would find some excuse or other to see her, and when he'd learned that her ex had been let out on bail, he had made it a point to drive by her house a couple of times a night just to make sure she was okay. Most of the time they would sit in her living room and talk.

During that time Summer had shared a lot about her life. He knew she had been raised by an aunt and that she had left her hometown of Birmingham, Alabama, for California with dreams of becoming an actress or, better yet, to find a rich older man to marry. At the time he'd thought she was teasing, but he'd discovered a few months later she'd been dead serious.

He'd found out the hard way that while he had been falling in love with her, she had been looking for a man with a lot more money than he'd had.

He fought back the anger that tried consuming him all over again, anger that seven years hadn't erased. He must have muttered something under his breath because she looked up and again their eyes met.

He tried looking away but couldn't. And when he moved to close the closet he told himself to head straight for the door and walk out. However, he couldn't do that, either.

Instead, he found himself crossing the room to where she was sitting. Although he had tried to forget it, he was still bothered by the fact that she had left him for another man. A man who had been old enough to be her father from what he'd heard.

By the time he reached her, she was standing. "What is wrong with you?" she asked, backing away from him until her back hit a solid wall and she couldn't go any farther.

His lips curved into a forced smile. "There's nothing wrong with me, Summer."

"Then what do you think you're doing?" she asked in a whisper.

"You still ask too many questions," he murmured, just seconds before leaning in and capturing her mouth with his.

The instant their mouths touched it registered in Summer's brain that she didn't have to accept his kiss. She could outright refuse it. However, any thoughts of doing so tumbled from her mind as he expertly took control of her mouth in a way she remembered so well.

His tongue surged between her parted lips and the moment it tangled with hers, she was a goner. Instead of being swamped with memories of the past, she was overtaken by sensations from the present, where he was causing a stir within her so effortlessly.

And it wasn't just about tongue play; it was a lot more than that. It was about body heat and the way she felt pressed against him, with his arms wrapped firmly around her waist and hers finding their way around his neck.

And then it was about a need. She could not characterize his, but she could certainly define her own. It had been seven years since she had been kissed by a man. Seven years of denying herself this one particular pleasure as well as numerous others. Those denials, especially the primal ones, were coming back to haunt her in the worst kind of way, thanks to him.

And then, she thought, when he pulled her body closer to his, closer to his heat, there was the idea, the very fact, that after all this time she was still attracted to him and he to her. Some things couldn't change. There was the chemistry, physical attraction, sexual tension. Lust was a strong benefactor, especially when motivated and fueled by sexual need.

He changed the angle of his mouth to deepen the kiss and tightened his hold around her waist. And then he used his tongue to taste her in a way he'd never done before. It was as if he were trying to get reacquainted with her flavor, sliding his tongue from one side of her mouth to the other.

Then, in a move she could only deem as sensuously strategic, he captured her tongue with his and began mating with it in a way that nearly brought her to her knees. He was building desire within her, slowly escalating their fiery exchange. Her hands moved from his neck to his shoulders, and then she spread her palms over his back as he elicited a response from her that she felt in every pore of her body.

Despite the greedy protest of her lips, he finally pulled his mouth away from hers. She drew in a much-needed breath. The kiss had been totally unexpected—completely without warning—and had managed to leave her breathless, speechless, with her senses heightened to their full capacity.

And then reality returned. She stiffened, determined that he would not assume the kiss would be the first of many, or that he was on the verge of finding his way back into her heart with the sole purpose of finding his way back into her bed.

Too late she began berating herself for letting the kiss last as long as it had. He was staring at her and she wondered if the kiss—especially the intensity of it—had been some kind of point he'd wanted to make. Probably, but she had news for him.

"If you want to keep your job, Darius, I would advise you to never do that again," she said in a cutting tone. "If you do, I will report your actions to the Texas Cattleman's Club. I'm sure there are other security companies they could use to do what you were hired to do."

She thought she saw a smile touch his lips before his gaze narrowed slightly. "Does it matter that you kissed me back? Moaned in my ear? Rubbed your body against mine?" he asked with a hint of scorn in his voice.

Summer felt heat flush her cheeks. Had she actually done all those things while they'd been kissing? Okay, she had returned his kiss, possibly even moaned a few times in his ear, but had she really rubbed her body against his? Due to the intensity of the exchange, that may very well have been a possibility. But that didn't mean she'd given him free rein to enjoy her mouth anytime the mood suited him. She needed to make sure he understood that.

"Fair warning, Darius. Kevin Novak of the TCC will be meeting with me this week to see how things are going at the shelter, and we'll be discussing ways that things around here can be improved. I'm sure getting this job was a feather in your cap and I'd hate to ask that you be replaced, but I will if you don't keep your hands to yourself."

His gaze locked on to hers for longer than necessary, and then he stepped back. Evidently, he realized she hadn't just made an idle threat. There was a long silence as they stood there staring at each other and then to her surprise, he smiled and said, "You enjoyed that kiss just as much as I did and I will bring up that fact to Mr. Novak if he questions me about anything. If you're thinking about putting me on the hot seat, then be ready to join me there. The TCC hired you to do a job, just like they hired me."

His dark eyes hardened. "And need I remind you that I've been living in Somerset a lot longer than you have? People around here know I'm a professional who's selective when it comes to friends. I have a tarnish-free reputation. This is a nice town, close-knit. You're the stranger here, Summer, not me. But I will heed your wishes. The next kiss, you'll initiate. Until then, you're safe with me."

She lifted her chin, wondering when he had become so arrogant, so sure of himself. For him to assume she would make a move on him was outright preposterous. "That won't happen."

He smiled. "Then I guess that means you're safe with me."

She was about to give him a blistering retort when his cell phone rang. "Excuse me," he said, and Summer watched as he quickly pulled it from his belt clip. She figured it was probably some woman calling him.

He muttered a few words to the caller and then glanced back at her and said, "I need to take this call. Remember what I said." And then he turned and walked out of her office.

Darius strolled into the lobby of the shelter, a safe distance from Summer's office, yet close enough so he could see if she left. He pulled in a deep breath and then remembered he had Kevin holding on the phone.

"Okay, Kev, I can talk now. What's up?"

"Just a reminder we're meeting at the TCC's game room Thursday night to shoot pool."

Darius couldn't help but grin. If Kev was calling to remind everyone, that meant he was feeling lucky. "I won't forget."

"Where are you?" Kevin asked.

"At Helping Hands. I decided to install the security system myself since I'm the one who's going to set up TCC's billing account for the shelter. Besides, all my men are handling other projects."

Darius then remembered something. "Your name came up in a conversation I had with the social worker here, Summer Martindale. You're supposed to meet with her sometime this week."

"Yeah, don't remind me. That was something Huntington was supposed to do and he delegated it to me like he's the king and I'm one of his lowly subjects. That man really grates on my last nerve."

Darius understood just how Kevin felt. He, Lance, Mitch and Justin all felt the same way. The five of them, along with Alex Montoya, were the most recent inductees into the Texas Cattleman's Club. This didn't sit well with some of the club's old guards—namely Sebastian Huntington and his stuffy cohorts—who for some reason felt the younger men really weren't deserving of membership in what was known as the most exclusive social club in the state of Texas.

"Hey, man, I thought all of us agreed to just overlook Huntington and his band of fools," Darius reminded his friend.

"Yeah, but he just rubs me the wrong way at times. He doesn't want to put his full support behind the shelter since the funding of it was our idea and not his."

"But he was outvoted, so eventually he'll get over it," Darius said. "And if he doesn't, then that's too bad. Maybe it's a good thing that he's having you do it instead of him. He wouldn't do anything but find fault with everything anyway."

"You're probably right. So, you've met Ms. Martindale?"

"Yes. She's the Summer I was involved with before moving here to Somerset."

"Damn, man, she's *that* Summer?"

"Yes, she is *that* Summer." Kevin didn't know as much about what had happened as Lance, but both of his best friends knew Summer had screwed him over in a bad way, which was the reason he'd wanted to leave Houston and start a new life here in Somerset.

"I need you to do me a favor," he said to Kevin.

"Sure. What do you need?"

It had always been this way between him, Lance and Kevin since their college days. Kevin had agreed to the favor without even knowing what would be required of him. The three trusted each other implicitly. "I'll go into full details when I see you Thursday night, but when you meet with Summer Martindale, if my name comes up, I don't want it mentioned that I'm affiliated with the TCC."

"No problem."

Darius had made the decision to tell Summer the truth when he was good and ready. He couldn't wait to see her face when she realized he was probably just as wealthy as the old man she had left him for.

He and Kevin began talking about the update he'd gotten on the fire at the Brody refinery. Darius was listening to Kevin's take on why he thought Alex Montoya was responsible when he heard footsteps on the tile floor. He glanced up to see Summer walking out of her office. He was standing behind a pillar, so she didn't have a full view of him, which to his way of thinking was a good thing. That way he could check her out at his leisure.

She walked over to a row of file cabinets and he quickly recalled that he'd always thought her walk was a turn-on. There was a sexy sway to her hips with every step she took. She was wearing a pair of brown slacks and a light blue blouse. The lush curves of her hips and the firm swell of her breasts were outlined to perfection by her outfit. He couldn't help standing there staring, taking in everything about her. He easily picked up on the differences in her, differences that, considering everything, he still couldn't help but appreciate.

She seemed a lot more self-assured, had taken owner-ship of her life and didn't easily back down from a fight. She certainly didn't have any problems trying to put him in his place earlier. The key word was *trying*. As far as he was concerned, when it came to her, he didn't have a place, especially not one she could put him in.

He should not have kissed her. But in all honesty, he could not have *not* kissed her. And now that he had, he wanted to kiss her again. Hold her in his arms. Take her to bed.

Darius tightened his hand in a fist at his side, not lik-ing the way his thoughts were going and liking even less that he wanted to do those things with the same woman who had crushed his heart. But her response to the kiss had caught him off guard—her complete surrender had made him hard in a way he hadn't been in years.

He had forced himself to end the kiss before he'd taken a mind to do something stupid like take her on her desk. He had been that far gone and she had been right there with him, although she'd gotten a little hot behind the collar later.

"Darius? You still there?"

His concentration was pulled back into the phone conversation, and he was trying like heck to recall what Kevin had just said. "Look, Kev, I'll get back with you later. There's something I need to do before it gets too late."

"Sure, man."

After snapping the phone shut, Darius walked toward Summer. She glanced in his direction with a surprised look on her face. "I thought you had left."

He forced a smile. "I'm sure you were hoping so, but I'm not the type who takes off without letting a person know why, unless there is reason outside of my control. Not like some people."

She glared at him. "And just what is that supposed to mean?"

"Think about it. When you do, it won't take you long to figure things out. I'll be back tomorrow."

Without giving her a chance to say anything else, he walked away.

Darius tried to keep his composure as he eased his long legs into his car. Moments later, after he'd driven away from the shelter and was headed toward home, he let out the expletive that he'd been holding back. Summer was certainly playing the innocent act well, having the gall to pretend she hadn't a clue what he was talking about when he'd thrown out his dig. He couldn't help but wonder what else she was concealing. For all he knew she could very well know about his vast wealth or his membership in the TCC.

He tightened his grip on the steering wheel. Despite the deep animosity he was feeling toward her, his body refused to deny that it wanted her. She could stir embers of passion within him without saying a word. All it took was a look, her presence or her scent to bring his libido to full awareness. He had to do something about her. She had invaded his comfort zone. His space.

For six years he'd been living in Somerset, enjoying peace and harmony. Of all the cities for her to relocate to, why Somerset? Avoiding her wasn't an option, although it would make his life a whole heck of a lot easier. Her very presence unsettled him in the worst way.

He breathed in deeply and fought back the anger that was getting him riled all over again. If she wanted to pretend, then two could play that game. He was in a position to teach her the very lesson she deserved to learn. She'd wanted a rich husband and in his own way, he would let her know just how she'd lost out on one. He would bide his time, get on her good side and then, when she assumed things were going great between them, after he'd gotten her back in his bed, he would do the very same thing to her that she had done to him.

Walk away without looking back.

Chapter 3

The following morning, with butterflies floating around in her stomach, Summer swiped her security card through the scanner before stepping into the shelter, hoping she was early enough to have arrived before Darius. He was the last person she wanted to see. She hadn't gotten much sleep last night and he was the reason. She'd been unable to get the kiss they'd shared yesterday out of her head.

As she made her way toward her office, she refused to even consider the reason why she'd taken more time getting dressed this morning than she usually did: Why she had spent a good ten minutes more putting on her makeup and why had she pulled out the curling iron for the first time in weeks.

When she stopped at Marcy's desk, she checked her watch. Marcy wasn't due in for another hour or so. Summer unlocked Marcy's desk to retrieve a clipboard that listed all her appointments and meetings for that day. Perusing the clipboard, she began to see what her day was going to be like.

"You look nice today."

Summer didn't bother to turn around. She didn't have to. She had left home with a made-up mind that no matter what, she was not going to let Darius rattle her. She was not going to allow him to make her come unglued and she would not look for condescension in his every word. So with that resolve, she would take his compliment in stride and assume he meant no more by it than what was said.

She turned around and her hands automatically tightened on the clipboard the moment she did so. She then swallowed deeply as the nervous sensations stirring in her stomach escalated. How was it possible that he looked even better today than yesterday? He was casually but impeccably dressed. A different pair of jeans and a different shirt, but the utterly breathtaking look was still there. All lean. Well-defined muscles. Perfect abs. And with the tan-colored Stetson sitting on his head, tilted at an angle that shadowed his dark brows, she couldn't help but admit he was truly a fine, handsome specimen of a man.

"Thank you for the compliment. You look nice, also," she heard herself say, determined not to get in a sparring match with him. "Will you need to be in my office today?"

"No, I'll be working in the other offices the majority of the day, other than when I start setting up the accounting for the TCC. It will be a while before I start on that."

She nodded, not wanting to prolong her time with him. "Then I guess I need to let you get started."

"How about lunch?"

She stared up at him, certain she had misunderstood. "Excuse me?"

He smiled and she felt a semblance of heat stirring in her blood, through her veins, in a number of other places she didn't want to think about. "I asked if you wanted to do lunch with me."

"Why?" She couldn't help but ask.

"Why not? You gotta eat and so do I."

"But that doesn't mean we have to share a meal," she pointed out.

His smile widened and the heat stirring in her blood intensified. "No, but it would mean that we're trying to put the past behind us and move on," he said. "It's not like we're going to become bosom buddies, because we aren't. But I'll be hanging around here for the next couple of weeks, so we might as well learn how to get along. I'm not going anywhere and I doubt you are, either. So, what about lunch?"

"I'm not sure that would be a good idea, Darius."

"What was it that you said yesterday? Oh, yes, your very words were, 'We're professionals and are mature enough to make the best of it.'"

Summer breathed in deeply. Yes, those had been her very words.

"I promise not to bite."

She opened her mouth to say something and changed her mind, quickly shutting it. A twist of emotions rumbled in her chest and she knew why. Darius was offering the olive branch, the chance to move on and put what they'd once shared behind them since there was no way it could ever happen again. And deep down she knew she needed that.

She couldn't continue carrying the bitterness of the last seven years. If they were doomed to live in the same town and would be running into each other on occasion, at least they could be civil to each other. But there was no chance of them ever getting back together. For her, the pain had gone too deep.

"Lunch will be fine," she heard herself say, hoping she didn't live to regret it.

"Great. You pick the place, just as long as they sell good hamburgers."

She couldn't help the smile that touched her lips. Some things evidently never changed and his love for hamburgers was one of them. "Too much ground beef isn't good for you," she said, quoting what she'd told him over a hundred times in the past.

And as expected, he rolled his eyes. "Yeah, yeah, I know, and the key words are *too much*. I've become a physical fitness addict, so I don't indulge in too many things that aren't good for me, but there's nothing wrong with enjoying a big, juicy hamburger every once in a while."

Summer decided not to say anything more on the matter. It was evident by his perfect body that he was into physical fitness. "I guess not. I'll be in the lobby at noon."

Darius stretched his neck to work out the kinks as he leaned back in the chair, away from the computer. He glanced up at the clock. It was almost noon.

He stood and stretched his entire body, refusing to acknowledge the anticipation he felt over joining Summer for lunch. Instead, he tried convincing himself that his nerves were the result of knowing he was slowly but surely breaking down her defenses and in good time, he would have the upper hand.

He was leaving the small office when his ears picked up the sound of commotion coming from the front of the building, near the lobby. He quickened his stride and when he rounded the corner, he saw a man standing outside the building with a baseball bat in his hand, threatening to break the glass door if he wasn't allowed to come in to get his wife and children. Summer, Darius saw, was talking to the man on the intercom, trying to reason with him.

He watched her, amazed at how calmly she was speaking to the man, clearly determined not to get ruffled by the vulgar language he was using and the threats he was making.

He glanced over at Marcy, who was sitting at her desk. "Have the police been called?" he asked, shifting his attention back to the scene being played out a few feet away. "And where the hell is security?" he continued, keeping his gaze fixed on Summer. She continued to appear composed as she tried to settle the man down and convince him to go away.

"The police are on their way. Our security guard called in sick this morning."

Darius looked at Marcy. "They didn't send a replacement?"

"Not yet."

Darius frowned. Huntington and his group had voted against the idea of Darius's firm being in charge of all the security for the shelter. Instead, Huntington had recommended a security company the TCC had used in the past, claiming it was top-notch. The majority of the members had gone along with him except for Lance, Kevin, Mitch and Justin. When they had been outvoted, as a compromise, they had pushed for the club to consider Darius to handle the security for all the computers and to set up the billing system.

Huntington had fought hard against it, saying Darius was too new to the club to take on such tasks, but he had lost the fight when Alex Montoya had sided with them instead of Huntington's group. Darius got the feeling that in addition to the bad blood between Alex and the Brodys, there was bad blood between Alex and Huntington. But then it seemed Huntington had a beef against anyone under the age of forty who joined the club.

The sound of breaking glass recaptured Darius's attention and in a flash he raced forward and placed himself in front of Summer just as the man who was wielding the bat forced his way through the broken glass toward her.

"Be a man and hit me instead of a woman. I dare you," Darius snarled through gritted teeth, not trying to hide the searing rage coursing through him.

The man evidently thought twice about following through on Darius's offer and dropped the bat, taking a step back. Within seconds, the shelter was swarming with police officers. Two of them quickly came through the broken glass door to apprehend the man, who didn't put up a fight.

Darius turned to Summer. "Are you all right?" he asked in a low voice. He hadn't realized just how angry he was until now. If that man had harmed a single strand of hair on her head, Darius would have gone ballistic.

In a way, Darius wished the man had taken him up

on his offer. That would have given him the excuse he needed to flatten him. The man had just proven what a coward he was. He was willing to take a bat to a woman, but had wasted no time backing away instead of squaring off with a man equal to his size and weight.

He watched Summer breathe in deeply. "Yes, I'm fine. It's not unusual for a husband to show up wanting to see his wife and children, and when we tell them they can't, most move on. Once in a while, we get someone like Mr. Green who refuses to abide by our rules and causes problems. Usually when that happens, security handles it."

Darius nodded. He would be calling a special meeting of the TCC to make sure something like this didn't happen again. He didn't want to think what could have happened had he not been there. There was no doubt in his mind that the man intended to use that bat on someone.

Before he could say anything, a police officer approached them to obtain their statements. After recording all the facts, the officer advised Summer that she would need to go down to police headquarters so formal charges against the man could be filed.

No sooner had the officer walked away than a woman Darius recognized as a staff member walked up. "Excuse me, Ms. Martindale, but some of the women are upset. They heard a man was trying to force his way inside."

Summer nodded. "Okay, I'm on my way to meet with them."

She then turned back to Darius. "Thanks for your help. I really didn't think he would go so far as to break down the glass. I was hoping that I'd be able to talk some sense into him."

She glanced at her watch. "I need to calm down the

women and then go to the police station. I guess lunch is off now."

He shook his head. "No, it's not. Go meet with the women and then I'll drive you to headquarters. Afterward, on the way back, we'll grab something to eat."

"Okay. Thanks." She started to walk away and then glanced at all the glass around the door.

"Go on. I'll make sure this mess is cleaned up and get the glass replaced," he said.

She gave him an appreciative smile before hurrying off with the staff member.

When she'd rounded the corner, Darius released a curse and pulled the cell phone from his belt, hitting the speed dial for Lance's number. His best friend answered on the first ring. "Hey, what's up, Darius?"

"There was an incident here at the shelter and security was not in place. We need to call a TCC meeting."

"I thought we were never going to get out of there," Summer said as they left police headquarters. Darius led her over to his car.

After calming down the women and children, she'd had to meet personally with Gail Green to let her know what her husband had done. Then Summer had to assure Gail that the shelter wouldn't be putting her and her two children out because of the incident.

Gail and her two little boys had arrived at the shelter three days ago after fleeing from their home in the middle of the night. The bruises on her body were evidence enough that she'd been in an abusive situation, but like a number of other women who sought refuge at the shelter, she had refused to press charges.

"I thought they handled everything in a timely manner," Darius said, smiling faintly as he opened the car door for her.

She rolled her eyes. "Spoken like a true ex-cop."

He chuckled before closing her door and moving around the car to the other side. The clock on his console indicated it was after three and they still hadn't eaten lunch.

"Where to?" he asked when he got settled behind the wheel with his seat belt in place. "And don't say back to the shelter because it won't happen. I'm taking you somewhere so we can grab something to eat. I'm hungry even if you're not."

As if on cue, her stomach growled and Summer couldn't help but grin. "Sorry. I guess that means I'm hungry, too. Have you tried that café around the corner from the shelter? The Red Sky."

"No. I've passed by it a few times but have never eaten there."

"Then I guess this is your lucky day because that's where I want to go."

"All I want to know is do they make good hamburgers?" he asked, easing his car into traffic.

"I've never eaten one of their burgers. I'm a salad girl."

He glanced over at her and grinned. "So, you haven't kicked that habit?"

"You want to consult Dr. Oz to determine which of us is eating healthier?"

"No."

She couldn't help but laugh. "I figured as much."

It felt good to laugh. She would never admit it to anyone, especially to Darius, but Samuel Green had truly frightened her and she was glad Darius had been there. When Mr. Green had burst through that door after breaking the glass, she'd had flashbacks to that time with Tyrone when she'd been exposed to his true colors. She had seen his anger out of control, and that anger had been directed at her. A backhand blow had sent her sprawling across the room but she had been quick enough to make it to the door before he could do anything else.

That had been the one and only time Tyrone had raised a hand to her, and she made sure it was the last. A courier had returned her engagement ring to him in the same box it had come in and later that same day, he'd been notified of the restraining order she'd filed. Thinking about it now, she appreciated the fact that she'd gotten out of an abusive situation. She had known when it was time to part ways even if Tyrone hadn't.

She glanced over at Darius. "Did you get much work done today?"

He shrugged. "Not as much as I would have liked, but that's okay. Typically, a job of this sort wouldn't take a whole lot of time, but security is a concern at the shelter, as it should be."

There was no way she would argue with that.

"And as far as the billing system goes," he continued, "I understand the TCC has money, but they want a firm accounting of how their money is being spent."

"Yes, and rightly so," she said, wondering if he thought she felt otherwise. "This shelter is fortunate to be funded by such a distinguished group of men. Do you know any of them?"

He lifted a brow. "Any of whom?"

"Members of the TCC?"

"Why would I know any of them?"

She noted that he sounded offended by her question.

"I didn't mean if you knew them personally. I was just wondering if you've ever met any of them. After all, you were hired by them."

He didn't say anything for a moment. "Yes, I've met some of them. They're okay for a bunch of rich guys, and I respect the club for all the things they do in the community. It's my understanding that some of the members prefer not having their identities known. They like doing things behind the scenes without any recognition."

Summer nodded. She could respect that, knowing there were a number of wealthy people who preferred being anonymous donors. She appreciated everything the TCC had done so far and all the things they planned to do. She was definitely looking forward to her meeting with Mr. Novak on Friday. Presently, Helping Hands could accommodate up to fifteen women and children that needed shelter care. Already the TCC had plans in the works to expand the shelter's facilities to triple that amount.

"You've gotten quiet," he said.

She glanced over at Darius and couldn't help but feel a rush of gratitude. He had stood back and let her handle things until the situation had gotten out of control. She appreciated his intervening when he did, playing the role of knight in shining armor once again.

She continued looking at him. His eyes were on the road and her mind couldn't help but shift to another time when he'd been driving her someplace. It had been their first official date. They had gone out for pizza and afterward he had taken her home. She had invited him inside and later, sitting beside him on the sofa, the kissing had begun. A short while later she had been lying beneath him in her bed as he made love to her in a way she hadn't known was possible. The intensity of the memories of that night was almost enough to push everything that had happened over the past seven years into the background.

Almost, but not quite.

"Summer?"

She blinked when she realized they had come to a traffic light and he had glanced over at her, catching her staring. "Yes?"

"Are you sure you're okay? I guess incidents such as what happened earlier are expected to some degree, which is the reason I'm installing state-of-the-art security software on all the computers—to reduce the risk that the location of the women seeking refuge is discovered. But still, it has to be unnerving when one of the husbands or boyfriends shows up."

If you only knew. "Yes, and what's really sad is the fact that the women have to go into hiding at all. The Greens have two beautiful little boys and today their father showed up demanding them back with, of all things, one of their baseball bats. The person we saw today was not a loving father or husband but a violent and dangerous man."

Summer frowned and then she sighed deeply. Tonight she would get a good night's sleep and try to forget the incident ever happened. Fat chance. She would remember it and she would imagine what could have happened had Darius not been there.

"Here we are."

She looked around. Darius had pulled into the café's parking lot and brought the car to a stop. She glanced over at him. He was staring at her with an intensity that sent shivers of awareness through her body.

Sexual chemistry was brewing between them again.

She could feel his body heat emanating from across the car. Summer forced the thought to the back of her mind.

"Umm, I guess we should go on inside," she forced her mouth to say. The way he was looking at her made her want to suggest that they go somewhere else, but she fought the temptation and held tight to her common sense.

She decided now was as good a time as any to thank him. "I really do appreciate what you did today, Darius, and I want to—"

"No, don't thank me."

His words stopped her short. "Why?"

"Because I didn't do any more than what was needed. No more than any other man would have done."

She contemplated his words. He was a man of action. Twice she had seen him in full swing and neither time had he accepted her words of gratitude. "I *will* thank you, Darius Franklin, because you deserve to be thanked."

And before he could respond, she got out of the car.

"Hey, Ms. Martindale, do you want your usual spot?" Tina asked when Summer walked in.

"Whatever is available," Summer answered, feeling the heat of Darius's chest close to her back. His nearness was almost unsettling.

"You must come here often," he said, moving to stand at her side.

She glanced over at him and smiled. "Practically every day. It's not far from the shelter and I enjoy the walk. And I like their grilled chicken salads."

Moments later they were being escorted to a table in the rear. Darius shifted his full attention to the people whose tables they passed. They either greeted her by name or smiled a hello. "You're pretty popular, I see," he said when they had taken their seats.

She shrugged. "Most are regulars who know that I work at the shelter. They believe it benefits the community and appreciate our presence."

They halted conversation for a while to scan the menu. Darius was the one deciding what he wanted since Summer was getting her usual. However, she was inclined to check out the soup of the day, or at least pretend that she was doing so. It was hard concentrating on anything, even food, while sitting across from Darius. As he studied his menu, she studied him over the top of hers.

She almost laughed out loud at the intense expression on his face. Deciding what hamburger he wanted couldn't be all that serious. But then Darius had always been a very serious man. Especially when it came to making love.

For a heart-flipping moment she wondered why a memory like that had crossed her mind, but she knew. Darius was the kind of man that oozed sexuality as potent as it could get, making those incredible urges consume the lower part of her body. They'd only had one night together, but it had been incredible. No matter what had happened after that, she could not discount how he'd made her feel.

He was the most gifted of lovers. Pleasing her had seemed to be the most natural thing in the world to Darius. She hadn't realized just how selfish Tyrone had been in the bedroom until after she'd made love to Darius. How could she have realized when Tyrone had been her first? No matter what her sexual experience had been with Tyrone, one time with Darius had made everything just fine.

Darius glanced up and she took in a lungful of air. The intensity of his gaze—she wanted to look away, but she couldn't. It was as if she were held captive by his deep, dark eyes.

"Here are your waters."

Summer almost jumped when Tina appeared with two glasses of water. "Thanks." Barely giving her a chance to set the glass down in front of her, Summer picked it up and took a long gulp, feeling the need for the ice-cold water to cool her down.

Tina hung around long enough to take their food and drink order before moving on again.

"So, what do you like about your job?"

She glanced over at him to answer his question, making an attempt to keep her gaze trained on his nose instead of his eyes. "Everything, but mostly the satisfaction I get from helping women in distress, those who might feel broken up because of what has happened. I like letting them know they aren't alone and somebody cares."

What she didn't add was that she enjoyed giving them the same support he had given her during those first crucial days, when she had begun doubting herself, second-guessing the situation and believing that maybe she had been the cause of Tyrone's problems instead of the other way around.

"I notice there's not a director at the shelter," he said.

Her gaze drifted down from his nose to his lips. Focusing on his mouth was just as bad as looking into his eyes. He had a sexy mouth. It was a mouth that could move with agonizing slowness when talking…or when being used for other things. She swallowed before responding.

"When I was hired by the TCC it was decided that

I could handle it all for now. When they complete the proposed expansions and decide to fill the position, I'm hoping I'll be considered for the job."

Darius nodded. He had not been a part of the TCC committee that had done the hiring for Helping Hands, which was one of the reasons he'd been surprised to discover her working there. He would have recognized her name the second it came across his desk.

"The shelter is pretty full now. How do you manage it all?" he asked.

She shrugged. "It's not so bad. I think the most challenging times are when I'm called in the middle of the night to a police station or hospital to comfort a woman who's been beaten or raped."

Darius's jaw twitched at the thought of anyone treating a woman so cruelly. Mistreatment of a woman was one thing he could not tolerate.

"It's also difficult at times when manning the abuse hotline. Someone is there to take calls twenty-four hours a day—usually a volunteer trained to do so. Every once in a while, a call will come through that I need to handle. Those are the ones that can get pretty emotional, depending on the circumstances."

Darius could tell from her voice that she was dedicated to what she did every day. To stay on safe ground and not stray on to a topic neither of them wanted to deal with, he decided to keep her talking about her work at the shelter.

For the first time since seeing her again, he was lowering his guard a little.

When the waitress finally delivered their order, he had to admit the food looked good. And after a bite into his hamburger, he had to own up that it tasted good, too.

One of his uncles in Charleston once owned a sandwich shop that used to make the best burgers around. As a kid, he enjoyed the summers he spent there and the older he got, he found himself comparing every hamburger he ate to his uncle Donald's. None could compare, but he had to admit this one came pretty close.

"How does it taste?"

He glanced over at Summer and could only smile and nod, since he couldn't talk with a mouth full of hamburger.

A half hour later, on the drive back to the shelter, he reflected on a number of things he hadn't expected. Mainly, he hadn't figured on sitting across from her for almost an hour and enjoying her company without animosity or anger seeping in. However, what couldn't be helped was the sexual tension. Although they had tried to downplay it with a lot of conversation, it was there nonetheless.

There was a lot about her he could barely resist. Her scent topped the list. Whatever perfume she was wearing filled his nostrils with a luscious fragrance that seemed to get absorbed right into his skin. And then there were her eyes. He was fully aware that she'd tried to avoid looking at him, which had been hard to do since they were sitting directly across from each other. Each time he would catch her staring at him, he would feel a pull in his stomach.

Thankfully, his hands were gripping the steering wheel because at that moment, it wouldn't take much for him to reach over and touch her, stroke that part of her thigh exposed beneath her skirt. Seeing her flesh peeking at him was making his mind spin, so he tried focusing on the road and decided to get her talking again. Anything to keep his mind off taking her.

"So, where do you live?" he asked.

He kept his gaze glued to the road. She didn't need to see the heat in his eyes, a telltale sign that although he wished otherwise, she was getting to him.

"I bought a house a block from the post office," she said.

He noted she didn't provide him with the name of her street. There were a couple of new communities sprouting up near the post office, as well as a number of newly renovated older homes that had been for sale. "Nice area," he heard himself say.

"I like it. My neighborhood's pretty quiet. Most of the people on my street are a lot older and are in bed before eight at night."

He nodded. From the information she had just shared he could safely assume that she had purchased one of the renovated homes in the older, established communities. Doing so had been a smart move on her part; they were a good investment.

She then opened up and began telling him about it, saying she was having a lot of fun decorating the house. He didn't find that hard to believe. When she'd lived in Houston, her apartment had been small but nice and he'd been surprised to learn she had done most of the decorating herself.

All too soon he was pulling into the parking lot of the shelter. "Thanks for taking me to lunch," she said, reaching to unsnap her seat belt even before he could bring the car to a complete stop. "Although I have to admit, riding in the car instead of walking only means I have to get my daily physical activity some other way," she added.

He came close to saying that he knew another way she could get her physical activity, and it would be something she would enjoy—he would make sure of it. Instead, he decided it would be best to keep his mouth shut.

"But since it will probably be dark when I leave today, I'll take the day off from exercise," she tacked on, getting out of the car.

He glanced over at her. "Why are you staying late?"

"Because I have a lot of work and can't leave until I'm finished. I'm meeting with Mr. Novak on Friday and there are a number of reports I have to run. More than likely, the TCC will have heard about the incident today and will want a full report on what happened."

He tightened his mouth after almost telling her that he'd already given them one. While at police headquarters, he had gotten a call from Mitch, Justin and Kevin. Lance had told them what had happened. Minor details had been given on television—since it was a women's shelter, no television crews or reporters were allowed to show up in order to protect the women staying there.

He knew if Summer stayed beyond five o'clock, she'd be pulling a long day. But for some reason, he had a feeling that was probably the norm for her. "Isn't there someone who can help you with those reports?"

"Afraid not. Besides, I'd rather run them myself, especially since I plan on pleading my case to Mr. Novak for an expansion of the shelter sooner rather than later."

Darius didn't say anything, but considering what had happened earlier that day, he wasn't crazy about her walking out to her car alone. Although the parking lot was well lit, he still didn't like it. Two security guards had shown up after the incident. He decided that before he left for the day, he would talk to the guards and make sure one of them walked Summer to her car.

When they reached the door he decided that unlike her, he intended to leave at a decent time. He had a meeting with the fire chief later, and it was a meeting he didn't want to miss. And besides, the last thing he needed was to end up in the office late at night with Summer—alone.

Chapter 4

Darius grabbed a beer out of the refrigerator and popped the top before tilting the can to his mouth, appreciating the cool brew that flowed down his throat. When the can was empty, he scowled before crushing the aluminum and tossing it into the recycling bin.

His frown deepened as he sat down at the kitchen table, thinking that today had certainly not gone like he'd planned. He was convinced that the incident at the shelter was the prime reason his protective instincts toward Summer had kicked in. He had been ready to do bodily harm to anyone who even thought of hurting her. And he could admit that the reason he had driven her to police headquarters and then later to lunch was because he hadn't wanted her out of his sight. He was becoming attached again, and that wasn't good.

He rubbed a hand down his face. Maybe he needed to

rethink the notion of exacting some sort of revenge on her and instead, just put distance between them and let it go at that, treating her the way he would other groupies or gold diggers whenever they crossed his path.

But he wasn't able to do that. If anything, today proved that when it came to Summer, he didn't think straight or logically. Right now, the only thing he should be thinking about was hurting her the way she had hurt him. Therefore, regardless of any protective instincts he might have, he would continue with his plan to make her think something special was going on between them. Then, at the right time, he'd drop the bomb that she meant nothing to him, and she'd discover she had gotten played, just like he had.

When his cell phone went off, he stood and pulled it off his belt. "What's up, Lance?" After his meeting with Chief Ingle, he had stopped by the TCC Café and had dinner with Kevin and Justin. Lance and his wife had driven to Houston to attend some sort of function there.

"I got your message. So Ingle thinks the fire was started with some sort of petroleum-based product?" Lance asked.

"He's pretty sure of it. But it wasn't one that could easily be detected, which is the reason the investigation took so long. They're trying to narrow the components down. However, he believes it's the same kind found in lubricating oils used for ranch equipment," Darius responded.

"Something that Montoya could easily get his hands on, since he owns that cattle ranch," Lance was quick to point out.

Darius shook his head. "His men are the ones working his ranch the majority of the time, Lance. Montoya's heavily involved in his import/export business."

"For crying out loud, Darius, you just don't want to believe he's responsible for that fire, do you?" Lance asked with frustration in his voice.

"What I don't want is for you to be so convinced Montoya is behind the fire that you start overlooking any other possible suspects."

"There aren't any other possible suspects, Darius. Montoya is the only one who hates me and Mitch bad enough to do such a thing. At the end of your investigation, you'll see that all the evidence points in Montoya's direction."

A few hours later, the fire investigation was the last thing on Darius's mind when he finally eased into bed, determined to get a good night's sleep. Moments later, after a number of tosses and turns, he discovered doing so wouldn't be easy when thoughts of Summer filled his mind. When he thought of what could have possibly happened had he not been there today. Even now he was worried that she was still at the center working, and he was tempted to go check for himself to make sure she was all right. But then he quickly recalled he had spoken with security to make sure someone escorted her to her car whenever she did work late.

He breathed in deeply, getting angry with himself that his concern for her, this feeling stirring deep within him, was making him weak. He refused to let that happen. But each time he closed his eyes, he saw her, remembered a better time between them, a time when she had been his whole world.

He stared up at the ceiling, determined to remember that she was not his whole world any longer, would never be it again. It was something he couldn't lose sight of. He would keep up his guard with her, no matter what.

"Thank you for walking me to my car, Barney, but it really wasn't necessary."

"No problem, ma'am. Besides, it was Mr. Franklin's orders."

Summer raised a brow at the uniformed guard. "Was it?"

"Yes."

Summer pondered that. How could Darius give an order to a guard who didn't work for him? Evidently, Barney had no problem following an order from someone who wasn't his boss.

"Well, good night," she said, opening her car door and getting inside.

"Just a minute, Ms. Martindale. This was pinned to your windshield beneath the wipers," he said, handing the piece of paper to her.

Summer tossed the flyer onto the seat beside her. "Good night."

"Good night."

Summer drove off, noticing Barney was still standing there, watching her pull out of the parking lot. No doubt he was still following Darius's orders. After what happened today, she could understand his concern and appreciated him wanting to make sure she was all right. Just like she had appreciated him taking her to lunch.

There had been something strange about sitting across from a man who had once undressed her, rubbed his hands all over her naked body and made love to her in a way that thinking about it took her breath away. A man who'd shown her that foreplay was an art form that could be taken to many levels, and that a person's mouth was just as lethal as his hands when making love.

When her car came to a stop at a traffic light, she turned on the radio, hoping the sound of music would drown out her thoughts of Darius. That wasn't going to happen, she thought, when she recalled how long after she'd left Houston she would lie in bed and think of him.

Her stomach growled and she remembered she'd missed dinner. When she got home she would make a sandwich and a glass of iced tea. It was one of those hot August nights.

As she waited for the light to change, she glanced over at the flyer she'd thrown on the seat and picked it up. Her breath caught in her throat and chills ran up her spine when she read the words, "I take care of my own."

The light turned green but she didn't realize it until the driver behind her blasted his horn. She accelerated, wondering which husband or boyfriend had placed the note on her car. It wouldn't be the first time one of the abusers of the women at the shelter blamed the staff for keeping his family from him. Mr. Green had taken the same position earlier that day. She wouldn't be surprised if it had been Mr. Green who had placed the note there, since her car had been parked in one of the spaces reserved for shelter personnel.

Summer tossed the paper aside, thinking of Mr. Green and the baseball bat, and his terrified wife. She sighed. She had long ago stopped trying to figure out why some men could treat a woman they claimed to love so shabbily.

The next day, Darius studied the computer screen in front of him and tried not to think about the woman a few doors down. She had been holed up in her office all morning and it was almost noon. He would bet any amount of money she would not be stopping for lunch.

A part of him knew it was really none of his business whether she ate or not, but another part decided to make it his business. Just as well, since he hadn't been able to concentrate worth a damn anyway.

Before arriving at the shelter, he had dropped by the refinery to take a look around the area damaged by the fire, hoping he would find something that had been overlooked previously. He hated admitting it, but Lance was right. All the evidence accumulated so far was pointing at Montoya, especially since the man didn't have an alibi for that night and he'd been seen in the vicinity of the refinery. However, the evidence was too cut-and-dried to suit Darius—way too pat. As far as he was concerned, if Montoya wasn't guilty, then someone who knew about the feud between Montoya and the Brodys was certainly making it look that way.

Darius stood as he checked his watch, deciding it was time to feed his stomach and satisfy his desire to see Summer again. He had fought the impulse to drop by her office and say hello when he had arrived at the shelter. But he couldn't fight it anymore.

Her office door had been closed, which meant she was either counseling someone or buried knee-deep in work. She had mentioned getting ready for that meeting tomorrow with Kev. But still, she had to eat, and he kind of enjoyed that café where they had eaten yesterday. The hamburger had been delicious.

Walking down the corridor, he went to the secretary's desk. "Is Ms. Martindale in a meeting with someone?" he asked Marcy.

Marcy stopped thumbing through a bunch of folders on her desk long enough to look up and smile at him. "No, she's going over some papers. If you need to talk with her about something, just knock on her door."

He returned her smile. "I think I will. Thanks."

Strolling back the way he'd come, he came to a stop in front of her door, hesitating a moment before knocking, convincing himself he was only pretending to be a nice guy when in fact, she really didn't deserve his kindness.

"Come in."

He opened the door and walked into her office, closing it behind him. She didn't look up. "Ready for lunch?" he asked.

She lifted her gaze from the document she'd been reading to fix it on him. The moment their eyes met, a slight tremor touched him. And if that weren't bad enough, he could feel a deep stirring in his gut. He stood there, fully conscious of the effect she was having on him and not liking it, but unable to do anything but stand there and take it like a man who wanted a woman, a woman he should have gotten from under his skin long ago. She broke eye contact with him and looked back down at the document she'd been reading. "I can't today."

You can't or you won't? Instead of asking, he said, "Yes, you can. You'll think better on a full stomach."

When she looked back up at him without saying anything, as if giving his words some serious thought, he decided to add, "Besides, that hamburger I ate yesterday was pretty good and—"

"And you probably don't need another one today. Too much beef," she finished for him, pushing her papers aside. "Why don't you try a salad?"

He chuckled. "That's rabbit food."

She rolled her eyes. "That's healthy." And then she said. "Okay, I'll have lunch with you, but only if we walk to the café."

He felt the amusement leave his face. "Walk?"

"Yes. Walk."

He noticed she was watching him intently, probably expecting him to back down. He couldn't help the smile that touched the corners of his lips when he said, "Fine. We'll walk."

"You really didn't expect me to do it, did you?"

Summer glanced over at Darius. They had been walking for the past few minutes in silence, which gave her the chance to wonder how, for the third day in a row, she'd been in his presence. He was right. She hadn't expected him to agree to walk to the café with her. Not that she thought he wasn't in any kind of shape to do so, but mainly because he didn't have a pair of walking shoes tucked away in a desk like she had. He was wearing cowboy boots, and they complemented his jeans and chambray shirt. And he had grabbed his Stetson off the rack to put on his head, which, considering the heat of the sun, had been a good idea. He looked good in his Western attire, too good to be walking with her on the dusty sidewalk. Every so often when someone needed to squeeze by them, Darius's denim-clad thigh would brush up against hers, making her very aware of the strength of his masculinity.

"No, I really didn't," she said finally. "But you have to admit it's a beautiful day outside. A perfect day to walk."

She couldn't help remembering the last time they had taken a walk together, late one afternoon when he'd shown up at her place after getting off work. They had strolled to the neighborhood park and on the way back had stopped at a corner store for ice-cream cones. That had been a perfect day to walk, too.

She breathed in deeply in an attempt to erase the memory from her mind. For three days, she had allowed him to invade her personal space and she wasn't exactly happy with the fact that he'd done so. She had appreciated his help yesterday, but somehow she needed to get him to understand that being cordial to each other didn't mean they had to share lunch every day.

"How is Aunt Joanne?"

She nearly missed a step and felt his hand on her elbow, reaching out to steady her, keeping her from falling. She stopped walking and glanced up at him. He was standing a scarce few inches in front of her and met her gaze. Darius had met Aunt Joanne when she had come to Houston to give Summer much-needed support during Tyrone's trial. Her aunt had liked Darius, and Summer wanted to believe that Darius had liked her aunt, as well, that his feelings toward Aunt Jo had been genuine and not fake—like the ones he'd displayed toward her.

"Summer, what's wrong?"

She swallowed and fought back the tears that threatened every time she thought of losing her aunt. "Aunt Jo died two years ago."

She saw surprise and then sorrow in his eyes. "I'm sorry. What happened? Was she ill?" he asked. He moved his hands from her elbow to her hand, and she could feel him wrapping his fingers around hers.

She shook her head. "No, in fact she'd had a physical the day before and had called to tell me how well it went, and that the doctor had even joked about her being fifty-five and would probably live well past ninety-five because she was in such good shape."

Summer paused a moment and then continued. "On her way home from work one night, she stopped at an ATM. A guy came up, demanding her money. She emptied her account and gave him all she had, but he shot and killed her anyway."

"Oh, Summer, I'm sorry to hear that," he said, pulling her into his arms. And she went without hesitation, ignoring the fact they were standing in the middle of the sidewalk. She was being given the shoulder to cry on that she had needed so badly two years ago. Burying her aunt had been the hardest thing she'd ever had to do. Less than a year after graduating from college, she'd lost the only person who'd been there for her consistently.

"That's it, Summer, get it all out," Darius urged gently in her ear. "Let it go." She felt the strength of his arms wrap around her shoulders, drawing her close.

Summer wasn't sure just how long she stood there, on a public street, being comforted by the only man she had ever loved—and who had done her wrong. She wasn't sure if she could ever forgive him for breaking her heart.

Pulling herself together, she eased back out of his arms, breaking all physical contact with him. "Sorry about that," she said softly.

"Don't apologize. Are you okay?"

"Yes, I'm fine." She nudged her hands into the pockets of her slacks and glanced down at the pavement. "It's still hard for me sometimes."

"I imagine that it would be, and I really meant it when I said that I'm sorry, Summer."

The sincerity in his voice as well as the warmth of his

tone touched her in a way that it should not have. She lifted her head to glance back up at him. "Thank you."

"You're welcome."

As they continued their walk toward the café, Summer's head was spinning with confusion over whether she could trust this man who had crushed her heart once before but seemed filled with pure compassion for her. Should she listen to her head, her heart…her body? She suddenly felt like she was nineteen again, and she didn't like it at all. Not at all.

Chapter 5

"You haven't been listening to a thing I've said," Justin Dupree complained while eyeing Darius curiously. The two men were enjoying a meal at one of the exclusive restaurants in town with plans to drop by the TCC later and play pool with Lance, Mitch and Kevin.

Darius took another sip of his beer and gave his friend an apologetic smile. "Sorry, what did you say?"

A smile touched the corners of Justin's lips. "I said Monica Cooper has been giving you the eye all night."

Darius raised a brow. "Who?"

Justin rolled his eyes. "Monica. You know. Sultry lips Monica."

Darius couldn't help but grin as he leaned back in his chair and took another sip of his beer. "No, I don't know her, but I'm sure you do."

There weren't too many single women with sultry lips that Justin didn't know. He had a reputation of being

Somerset's number one jet-setting playboy. Heir to his family's multimillion-dollar shipping company, Justin could probably talk a nun out of her clothes. He could also close any business deal he wanted—he had a reputation of being a tough-as-nails, ruthless businessman. Darius was proud to consider him a friend.

Justin smiled. "Yes, I know her. Her dad owns a nice spread outside of Austin. She comes to Somerset every summer to visit her aunt. She seems taken with you."

Darius didn't even bother looking over his shoulder at the woman. Instead, he said, "That's nice." He knew Justin had to be wondering why he wasn't showing Monica, or any woman for that matter, any interest tonight. Even their waitress had given him a flirty smile. But the only woman he could think about at the moment was the one he'd had lunch with today. The one he couldn't get out of his mind.

The one he had held in his arms while she'd cried.

"Okay, Darius, what's going on in that brain of yours? Lance said you still don't want to believe that Montoya was behind that fire."

Darius studied the contents of his beer bottle before glancing over at Justin. The two of them were best friends to the Brodys. Justin was Mitch's best friend like he was Lance's.

In a way, Darius felt guilty. He hadn't been thinking about Montoya and the fire, and he really should be. He had been thinking about Summer. But now that Justin had brought it up…

"I'm just not as convinced as everyone seems to be. Like you, Montoya is a shrewd businessman. Always on top of his game. Smart as a whip. I can't see him being stupid enough to set fire to his enemy's refinery, not when all fingers would point his way. He has no motive."

Justin shook his head. "Sure he does. You just said it. He and Lance are enemies."

"But that's just it, Justin. They have been enemies for years. That's nothing new. According to Lance, that goes as far back as high school. Competing against each other every chance they got."

"Yes," Justin said, "and they are still competing against each other today, in practically everything. The only reason Montoya decided to join the TCC was to be a deliberate thorn in Lance's side. On top of that, Montoya is friends with Paulo Ruiz, and everyone knows that guy has underworld connections and is as shady as they come. For all we know, Ruiz may have been the one to arrange the fire for Montoya."

Darius nodded, but he still wasn't convinced. "Well, all we got now is circumstantial evidence that wouldn't hold up in court. Unless there is valid proof, then—"

"I'll get it," Justin said, interrupting Darius.

Darius raised a dark brow. "And just how do you plan to do that?"

Justin smiled. "You'll find out when I lay all the evidence you need at your feet."

Hours later on the drive away from the TCC, Darius couldn't help but reflect on what Justin had said over dinner. Granted, he didn't know Montoya as well as the others since he hadn't lived in Somerset all his life, but he couldn't help but admire someone who had worked hard to propel himself from rags to riches. He'd heard that Montoya had once been a groundskeeper at the club.

And Darius had a hard time believing that someone

that driven to succeed would risk losing it all in a situation where he would automatically be labeled the guilty party. Darius was convinced that if Montoya had been involved in the fire, he would have done a better job of covering his tracks. The man didn't even have a valid alibi, for crying out loud. Definitely not the stance of a guilty arsonist.

Darius decided that before going to bed he would go back over the information he had collected so far, especially his interviews with a number of employees who had left the company within the past couple of years on bad terms. He then cursed under his breath when he realized he'd left the file with his notes back at the shelter.

Darius turned on the radio, deciding he needed to hear some music. He let out a deep breath as he recognized the song as one that had been playing earlier today at the café while he and Summer had shared lunch.

The image of Summer sitting across from him as she tried to put the pain of losing her aunt behind her flooded his mind. He'd liked her aunt and thought it was tragic how the woman had lost her life. He could just imagine what Summer had gone through during that time. But he really didn't want to think about that. Then why was he? Why did he have to constantly remind himself that he couldn't—and shouldn't—care?

He glanced at the clock on his car's console. It was close to ten. Tomorrow he would spend the day at the refinery, checking out a few things and questioning a number of the employees, including one who claimed he saw someone fitting Montoya's description in the refinery's parking lot the night of the fire.

The moment he stopped at a traffic light, his cell phone went off. He quickly slid it open. "Yes?"

"Darius, this is Walt. I got a message that you called."

Darius smiled. Hearing his old partner's voice reminded him of working as a detective in Houston. They'd had some good times together, despite Walt's miserable attitude. "Yes, Walt, how are things going?"

"Pretty much the same. I'm sure you heard that Smothers finally retired. We were all glad about that."

"Yes, I heard." John Smothers was a tough detective who should have retired ages ago.

"So, what's up? You said you needed my help with something," Walt said.

"I'm investigating a case of arson here in Somerset and need you to do a background check on one of the company's employees. I heard from another employee that the man used to work for a company that burned to the ground a few years ago in Houston."

"Sure, what's the employee's name?"

"Quincy Cummings," Darius said, hoping Walt would be able to obtain information about the guy.

"I'll let you know something in a day or so," Walt said.

"Thanks, I appreciate it."

"So, what's been going on with you, Darius? The last time we talked was over a year ago. I thought you were calling to let me know you had gotten married or something," Walt said in a joking tone. But for some reason Darius was annoyed by Walt's words—they had definitely hit a nerve. It could be because Walt had been the one to tell him about Summer and the things she had said about him.

"Not hardly. I plan to stay single for the rest of my days," Darius said, wondering why each and every time he talked to Walt, his marital status came up.

"Same here, man. Women are nothing but liars. None of them can be trusted. Hey, remember that good-looking broad you had the hots for when we were partners? The one who dumped you for some rich old man when you were out of town? I don't recall her name but I—"

"Summer," Darius cut in, trying to keep his tone from showing the irritation he felt.

"What?"

"I said her name was Summer. Summer Martindale," Darius said, ready to end the call.

"Oh, yeah, that's right. I wonder what happened to her after she left Houston. If she and that old man she ran off with are still together."

"I wouldn't know," Darius said shortly, deciding not to mention that Summer was now living in Somerset and he had not only run into her but had kissed her again. "Look, Walt. I appreciate you calling me back. Let me know if you find something out on that employee."

"Sure thing, pal."

Darius hung up the phone. Walt was the kind of man who believed misery loved company and had always seemed miserable, mainly because he'd had a tough time when it came to women.

Deciding he needed that file he'd left back at the shelter, he made a turn at the next traffic light. A few moments later, he was pulling into the parking lot and was surprised to see Summer's car in the usual spot. Why was she still here?

It didn't take him long to get out of his car and walk toward the shelter's entrance. The security guy named Barney recognized him but followed security procedures before allowing him entry.

"Is Ms. Martindale in her office?" he asked the man as he stuffed his ID back into his wallet.

"Yes, sir, and I did as you asked and walked her to her car last night."

"Thanks. I appreciate it."

Walking toward Summer's office, he stopped at the night-duty secretary's station. He had met the older woman, Raycine Bradley, the evening before. "Good evening, Ms. Bradley, is Ms. Martindale meeting with someone?" he asked.

The woman smiled at him. "No. I think she's packing up to call it a night. Finally."

Darius nodded, thinking Summer should have done that long ago. "I think I'll go hurry her along," he said, heading to the corridor that led to Summer's office.

Moments later he knocked on her door.

"Come in."

He stepped into her office and closed the door behind him. She was standing at a table with her back to him sorting out papers. Without looking his way, she said, "I promise I'll be leaving in a few minutes, Raycine."

Darius crossed his arms over his chest and leaned against the closed door. "That's good to hear. I intend to do everything in my power to make sure that you do."

Summer swirled around and stared at Darius in surprise. From the look on his face, he wasn't a happy camper. "What are you doing here?" she asked.

"I need to ask you that same thing," he said in a curt tone, moving away from the door to stand in the middle of her office with his hands braced on his hips.

Now she knew what had him upset. He didn't like the fact she was still there. She couldn't help wondering why he was making it his business. "I had a lot to do for tomorrow's meeting with Mr. Novak. In addition to that, a new woman checked into our facilities today."

She saw the look of concern that immediately showed on his face. "How is she?"

"She was a lot better once we got her settled in and assured her that if her husband showed up here, we wouldn't let him near her."

Darius shook his head. "It's sad that any woman has to worry about something like that."

Summer sighed deeply. "Yes. Been there. Done that."

But she didn't have to remind him of that since he'd been a part of that particular drama in her past. She had truly believed a restraining order would keep Tyrone away from her. He had proven her wrong. She didn't want to think about what might have happened if Darius hadn't shown up when he did, putting his life on the line for her.

Not wanting to think about Tyrone any longer, she asked, "So, are you going to tell me why you're here?" His gaze stroked her like a physical caress she couldn't ignore.

"I left something I need for tomorrow. I forgot to mention that I won't be back here until next week, when I start setting up the billing account."

"Oh." She should have been thrilled that she wouldn't be seeing him for the fourth day in a row but a barrage of emotions she couldn't explain tried to engulf her. She fought them back.

"I'm working on a case that requires my attention elsewhere," he added.

She wanted to tell him that he owed her no explanation. Instead, she said, "Sounds real serious."

"It's a case involving arson. You probably read about it in the papers a few weeks back. A fire at the Brody Oil and Gas refinery."

"Yes, I do recall reading about it," she said, leaning against the table. "And you think it was deliberately set?"

"It looks that way. I've been asked by the Brody brothers to find out who did it."

Summer eyed Darius. She recalled how much he'd enjoyed his job as a detective. Once in a while he would tell her about a particular case he was trying to solve. "Got any leads?" she asked.

"Not enough to suit me, which is the reason I need to spend a day at the refinery." He moved over toward her. "So, what do you need me to do?"

She straightened her stance. "About what?"

"About helping you pack up and get out of here, like you should have done hours ago."

"I told you why I'm still here."

"But your reason isn't good enough. I can see you staying over for an hour or so, but damn it Summer, it's going on eleven o'clock and knowing you, you'll be back here first thing in the morning."

"Of course. My meeting is at eight."

Darius wondered how she would feel knowing he had just finished playing a game of pool with the man she would be meeting with. And now Kev knew she was someone from his past, someone who had once meant a lot to him. His friend knew how much she had hurt him, as well. "So, what can I do to help?" he asked.

When Darius came to a stop in front of her, Summer released a resigned sigh. It wouldn't do any good to argue with him. Besides, she was too tired. "I guess you can help by stapling these papers that I've already sorted."

"Okay."

She tried to scoot over when he joined her at the table but their arms touched nonetheless, and she felt it—a spark of sensations that swept through her. She inhaled a sharp breath.

He glanced over at her. "You're all right?"

She breathed in deeply before saying, "Yes, I'm fine. Why wouldn't I be?"

"No reason."

There was a reason and they both knew it. Memories filtered through her mind of a night she just couldn't forget. There was no way she could deny that over the years she had lain in bed missing a warm, hard body beside her, and being awakened by the taste of a desire so potent it could blind you.

"If you're meeting just with Kevin Novak, why are you making all of these handouts?"

His question cut into her thoughts and she glanced over at him. "For the other members of the TCC, for him to share with them. I want everyone to know what's going on here at the shelter, that we're benefiting the community and that I'm competent enough to handle things."

Darius reached out and touched her arm. "You're worried for nothing. If they thought you weren't competent enough to handle things, you wouldn't be here."

"But what if—"

He reached for her. "For crying out loud, woman, you worry too much."

She should have seen it coming and backed away from him. But the moment his mouth touched hers she knew she could not have moved an inch. And now that her stomach was contracting with desire, there was no way she wasn't going to enjoy it while it lasted.

That was one thing she was truthful about, the fact that Darius knew how to kiss, even during those times when he should be doing something else. Like now. He had offered to help her, not seduce her. Awareness, bold and daring, raced through her, made her acknowledge that Darius was the only man who could ever make her purr in his arms. The only man who'd made her feel she'd been cheated out of many more nights with him.

If only...

She didn't want to think about if only. She only wanted to think about now, not what did or didn't happen seven years ago and during the years in between. She didn't even want to think about why being in his arms felt natural, like a place she should be. A place she belonged. His mouth felt in sync with hers, also totally natural, connected to hers while kissing her so perfectly.

When he finally ended the kiss, she couldn't do anything but pull in a deep breath, still tasting him on her lips. She didn't bother giving herself a mental shake and questioning why she had let him kiss her. She knew very well why. She wouldn't do as she'd done the last time, pretending she hadn't wanted any part of it since, like before, she hadn't resisted. She doubted that she could have even if she'd wanted to.

But she didn't want to talk about it. Without saying anything, she turned back to the table and gathered up what was left of the papers she had sorted. She was fully aware that he was watching her, but following her lead, he didn't say anything, either. Out of the corner of her eye, she could see him neatly stacking the handouts she'd made. They turned at the same time and their gazes locked for a mere second before simultaneously, they stepped into each other's arms again.

It seemed what was happening at the moment was Summer's mind was refusing to remember the bad times, only the good. And there had been good times, as good as good could get. They had only shared a bed once but before then, they had shared companionship, although she'd found out later he'd had an ulterior motive for doing so. But she wouldn't dwell on that now. The only thing she wanted to dwell on was the way his mouth was taking hers, with a hunger she could feel all the way to her toes, with an intensity that had her stomach churning as they were enjoying this kiss to the fullest.

It didn't even bother her that he was holding her in a possessive and intimate way, with his hands cradling her backside to fit her pelvis snugly against the front of him. She could feel the muscled tone of his body and his erection, hard and strong, pressed against her.

Taking his cue, she wrapped her arms around his neck as he sank deeper into her mouth, sending points of pleasure all through her. She felt sensations in her fingers as she caressed the back part of his neck, and through the material of her skirt where she was making contact with his denim-clad thigh. And she was very well aware of when he changed the angle of his mouth to position hers more to his advantage.

His efforts had her mind reeling, filling her with an urgent need to recognize and accept what was taking place, giving her the resolve to simply stand there, indulge and take it like a woman. And she was. She was taking it like a woman who needed every stroke of his tongue, every bit of his taste and every mind-blowing, tantalizing sensation his mouth was making her feel.

When the kiss ended moments later, she couldn't resist placing a lingering heated kiss on his jawline. Nor could she resist taking the tip of her tongue and tracing along his upper lip before finally taking a step back.

Darius drew in a deep breath and fought the urge to pull her back into his arms again, ask if he could follow her home and make love to her with the same intensity that he had made love to her that night. But this time, his heart wouldn't come into play, only his lust.

He wished the kiss could have wiped away all the wrongs of the past and he could move on without feeling animosity in his heart. Unfortunately, it hadn't. What it had done was make him fully aware of how vulnerable his heart still was when it came to Summer, and just how hot and strong his desire for her still burned within every part of his body.

"Finish up in here so I can walk you to your car," he heard himself say in a deep, throaty voice. A yearning for her was stirring his insides, thundering all the way through his veins, making him want to say the hell with it and take her on that very table.

But he couldn't. He wouldn't.

"I'll be fine, Darius. I don't need you to walk me to my car."

As he studied her, he saw the way her eyes glowed in a seductive lure. He doubted she even realized it. He needed to act accordingly and not give in to what she was asking for without even knowing she was doing so.

"I'm walking you out anyway, Summer."

He saw the lure in her eyes quicken to a sharp edge

and he wouldn't be surprised if she stood her ground. Then it would become a standoff, since he had every intention of walking her out. In fact, he intended to follow her home to make sure she got inside her house safely.

"Fine. Suit yourself, Darius."

Her words ripped through the air. He could tell by her tone that she wasn't happy, but that didn't bother him. When it came to her safety there was no compromising. He moved from the table to stand in front of her desk, convincing himself that it was his protective instincts kicking in where she was concerned, and nothing more.

Darius watched as Summer grabbed her purse and then he followed her out the door, pausing in the hall while she locked up her office. The shelter was quiet since most of the people in residence were probably in bed, asleep. "What did you have for dinner?" he asked when they began walking down the corridor toward the lobby.

"I worked through dinner."

Darius pressed his lips together to keep from saying a word that might have burned her ears. Knowing she had missed a meal bothered him a lot more than he cared to admit.

"And please, Darius, no sermons. I'm too beat to listen."

He glanced over at her. "I don't do sermons."

"Could have fooled me."

He halted his steps and brought her to a stop before rounding the corner that led to the lobby. She might be too beat to listen to what he had to say, but there was no doubt in his mind that she had plenty of energy for an argument and was gearing up for one. However, he had no intention of obliging her.

He leaned forward and placed a light kiss on her lips. "You're much prettier when you're not trying to be difficult."

She frowned up at him, clearly caught off guard. "I'm not trying to be difficult."

He couldn't help but smile. "Could have fooled me."

He didn't even try to hold back a chuckle when she narrowed her gaze at him. Ignoring the look, his hand took hold of her elbow. "Come on, Summer, let me grab that file off my desk and then get you home before you fall flat on your face from exhaustion."

Summer glanced over her shoulder before opening the door to her house. She had been fully aware that Darius had followed her home. She could have been nice and invited him in, but she'd decided not to. There was only so much Darius Franklin she could take, and after the kisses they'd shared in her office tonight, she had reached her limit for today.

She didn't have to wonder what there was about him that made her feel so raw and exposed yet at the same time so well protected. Whenever they kissed, she couldn't help but recall the passion. And then there were the memories of the hopes and dreams that had blossomed in her heart of what she'd assumed was a promising future between them. She had even allowed her dreams to include marriage and babies.

She headed for the bathroom to take her shower, wondering if at any time during the past seven years Darius had regretted bragging about their night together in such a degrading manner to his partner, Walt Stewart. She appreciated the fact that Walt felt she needed to know just what Darius had said.

Pain tore into her heart every time she realized just how wrong she had been about him, and that made her determined not to make another mistake by giving him her heart a second time. But she *had* enjoyed their kiss. In her mind, one didn't have to do with the other, just as long as she knew where she stood with him and where he stood with her.

He was now a dedicated businessman who seemed to enjoy what he did for a living and she had a new life, a new career and was no longer looking over her shoulder, fearful of seeing Tyrone. The past seven years had been good for her, although lonely. When it came to men she had learned the hard way to play it safe, and she would continue to do so.

And one sure way to do that was to make sure she didn't assume anything where Darius was concerned.

Darius needed a shower to relax. After making sure Summer had gotten home okay, he had driven straight home with memories of their kisses running all through his mind. Having her in his arms had felt natural, like that was where she belonged. Considering what she'd done to him seven years ago, was that weird or what?

When he had reluctantly ended their kiss, she had taken her tongue and swept it across his lips. He still felt a stirring deep in his gut just thinking about it. It had been unexpected. It had felt good.

And now he knew where she lived and would make it his business to get her to invite him over to her place one night. It might take a while to work up to that, but he would get there. He wouldn't see her again until Monday, which was just as well since he of all people knew Summer was the type of woman who could grow on a man.

She was the type of woman who could easily get under a man's skin. And he had to admit that she had gotten under his tonight. She had made sensations he hadn't felt in years rush through him, reminding him what it was like to lose control with a woman.

Darius headed toward the shower with a deep frown on his face. No matter what Summer evoked within him, he was determined to remain immune to her charms. He had no intentions of making the same mistake twice.

Chapter 6

"How did your meeting go on Friday?"

Summer glanced up and met Darius's gaze. She had wondered if he would be dropping by the shelter today. She hadn't expected to see him Friday, but she hadn't known for sure when he would be back to complete the project he'd been hired by the TCC to do.

"I think the meeting went great. Mr. Novak appreciated the handouts and was very attentive to what I had to say. He agreed that based on our occupancy log, it would be a good idea to consider expanding the facilities sooner than later. He said he'd take his recommendations back to the other members of the TCC."

Darius nodded. "And how was your weekend?"

"Busy as usual. And yours?" she asked, watching him carefully. She used to have the ability to read his thoughts, but now his expressions were unrevealing and she didn't have a clue as to what he was thinking.

"It was okay. After spending Friday at the refinery, I had to follow up several leads," he said, stepping into the room.

She immediately felt his heat, breathed in his scent and admitted to herself that she had missed seeing him around. "And you're still certain the fire was intentionally set?"

She tried not to notice how good he looked standing in front of her desk with a cup of coffee in his hand. All it took was a glance at his mouth to remember their kisses right here in this office last week.

She refused to admit she had purposely left her office door open on the off chance he dropped by Helping Hands today. On a number of occasions he had caught her unaware and she didn't want that to happen this time. She also refused to admit that she had thought about him a lot over the weekend, wondering how he was spending his time—and with whom. The latter was something she had no right to concern herself with, but she couldn't help it.

"I'll pick up the official report from the fire marshal this week, but so far, all evidence still points to arson," he said.

"Then I'm sure you'll be the one to solve this case."

Darius didn't want to think about what effect her confidence had on him at that very moment. She'd always had a way of making him feel that he could leap tall buildings with a single bound if he had to. He used to tell himself the reason she felt that way was because he had been the one to save her from a dangerous situation, and he shouldn't put much stock into it. But he had anyway.

"So, what's next?"

That was another thing that had drawn him to Summer, her interest in his job. She would ask questions and seemed to understand his excitement about it as well as his frustrations. He would enjoy getting off work at the end of his shift and dropping by her place to tell her how his day had gone.

"I'll continue to conduct an investigation over at the refinery while working on the security and the accounting systems here. Since the TCC wants me to personally handle both, I've delegated my other projects."

There, he'd just told her his plans which meant, whether she liked it or not, he would be hanging around for a while. He wondered if she had assumed he would be moving on and assigning the shelter job to someone else, but he couldn't read her expression.

"Well, I'll let you get back to work. I'll see you at noon."

He watched as her brow lifted. "Noon?"

He smiled. "Yes. We're doing lunch."

She stared at him. "Are we?"

"Sure we are, and I'll even let you twist my arm into getting one of those salads you seem to like so much."

There was a pause, and Darius sensed she was trying to determine whether it was worth the effort to start an argument with him. When she began speaking, she spoke her words slowly as if to make sure they were understood. "I don't want you to assume we're going to lunch together every day, Darius."

"Don't you like my company?"

She hesitated, and he watched her nervously lick her top lip with her tongue before she answered. "Whether I like your company or not has nothing to do with it. We have issues we haven't yet resolved."

They had issues yet to be resolved? She made it sound like she had been the injured party and not the other way around. He hadn't been the one to skip town with a man old enough to be her father who could buy her all the things Darius couldn't afford on his detective salary. They would resolve things all right, but his way. Pretty soon she would see how it felt to have someone you assumed loved you turn around and leave you high and dry with a broken heart.

"Some things can't be resolved and are better left alone," he said. "And in our case, maybe that's the way things should be, Summer. What happened between us was seven years ago. People change and they grow to regret things they did when they were young and foolish."

Darius maintained eye contact with her, assuming she was thinking about what he'd said. He made it sound as if he was giving her a chance to redeem herself, and that he was willing to forgive her for what she had done. Little did she know how far from the truth that was.

"Maybe you have the right idea," she finally said. "It *was* seven years ago and we've grown a lot since then."

"I'd like to believe we have." Deciding he didn't want to discuss it any further, he asked, "So, do we have another date for lunch?"

She hesitated and then said, "Yes, we do."

After Darius walked out of her office, Summer couldn't help wondering if she was making a mistake by agreeing to put the past behind them. He evidently found it easy to do so, but he hadn't been the one to get his heart broken. But then, on the other hand, she couldn't discount the fact that Darius had saved her life. And then another part of her wondered if perhaps she had put more stock in their affair, and had expected more from the relationship than he had.

She had gone a long time without getting involved with a man and she wasn't so sure if she could handle Darius—she wasn't even sure if she wanted to. She had gotten used to being by herself. Why was he determined to invade her space?

The only thing she was certain about was the way he made her feel whenever he touched her. To be honest, he didn't even have to touch her to make her hormones react. He could stand five feet away and she had the ability to feel how the tension in the air surrounding them seemed to vibrate, emitting all sorts of sensuous stirrings and longings. He had been in her office less than fifteen minutes and already her vital signs were at their highest peak.

But she was no longer concerned by the staggering degree of physical chemistry flowing between them. It had always been there, from the first. What she was concerned about was how easily she wanted to forgive him and believe that what Darius had said was true. Seven years ago, they had been different people with different values, at a different place in their lives. People change. And they come to regret decisions and actions of their past. Decisions and actions that they can't change.

She knew some men didn't like confrontation and Darius was probably of the mind that even if they hashed the issues out, it would not change anything. But still, was it too much to expect an apology for sharing something private and personal with his partner? Couldn't he see that doing so had degraded what they'd shared?

Even now she could vividly recall that day, after she and Darius had spent the night together. He had left her bed that morning seemingly in a good mood, making plans for them to spend the day together. But first he had to go home to get a change of clothes and stop by police headquarters to complete some paperwork, and she had to work a few hours at the restaurant where she was a part-time waitress.

When she'd returned home, she had waited for Darius. When hours passed, she had gotten worried. That evening, Walt had appeared on her doorstep with a message from Darius saying he'd had to leave town unexpectedly on police business. After delivering that message, Walt had asked if he could talk to her privately. That is when he'd told her how Darius had come to the station that day and bragged about finally sleeping with her. He had made a bet with Walt that it would take less than a month to share her bed. Discovering their one night together hadn't been anything more than a chance for him to win a bet had hurt her deeply. And then to know he'd gone back and told his friend had been another crushing blow.

While listening to Walt level with her about what Darius had done, she had barely been able to maintain her composure. Only after Walt had left did she break down and let it all out. She knew she had to leave Houston immediately and did not want to see Darius again, ever. It had been bad enough with Tyrone, but the hurt Darius had inflicted was even worse because in just a short time, she had fallen in love with him.

She had been too ashamed to call her aunt to tell her what had happened, so in the days that followed, she'd made some quick decisions. One of her regular customers at the restaurant, an author of academic books named Jack Lindsey, would be spending a year in Florida with his wife while he penned his next book. Jack had offered her the chance to accompany them as his assistant, to organize and edit all of his notes. He had made the offer before, but she had turned him down because of Tyrone's threats regarding what he would do if she ever left town. But with no future for her in Houston, she had quickly packed up and left town with the Lindseys.

The Lindseys had been wonderful and she had enjoyed the year she had spent with them on their beach property in Miami. She had buried herself in her work, determined to put Darius out of her mind and go about healing her heart. When she hadn't heard from him in over two weeks, that had only verified everything Walt had said. Their night together had been a conquest for him and nothing more.

Since both Mr. and Mrs. Lindsey were former teachers, they had encouraged Summer to pursue a college degree, and Mrs. Lindsey had even tutored her on those subjects Summer had felt would hold her back from getting accepted to any college. Using the money she'd made working for the Lindseys, along with a very nice bonus they had given her at the end of the year, she had remained in Miami to attend college there. She had poured all her time and energy into her classes, determined to reach every goal she had established for herself and refusing to wallow in the hurt and pain Darius had caused her.

Summer got up from her desk and looked out the window, not sure how she would handle the one man she thought she would never see again.

What she was up against now was how he could make her feel. Whenever she was around him, he was capable of bringing out feelings and desires that she wished would stay buried. In seven years, no man had made her remember how it felt to be a woman. A desired woman. It was something Darius could do so effortlessly.

When he met her gaze, she could see the desire in his eyes, and on most occasions he wasn't trying to mask it. It was as if he knew exactly what he was doing to her, what buttons to push, what words to say.

She had thought about him a lot over the weekend, wondering how and what he was doing. And, she thought as she bit her lower lip, with whom. She wished she could claim she didn't care, but she did. She couldn't help but notice how ladies would glance their way whenever they walked into the café together. There was feminine interest in their eyes and she couldn't very well blame them for it. After all, she was a woman, too.

She sighed deeply before checking her watch. It was time to make her rounds and greet everyone. She would keep herself busy until lunchtime.

Darius stared long and hard at the computer screen, thinking he must have missed something while setting up the billing system. He needed to go back and recheck. Or better yet, he thought, leaning back in the chair and rubbing the bridge of his nose, it would probably be a good idea if he kept his mind on what he was doing and stopped thinking about Summer. Having her on his mind was probably the reason he'd thought he'd found a number of irregularities in the TCC's accounting.

Deciding to give both his eyes and his mind a break, he pushed away from the desk and stood, needing to stretch his body. He had been sitting at the computer practically all morning and the limited space under the desk had been murder on his long legs.

He glanced at his watch. He had another hour to go

before lunch and he couldn't deny he was looking forward to dining with Summer again. He tried convincing himself that spending time with her meant absolutely nothing, and was just a part of his plan for revenge. There was no reason to think it was anything more than that.

He breathed in deeply, truly wishing he believed that. But he knew if he wasn't careful, he would be succumbing to Summer's charms all over again. And he didn't want that. He had given his heart to her once and what she'd done had almost destroyed him, made him unable to put his complete trust in another woman.

He had asked her how her meeting with Kev had gone, but he'd already been privy to that information. To say she had impressed Kev was an understatement. Besides stating the obvious about what a good-looking woman she was, Kev had been taken with her keen sense of intelligence as well as her concern for the women who sought refuge at the shelter. Kev also felt she had a lot of good ideas that the TCC should definitely take under consideration.

Sitting back down at the computer, he resumed setting up the Helping Hands account, trying to push thoughts of Summer to the back of his mind. However, once again a few discrepancies within TCC's accounting system popped up.

He pulled back when his cell phone went off. It was Lance. "Yeah, Lance, what's up?"

"Kate's fixing dinner tonight and wants you to come eat with us."

Darius smiled. He liked Kate and would be the first to say she was just what Lance needed. "I'd love to."

"Great. I'll let her know."

"Lance?"

"Yeah?"

Darius paused, not sure if he should mention anything about the discrepancies he'd found in TCC's accounting. Huntington and his band of tightwads managed the accounting for the club—namely the money they got from fundraisers and endowments. And everybody knew his group kept a tight squeeze on TCC's money supply. If there was anything wrong with the club's funds, they would know it. But still…

"Darius? What is it?"

Darius breathed in deeply. "Nothing," he finally said, deciding not to jump to any conclusions about the discrepancies until he'd had a chance to look at them more carefully.

"How are things going with you and Summer Martindale?"

Darius frowned. "You talk as if we're a couple."

"Aren't you?" Lance countered.

"Not yet."

There must have been something in his voice that gave him away.

"I don't know what your plans are regarding her, Darius, but be careful. They can backfire on you. If you're going to pursue her, then you need to forget about what happened seven years ago and move on."

Darius didn't say anything for a moment and then admitted, "I can't."

"You should try, man. When the shit blows up in your face, don't say I didn't warn you."

"Today I came prepared," Darius said, glancing down at his feet.

Summer followed his gaze and noted he had removed

his boots and was now wearing a pair of leather loafers. That meant he had come to the shelter today prepared to walk over to the café, and *had* assumed she would have lunch with him. She wasn't sure whether she liked the fact that he'd known she would give in.

She returned her gaze to his face. "So I see. You're ready?"

"I'm always ready, Summer."

She had absolute confidence in the truth of that statement. "Excuse me for a second. I need to let Marcy know I'm leaving."

She walked over to Marcy's desk. Marcy was in her late fifties and was someone Summer had become close to since working at the shelter. "I'm going to lunch now, Marcy."

Marcy smiled. "Okay. Did you ever get that dripping faucet at your house fixed?"

Summer shook her head. "Not yet, but I better do so soon, since it's keeping me from getting a good night's sleep." She then turned to rejoin Darius and together they left the building to walk over to the café for lunch. Her morning had been busy and she needed time away from the shelter. She always enjoyed her lunch, at least whenever she could make time for it.

It was a beautiful day and for some reason, Summer couldn't push aside the pleasurable sensations she was feeling with Darius beside her. She felt lucky today. She had counseled two women that morning and after listening to their stories, a part of her felt blessed that she had cut her ties with Tyrone when she had, otherwise she could have been one of them. And although Tyrone had caused unnecessary drama that had landed him behind bars for twenty years, she was free to make choices about her life. Now it was her job to convince those two women they could make choices about their lives, as well.

"So, how has your day been so far?" Darius asked.

She began sharing bits and pieces of how busy she'd been as they continued their walk to the café. Although his legs were a lot longer than hers, he adjusted his steps to keep in line with hers. More than once, while sharing her ideas about a number of things she would like to see happen at the shelter, she would glance up and see how absorbed he was in what she was saying. They were ideas she hadn't shared with Kevin Novak for not wanting to overwhelm the man since everything she had in mind included a hefty price tag. But they were expenditures she felt would greatly benefit the women who sought refuge at the shelter.

Then, while it was on her mind, she asked about his brother, something she should have done long before now since she knew how close the two of them were. Like her, he had lost his parents at an early age, and he and his brother had been raised by their grandmother.

"Ethan is doing fine now."

She opened her mouth to ask what he meant by that when suddenly a warm, masculine arm snaked around her waist to stop her from stepping in a rut in the cement sidewalk. "Thank you."

"Don't mention it," he said, releasing her.

Summer tried to ignore the sensations that raced through her veins at his touch. When they reached the café and he opened the door, she quickly moved past him, wondering how she was going to get through her meal.

Kate Thornton Brody smiled up at Darius. "You need a woman in your life," she said.

Darius lifted a brow, wondering where that had come from. He glanced across the living room and shot Lance a questioning look, but all his friend did was smile and shrug his shoulders. Damn, he hadn't been in the house five minutes and already Kate was on him about being single.

Seeing that Lance wouldn't be giving him much help, Darius reached out and placed a friendly arm around Kate's shoulder. "Sweetheart, you know I prefer being single."

She gave him one of her sidelong looks that said she'd taken what he'd said with a grain of salt. "So did Lance at one time."

"But now he has you and he's a lucky man," Darius said truthfully. He had known Kate ever since she began working for Lance as his very competent administrative assistant when he took over Brody Oil and Gas a few years back, and had always liked her.

"What's for dinner? I'm starving," he quickly said, before Kate could make another comment about the state of his affairs or lack of them.

"Didn't you eat lunch?" Lance asked, finally moving off the sofa.

Lance's question reminded him of Summer…not that he could forget. He hated admitting that whenever he had lunch with her, it was a pleasant experience. She was a great conversationalist. Always had been. And today she'd seemed more relaxed with him, more at ease. And as usual, she had looked beautiful sitting across from him.

"Yes, I had lunch," he finally said. "A salad."

Humor lit Lance's eyes. "A salad? What kind of foolishness is that?"

"Don't let Lance tease you, Darius. There's nothing

wrong with eating a salad," Kate said, walking back toward the kitchen.

When she was gone, Lance looked at him and chuckled. "I take it you had lunch with Summer."

Darius met Lance's amused look. "What makes you think that?"

"She's the salad girl."

Darius couldn't help but smile. When he'd left Houston because of Ethan's accident, Lance had shown up in Charleston to give him the support he needed. It was during that time that he had told Lance all about Summer, even how much she liked eating salads.

"I'd like to meet her. Invite her over one—"

"It's not that kind of relationship, Lance, and you know it," he said quickly, deciding to squash any foolish ideas that might be floating around in his best friend's head.

"Whatever you say," Lance said, smiling.

"I'm serious, Lance."

"Of course you are. I believe you."

Darius frowned. He could tell his friend really didn't believe him. "It's hard to love someone who has hurt you deeply," he said.

The amusement disappeared from Lance's face. "I'm glad everyone doesn't feel that way, Darius, or I wouldn't have Kate as my wife. If you recall, I almost lost her when I announced my engagement to another woman. But she still found it in her heart to give me another chance."

Darius's frown deepened. "So, what are you trying to say?"

Lance held his friend's gaze. "What I'm trying to say is that if you love someone, there can always be forgiveness."

* * *

"I really appreciate you walking me out to my car again, Barney, but it's really not necessary," Summer said to the security guard at her side.

"No problem, Ms. Martindale. Besides, it's Mr. Franklin's orders."

Summer shook her head, still not sure how Darius could give orders when he wasn't paying the man's salary. She was just about to ask Barney how that was possible when he suddenly said, "Someone has slashed your tires."

"What?"

"Your tires," he said, pointing his flashlight on her car. "They've been slashed."

Summer followed the beam of light and saw what he was talking about. She hauled in a deep breath, recalling the last time her tires had been slashed and who had been responsible. She forced herself to calm down as old fears tried to resurface.

That was all seven years ago. Tyrone was locked up and couldn't touch her. More than likely, the husband or significant other of one of the women at the shelter was venting his anger on her since the shelter was standing in the way of the person he really wanted to take it out on. But it couldn't be Samuel Green, since he was still locked up, held without bond.

"I need to follow procedures and report this to the police, Ms. Martindale," Barney was saying, interrupting her thoughts. "Please come back inside while I contact the authorities and complete an incident report."

Summer turned her attention away from her tires. "Yes, of course."

She moved to follow him back inside. She'd heard reports of acts of revenge being directed at staff members who work with victims of violence. Incidents of rock throwing, drive-by shootings and even bomb threats had been reported. As far as she was concerned, the person who damaged her tires was nothing but a bully.

"Are you all right, Ms. Martindale?" Barney asked with concern when they had reached the door to go back inside.

She forced a smile on her lips. "Yes, I'm fine." She heard the words she'd just spoken, but wasn't sure she believed them herself.

Chapter 7

"What's this about your tires getting slashed last night?"

Summer glanced up and saw Darius leaning in her office doorway. News had spread quickly. The evening crew from last night had a lot to share with the staffers that had arrived that morning. She'd figured he would hear about the incident sooner or later. She wished it had been later, since she really didn't want to talk about it right now.

"I'm sure you've heard the story, Darius, and I'm not in the mood to rehash it."

"Humor me," he said, crossing the threshold and closing the door behind him. She couldn't help but study his features. There was something different about his eyes. Their darkness was still striking, but now they contained an element of hardness she hadn't seen since that first day he had discovered her working at the shelter. And his lips were pressed together in a tight line. On most days, it wouldn't take much to look at his lips and re-member how they had introduced her to pleasures of the most decadent kind in a single night.

"I'm listening."

Summer blinked. While she had been staring at him, probably like a lust-crazed woman, he had taken a seat in the chair in front of her desk. She leaned back, trying to relax under the intensity of his direct gaze, but found it difficult to do so.

"What you've already heard is probably correct," she started. "Barney walked me out to the car like he's been doing since that incident with Samuel Green and noticed my tires had been slashed. We came back inside, called the police to report it and he filled out an incident re-port. End of story."

"I don't think so."

She heard the near growl in his voice. He was angry, she could tell. And she knew his anger was not directed at her but at whomever had slashed her tires. Given his mood, that was a comforting thought.

"I want to find out who did it," he said in the same tone of voice. "What did the police say?"

She shrugged. "Not much. They would have liked a list of the women residing here to check out the names of husbands and boyfriends, but because of our confi-dentiality policy, we couldn't provide it for them. I con-tacted the TCC earlier today to see if we could have two guards here at night instead of one."

"I thought there were two guards here since the night of that incident with Green."

"That lasted all but two days before one of them was pulled. Evidently, the TCC rehashed the idea and felt only one was needed. That's why I called them—to see if they would reconsider since the staff members around here were beginning to get nervous. However, the man I spoke with at the TCC said adding an additional guard wasn't going to happen."

"Who did you talk to?"

"I asked for Kevin Novak but the person I talked to was an older gentleman by the name of Sebastian Huntington." She saw his jaw twitch. "You know him."

"Yes, I know him."

Summer noticed that he'd said the words in a tight voice with more than a little distaste. "He wasn't very friendly," she added. "Nothing at all like Mr. Novak."

He didn't say anything but from the way he was looking at her, she knew he was taking it all in. And then he asked, "Is there anything else?"

She shook her head. "No, nothing other than the piece of paper that had been placed on my car, which I also mentioned to the police last night."

He lifted a brow, his posture on full alert. "What paper?"

"One night last week someone placed a note under the wiper blade. Barney had walked me to my car, and he pulled it off and gave it to me, thinking it was some kind of sales flyer. It wasn't until I stopped at a traffic light and glanced at it did I notice what it said."

"And what did it say?" he asked, leaning closer and moving toward the edge of his seat.

She swallowed, remembering precisely what was written in bold letters on the paper. "It said, 'I take care of my own.'"

The moment Darius left Summer's office he darted into an empty conference room and called Kevin. He picked up on the second ring. "This is Kevin."

"Kev, were you informed that Huntington had reduced the number of security guards at Helping Hands?"

"No."

An angry Darius went on to tell Kevin about the incident that had occurred last night.

"Huntington has no right to make those kinds of decisions without discussing it with the committee first, and I am part of that committee," Kevin said, almost livid.

"The man's been a part of the TCC for so long I believe he thinks he owns it, which is why he constantly overlooks anything the younger members have to say," Darius said.

"And how is Summer Martindale?"

"She's a little shaken up, although she was trying not to show it. The staff here is nervous—first Green breaking doors down and now this tire-slashing incident. It doesn't bode well. There have been revenge-type incidents reported in various cities around the country, and they are aware of it. We need to make sure they feel protected."

Darius tried to convince himself that his concern for Summer was no different than his concern for any other woman he'd once been involved with, but deep down a part of him knew that wasn't true. He would even go so far as to admit missing her whenever he spent time away from Helping Hands.

They were feelings that he didn't want to feel. One way to remedy that was to start keeping his distance, but then he wouldn't be able to make her feel the way he had felt when she'd left. He just needed to make sure he kept things in perspective.

"I totally agree," Kevin said, bringing Darius's attention back to the matter at hand. "I'll confront Huntington myself, and if I have to, I'll call a special meeting of the board."

Moments later, Darius hung up the phone feeling a lot better than he had before making the call to Kev. He knew his friend wouldn't like the "executive" decision Huntington had made regarding the security at the shelter any more than he did. As usual, the man was trying to throw his weight around, fighting for power he really didn't have. But Darius relaxed a bit, knowing Kev was on it.

He glanced at his watch. He needed to leave for a while to attend to business concerning the fire at the refinery—he had to talk to several guys who had been off work the day he'd met with the employees the last time. But he intended to return to the shelter before Summer left for lunch. The thought of her walking anywhere alone troubled his mind.

From now on, he would make sure that she was well protected. At all costs.

Three days later, Summer glanced over at Darius before looking down at her watch. It was a little past eight in the evening. She had volunteered to stay for a few hours to help man the abuse hotline, and he had surprised her when he volunteered to assist her.

At first, she hadn't been sure whether women on the other line would want to unload their pain and anguish to a man, but from overhearing bits and pieces of his conversations, she could tell he was handling things quite nicely. She would be the first to admit that he had a good demeanor for assisting those who called in, male or female.

"What time are you leaving?" she asked him. Since the night her tires had gotten slashed, he had made it his business to return to the shelter every day after being at the refinery in the mornings, to walk her to the café for lunch. And if she remained late in the evenings, he did so, as well. Then he would not only walk her to her car, but would follow her home to make sure she got in safely.

"I'll leave when you leave," he said, glancing over at her.

In a way, his protectiveness irked her. She didn't want him to feel like she needed him in any way. "There are two security guards now, so I'll be all right." She really hadn't been surprised when, the day after the tire-slashing incident, two guards were on duty. There was no doubt in her mind that Darius had had something to do with it, although what exactly, she wasn't sure.

"I plan to leave in a few minutes," she said.

He smiled over at her. "Then so will I."

And he did. After she had handled the last call she would take, she gathered up her belongings and headed for the door with him by her side. He nodded to the guards on duty as they passed.

"Nice night," he said.

She looked up at the sky and saw the full moon and the stars, and how they illuminated the otherwise dark sky. He was right. It was a nice night.

"I'll be following you home again."

She glanced over at him. "It's your gas."

She said nothing as they continued walking. When he opened the car door for her, she slid inside, noticing how his gaze shifted to her legs when her skirt accidentally showed a little bit of flesh. She started to say something about his wandering eyes and decided not to. It probably wouldn't do any good anyway.

The drive to her place was uneventful and whenever she glanced in her rearview mirror, he was there. She would admit that, considering the incidents of the past two weeks, she felt a semblance of security knowing he was near, just like the days and nights following that episode with Tyrone.

She parked her car in the driveway and was surprised when he parked behind her and got out of his vehicle. The other times he had followed her home, he had stayed in the car while she went inside and then left. She wondered why he had changed the routine, and she didn't like the way her skin seemed to feel warm all over as he came closer.

"You have a two-car garage. Any reason you aren't parking in it?" he asked, coming to a stop in front of her.

"It's full of boxes. I haven't unpacked everything yet." She paused. "Why did you get out of the car?"

She appreciated him seeing her home, but she had no intentions of asking him inside. Her house was her place. Her own private space. When she had moved to Somerset and found what she thought was the perfect neighborhood along with the perfect house, she had moved in, determined to keep bad memories from past experiences outside. Darius was a reminder of a bad past experience.

"I overheard you mention to Marcy that you had a dripping bathroom faucet that was keeping you awake at night. I thought I'd take care of it for you."

"Now?"

"I don't have anything else I have to do."

Summer sighed. She did. She wanted to take a shower and go to bed. "Thanks for the offer, but I'll get around to calling a plumber later this week."

"No need. It will only take a minute. Then I'll be out of here."

Standing in the shadows, she could barely see the features of his face in the moonlight. But what she did see was a man who had first been her friend and then her lover. She didn't know what he was now, aside from very determined to look out for her.

From the look of things, his mind was made up. She really wanted the faucet fixed. Since he *had* volunteered, she might as well take him up on his offer. "All right, then. Thanks."

"I've told you more than once that you don't ever have to thank me for doing what I do when it involves you, Summer."

She swallowed. Yes, he had said that more than once. Most times had been when they were sitting on a sofa, hugged up while watching television. She'd enjoyed those nights when they would sit curled up with a movie, sharing a bowl of popcorn in her living room, talking.

Another thing she had appreciated about him was that he had never tried pressuring her into sex. That night when they had finally made love, it was because it was something they both wanted, not something he had pushed her into doing.

"Yes, I know you don't need my thanks, but I don't want you to think I don't appreciate it," she finally said.

"Fine. Let me grab my toolbox out of the car."

She waited while he went back to his car. Moments later, she grabbed her mail out of the box and opened the door, hoping she wasn't making a mistake letting him inside.

He followed her and closed the door behind them. The click of the lock made her fully aware that they were alone, totally and completely. Trying to ignore her nerves, she threw the mail on the table. Since she paid most of her bills online, she knew the majority of it was nothing but junk mail anyway.

"Nice place," he complimented, glancing around. She knew he was taking stock of her place.

She tried to ignore how at home he looked in her living room. Like he belonged there. "Thanks."

This house was a lot more spacious than her apartment had been, and since she had a job that paid well, she could afford nice furniture.

"Which bathroom has the dripping faucet?"

"The one in my bedroom." Too late she realized that he was going to go into her most private room.

"Which way?"

"Down the hall to your right."

When he disappeared around the corner, she inhaled deeply, deciding she needed to do something other than just stand there while he repaired the faucet. She needed to at least appear busy. Unfortunately, there weren't any plants she had to water, nor were there dishes in her sink that she needed to wash. Her gaze lit on the junk mail that she had placed on the table and she decided now was as good a time as any to go through it.

Darius moved down the hall toward Summer's bedroom, thinking she had a lovely home. It was an old house, but very well cared for and maintained. He also liked the vibrant colors that suited her decor and the furnishings that blended in so well. And she was still neat as a pin, he thought, entering her bedroom and glancing around. His gaze came to a stop on the queen-size bed and he couldn't help but wonder what man had probably shared it with her. A rich, older man, no doubt.

Overhearing the conversation about her dripping faucet had given him the perfect excuse to invite himself in. For some reason, he had wanted to see the house that she was living in without him. Although they'd never actually discussed marriage seven years ago, as far as he was concerned, it had been the next thing on the agenda for them. He'd known that after what Whitman had put her through, it would be hard for her to put her trust in any man, but he had been willing to be patient and give her whatever amount of time she needed to learn to trust a man again. She'd needed to know that he was someone she could depend on. Someone who would always be there for her. Too bad she hadn't given them a chance.

Forcing those thoughts from his mind, he headed toward her bathroom. He had just stepped over the threshold and placed the toolbox on the floor when she frantically called out his name.

He rushed to the living room and saw total shock on her face. "Summer? What's wrong?"

She stared up at him, barely able to force words past her lips. But he did hear the one single name she said.

"Tyrone."

He looked at her, confused, not sure why she was bringing up the man who'd caused her nothing but grief. "What about Whitman, Summer?"

She glanced down and he followed her gaze to the mail sprawled at her feet. He quickly figured that something in one of the letters must have upset her.

He bent down, picked up the envelopes and flipped through them. Then he saw a letter from the Texas Parole Board. From the look of the envelope—specifically, all the stamp marks all over it—the post office had made several attempts to deliver it to her.

He pulled out the letter and read it, and then took a deep breath. As a former police officer, he was familiar with Texas law regarding those who'd been victims of violent crimes. A standard letter was issued to notify victims of the parole board's decision to release an inmate.

Darius glanced up at the date of the letter. It had been sent over a month ago. Tyrone Whitman was now a free man.

"I want you to drink this and please don't tell me that you don't need it because you do," Darius said, walking over to where Summer sat on the sofa with a cup of coffee laced with brandy in his hand.

Something had had him on edge all day, and he hadn't been able to figure out what. But now he knew. The thought that the man who had caused Summer so much grief had only served seven years of a twenty-year sentence made him very angry. But right now, Summer didn't need his anger. More than anything, she needed his support.

Surprisingly, she took the cup without giving him a hard time and took a sip. A frown appeared on her face and he knew why—he had made it a little too strong but if anything, it would help her sleep.

"I can't believe it," she said, breaking the quiet stillness of the room and leaning forward to place the cup on the coffee table. "How can Tyrone be out of prison? That makes no sense."

Darius had to agree with her. It definitely made no sense given the man's crime. They should have put him in jail and thrown away the key. There was no way Whitman should be free to walk around. At least not on this planet. How could they have done such a thing?

He cringed whenever he thought about the final days of the trial and the threats Whitman had shouted out to Summer, saying what he would do to her if he ever got out. He wondered if Summer was remembering those days. He doubted she could forget. She stood and began pacing the floor. He watched her. He of all people knew how she felt, how upset she had to be.

"Tomorrow I'll make a few calls and try to pinpoint his whereabouts," he said, trying to make her feel secure. "Usually when someone who has committed a serious crime is paroled, they're released with a number of restrictions. I bet Whitman can't leave Houston."

She stopped pacing and glanced over at him with blatant hope in her gaze. "You think so?"

"I'll find out tomorrow."

Seeing the panic she was fighting to control gave him pause. At that moment she was no longer the confident, self-assured woman he had watched over the past two weeks. Now there was real fear in her eyes and a sign of helplessness in her voice, and he didn't like it.

Crossing the room he pulled her into his arms. And when she began to tremble while he held her close, whatever hard casting surrounding his heart began to crumble. She needed him and there was no way he could not be there for her.

As if she was relieved to be able to hold on to something solid, she wrapped her arms around him. He was unprepared for the slew of emotions that rushed through him. He would protect her with his life if he had to, and would never let Whitman get close to her again.

He pulled back slightly, wanting to look at her, to make sure she was okay, and when his gaze settled on her lips, he was drawn to them like a magnet. Without any control, he lowered his mouth to hers.

The moment he drew her tongue into his mouth and began feasting on it, he felt sensations all the way to his toes and couldn't do anything but shiver with the pleasure of their intimacy. He drew his arms around her, tightening his hold to bring her body flush with his.

Summer felt his hardness, firm and rigid, pressing against her and marveled that his body was letting her know how much he wanted her. The only times she'd ever been kissed with such heat and passion was when he did the kissing.

He shifted the angle of his head, which caused her to follow as she tilted the curve of her mouth to his and nearly moaned out loud when his tongue took hold of hers with an intensity that made her weak in the knees.

When he finally released her lips, she leaned into him and sighed deeply. She had needed that kiss. She had needed the connection.

He felt firm, warm and solid—everything she needed at that moment. And in his arms she felt safe and secure. Protected. The thought that Tyrone was no longer locked up behind bars sent real fear through her, fear she was trying hard not to show. But every time she remembered those threats he'd yelled out in the courtroom while being taken away, she couldn't ignore the real panic that wanted to overtake her entire being.

"I don't want you to stay here tonight. You should come home with me, Summer."

She leaned back in his arms and met his gaze. "I can't do that, Darius. I'll be okay and—"

"No, Summer, think about it. I don't want to scare you, but until we know for sure that Whitman is in Houston, I don't want you here alone. What if those two incidents at the shelter had nothing to do with a disgruntled husband or boyfriend? What if Whitman is in violation of his parole and is not in Houston but here in Somerset and responsible for leaving that note on your windshield as well as slashing your tires?"

Darius saw the glint of real fear in her eyes when she considered those possibilities. What he'd said was true. He was not deliberately trying to scare her but she had to face the facts. And until he checked to see just where Whitman was and what he was doing, he would not let her feel safe. Hell, as far as he was concerned, as long as Whitman walked the streets he wouldn't advise Summer to feel safe. She had become an obsession to the man. In Whitman's eyes, she had betrayed him and he intended to teach her a lesson for doing so. He had made that threat in the courtroom with a crazed look in his eyes. Darius would never forget it.

"I'll go back to the shelter and sleep on the sofa in my office, and—"

"And what if word gets around to the women at Helping Hands that you, the woman who counsels them, is in the same predicament they are? Will that offer them any real hope for a brighter future when the man who disrupted your life seven years ago is still doing so?"

Summer's throat tightened as she stared up at him. She wished she could go anywhere but home with him. Being in such close quarters when she was feeling so vulnerable would be temptation she wasn't sure she could handle.

"Go on and pack an overnight bag for now, at least until I find out a few things tomorrow. If I get information indicating Whitman is in Houston behaving himself under the watchful eye of a parole officer, then I'll bring you back here tomorrow. Until then, you're going to be with me, Summer."

Summer breathed in deeply. A part of her wanted

to scream out that this had all been a mistake, a nasty nightmare, and she would wake up any minute snuggled in Darius's arms for another reason, one that didn't have anything to do with Tyrone.

Darius released her, dropping his arms. "Get your bag so we can go. I'll wait here."

Summer looked at Darius, knowing his mind was set about her going home with him. There was nothing she could say to make him consider leaving her here tonight. But a part of her didn't want to be here tonight, the part that vividly recalled Tyrone's threats. She was well aware of what the man was capable of.

Because she hadn't lived in town for long, she hadn't gotten to know her neighbors. There were elderly couples that lived on either side of her that she would see on occasion. But other than the staff at the shelter, Darius was the only person she knew in Somerset. She had planned to join some community organizations but hadn't gotten around to doing so.

Making a decision, she said, "All right. It won't take me long to get my things."

A faint smile touched his eyes. "Take your time. I'm not going anywhere."

Her heart felt full. Some things had changed, but Darius was Darius, the man who'd always been and forever would be her knight in shining armor. The one person she could always depend on to be there for her.

Without saying anything else, she rushed off to her bedroom to pack.

Chapter 8

Summer fell in love with Darius's home the moment she walked through the door. Although it was too dark outside for her to see everything, she knew he had taken her to a sprawling two-story ranch house. When she stepped into his living room, she felt a sense of comfort. She knew it was strange for her to feel that way, but she couldn't help it. During the short drive he had made her feel safe, assuring her that he would find out everything he could about Tyrone's whereabouts and that until he did, she would stay with him.

She glanced around and wondered if he'd hired an interior designer to decorate his home. Everything was color coordinated perfectly, and the furniture complemented the decor. A huge brick fireplace took up one entire wall and a bevy of windows guaranteed sunshine deep in the house during the daylight hours.

To shield the foyer from the interior rooms, a glass-blocked wall was erected between the main living area and the front door. The furniture in the living room was dark, rich leather and looked comfortable as well as sturdy.

"You have a beautiful home, Darius," she said when he followed her inside, carrying her overnight case.

"Thanks. Come on and let me get you settled in the guest room. It's past midnight and you have to be tired."

She was, and couldn't wait to get a good night's sleep, or at least try, she thought. But then she figured that he had to be tired, as well. He had spent the day at both the shelter and the refinery.

Moments later, after following him up a flight of stairs, she stepped into the guest bedroom. She glanced around in total awe. The spacious room had a high roof beam with Old Hickory decor. The king-size bed appeared massive, and the bedspread was a colorful patchwork that matched the country curtains.

"Evidently, your security company is doing well," she said.

When he didn't respond, she glanced over at him and saw a hardness that had formed around his mouth. What had she said to irritate him?

"Darius?"

"Yes, it's doing well," he finally replied in a somewhat biting tone. "There's a guest bath over there with a Jacuzzi tub," he said, pointing across the room. "My bedroom is at the end of the hall if you need anything. Good night."

Summer held her composure as she watched him quickly leave, closing the door behind him. Again she wondered what she had said that had hit a nerve with him. Why had commenting on his success bothered him?

She moved toward the bed and decided that when she saw him in the morning, she would find out.

Darius lay in bed wide awake, staring up at the ceiling. After he'd left Summer, he had made his rounds, making sure everything was locked and secured before going to his bedroom. There he had continued to stew over her comment, which had reminded him that a man's wealth was all she cared about.

He rubbed a hand down his face, not wanting to think that, but what else was he supposed to think? Now that she knew he had a little money, would her attitude toward him change?

He had brought her to his home to protect her, but that didn't mean he had to forgive her for all her past deeds. He wasn't sure that he could. His hands tightened into fists. He heard a sound and glanced over at the illuminated clock on the nightstand. It was almost two in the morning. Since his state-of-the-art security system hadn't sounded to alert him of an intruder, he guessed that Summer was up and moving around in his home. Evidently, she couldn't sleep, either.

Easing out of the bed, he slipped on a pair of jeans. He walked out of his bedroom and immediately saw a light shining downstairs.

When he reached the living room, he didn't see her anywhere. He gently pushed open the kitchen door. She was sitting at the kitchen table drinking what appeared to be a cup of tea, wearing a silk bathrobe belted around the waist. And although he had a feeling she was fighting hard not to do so, he could tell by the trembling of her shoulders that she was crying. Tears from any woman were his downfall—and when they came from Summer, doubly so.

Crossing the room, he fought the tightening of his heart. Hearing his movement, she whipped her head around and met his gaze. But she hadn't been quick enough to wipe away her tears. Without asking what the tears were for, he reached out his arms. "Come here, Summer."

She stared at him for a moment and he wasn't sure exactly what she would do. Then she rose to her feet and crossed the distance separating them. He pulled her into his arms and when he did so, she buried her face in his chest.

"Shh. It's okay, sweetheart. Things are going to be okay."

She shook her head and wiped her eyes, pulling back slightly to look up at him. "No, they're not. I've gotten you upset with me and I don't know why."

At that moment, he felt like a total ass and wished there was a way he could take back his earlier behavior, but he couldn't. So he stood there and held her in his arms, remembering times past when he would hold her the same way just moments before he would claim her mouth with his.

He knew at that moment that his desire for her was just as keen as it had ever been and, unable to fight what he was feeling, he gazed into her face just seconds before using the tip of his tongue to trace a line across her lips.

He heard the catch in her breath and tried to ignore it. He eased closer, unable to stop his body from responding to it. His hard erection pressed against her, warming him in a way he hadn't been warmed in a long time. His tongue left the corners of her mouth to glide over her bottom lip before pulling it into his mouth to suck on it a little. And then there was the feel of her nipples pressing into his bare chest like hardened tips.

He released her bottom lip, but only long enough to press his mouth fully onto hers, needing this taste of her, liking how she trembled in his arms not from fear but from his safekeeping. He had thought about this part of their relationship many times, the moments when he would capture her mouth and take them both to another level. Then one night their kissing had driven them to lose control and they had made love. He continued to kiss her deeply, wanting to lose himself in the kiss again like he had that night. And wanting to lose himself inside of her. He couldn't for the life of him remember connecting to any woman and feeling this way.

"Darius."

The sound of his name sent shudders of arousal through him. It was spoken in a breathless tone, a voice barely able to do anything but purr out a sexy timbre. It made the heat within him rise to a temperature that could easily cause him to boil over.

He shifted his hips and thighs to plaster them closer to the juncture of hers. Every cell within his body felt vibrantly alive, sensitized to her. His mind was finally in sync with what the rest of his body already knew. He wanted her.

He had to have her.

There was no question about his wants and his needs, only about how long he could last without having them satisfied. He pulled back, separating their mouths, but his gaze held hers and he knew she saw in his features the desire he could not hide. His entire being was ruled by an urge to mate with her, to share a physical intimacy to a degree he hadn't had since the last time they'd been together.

While her eyes continued to hold his, she brushed the back of her hand across his cheek and the caress sent shivers through him. He let out the breath he'd been holding, and his hands dropped from her waist to cup her backside, bringing her snug against him.

He could feel the fluttering in her stomach stirring against his erection, making it throb. His nostrils picked up her scent and blood pounded through his veins. He felt himself losing what little control he had and fought to rein it back in. Then she did something he hadn't expected. She made a move he couldn't combat.

She reached out and eased down his zipper before inserting her hands through the opening to cup him, as if she needed to touch, stroke and massage his aroused body part, getting reacquainted with its size and thickness. She didn't break eye contact with him, and he grew even more aroused with her bold ministrations. The more she stroked, the more his body vibrated, making blood rush through his veins, all going directly to that throbbing part of his body.

Minutes ticked by as he continued to stand there and stare at her while she literally drove him over the edge with her hand. He studied her face, saw the intent look in her eyes, the need to touch him this way. There was a feminine glow in her gaze that stirred everything male within him, and then once again, catching him off guard, she leaned in closer, stood on tiptoes and slid her tongue all around his lips, leaving a wet path in its wake. She caressed his mouth with the tip of her tongue the same way her fingertips were now stroking his aroused shaft.

He heard himself groan at the pleasure easing up his

spine and he knew if he didn't stop her now, he would embarrass himself in her hands when he preferred being inside of her body.

Now it was his turn to catch her off guard. He gently pushed her hand away seconds before sweeping her into his arms. He leaned down and kissed her with a voraciousness that had her moaning in his mouth.

When he finally pulled away, he took in a deep breath and knew he had to get completely submerged inside her body before he lost it. He stared down at her kiss-swollen lips as he held her in his arms.

"Do you know what you've asked for?" He wanted to make sure they were on the same page.

She held his gaze. "Yes. I know."

"You sure it's what you want?" He had to make doubly sure.

She shifted in his arms and ran her wet, warm tongue across his bare chest. The muscles in his stomach tightened and he knew, without her uttering a single word, he had gotten his answer.

Without saying anything else, he carried her upstairs to his bedroom.

Summer felt hot.

And when Darius placed her on his bed and joined her there, she felt passion that had been bottled up inside of her, ready to boldly claim its freedom. Every bone in her body seemed to vibrate, needing a release.

Her head began spinning when Darius removed her clothes with a swiftness that sent pieces flying everywhere. Then he stood and in record time, dropped his jeans and put on a condom he'd taken out of the nightstand drawer. Moments later, when she lay flat on her back, naked, he towered over her and she felt her thighs quiver with a yearning she hadn't felt in years.

He leaned back to slowly peruse her body and she felt heat every place his eyes touched, especially around her feminine core where his gaze seemed to linger, making sensations stir deep within her. The look in his eyes gave her more than an inkling of what he was thinking, and when he reached out and lifted her hips, placing her legs across his shoulders, she literally cried out before his mouth had a chance to touch her.

She cried out again when his mouth did touch her. He pushed his tongue inside, working it around in her with a greed that sent sparks shooting off in her, scorching everywhere it touched and weakening every bone in her body, turning her muscles to mush.

He spread her legs wider as his mouth continued to inflict upon her torment that was unyielding. What he was doing had captured her senses, totally wrecked her brain cells and fractured all rational thought. Physically, she was beginning to feel herself break into pieces and she grasped the strong arms on each side of her, trying to let him know there was no way she could take any more.

As if determined to prove to her that she could, he continued his torment on her body, tightening his grip on her thighs as his tongue dived deeper inside of her. When he flicked across a sensitive part of her, she shattered, and helplessly screamed his name as an onslaught of sensations ripped into her.

It was only then that he pulled back and straddled her, and before her lungs could fill with more air, he entered her in one deep thrust as he captured one of her breasts into his mouth, sucking deeply on a nipple.

The joining had been so perfect it nearly brought

tears to her eyes. She grabbed hold of his head to hold him to her breast and wrapped her legs around him to keep him inside of her. But the movement of his body told her he wasn't going anywhere.

He began moving, retreating and then pushing back in. Over and over again. Harder. Deeper. Faster. She felt every hard inch of him, felt the strong veins of his erection throb deep inside of her and push her over an edge that had her moaning yet again.

And when he shifted his mouth to her other breast and began the same mind-wrecking torment, her moan turned into another scream. She felt every nerve in her body explode, and she began riding a wave that took her across the top of anything and everything. When his body stiffened and bucked mercilessly while he tightly gripped her hips, she knew this was the fusing of not only their bodies, but their minds and souls.

And at that moment, nothing else existed in her world but the man who continued to push in and out of her while screaming her name. This was the same man who'd first shown her how beautiful the joining of a man and woman could be. The same man who moments later slumped down on the bed beside her and pulled her into his arms, holding her as if he never, ever wanted to let her go.

Summer awoke with the sunlight shining on her face and a strong, hard body plastered to her own. She shifted slightly and looked over at the man sleeping beside her, the man whose strong masculine leg was thrown over hers and whose arms, even in sleep, were wrapped around her.

Memories of last night flowed through her mind. It was the first time she had made love in seven years and it had been everything that she had remembered and more. Same man. Same passion. Same love.

She closed her eyes thinking that by rights, she should be upset with herself for still loving him and for the weakness that allowed her to tumble back into bed with him, especially after the way he had cheapened their first night together. But then she couldn't feel remorse when every part of her body was rejuvenated, like it had been awakened from a long sleep by pure pleasure. It had been making love with Darius the last time that had made her appreciate the fact she'd been born a woman, and it was his lovemaking now that was deepening that appreciation.

But still…memories of her pain, her humiliation wouldn't completely go away. How could a man who was so caring when it came to her so easily dishonor her the way he had? She had fallen in love with him completely and when he had made love to her that night, that love had intensified to a point that totally overwhelmed her.

He hadn't said the word *love* to her, but she had been certain of his feelings and had felt he'd displayed with his actions what he hadn't spoken. But she'd discovered her assumptions had been wrong. She did not intend to make the same mistake twice. All she and Darius had just shared was a sexual release. For her, it was a long time coming. She would not assume anything about their relationship ever again. She would accept it for what it was.

He shifted in bed and she tilted her head to look over at him. Before she could say a word, he leaned over and kissed her with a tenderness that made her groan. She didn't have to mull over what they were about to do again, this time in the brightness of the sunlight. And when he eased his body over hers, she wrapped her arms around his neck and eagerly gave him the mouth he seemed so intent to claim.

Summer stood at the window in her office. She kept replaying in her mind what had transpired last night and this morning. Although Darius had made love to her with an intensity and passion that nearly brought tears to her eyes, on the drive back over to her place this morning, she could sense him withdrawing. Why? Was he afraid she might assume just because they had slept together that she would think he wanted her back in his life? If that was the case, then he didn't know how wrong he was about it. She knew better than to think that way. She had learned her lesson well.

He had insisted on driving her to the office after he'd taken her home to dress, and he hadn't had a lot to say about what they had shared last night. Instead, he'd kept the conversation centered on Tyrone and all the things he would be checking on, saying he would take a trip to Houston if he had to.

He was still displaying those protective tendencies, but she could feel him putting up his guard, shielding emotions from her, keeping them out of her reach. More than once while in his arms last night and this morning, she had been tempted to ask him why he had done what he did seven years ago. But then she would decide to leave well enough alone. What happened was no longer a threat as long as she kept her heart out of the mix. Besides, she had bigger fish to fry. Tyrone Whitman and his whereabouts were what she needed to stay focused on. It was the only thing she should care about, the only thing that mattered.

The thought of Tyrone being free made her skin

crawl, but she refused to allow him to make her live in total fear. More than ever she was convinced he was the one who'd left that note on her windshield and slashed her tires, mainly because those were things Tyrone would do. Saying he took care of his own was something he'd said to her more than once. The reason she hadn't made the connection before was because she had assumed he was still locked up in prison. But now she knew that was not the case.

She glanced up at the clock on the wall. Darius said he would be coming back to walk her over to the café for lunch, and not to leave without him. This would be one time she did what he asked without any hesitation.

The phone on her desk rang and she immediately went to pick it up, hoping it was Darius with good news. "Hello?"

The person on the other end didn't say anything. "Hello?" she repeated. Chills ran down her spine when the person finally hung up. She tried to convince herself it was probably just a misdialed number. But deep down she had a feeling that wasn't true.

Darius's hands tightened on the steering wheel as he turned down the street that would take him to Helping Hands. Already he was regretting the news he was about to deliver to Summer.

He had made a call to the Houston Police Department as soon as he'd dropped Summer off at work. He'd been told Walt was out of town on an investigation, so he had spoken with Manny, another detective he knew. It had taken Manny less than an hour to find out what he wanted to know.

Manny had verified Whitman was out on parole with

an order not to leave Houston. However, according to Manny, Whitman could not be found at what should have been his current address, and his landlord hadn't seen him in weeks. Since Whitman had a week or so left before they could haul him in for violating parole, so far he hadn't broken any laws…unless it could be proven he had left Houston.

There was no doubt in Darius's mind that Whitman had been in Somerset and was possibly still around. Since Somerset was such a small town, it would be easy for Whitman to find out where Summer worked—as well as where she lived. The thought of her being at Whitman's mercy again was enough to make every fiber of his being roar in anger.

He shifted his thoughts to last night and this morning. While making love to her, he had tried holding himself back but he hadn't been able to control his emotions. Never had he been so affected by making love to a woman. It was as if the last seven years hadn't existed and there had never been a wedge between them. Last night and this morning fit perfectly into his plans. After this morning, he was supposed to take her back home, tell her about all the wealth he had accumulated over the years, that he was a member of the TCC and that not only did he know Kevin Novak but that Kevin was one of his closest friends. He had wanted to see the hurt in her eyes.

But Whitman's parole made that impossible—at least that's what he told himself. If it was determined the man was a threat to Summer, that would mean she'd stay with him for a while. She wouldn't like the idea, but he was determined to protect her at all costs.

* * *

Summer had been hoping, praying that the last seven years in jail would have changed Tyrone and she would no longer matter to him. It was disheartening to know she had been wrong and there was a strong chance he was stalking her again.

She told Darius about the strange phone call she had gotten that morning, and he, too, was convinced it had been Tyrone.

"Come on, let's go to lunch."

During lunch at the café Darius received a call. After the conversation ended, Summer knew from the look on his face that she was not going to like what he had to say.

He proved her right. "Before coming to the shelter I stopped at police headquarters to alert them that Whitman might be in the area. I provided them with a description of how he looked the last time I saw him, figuring his looks hadn't changed much over the years. But even if they had, Somerset is a small enough town that a stranger would stick out like a sore thumb."

He stopped talking, but she could tell there was more. "And?" she prompted.

"And they think he's been seen. A couple of the police officers who were cruising the area a few blocks from the shelter got suspicious of a guy who met Whitman's description. When they tried to approach him to question him, he ran."

Summer didn't say anything for a moment. "I refuse to let Tyrone scare me again, Darius. Although it didn't work the last time, I'm going to get another restraining order."

"That's a good idea. If he is taken into custody here

in Somerset for any reason, his parole will automatically be revoked."

Darius hesitated a moment and then said, "Although you're refusing to let Tyrone scare you, I'm hoping you'll continue to stay with me until this issue with him is resolved. It will only be a matter of time before he finds out where you live, if he doesn't know already. Alarm or no alarm, if he ever breaks inside your home again, depending on his frame of mind, there's no telling what he will do. If knowing he will go back to jail and serve out the rest of his sentence hasn't deterred him, that can only mean he doesn't care. And people who don't care will do just about anything to get back at the person they think has betrayed them."

Summer knew what Darius said was true. Tyrone had held a gun to her head, willing and ready to end her life as well as his own. She really didn't want to go home with Darius again, but she didn't have a choice. Even after what they had shared last night and this morning, she could still feel tension between them. She could tell he still had his guard up.

"Summer?"

She met his gaze, felt the heat in the dark depths of his eyes. He wanted to keep her safe. And he wanted her. Summer knew that no matter how guarded he was being, he couldn't deny he enjoyed having her back in his bed, and she would admit she enjoyed being there. Intimacy between them wasn't just good, it was off the charts. Sexual tension was always oozing between them, even when she didn't want it to, like now.

Knowing he was waiting on an answer, she said, "Okay, I'll move in with you for the time being if you think it will be for the best."

Chapter 9

A week later, as Darius sat in the TCC café waiting to meet with Lance, he was convinced that Summer moving in with him had been the best thing to keep her safe. Although he wasn't sure just what her being underfoot was doing to his peace of mind.

At first, he had put up his guard, finding excuses to work outdoors in the evenings to stay away from the house. But living under the same roof made it difficult to deny his desire for her when she was near.

Evidently, she hadn't been sure just where she should sleep the night she had returned to his place. They had stopped by her house to get more of her things, and after she had gotten settled at his place and taken a shower, she had gone to sleep in the guest bedroom.

He had stayed outside deliberately talking to his ranch foreman, and when he had come inside and found her asleep in the guest bedroom, he tried to convince himself that her sleeping arrangements were fine with him.

He'd taken a shower and crawled into his own bed. But knowing that she was asleep in another bedroom didn't suit him. However, his stubbornness, the cold hard casting around his heart, just wouldn't thaw any.

After the third night, he realized that he had finally reached his limit. He got out of bed and went into the guest bedroom to discover her wide awake. She had been unable to sleep those nights, too.

He could vividly recall that particular night, and how he had stood in the doorway and stared at her across the room, wanting so much to despise her, and also his weakness for her. Without saying a word, he had reached out his hand to her and she had eased out of bed, crossing the room to place her hand in his.

Darius sighed deeply thinking it had been at that particular moment that he could no longer deny that she was and would always be a part of him. He had faced the truth that the reason he was so determined to protect her was because he still cared for her. Deeply.

Since then she had shared his bed every night and he'd enjoyed waking up with her beside him each morning. And he was getting used to her being in his home, in his space. Being under the same roof with her gave him a chance to get to know the new Summer, the one that had grown up without him. And he couldn't help but admire the woman she had become, the dedicated social worker who understood what it was like to be a woman in jeopardy. A woman who had been abused.

In the evenings he no longer found reasons to stay away from his home. Together they would prepare meals, clean up the kitchen and talk about the day's events, only bringing up Whitman when they needed to. He had been sighted several more times in Somerset. Darius had even approached the Texas Rangers about Whitman informing them that he had violated parole. Although he had yet to be apprehended, Darius was convinced that eventually he would be, and was glad, in the meantime, that he was keeping Summer safe.

"Sorry I'm late. I sort of got detained," Lance said, breaking into his thoughts and sliding into the chair across from him.

Darius couldn't help but laugh. Based on the satisfied smile on his best friend's face, he could only assume Kate was the reason he was late, and now he understood what it was like to have a woman under your skin and close at hand.

"No problem. I just wanted to give you a copy of the official fire department report and provide an update on my investigation. I checked out all your employees who were questionable and was able to rule out each and every one of them."

Lance nodded. "I figured you would. I told you who I suspect."

Yes, Lance had told him, Darius thought, several times. But Darius still wasn't convinced. Something didn't sit right with him.

Darius checked his watch. It had become a routine for him to drive Summer to work every morning and pick her up in the afternoon, and he did not want to be late. It was a routine he was beginning to get accustomed to. And it was one he liked, whether he wanted to admit it or not. Business would have to wait.

Summer came down the stairs and looked around, not seeing Darius anywhere. She went into the kitchen, deciding to make a cup of tea. It wasn't unusual for him to go outside and spend time with the men who ran his ranch in the afternoons, and she had been fully aware that when she'd first come to stay with him he had used that as an excuse to put distance between them.

Now that had changed. He no longer avoided her in his home and she spent every night in his bed. She still wasn't assuming anything and knew once Tyrone had been captured, Darius would expect her to leave and return to her home. She wouldn't be doing herself any favors if she became attached to his beautiful home, which she already loved. It was far enough from town to offer peace and quiet that anyone would cherish, yet at the same time it was a place where a family could be raised.

She shook her head, determined to get such foolish thoughts out of it. What she and Darius were sharing was physical and nothing more. She turned at the sound of footsteps and knew it was him.

He walked through the back door, saw her and smiled. He might not love her but there was no doubt in her mind that he enjoyed having her around. He closed the door behind him, locked it and just stood there, staring at her. When he had brought her home from work she had gone upstairs to take a shower. Now she felt refreshed but at the same time, hot. And the way he was looking at her was making her feel even hotter.

Without a word, she crossed the kitchen floor and wrapped her arms around his neck. Then, leaning upward she captured his mouth with hers. His response was immediate and he didn't waste any time letting her know it, or letting her feel it. His thick erection was throbbing against her, making her senses come unglued and sending sensations rushing through her veins and all over her skin.

Moments later she pulled back and met his gaze. "We need to prepare dinner," she said in a ragged voice, barely able to breathe.

"Later." And then he swept her off her feet and headed upstairs to his bedroom.

Bodies joined. Summer moved with Darius as his lips brushed a kiss beneath her ear and whispered just how much he enjoyed being inside of her, making love to her, being one with her.

The rhythm he had established was perfect, and floated them toward fulfillment. The air surrounding them was charged and the more he thrust into her body, the more her senses seemed whipped with a pleasure so profound it took her breath away.

"Now!"

As if on cue, her body began convulsing right along with his, endlessly, as shivers tore through them, pulling them down yet at the same time building them up. And when she cried out in pleasure, every pull of her feminine muscles was regulated by his steady yet rapid strokes into her body, making her lift her hips and use her thighs to squeeze him tight, clench him for all she was worth.

She tossed her head back when he surged even deeper inside of her, gripping her thighs and taking her all over again, pushing her toward another orgasm and doing everything in his power to make sure they both got there.

They did.

Instead of letting up, the heat was on yet again, and the workings of her inner muscles signified that such a notion made perfect sense, given the depth of their desire, their passion and their sexual hunger. It was as if they were making up for lost time and then some, filling a drought, satisfying a yearning, soothing an ache.

And when he began moving inside of her in quick, rapid successions, she cried out his name as shivers of pleasure tore through her once again.

"Do you know how beautiful you are? And you're even more beautiful after making love."

Summer glanced over and saw Darius had awakened. He was smiling, and the look in his eyes was filled with the same heat she still felt on some parts of her body. "Thank you."

She knew at that moment she would have to broach the subject she had tried putting behind her since seeing him again.

His betrayal.

"And you are a very handsome man, making love or not," she said softly. Truthfully. She paused a moment and then asked the one question she needed answered. One she could not put off asking any longer. "Why did you make that bet?"

A confused look appeared on his face. "What bet?"

Summer was certain there was no way he could not know what bet she was referring to. But if he wanted to pretend to have a loss of memory, she could remedy that. "I'm talking about the bet you made with Walt about how quick you could take me to bed."

In an instant, he was up, leaning over her. The look on his face was one of incredulous fury. "What the hell are you talking about? I never made a bet like that."

She wondered why he was not going to own up to it now. "That's all right, Darius. It doesn't matter."

"Yes, it does matter," he said in a hard voice. "Especially if you believed it."

She frowned. "Why are you denying it?"

"Because I never did such a thing. How could you have believed something like that?"

She drew in a deep breath and held his gaze. "Because Walt told me what you did. He felt that I had a right to know."

His face hardened. "Walt!" he all but roared.

"Yes," she countered in a voice filled with just as much conviction. "Yes, Walt Stewart. He was your partner at the time. Or have you forgotten about him, as well?"

"No, I haven't forgotten about Walt. In fact, I spoke with him just last week about that arson case I'm investigating. What you're saying doesn't make sense, Summer, because Walt knew how I felt about you. There's no way he could have told you something like that."

Summer's head began spinning and it took her a second to find steady ground. *Walt knew how I felt about you...*

Could he be saying that he had cared as deeply about her as she had about him? She continued to stare at Darius and noted the way he was looking back at her. Then he asked slowly, with disbelief, "And Walt actually told you that?"

"Yes."

Darius released her and eased out of bed, seemingly barely able to keep the lid on raging anger. She swallowed, slowly realizing the impact of what now appeared to be a blatant lie. But why?

"Put on some clothes. We need to talk, and this is not the place for us to do it," he said, interrupting her thoughts. He picked up his jeans and eased into them. "Please meet me in the living room."

Summer stared at his back as he walked out the room.

* * *

Darius paced his living room with his hands in tight fists. Why in the hell had Walt told Summer something like that? How could he have told her?

He could vividly remember sharing a beer with Walt one night after their shift had ended and telling him just how much Summer had come to mean to him. Walt had sat there listening, not saying anything, mainly because Darius hadn't given him a chance to say anything. His heart had been filled with love, and he had wanted to share those emotions with someone he had considered a friend.

He and Walt had gotten hired around the same time and had easily become friends. He was well aware of Walt's issues with the opposite sex because of his ex-wife's betrayal, but Darius had overlooked them because it hadn't been his issue or concern.

Now he had to wonder just how deep Walt's deception went. He knew what Summer had been told, but what about what Walt had told him about Summer, and the message she had supposedly left for him? According to Walt, Summer had left town with an older man. A rich man.

"I'm here now."

Darius stopped his pacing and turned around. She stood there, not in the shorts and blouse he had taken off her earlier that night, but in one of his T-shirts that had been thrown across a chair in his room. Whether it was her intent or not, her wearing his shirt meant something to him. It was as if she was giving him an unspoken acknowledgment of their connection, a connection that had started seven years ago and by some work of miracle was back in full force.

Making love to her over the past weeks had closed old wounds. But now he was discovering that those wounds were self-inflicted due to his belief of Walt's lies. "Let's sit and discuss this, please. I'm beginning to think we've been played."

He watched as she took a seat on the sofa, trying not to notice that his shirt hit her mid-thigh, and how sexy she looked in it. More than anything, he had to keep his mind on the issues at hand, issues they needed to dissect and resolve. After she was seated, instead of sitting beside her on the sofa, he took the leather wing chair that sat not far away.

"To take up the conversation we started in bed, I want you to know, I want you to believe, that at no time did I discuss sleeping with you with Walt. There was no bet."

He watched her features. She held his gaze as intensely as he was holding hers. He saw in her eyes a desire to believe what he said. But…

"Then how did he know about that night?" she asked. "He knew that you had spent the night over at my place."

Darius thought about her words. "He must have driven by your apartment and seen my car parked out front."

He could tell from her expression that she was taking his explanation into consideration, agreeing that it was possible. However, there was still lingering doubt in her eyes.

"Why didn't you contact me?" she then asked him. "He told me you left town and would be gone for a few days, but I never heard from you again. It was like you *had* scored and put me out of your life."

Darius leaned back in his chair. "Did he not tell you why I had to leave immediately or where I had gone?"

"He didn't go into any details. He just said you'd been called away on police business and would be gone a few days."

Darius jaw tightened. "The reason I had to leave when I did was because I got a call that Ethan had been critically injured in a car accident and was being wheeled into surgery. Since I'm his only family, I had to get to Charleston. For a while, I wasn't sure Ethan was going to make it. I was by his bedside day and night and did not have use of my cell phone. And when I did call, I got a message that you had gotten your cell number changed."

He saw the shock in Summer's gaze and before she could say anything, he knew she hadn't known. "Walt didn't tell me that," she said angrily, getting to her feet. "I didn't know."

Connecting his fingers in a steeple, he placed them under his chin. "When I returned to town almost two weeks later, after Ethan's condition had stabilized, I went straight to your place from the airport, only to be told by your landlord that you had moved out a few days earlier, and that an older man in a Mercedes had picked you up and that you had left with him."

She nodded. "Yes, that was Karl Lindsey."

He paused for a second and then said, "Walt is the one who told me why you had left."

She shifted in her seat and his gaze was drawn to a flash of her thigh. His attention went back to her face when she said, "Yes, Walt just happened to drop by that day Karl was there, and just on the off chance you cared enough to ask, I told him that I had taken a job with Karl and would be moving to Florida for a year."

Darius raised a brow. "A job?"

"Yes, Karl had been one of my regulars at the restaurant. He's a writer. He offered me a job as his assistant, editing and organizing his notes. He had offered me the same job before but Tyrone had forced me to turn it down. When I hadn't heard anything from you, and after Walt told me what you did, I decided to take Mr. Lindsey's offer and moved to Florida with him and his wife and—"

"His wife?"

Summer didn't say anything for a moment as she studied his expression. Then she said, "Yes, Lola, his wife. You sound surprised."

Darius stared at her as a deep sharp pain ripped through him. For the first time he was seeing that trust on both sides had been shattered because he and Summer had been quick to believe the lies of others. He had been so quick to believe the worst of her and she of him. Not because they thought of each other as devious people, but because their relationship had been in the early stages, at a very delicate period when trust, faith and love was building. He didn't want to think of how strong their relationship would be if it had been given a chance to grow.

"Darius?"

He hated telling her what he'd thought, what he'd assumed, but knew that he had to do so. "The message Walt gave me, the one he claimed you left, was that you had met this old, rich man and that you couldn't waste your time with someone who was nothing but a college-educated cop with no aspirations of being anything else."

She stared at him. He saw the hurt and pain in her eyes and knew why. Just like she had believed Walt's lies about him, he had believed the man's lies about her.

"Why were we so quick to believe the worst of each

other?" she asked in a whisper that he could barely hear. "We played right into Walt's hands," she added. "That's sad."

As far as he was concerned, it was worse than sad. It was pathetic. Seven years wasted. He then said the only thing that he could say at that moment. "I'm sorry."

She breathed in deeply. "And I'm sorry, as well."

Darius could only sit there silently for a moment, wondering how one went about repairing a love that had been destroyed by lies. Lies that had been so easy to accept. Inside of him, a voice said, *One day at a time.*

"Summer, I—"

"No, Darius, I think we both need time to come to terms with what happened, the lies that were told and why we were so quick to believe them. I haven't been in a relationship with anyone since you, serious or otherwise. I've grown accustomed to being by myself, not wanting a man to share my life. I don't trust easily anymore. I'm more cautious. I really don't know if that can change."

He could read between the lines. She was letting him know when it was all said and done, regardless of the fact that they had lived together for the last few weeks or so, getting along marvelously, complementing each other's personalities, she was not all that certain that she wanted to give them another chance because of their lack of faith and trust in each other. From what she was saying, she still didn't want a man in her life. Things had changed. She had changed. In a way, he understood.

Over the years he had kept most women at bay, being selective about who he wanted to spend his time with and not allowing himself to get serious about anyone. But he could see all that changing and wondered if she could. Their relationship—and he considered them to be in a relationship—had to undergo some serious repairs. Major repairs. But he thought they could do it.

They had uncovered a lot tonight. But he still had something else to come clean about—his association with the TCC.

"Summer. I—"

"Will you contact the authorities to see if anyone has seen Tyrone again?" she cut in to ask.

He knew she was trying to get off the subject. He would let her do so for now since tonight had been over-whelming, to say the least, and he wasn't sure how she would handle the unveiling of another lie. One that had been his own, as a way to hurt her. He would tell her another time. Soon. Tomorrow.

"Yes, I'll do that."

There was no need to tell her that he planned on kill-ing two birds with one stone by driving to Houston to-morrow to meet with Tyrone's parole officer and that he would also be paying a visit to Walt.

He studied her, wondering if she knew the signifi-cance of what she had admitted moments ago. He was the last man she had made love with. She hadn't wanted a man in her life in seven years, yet she had shared her-self with him.

At that moment, all he could think about was what they had shared. The heat. The passion.

"I guess we could sit here and stare at each other all night," she finally said, "but I prefer going back to bed."

He rose to his feet, accepting the gravity of the mis-takes they'd both made. But he also accepted that she needed him now like he needed her. "Then I don't plan to keep you up any longer."

He crossed the room to her. They had a lot left to talk

about, still more truths to tell. But at that moment, they needed to be together and they both knew it.

Darius held his hand out to her and she took it. Together, they returned to his bedroom.

While en route to the shelter the next morning, Darius received a call. "This is Darius."

He listened attentively to what the caller was saying and then he said, "That's good news and I appreciate you calling to let me know. I'll pass the information on to Ms. Martindale."

He clicked off the phone and glanced over at Summer. "That was a Texas Ranger friend of mine. He was calling to let me know that they picked up Whitman this morning."

Darius saw a wave of relief pass through her. "Where?" she asked.

They had come to a stop at the traffic light and Darius glanced over at her. "Less than a block from your house."

He hated telling her the next part but knew that he had to. "He had a gun and a rope in his possession."

Summer stiffened and Darius understood why. Chances were Whitman had discovered where she lived, and a good possibility existed that he had planned on using that information for no good. Since he had violated parole in more ways than one, Darius knew he would return to prison and serve his entire sentence.

She didn't say anything, staring straight ahead, out the windshield.

"You okay?" he asked.

She turned to him. "Yes, I'm okay."

She might be okay, but he wasn't. How could he have been so wrong about her? He couldn't wait to confront

Walt about the lies he'd told. "I have something to take care of this morning and won't be back in time to join you for lunch."

"All right."

She didn't seem to be in a talkative mood and he figured she needed time to digest everything he had told her about Whitman.

"Since Tyrone is in police custody, there's no reason I can't return home now, is there?"

None other than I don't want you to go. I've gotten used to having you around. I've fallen in love with you all over again. "No, there's no reason you can't," he said.

He breathed in deeply and at that moment, he knew there was no use denying what he'd known all along. He loved her. He had not stopped loving her.

And all this time he had tried convincing himself that he would seek revenge for what she had done, when he knew he couldn't have gone through with that plan no matter how much he'd thought he wanted to hurt her.

From the first moment she had turned her eyes on him he had been a goner, and although he'd convinced himself over the years that he had gotten over her, the simple truth was, he hadn't. Coming to terms with his love for her was a monumental release of the hold he'd placed on his emotions. All the built-up tension and anger he'd felt since seeing her again left his body, flowed out of his muscles. It strengthened his heart, propelling him to do whatever he had to do to make her his again.

Chapter 10

A few hours later, Summer slipped into her walking shoes to go to the café for lunch, reflecting that this was the first time in quite a while that she would be doing so without Darius by her side.

She drew in a huge breath of profound relief, knowing what could have been another nightmare with Tyrone was now over. She shivered when she thought of the items that had been in his possession. There was no doubt in her mind he intended to do her harm, and she was grateful yet again to Darius for keeping her out of harm's way.

Darius. The man she still loved.

She wondered if she'd sounded convincing when she told him that she didn't want a man in her life. A part of her did want to belong to him, totally and completely, but was afraid to get her hopes up again. Even though she knew the truth now, it couldn't erase the pain she had felt for seven years.

Besides, there was nothing Darius had said to make her think that he wanted to renew what they'd once shared. When she'd mentioned returning to her place now that the threat with Tyrone was over, he hadn't said anything to talk her out of it, he hadn't said that he didn't want her to leave.

He had apologized for believing the lies Walt had told him. And she had apologized to him, as well. Later, they had made love but no promises had been made. There had been no discussion of a future together. Although he hadn't said as much, she had a feeling that he didn't want a woman in his life.

That left her with the same life she'd been living since leaving Houston. The kind of life she had gotten used to. It was somewhat lonely but safe. She would continue to live it without the man she loved.

The anger within Darius told him to strike out the moment he saw Walt walking toward him. But he fought to hold his rage in check. There was only one thing he wanted from the man and that was for him to explain why he'd done what he did.

Without telling Walt why, he had called and requested to meet with him in Laverne Square, a newly developed area of Houston near the Madaris Office Park. He rose from the bench when he saw the curious look in Walt's eyes.

"Darius, didn't you get my message that the guy you wanted me to check out was clean? I left it on your voice mail last week."

"That's not why I asked you to meet with me," Darius answered, trying to keep the bitterness out of his voice.

Walt lifted a brow. "Oh. Then what's up?"

Darius looked directly into his eyes. "I'm here about the lie you told me about Summer Martindale."

Walt held his gaze for an instant before shifting his eyes to look out over the pond in the square. Time stretched on and for a moment, Darius wondered if he was going to say anything. Then Walt turned his gaze to Darius.

"She came with a lot of baggage and was trouble with that crazy boyfriend of hers. You didn't need her."

His words, spoken as if he'd had a right to make that decision, slithered down Darius's spine. "You were wrong, Walt. She wasn't trouble and you knew how I felt about her. I not only needed her but I loved her."

"You have a lot to learn about women, Darius. You can never let one get under your skin, and you can never admit to loving one."

Darius stared at him for a moment. "Actually," he said in a deep, cutting tone, "there's a lot that *you* need to learn about them, and recognizing a good one when you meet her is at the top of the list."

A deep frown settled on Walt's face. "There aren't any good ones."

Walt had extreme issues, but Darius couldn't concern himself with that right now. As far as he was concerned, what Walt had done was unforgivable. When he thought about all those wasted years when he and Summer could have been together, years when he had loathed her very name, he practically wanted to kill the man. It was all for nothing. All for lies.

Filled with total disgust and having nothing else to say, Darius started to leave.

"Hey, wait, man, we're okay, aren't we? We're still friends?" Walt asked in a lighthearted tone.

Darius stopped walking and looked over his shoulder. Their gazes locked. The message he was certain Walt saw in his eyes was blatantly clear.

"No. Our friendship died the day you lied to me. I loved her, but because I thought you were my friend, I believed you. A true friend would not have done what you did."

Without saying anything else, he walked off, leaving Walt standing there.

Summer was just about to go to the café when one of the security guards escorted a very well dressed, distinguished-looking older man through the entrance. It didn't take a rocket scientist to figure out from the way the man was carrying himself that he was someone of authority, someone of importance, which could only mean he was a member of the TCC. Kevin Novak had given her a heads-up that over the next few months, members of the TCC would probably be dropping by to check out the shelter since he had asked them for more money.

Putting on her brightest smile, Summer crossed the lobby to greet the man. "Welcome to Helping Hands," she said, extending her hand to him. "I'm Summer Martindale, a social worker here."

The man took her hand and looked at her. "So, you're the young woman who's been causing so much excitement."

Summer forced her smile to remain intact when she recognized his voice. He was the person she had talked to on the phone when she'd called requesting additional security guards. "Am I?" she couldn't help but ask, not liking the way the man seemed to be staring down his nose at her.

"Yes. I'm Sebastian Huntington, a member of the Texas Cattleman's Club."

"Nice to meet you, Mr. Huntington."

He didn't say anything to indicate that the feelings were mutual. Instead, he glanced around. "Things seem calm enough around here. I really don't see why two guards are needed. But then, you've managed to convince Kevin Novak differently."

She was about to say the reason things appeared calm was because everyone felt safer with two guards when he once again looked down his nose at her and arrogantly said, "And then there's Darius Franklin, who's evidently quite taken with you. He's also been singing your praises at the TCC meetings." A sneer touched his lips as he studied her features. "Now I see why."

Surprise flickered in her eyes. "Darius?"

"Yes. He's one of our newest members."

Now she was confused. *Darius was a member of TCC?*

"How long has he been a member?"

The man frowned down at her like she'd asked a stupid question. "Not long enough for him and his friends to be throwing their weight around. He's only been a member for over a year."

Summer nodded. "Oh, I see." And the sad part of it was that she really did see. Darius had lied to her.

"Ready to go?"

Summer slowly lifted her gaze from the document at

the sound of the deep, husky voice. Had it been nearly three weeks ago when here in this office she had heard that voice again for the first time in seven years?

After Mr. Huntington left, instead of walking to the café, she had gone to the library. There she had researched information on the Texas Cattleman's Club branch that was located in Somerset. Darius was listed as a member, having joined the same day as Kevin Novak and several other men, and from the photographs she had seen, it was apparent that he and Mr. Novak knew each other very well. Why had he pretended otherwise when she'd told him of her meeting with Mr. Novak? Why had he deliberately kept his membership in the TCC from her?

Instead of answering his question, she asked one of her own.

"Why didn't you tell me you were a member of the Texas Cattleman's Club?"

She saw surprise light his eyes and knew he was probably wondering how she'd found out. "Mr. Huntington dropped by to check out the place and mentioned you're a member," she said, leaning back in her chair.

"So, my question is, why didn't you tell me, Darius? You had several chances to do so when I was preparing for my meeting with Mr. Novak, and many after that. Why didn't you tell me?"

A part of Darius wished he'd have told Summer everything last night. How would she react to finding out he had withheld the information because of his plan to hurt her?

Any chance of rebuilding a relationship with her would probably be destroyed now. But still, he had to be upfront and honest with her. Lies were the reason they were in the situation they were in now.

Sighing deeply, he entered her office and closed the door behind him, leaning against it. "The reason I didn't want to tell you is because I was still operating under the belief that you had left Houston with a rich man. A man you had chosen over me because of his wealth. With that belief festering in my mind as well as my heart over the years, I had grown to resent you for choosing wealth over love."

When she didn't say anything, he continued. "I figured that if that was true, once you found out about my wealth, the fact that I had become successful, I could get my revenge by seducing you, taking you to bed and then walking away from you the same way I thought you had walked away from me. I wanted to hurt you the way you had hurt me."

Summer still didn't say anything for a moment, and then in a low voice, she asked, "You hated me that much?"

Darius breathed in again, hearing the deep hurt in her voice. "I thought I did, but once I got to know what I thought was the new Summer Martindale, the one who's dedicated to the women at the shelter, the one who works tirelessly after hours when her shift is over, I realized that no matter how much I wanted revenge, I couldn't have gone through with it. And do you know why, Summer?"

"I have no idea," she said in a sharp tone.

He held her gaze. "Because I realized that although I'd tried over the years, I couldn't replace love with hate. Although I wanted to hurt you, I couldn't because I still love you."

Their gazes held and for a moment, he wondered if she believed him. He hoped and prayed for some sort of sign that she did. He had been wrong for wanting to get even with her, but at the time he'd felt it was something he had needed to do because of his pain.

"So many years have passed, Summer. We owe it to ourselves to try and rebuild the relationship that was destroyed because of our lack of faith and trust in each other. In Houston today, I made a point to see Walt. I had to know why he'd done what he did. His reason was he saw me falling for you and figured I'd get hurt. But the truth of the matter is that I was hurt in the end anyway. Not by you, but because I'd believed the worst about you."

He moved away from the door to stand in front of her desk. "I'm asking that you give me a chance to do what I wanted to do seven years ago and that is, love you the way a man is supposed to love a woman. Please allow me into your heart, Summer. Give me a chance to prove that I am the right man for you."

He took another step closer. "Will you put behind you all the hurt and lies of before and move forward in the way we should have years ago? Can you find it in your heart to love me as much as I love you? To work on re-building a relationship of love, trust and faith?"

He saw the single tear that fell from her eye and literally held his breath before she began speaking.

"Yes," she said slowly. "I can work on rebuilding our relationship because I love you, too, and I want you in my life. I want a future with you, not because of your wealth but because you are a man who's proven more than once that he can be there when I need someone, that he has my best interests at heart, and protects me when I need protecting."

She pushed her chair back and walked around her desk to him. "We have a lot of years to make up for, but I knew that night we made love again it was something I wanted. I was just afraid to hope for it."

Darius pulled her into his arms and held her tight, close to his heart. And then he lowered his mouth to hers. He wanted her with him always and from the intensity of their kiss, it seemed she wanted the very same thing.

Moments later, he pulled his mouth away from hers. "Ready to go home, sweetheart?" And to make sure she understood, he added, "Not to your place, but to mine. A place that you will one day consider ours, I hope."

She smiled up at him. "Yes, I'm ready."

He took her hand in his and they walked out of her office together. He knew there was a lot of work ahead, rebuilding their relationship into the kind they both wanted, the kind they deserved. Lies had destroyed their relationship, but love had restored it. Their love would make it all happen for them.

They would make sure of it. Together.

Epilogue

Three weeks later

Summer stepped outside on the porch and glanced around. It was a beautiful day and the smell of flowers was everywhere.

She felt butterflies move around in her stomach at the same time she saw the car pull into the yard. She smiled. Darius was home.

She glanced around again, thinking how easy it was to think of his ranch as home. She never returned to her place, and every week more and more of her things would show up here.

And then one night while they were busy unpacking some more of her boxes, he had got down on his knee and proposed to her. He asked her to be his wife, the mother of his babies and his best friend for life. Somehow through her tears she had accepted. The moment he had slipped the ring on her finger, more love and happiness than she'd ever thought possible filled her heart. They hadn't set a date yet, and had decided to take things one day at a time.

She had met his friends and could see the special friendship they shared. She liked them a lot. Tonight they would be joining Lance and Kate at the TCC for dinner.

As soon as the car came to a stop, she moved down the steps, and when Darius opened the door and got out, she was there waiting.

He pulled her into his arms and kissed her, making her feel wanted and loved. Things were so good between them that she would occasionally pinch herself to make sure it was real. And over and over he would prove to her that it was.

He pulled back and studied her face with concern. "Are you okay? I stopped by the shelter and Marcy said you had left early."

She smiled up at him. "Yes, I'm fine. I just wanted to be here when you got home. I thought that I would pamper you a little before we left for dinner."

A grin curved his lips and she could tell he liked the idea. "Pamper me?"

"Yes. Are you interested?"

Instead of answering, he swept her off her feet into his arms and carried her up the steps. *Yes,* she thought, *he was interested.*

She laughed, knowing once he got her inside the house he intended to show her just how interested he was.

* * * * *

Synithia Williams has loved romance novels since reading her first one at the age of thirteen. It was only natural that she would one day write her own romances. When she isn't writing, Synithia works on water quality issues in the Midlands of South Carolina while taking care of her supportive husband and two sons. You can learn more about Synithia by visiting her website, synithiawilliams.com.

Books by Synithia Williams

Harlequin Kimani Romance

A New York Kind of Love
A Malibu Kind of Romance
Full Court Seduction
Overtime for Love
Guarding His Heart
His Pick for Passion

HQN

Forbidden Promises
Scandalous Secrets
Careless Whispers

Visit the Author Profile page at Harlequin.com for more titles.

FULL COURT SEDUCTION

Synithia Williams

For Ashley and Toya,
my ride-or-die sisters since forever.

Acknowledgments

The biggest thanks to Farrah Rochon for organizing the Destin Divas Retreat. I plotted *Full Court Seduction* at that retreat and made a few new writing friends. I have to give special thanks to Destin Divas Jamie Wesley, Carla Freed and Lena Hart for helping me define a "Hollywood ending" for Jacobe and Danielle, and Divas K.M. Jackson and Kaia Danielle for their valuable feedback on the draft. Finally, to my wonderful hubby, I truly appreciate you watching our two boys while I'm off in the writer world. Writing would be much harder without your support.

Chapter 1

Event planning would be the death of her.

Which was why Danielle had taken a break from planning the next few events for the St. Johns River Watchers to get a cup of coffee. She was pretty sure that if she hadn't taken the break, her heart was going to wave the white flag and go on permanent strike against the stress she put herself through.

The sound of footsteps running toward the kitchen of the small beachfront cottage that served as the River Watchers office preceded the appearance of Danielle's education-and-outreach coordinator, who was rushing toward the door.

"Danielle, have you heard?" Debra said between huffs. Her cheeks were red from the sprint. She pushed her thin jet-black hair behind her ears, making her gothic-inspired cross earrings swing against her pale neck. Her black pants, boots and *Nightmare Before*

Christmas T-shirt were splattered with glitter, a leftover from a presentation at a kindergarten class earlier today.

"Heard what?"

Debra looked to the ceiling and shook her head. "You're not angry, so I'm assuming you haven't heard. I spoke with Mr. Springfield today—the state hasn't automatically denied the permit allowing Clear Water to discharge into Springfield Creek."

Danielle set the mug on the counter, coffee and gala temporarily forgotten, and crossed to the small wooden dinette table. "What? They should be shutting down, not expanding."

She'd fought on behalf of the River Watchers all last year to get Clear Water's permits revoked. The small wastewater provider couldn't handle the sewage from the rapidly growing area coming to them and had exceeded their permit limits for pollution levels going into a tributary of the river. The state had agreed and ordered Clear Water to come up with a plan to reduce pollution or shut down.

"They think that expanding their operation and adding another discharge point will make them meet our demands."

"The creek can't handle that."

Debra nodded. "I know that. Mr. Springfield certainly doesn't want it going into the creek. He worked too hard with us to put the easements in place that will stop it from future development. Now all those efforts are threatened if this happens."

Danielle's brain buzzed with a variety of ideas. They needed to do something. "We need to get in front of the county commissioners at their next meeting. Get them to deny any permits for the expansion. If this goes through it doesn't just hurt Mr. Springfield, it had the potential to hurt everyone living in the Crescent Acres community."

Crescent Acres was a low-income neighborhood in an area just south of Jacksonville, Florida. Springfield Creek flowed right through the neighborhood before it entered Mr. Springfield's property. Many of the people who lived there fished and played in that creek. If a sewer provider that already couldn't meet their current permit limits started dumping poorly treated wastewater into the creek the effects could be devastating.

"I'm already talking to the commissioner's clerk to see about getting on the agenda," Debra said.

"Any idea what stance the county wants to take?"

Though the county leaders sometimes voted to preserve the areas going into the river, they also rarely took a huge stance on environmental issues.

Debra shook her head. "No idea."

Danielle slapped her fist into her opposite palm. "We've got to get them to fight this."

Debra chuckled. "I think they're already expecting your call. The clerk remembers how much you hounded the state to go after Clear Water last year."

"I only scheduled a small press conference."

Debra smirked. "You put out a rally cry to our supporters to show up in front of the Clear Water gates with old toilets and signs that said 'Poop in the toilet, not our river.'"

Danielle shrugged and smothered a grin. She was pretty proud of that idea. "It got everyone's attention. We'll need something equally big to get people paying attention again. That was just a year ago, but no one is watching what Clear Water is doing now. I can't believe they have the nerve to try and dump into Springfield Creek."

"They'll be ready for battle after you gave them so much grief before."

Danielle had been with the River Watchers since graduating from the University of Miami five years ago. When her sampling efforts proved Clear Water was dumping catastrophic amounts of pollution into the river, she'd spearheaded a movement against the provider. Her actions quickly turned the small organization into the most well-known conservation watchdog in the community. She'd gone from organizing their monitoring program to an executive director in a record five years.

"Does it look like I can't go to battle with them?" Danielle turned, picked up her coffee mug off the counter and took a sip.

"Of course you don't look like you're ready for battle. That's why you win. You surprise people with ferocious tenacity beneath your girl-next-door exterior."

"I do not."

"Yeah. You do." Debra eyed Danielle from head to toe.

Danielle straightened her glasses and smoothed the front of the white cardigan she wore over a navy sundress. "Maybe I use that as a slight tactical advantage."

"You're never afraid to do battle with anyone, which is why I love working with you."

"Don't try and butter me up for a raise," Danielle teased. "I won't be able to cover the part-time salaries of the interns next fiscal year if we can't get any more donors."

"I'm not worried. Since you became executive director a year ago the donations have improved. The idea for the River Gala and silent auction this year was smart. I'm sure that'll help raise some funds."

Debra nodded and looked at Danielle like she was the great black hope. Danielle's earlier freak-out about the success of the events she planned came back full force. They would need several successful events, not just the gala in a few weeks, to keep their doors open.

"If it makes you feel any better," Debra said. "I think Mr. Springfield knows this is going to be a huge battle for us. He gave us a gift to thank us for our efforts."

"A gift?"

"Two tickets…wait let me start over. Two—*court-side*—tickets for tonight's Jacksonville Gators game." Debra pulled the tickets from her back pocket. "He said to go, enjoy and relax before the fight. I know you're a huge fan. I figured you'd be excited."

Danielle rushed over to Debra's side to snatch the tickets. "Are you for real?" She scanned the tickets to confirm the unbelievable news.

"Yep. Mr. Springfield has to go out of town tonight. He said he couldn't think of two more deserving ladies than us."

"Tonight's game is a big one for them. They're playing Miami."

"Ooh, double the eye candy. Miami has some sexy players." She bumped Danielle with her elbow.

"I wasn't thinking about the sex appeal of the players. If this game was after the gala it would've made a great prize for the auction."

Debra poked Danielle's shoulder. "Will you stop thinking about the gala for a second and accept this completely fantastic gift?"

Danielle rubbed her shoulder even though the spot didn't hurt. "I don't always think about work. And we had drinks a few weeks ago."

"Drinks with the other river rats a month ago doesn't count," Debra said, referring to the other conservation leaders in the area.

They'd gotten the nickname after a snarky reporter accused the environmental community of "scurrying around the river looking for problems" like rats. Instead of getting offended, Danielle insisted they accept the nickname. They did look for problems, and they made sure the problems were fixed.

Some called her overzealous. She didn't care. There wasn't much she could hold on to in her life. She was single, her parents were always busy with other things, she had no siblings, and she hadn't had a significant relationship since college. Her passion for protecting the river was about the only thing to keep her warm at night. A state some would consider depressing if they didn't consider her reasons.

The Ridgeport area was her home. She'd inserted herself in the community, made connections with residents and other activists there. What she did to protect the people hurt by industries like Clear Water, and their appreciation for her efforts, was the only proof she had that she mattered to someone.

"Come on, Danielle. We've got courtside seats. We have to go."

Danielle did a quick count in her head. It had been over a month since she'd done anything remotely fun that had nothing to do with raising money for the River Watchers. "Why not?"

Debra did a quick shimmy of her hips and grinned. "Yay! It's going to be so much fun. Hey, we're right behind the bench. Maybe you can put that unassuming girl-next-door charm on blast and snatch a towel from one of the players."

"Really, Debra, how am I supposed to do that?"

"They won't suspect you of stealing a towel," Debra said with a wiggle of her eyebrows. "Try to go for one that Jacobe Jenkins uses to wipe the sweat from his brow. Since you salivate every time you see him on television or on a billboard."

Danielle waved a dismissive hand, but her heart wasn't so indifferent. It jumped with a secret thrill of excitement. "I do not salivate."

Debra's smirk screamed, *Yeah, right.* "Yeah. You do. You both were at the University of Miami at the same time. Did you drool over him then, too?"

Drooling over Jacobe Jenkins was an understatement. Hiding how much desire gripped her whenever he came near had become her number-one priority. Except for that one night. Danielle tried to force the long-ago encounter from her mind and focus on the myriad of ways Jacobe Jenkins had irritated her, when he wasn't sending her estrogen levels through the roof.

"Every time I was around Jacobe he was being a cocky jock who thought the world was his to command, or he was on his way to a party."

Debra held up both hands in front of her body. "Shut the front door. You did not tell me you know Jacobe Jenkins!"

"I don't *know* Jacobe. I knew him. A hundred years ago when we were freshmen in college. I tutored him a few times in Biology 101. He left for the draft right after freshman year, and I never saw him again. A few brief interactions do not count as *knowing* him."

One night of fast and hot sex the night before the draft

could count as knowing him, but Danielle was taking that secret to her grave.

"It's still cool that you kinda know him. It'll be fun to sit right behind him and the rest of the team at the game. Maybe he'll see you and recognize you. Then he can introduce me to one of his sexy teammates. That team is full of grade-A, prime-choice, hot-guy sexiness."

"First of all, I doubt he'd recognize me. Second, if he did I doubt even more that he'd speak to me. Third, prime-choice, hot-guy sexiness? What is that?"

"Um, every single man on that team."

Debra and Danielle both laughed. Someone cleared their throat. They both stifled the laughter and turned toward the door. One of the female interns who took water samples along the river stood there with a cooler in her hand. "I'm going to take some samples on the beach today. You need anything before I go?"

Danielle shook her head and tried to look professional. Hard to do after being caught talking about prime male sexiness. "No, Marie, we're good."

As soon as the young woman walked away, Danielle bumped Debra. "We've got to stop talking about the men of the Jacksonville Gators like they're pieces of meat. It's not professional in front of the interns."

"The interns drool over those men, too," Debra said, grinning. "So, are you really good to go? Don't you want to see the super-hot men on this team up close?"

A shiver of anticipation raced through Danielle. Seeing Jacobe up close and in person would be fun. Based on media reports, he was cockier and even more arrogant than she remembered. Shortly after joining the league he'd gotten into some trouble for fighting and partying hard. The team that had drafted him had traded him to Jacksonville two years before. Jacksonville had been a laughingstock of the league until Jacobe joined and they picked up a few more free agents and draft picks. Some were even talking play-offs this year. Of course he wouldn't recognize her, but she was a fan of the team, and seeing him again even if from afar would be kind of thrilling.

You seriously need to find a man.

Danielle pushed that thought aside. She didn't need anyone to validate her. She had her work. People moved on. The cause remained the same.

She looked at Debra and nodded. "I'm in."

The Jacksonville arena buzzed with the excitement of the rivalry game. The same energy pumped full throttle through Danielle and Debra. Danielle had only been to two other Gators games. Each time she'd sat in the nosebleed seats. The Gators had almost made it to the play-offs last season, but had lost in overtime. That was the last game she'd come to. She and the rest of the fans had felt the team's disappointment that night. This year they'd played each game as if it were a rematch of that heartbreaking loss. With each win, ticket prices increased. Nosebleed seats were getting to be out of her budget. Courtside had only been a dream before Mr. Springfield's gift.

Debra gripped Danielle's arm. "Oh, my God, there he goes again!"

"Are you going to do that all night," Danielle said, swatting at Debra's hand. Every time Jacobe came anywhere near the bench Debra went into a fit of hormones. They both wore Gators T-shirts and jeans. Debra's proudly included Jacobe's number, 06, on the back. Jacobe wasn't on the bench often. He'd spent most of the first half contributing to his team's six-point lead over Miami. The few times he did come to the bench, Debra's enthusiasm rivaled that of someone who'd just won the Powerball jackpot.

Debra released Danielle's arm. "I can't help it. He's so damn fine."

Danielle couldn't argue with that. Instead, she took stock of Jacobe's fineness herself. And, boy, was that man fine. Six feet and four inches of long, lean muscle, smooth, terra-cotta skin and walnut-colored eyes. He played point guard and led the team with ease and confidence. His large body was a thing of grace and beauty. He handled the ball with self-assurance, ran up and down the court without hesitation and effortlessly faked out the opponent defending him. Since he'd been traded to the Gators she'd seen images of him everywhere, but being this close to him in action proved how inadequate billboards, television commercials and nosebleed seats were at portraying his skill and hotness.

Danielle alternated between greedily studying his powerfully built body and jumping up to cheer with the rest of the fans every time he scored. When she'd first come into the arena she'd considered keeping to her seat to try not to draw any attention to herself. That idea was immediately dropped after she was swept away by the buzz of electricity in the crowd. What did it matter if he did happen to look behind the bench? Jacobe had more than likely forgotten about her. Even if he happened to remember the tutor he'd slept with one night in college, she doubted he thought of her often or remembered much about her.

That night she'd known she would be treated as just another groupie, but knowing that hadn't kept her away. Despite the attraction that sizzled between them, Jacobe had never tried to hook up with her. He'd been dating a girl named Christy, and, unlike many of the jocks she knew, he'd been faithful to her. Getting Jacobe to stray from the girl he'd started dating in high school had been a game for so many girls. A game Danielle had prided herself on staying out of. Then she'd heard that Jacobe and Christy had broken up.

To this day she couldn't believe her audacity, but a switch had gone off in her head after hearing about the breakup. A part of her felt that if he was single she wasn't being just another girl trying to steal him away. The thought of that day crept into her head, dulling the noise of the crowd as she remembered how she'd lit into him for keeping her waiting for another tutoring session.

"Yo, I said I was sorry. I have a party to prepare for," he'd said.

"You know what, go to your party and quit wasting my time," Danielle shot back. *"I've got better things to do than babysit jocks."*

"You know what, I've got better things to do than get lectured by you," he'd said, then turned to his roommate, who'd come with him to the library. *"Come on, man, let's get out of here."*

His roommate had snickered and tapped Jacobe on the arm. *"Dude, why don't you two just hit and get it over with? You know all that fighting is just foreplay."*

Jacobe's sexy brown eyes had raked over every inch of her body. *"I'd love to. She doesn't want to handle all this."* He'd given her a cocky smile before turning and leaving.

That one simple statement had made her blood boil, though not from rage. She hadn't known if he was truly interested or just wanted to tease her, but she'd gone to his pre-draft party that night wearing a sexy black dress she'd bought on a whim a month earlier. She'd gotten her answer. He had been interested, and she was able to handle what he offered.

They'd left the room in an awkward silence. Jacobe had promised to call. She hadn't believed him. The next day he'd flown to New York for the draft, and she'd never heard from him again. Through the grapevine, she'd learned he'd reconnected with Christy.

She didn't regret their time together. Over time she'd gotten over him never calling. She'd gone over there to discover if he'd felt the same attraction she'd spent the year trying to ignore, and she'd gotten her answer.

The buzzer for the end of the second quarter sounded. Danielle jerked out of the past. Debra was too busy cheering to notice Danielle was distracted. The crowd clapped as the Gators ran off the court. Danielle joined in. Jacobe walked over to the chair right in front of where Danielle stood, snatched up a towel and wiped his face.

He looked up into the crowd, spread his arms wide and waved them up and down. "This is our house!" he yelled, getting the crowd hyped even more. His intensity burned off him in waves.

A tiny shiver ran through her. His gaze lowered from the upper stands and landed right on hers. Most of the air evacuated her lungs. He held her gaze barely a second before looking away.

He took a step, paused, frowned and then turned to stare directly at her again.

Danielle's heart thudded, and the remaining air in her lungs dissolved like cheap tissue paper. Her stomach clenched right before a thousand feathers tickled her inside. His eyes lightened, maybe with recognition—she couldn't tell—but the smile that spread his lips sent a bolt of lightning straight to her core.

Then he turned and walked with the rest of the team into the locker room. Danielle stood there, stupefied. Had the moment happened, or had she just imagined that? He couldn't possibly remember her, could he? No, not after all these years.

"Danielle, what was that?" Debra's excited voice zipped Danielle to the present.

"What was what?"

"He looked at you, and he looked happy to see you."

Danielle pushed her glasses farther her nose and shook her head. "No, he looked into the crowd. He wasn't looking at me."

"I saw the look."

"Forget the look. The look means nothing." She was going to make it mean nothing anyway. "Let's go to the concession stand. I want some popcorn."

The lines were so long that the trek for popcorn and sodas took most of halftime. By the time they made their way back to the seats, the teams were running onto the court to warm up. Danielle staunchly avoided watching Jacobe. She may have enjoyed that second of eye contact, but that didn't mean she had to visually stalk him for the rest of the night.

Debra chocked on her popcorn and grabbed Danielle's arm. "He's coming over."

No need to pretend she didn't know who she was talking about. "His chair is right in front of us."

"No, he's looking at you and coming this way."

"Will you stop it, Jacobe Jenkins isn't—"

"Danielle?" A male voice that didn't sound quite sure if he was getting her name right interrupted.

Danielle's hands became slick. Her heart fluttered like a hummingbird's wings against her ribs. *Oh, wow. It was him.*

She slowly pivoted in her chair to look into a pair of sexy brown eyes. He smiled at her with a hint of unsureness in his gaze.

"Oh…hi, Jacobe."

"Danielle Stewart…right?"

She nodded. "That's me."

"What are you doing here?"

"Enjoying the game."

He laughed. "Yeah, I guess so. What have you been up to?"

Danielle glanced around. Some of the courtside reporters were looking their way. A few even snapped some pictures. Danielle squirmed self-consciously in her seat. "I work for the St. Johns River Watchers."

"You live around here?" Sweat ran down his face, to his neck and into the jersey covering his wide, muscled torso.

Why in the world was a sweaty man so damn sexy? "Yep."

He ran the towel over his face, thankfully removing the distracting sweat. Unfortunately, the movement brought attention to his fantastically sculpted arms. "This your first game?"

"No. My first courtside seat, though."

He nodded. "Cool. What are you doing after the game?"

She blinked, thrown off by the question. "Going home."

He shook his head, dismissing her statement. "The guys from the team usually meet up at a pool bar downtown called The Hall. Meet me there after the game."

Debra's leg bounced like a supercharged Chihuahua

in Danielle's periphery. "The Hall?" Had her voice really just squeaked? She cleared her throat.

"Yeah. You know where it is? They're usually selective about letting people in after a home game because the team hangs out there afterward, but I'll call ahead and tell them you're cool. Come by. Let's catch up."

One of his teammates called. Jacobe looked over his shoulder to acknowledge him, then looked back at her. "I'll see you there later." Not a question.

She was too stunned to get angry at his direction or think of an excuse to say no. "Um...yeah. Sure, we'll stop by."

He grinned. "Cool." He spun and rejoined the team.

Debra leaned in. Danielle lifted her hand to stop her from saying anything. "Stop. The reporters are still watching. Save the gushing for after the game."

"Fine, but there will be tons of gushing in the car."

Danielle nodded and took a sip from her soda. She had to keep her composure for the reporters still looking her way. She knew they had to be wondering who she was.

For the entire third quarter, she replayed the conversation and wondered what it meant. He'd seemed almost happy to see her. Happy? Had he thought of her over the years? Maybe she'd jumped the gun in assuming he could so easily forget her and move on. Maybe Jacobe wasn't as self-centered as she remembered. Maybe the whole bad-boy persona that the media portrayed was just that—a persona.

All those maybes floated away when, halfway through the fourth quarter, Jacobe pushed a referee aside so he could deliver a right hook to an opposing player and left the guy knocked out cold on the floor. He smirked, then stepped over the downed opponent. Danielle sighed and shook her head. Apparently, Jacobe was still the arrogant, cocky jock she'd taken him for.

Chapter 2

Typically, when Jacobe entered The Hall after a game and heard the drum of old-school hip-hop and smelled the Buffalo wings the place was known for, he was instantly ready to party. Tonight, the tension that had taken over his neck and shoulders since he'd knocked out Rob Jackson wouldn't go away. He shouldn't have done that. The league would probably suspend him for that. Not what he needed right before the play-offs. Taking the Gators to the play-offs would secure his place as one of the best players in the league, which was something he knew, but the trouble in his past kept others from admitting it. It would also make the final argument for him to be signed by Phoenix next year. They were building a superteam, and Jacobe was aiming to be on that team.

He could see the years of winning the finals in his future if that happened. The chance was now a big if. His agent had already called and told him not to talk to any reporters while he tried to smooth things out with managers of both teams.

He shouldn't have hit Rob, but he damn sure didn't regret it. *How's your son? Oh, wait, you don't have a son.*

Rob had tossed out the low blow right before Jacobe knocked him out. Jacobe kept his private life private, but Rob had been his teammate four years ago when Jacobe had learned that the woman he'd dated since high school had played him for a fool.

Tossing aside thoughts of Rob, suspension and the worst mistake of his life—Christy—Jacobe scanned the crowded room. After home games The Hall was typically brimming with people. The team came there to play pool and celebrate after a win and the locals had figured that out. The high-top tables were filled with people, along with the chrome stools around the bar. There were people at the pool tables that lined the room, as well, except for the empty table at the end. That's where the Gators played.

His search wasn't just to check out the crowd. He looked for one person in particular. It wasn't long before his gaze landed on Danielle Stewart and the friend she'd been with at the game, sitting at the end of the bar sipping on fruity-looking drinks. His tension eased.

Danielle Stewart. Just thinking of her brought a smile to his lips. His prim-and-proper tutor who had lectured him about the importance of recycling and saving the planet while simultaneously giving him a raging hard-on. If it weren't for that one night in college, he never would have believed she'd felt any of the attraction that always bubbled up in him like molten lava when she was around.

"That's the girl from the game, right?" His teammate Kevin Kouky asked from his right. At six foot seven,

Kevin was taller than Jacobe's six-four. His golden-brown skin was hidden behind a myriad of tattoos and one-inch plugs filled his ears.

"That's the girl," Isaiah Reynolds, another teammate, said from his left. Where Kevin's appearance made old ladies cross the street when they saw him coming, Isaiah made them smile and want to pinch his cheeks. He and Jacobe were the same height, but the similarity ended there. Isaiah had "boy you could take home to mama" down pat with his prim-and-proper attire, right down to his signature bow ties.

Will Hampton nodded and grinned. "That's the girl alright." The mischief in Will's eyes sparkled brighter than the diamonds in his ears. The shortest of the group at six one, Will was also the jokester of the team.

Jacobe hadn't called any man a friend in years. Outside of accepting the mentorship of movie star Irvin Freeman and singer Dante Wilson, Jacobe kept most people at arm's length. History had taught him that. Away from the stadium, the only people he preferred hanging with were Kevin, Isaiah, and Will. They were cool, though he still wasn't sure if he could trust them.

"Her name is Danielle," he said. "We knew each other in college. I haven't seen her since the night before the draft."

Kevin bumped him with his elbow. "You seemed pretty happy to see her."

Jacobe shrugged. He had been surprised to see her. Pleasantly surprised. After Christy's betrayal he'd often wondered what would have happened if he'd called Danielle again. "I wouldn't mind reconnecting."

Especially in the bedroom. He didn't know what bit of fate had put Danielle in the courtside seats behind the bench tonight, but he had no intention of squandering the good fortune. He'd love nothing more than a repeat of their night together.

Danielle and her friend stopped their conversation to look their way. Her eyes widened behind those cute black-and-gold glasses she wore before she turned toward her friend. The dark-haired woman elbowed Danielle and said something. Danielle looked back his way and gave him a shy smile.

Ah, yeah, he was going to thoroughly enjoy reconnecting with Danielle Stewart. She'd driven him crazy back then, pestering him to use his popularity for good. The only person who'd seemed to think he could be good at something other than playing ball.

Her lectures had always fallen on deaf ears. Mainly because he couldn't stop himself from thinking of peeling off those cute little cardigan sweaters she seemed to always wear and kissing her until the passion in her warm dark eyes was because of him instead of whatever cause she was championing. He'd always wondered what she would do if she'd known that while she droned on about ecosystems or some other nonsense, he'd wanted nothing more than to plop her on top of the nearest desk and make her glasses fog up.

He lifted his head in acknowledgment, then crossed the room her way. Isaiah, Kevin and Will followed. People stopped and congratulated him and the guys on the win. He spoke, but kept his attention on Danielle. She wore a fitted gold-colored Jacksonville Gators T-shirt that made her luscious breasts look like twin works of art, ankle-length jeans that hugged her ass perfectly and flats. Her thick, dark, shoulder-length hair was parted on the side to sweetly frame her heart-shaped face.

"You came," he said when he got to her side. He

opened his arms and leaned in for a hug. He had to hug her. She was too cute and curvy to not hug.

Her eyes widened, but she leaned in from the waist and patted his back. Jacobe fought the urge to pull her in for a real hug instead of one that left enough space for two small kids to run through.

"Well, you invited me." Her eyes met his and she sucked in a breath, then looked away. "This is my co-worker, Debra." She straightened her glasses and gave another shy smile.

She was still attracted to him. Good, because if she'd shown up with any intentions of reliving their night together he was game. He needed a distraction. They'd won, but the price he'd have to pay for hitting Rob hovered over him like a cloud.

He reached out a hand to the pretty woman next to Danielle. "Nice to meet you, Debra. I'm Jacobe. These guys here are my teammates, Kevin, Isaiah and Will. Fellas, this is Danielle Stewart."

The guys nodded and shook the ladies' hands. Jacobe watched both of them for any signs that they were interested in Danielle. Interest did light up their eyes, but mainly in the way they darted glances between Jacobe and Danielle. He hoped his instincts were right. He didn't need another teammate sleeping with the same chick as him. He had definite plans to eventually sleep with Danielle again.

Debra grinned and shook his head. "I know who all of you are. We're both big fans."

Jacobe looked back at Danielle. "You're a fan?"

She nodded and met his eye without glancing away like she had before. "I am."

"How long have you been in Jacksonville?"

"Since right after college."

Jacobe frowned, upset by the idea that she'd been so close without him even knowing. Though he had thought of her over the years, he hadn't gone so far as to track her down. "I didn't know that."

"We don't exactly hang out in the same circles." She glanced at his teammates.

"I guess not."

Debra leaned forward. "So, Jacobe, how do you know Danielle?"

Jacobe met Debra's eyes and searched for any indication she already knew about his one night with Danielle. He couldn't fault Danielle for telling people about that night—a few of the women he'd had one-night stands with over the years had loved to brag about it afterward. He would be slightly disappointed if Danielle had done the same. That night had been spontaneous and wonderful, awkward but somehow special. A secret between them. He'd never expected her to brag.

"What did Danielle say?"

"That she helped you study, but that's about it."

Relief eased more of the tension. She hadn't bragged to her friend. "Danielle tried helping me out in biology. I was a little hardheaded then."

Danielle raised a brow. "Just a little."

Debra leaned forward and looked expectantly between him and Danielle. "Was she just as driven back then as she is now?"

"When it came to biology and giving back she was. I remember her always trying to get me to volunteer for various causes or skip parties to study."

Danielle smirked and leaned against the bar. "Tried

but was unsuccessful. You never wanted to volunteer, and there was always some party to attend."

"I gave back in my own way. You always liked to judge."

Her shoulders straightened. "I didn't judge."

"Yes, you did." He looked back at Debra. "When she rolled up the sleeves of those cute little sweaters she wore I knew she was pissed and that someone was about to get chewed out."

Debra laughed. "She still does that. In the office we say she's ready for battle."

Danielle held up her hands. "I'm going up against politicians and businessmen. I have to be ready for battle." The familiar fight-for-what's-right tone came to her voice.

Isaiah watched her with growing interest. "Politicians and business men? What do you do?"

"I'm the executive director for the St. Johns River Watchers."

Jacobe exchanged glances with the fellas to see if they recognized the organization's name. Isaiah nodded. Of course he would know. Kevin and Will shrugged.

"Impressive," Isaiah said.

"The River Watchers?" Jacobe asked. "What's that?"

Her look said she was disappointed but not surprised by his ignorance. "We're a watchdog organization that makes sure businesses, governments and citizens aren't doing anything to harm the river. Our goal is to protect the river and, ultimately, the beach."

Jacobe wasn't surprised by her career path. "You're still trying to save the world, huh."

Her shoulders stiffened. "And you're still turning your nose up at saving the world."

Kevin cleared his throat. "Oh, look, I think I see the

sign to get out of the cross fire." He looked at Isaiah, Will, and Debra. "Pool, anyone?"

The others agreed quickly and scuttled away. "Wow," Danielle said, watching the four leave. "We still know how to clear a room." She took a sip from the straw in her fruity drink.

Jacobe chuckled. "We didn't even have to raise our voices this time. Remember when they kicked us out of the library?"

She smiled. "Yes, the study session before our first test of the semester. You were so distracted and you kept pulling out your cell phone to do other things."

"The test right before a rivalry game," he replied. "I was trying to watch videos of the other team's footage."

"You couldn't wait until we'd finished? One hour, that's all we had."

"I couldn't help it. We met right after practice. I had basketball on the brain."

"How hard was it to focus for an hour?"

"Very." He thought of that day. Basketball hadn't been the only thing on his brain. "You had on that pink sweater with a tight white T-shirt under it." She'd buttoned the sweater to right beneath her breasts. The swell of her chest above it was like a beacon to his eyes. "I had to look at videos on my phone or stare and wonder how you'd squeezed into that shirt."

Her mouth snapped shut and her eyes were wide. He chuckled. "Yes, I was checking you out back then. I thought you would have figured that out by now."

"I hadn't. I thought it was just that night."

He shook his head. "I wanted you long before that night."

She tucked her hair behind her ears and stared into her drink. "You never said anything."

"I'm not into cheating. Too much drama." Something he'd learned the hard way.

Her eyes flew to his. "Neither am I. I only…did what I did because I'd heard you and Christy broke up."

"We had." They should have stayed broken up.

"But then I heard you two were back together."

"We got back after the draft. She said she was pregnant." He couldn't stop the anger from creeping into his voice.

Her eyes widened. "You have a kid?"

He shook his head. "Thought I did. Turns out he wasn't mine."

"Oh."

"That's why I hit Rob tonight. He brought it up."

She scowled. "In the middle of the game. That's a dick move."

Jacobe grinned. He'd always loved her candor. Her spark. "Some would say the same about me hitting him."

Her brows pulled together and she drew her lower lip between her teeth. "I'd thought that when you hit him and walked away so coldly. I guess I understand now. I'm sorry to hear about what Christy did."

"I don't want to talk about that." He shouldn't have told her. Only a few people knew about that situation. A part of him didn't want Danielle to think he'd slept with her that night and gotten back with Christy on a whim.

He needed to change the subject before the old familiar bitterness of that situation took a hold of him. He'd come here for a distraction. He let his gaze slowly roam over every inch of Danielle's sexy curves. "Instead of talking about the past, how about we get out of here?"

The sympathy in her eyes evaporated. "Excuse me?"

"I thought we could catch up. It's been years."

"Yeah, and we can catch up right here, right now."

"You don't have to be shy with me, Danielle. You popped up at my game, in the seat right behind me. Kind of reminds me of that night. I'm good with us hooking up again."

Danielle leaned back. "I was there because one of our donors gave us his courtside seats. I didn't think you'd even remember or recognize me."

"Why wouldn't I?"

"Because I never heard from you again after that night in college."

"That was my mistake. Believe me."

A vision of Christy in his hotel room after the draft, crying and saying they belonged together and that she was pregnant, popped into his mind. She'd dropped a positive pregnancy test on the bed when he'd accused her of showing up just because he'd been drafted. Would Danielle understand the sense of responsibility that had come over him when he'd seen that plus sign and Christy's tears? That nothing else had mattered other than being a better father than the one he'd had.

"You know you're just the same as you always were." Danielle broke into his thoughts.

He met her gaze, was surprised to see anger in her eyes. "Excuse me?"

"I came here because you invited me. I thought that maybe, despite that night together, you would be cool and decent. That we could... I don't know, talk like the adults we are. I didn't come here so you could try and sleaze your way into my bed." She hopped down from the stool. "You have a good night."

He watched her storm off. She said a few quick words to Debra, who glared at Jacobe before she dropped her pool stick and followed Danielle to the door. Kevin, Isaiah, and Will gave him confused looks. Jacobe cursed and rubbed the bridge of his nose. Damn. Now he'd have to go down to that River Watcher place and apologize for being a jerk.

Jacobe's shoulders were tense as he entered the main conference room for the Gators with his agent, Eric Jones. Eric had caught a red eye flight from Los Angeles to be here for this early morning meeting. Eric would probably be the only one who had Jacobe's back today.

Meetings with the management staff were never fun. He had a pretty good idea of the lecture he was about to receive. Tone down the aggression. We can't afford to lose you right before the play-offs. Try and keep your name out of the headlines. He'd heard the same lines constantly over the past few years. Never mind that he had toned down his behavior recently. The situation with Christy was a blow he hadn't known how to handle. He'd taken out his aggression on and off the court. For the most part, he considered himself over that blow. It was only when assholes like Rob used the situation against him on the court that his efforts to stay out of trouble were forgotten.

Three people sat around the conference table. Coach Simpson in the usual polo shirt and khakis he wore on off days. His teal-gray eyes met Jacobe's with determination. Rebecca Force, the team's public relations supervisor, sat primly next to the coach. Brian McClain, one of the team's owners, was the last person at the table. Jacobe's shoulders tightened even more. Brian reminded Jacobe of his high school principal with his graying brown hair, stiff suits and perpetual frown. Like his high school principal, Brian never saw anything good in Jacobe off the basketball court and made no qualms about his opinion that Jacobe joining the team would be a distraction. Only their joint goal of a play-off win for the Gators kept them civil toward each other.

"Are we waiting on anyone else?" Eric asked, after they greeted everyone and sat in the chairs to Coach Simpson's left.

Rebecca shook her head. "No, just waiting on you two."

"Sorry for keeping you all waiting," Jacobe said.

Rebecca gave him what he guessed was supposed to be a friendly smile. The tightness around her eyes contradicted the action. "You're actually right on time. We met for a few minutes before you got here to discuss a few things."

The hairs on the back of his neck stood up. "Let me guess—you met early to talk about me."

Eric held up a hand. "Wait a second, Jacobe. Before you get upset, let's hear what she has to say. Though I would have liked to have been included in any discussions regarding my client."

Jacobe would have liked that too. He looked at Rebecca. "What do you have to say?" He didn't bother to hide his frustration.

He didn't like being *discussed* beforehand like he was a threat that needed to be neutralized. Never had. Not when he was sent to the principal's office in school, or when his mom used to get on the phone with her girlfriends and discuss the latest note sent home from school and all the reasons Jacobe couldn't be well behaved like other kids.

Rebecca broke into his thoughts. "The league commissioner called this morning."

Jacobe scoffed. "Already? I guess he couldn't wait

to tell me I've messed up. So what is it? A fine? One-game suspension?"

Eric glared at Jacobe. "Let me do the talking."

Brian jerked forward in his chair. "Try a five-game suspension."

The words stunned Jacobe into temporary silence. "Five games?" He'd expected to miss a game, maybe two, not five. They were a few weeks away from the play-offs. If the team lost at this time they could miss their chance at being a number-one seed. Worse, they may not make it at all.

"Yes. Five," Brian said. "Your antics are hurting the team. When the rest of the owners overrode me and brought you here, I knew it would be a problem. You don't care about this team. You don't care about anyone but yourself."

"I care about the team." The words were automatic. Programmed. Though the guys on the team had grown closer to him than any other teammates he'd had since college, he cared mostly about making his way to the play-offs and, ultimately, Phoenix.

"Of course he cares about the team," Eric said. "He's done everything to dedicate himself to the team."

"If he cared about the team he wouldn't have knocked Rob out."

"Rob deserved a lot more than being knocked out."

Coach sighed and leaned his forearms on the table. "What did he say that set you off?"

"Something he shouldn't have."

Brian scoffed and tossed his hand toward Jacobe. "See, utter lack of caring about the consequences of your actions."

Eric held up his hands. "Look, he gets why he shouldn't have hit him during the game."

"After would be better?" Brian asked.

After the game Jacobe wouldn't have hit him just once, but that was beside the point. "I shouldn't have let my temper get the better of me. I want to take the team to the play-offs just as much as you want to get us there."

Brian didn't reply. He just sat back in his seat and crossed his arms. He might hate Jacobe, but they both wanted wins.

Rebecca glanced between Jacobe and Brian. When Brian didn't say any more, she focused on Jacobe. "Your popularity with the team's fans is high, but last night there was a lot of chatter on the internet about how you're not good for the team."

"You're winning," Eric said with a grin. "They'll get over it."

She lifted a hand. "That may be true, but Jacobe will be gone for five games. If the team starts to lose, then it'll be easy to blame your hot temper and lack of focus for the losses."

"If you're telling me to play nice, I hear you. No more fighting on the court."

Rebecca shook her head. "We need more than that."

"What?"

"We need a plan. Today."

Eric looked around the table. "You can't be serious?"

Coach Simpson nodded. "We are. We want Jacobe to remain a Gator, that's no secret. We also want *everyone* to see that he's an asset to the team." Coach tilted his head slightly in Brian's direction. The hairs on the back of Jacobe's neck twitched some more. He eventually wanted to go to Phoenix, but if that didn't pan out he didn't need the Gators refusing to sign him next year.

"We've finally hit our rhythm as a team," Coach continued. "If we keep playing like we're playing we've got a shot at the play-offs and, I believe, the title. We've built something great here. Let's keep it going."

"I hear you, Coach, but I can't play if I know every time I foul someone I'm going to be called into the conference room and told to behave."

Brian snorted. "That was a lot more than a foul."

Rebecca cut in before Jacobe could respond. "That's why we met before you were here. We *all* want you to remain a Gator next year."

Jacobe narrowed his eyes and studied them. Coach and Rebecca eyed him intensely, and Brian looked like he was tired of the entire fiasco. Wariness had his stomach churning.

Eric shifted in his seat. "You keep saying that. Are there plans to drop him?"

Rebecca and Coach both shook their heads and said simultaneously, "You know we want him."

Brian sat forward and nailed Jacobe with a hard stare. "You're a free agent next year. We won't keep a liability."

"Are you threatening my client?" Eric's voice turned hard.

Rebecca tried again for the friendly smile. "Of course not. Which is why I'm working on a plan to make you more likable."

Jacobe's shoulders tightened. "Excuse me?"

"You aren't seen out and about doing things in the community. If you take up a project or a cause, people will see that you're giving back instead of just…"

"Being a distraction and hindrance," Jacobe finished for her.

He gritted his teeth. Like many other athletes, Jacobe gave to various charitable organizations. Mostly to programs that mentored young boys and gave them direction and support. He gave his money but not his time. He was still getting his own life figured out—how could he possibly make a good mentor?

Eric gave him a reassuring look before turning to Rebecca. "What are you thinking?"

"We've come up with a list of organizations that you can be seen with."

Jacobe shook his head. This was his image problem. He'd find a way to fix it. "I've already got an idea."

Rebecca frowned. "You do?"

"How about protecting the river," Jacobe said. "It's a big part of our city. I've got a friend who works to protect the St. Johns River and the beach. You can't deny that seeing me out there saving sea turtles or some stuff like that would make people *like* me."

Eric nodded and tapped his finger on the table. "That could work. Being green is in right now."

He almost laughed. He'd known Danielle back when saving the planet wasn't just a fad and she was the earth's number-one champion. "I know it'll work."

"Can you set up something with them by the end of the week?"

"I'm sure I can." He already planned to see Danielle later that day to apologize. He still wanted to sleep with her, but he wouldn't assume she would readily fall into his bed. That night in college was a once-in-a-lifetime action. He had a feeling that the woman she was today wasn't going to come to him on a spontaneous whim. He'd have to earn a place in her bed.

Chapter 3

"I'm sorry, Danielle, but I don't think the River Watchers should push council to oppose Clear Water's expansion."

Danielle fought to keep calm as she stared at the board president. Liberty Meyer was only on the board as an attempt to prove the River Watchers were open to voices from all sides. After Danielle had gone for Clear Water and a few other industries like a pit bull on crack, some in the business community had accused the River Watchers of being too biased. Liberty was a vocal member of the manufacturers' alliance and the River Watchers' attempt to bring the business community in on the discussions. Much to Danielle's chagrin, Liberty ran and won a seat on county council after being assigned to the board. Making her a double pain on Danielle's backside.

"Our organization serves as champions to our natural resources," Danielle said in a surprisingly calm voice.

"If they're allowed to expand and dump into Springfield Creek it'll be devastating to the local ecosystem. Not to mention the neighborhood downstream that uses the creek for fishing and recreation."

"Clear Water expanding will bring jobs," Liberty countered. "If we don't bring jobs, that can be detrimental to the population. I care about the flowers and the fish and birds as much as everyone sitting around this table."

Danielle barely stopped herself from snorting.

"But I care more about the men, women and *children* that rely on me as a member of the county council to keep our economy strong and vital."

"I care about the people here, too. This isn't just about the birds and the flowers, Liberty. Clear Water can't meet their permit limits. There's an entire population who'll be swimming in sewage if they dump into the creek."

Liberty rolled her eyes and waved a hand. "Oh, Danielle, please. That's why we have engineers who can design and build a system that can properly treat the waste. People won't be in sewage. This is why I've always said you're too biased when it comes to these types of decisions."

Debra's hand gripped Danielle's leg beneath the table. The movement effectively stopped Danielle from pouncing onto Liberty. That wasn't the first time the woman had thrown out the comment. Danielle and Debra both believed Liberty was trying to make a case with the board to remove Danielle as director.

Mr. Springfield, who'd watched the exchange silently with the rest of the board members, rapped his knuckles on the table. "Ladies, ladies, you both make very good points. Since I'm directly affected by the expansion, I have to defer from voting, but I think this is important enough for the board to take both sides into consideration. If Clear Water can truly improve by expanding, it's better than having a poorly run system out there. If they cannot, then none of us here want them discharging into Springfield Creek. Let's take a little more time, talk to the people in Environmental Protection and see if Clear Water will come to a board meeting to discuss their plans."

There was a round of agreement at the table. Danielle and Liberty gave tight smiles and stiff nods. Mr. Springfield had made a valid point, though Danielle doubted Clear Water would be willing to come to the table and speak to them.

Danielle nodded. "I'll make the necessary contacts. I'll also speak with the Environmental Protection again and send my findings to the board."

Liberty sat forward and crossed her arms on the table. "Don't spend too much time on that. Remember the gala is the most important thing right now."

Danielle took a slow deep breath before responding. "The plans for the gala are coming along very well. We've got several sponsors." Five. "And ticket sales are promising." Two sold today bringing them to a total of twenty.

"Really? I thought it would be slow considering the lack of promotion."

Debra grabbed Danielle's leg again. The limited promotion was due to the budget cuts on the advertisement. Budget cuts Liberty recommended. "We've been lucky to have been picked up a media sponsor." The local free newspaper counted.

Liberty's smile was fake and tight. "That's good. I don't know how we'll keep things going as is if we don't bring in more funding."

Translation: make the gala a success or else Liberty had a good reason for Danielle's dismissal.

The meeting ended soon after. Danielle was too annoyed and wound up to sit in her office and work on the final preparations for the river cleanup that weekend.

Debra poked her head in Danielle's door. "Hey, I'm about to go pick up supplies for that school presentation later in the week. You need anything?"

"A hundred ticket sales," Danielle said.

"Don't let Liberty get to you. Sales always start slow. They'll pick up."

Danielle pushed aside her frustration with Liberty. She would make this gala a success. "I know they will." She filled her voice with confidence.

"Hey, I've got something to get your mind off of Liberty. Let's call the rest of the river rats and hang out tonight. Maybe we'll come up with some good ideas to shut up Liberty."

Danielle's first impulse was to say no. She'd rather figure out how to get more ticket sales for the gala. Maybe even do some door knocking for sponsors. But if she thought about it too much she'd go crazy. A night out with people who understood would help. "Set it up."

Debra clapped her hands. "Great! Look I've got to go. Most of the interns are out taking samples. We all have our cells if you need anything."

Danielle smiled and waved at Debra as she floated out of the office. With no one there to help distract her from the fact that Liberty wanted her gone, Danielle opted for the best thing to get her mind off of the uncontrollable things in her life. Kicking off her kitten heels, she slipped on a pair of rain boots and stomped out the back of the cottage and down to the beach. Having an office right on the very water body they were trying to protect was the best thing about her job. Every time she thought her work was getting nowhere or that no one was listening or cared, she could look out her window and see the sun reflecting off the waves and remember what she was fighting for. The one thing that she could hold on to in her life.

It was cloudy and drizzling, so she'd put on her pink North Face raincoat for the walk. She liked the beach when it was sunny, but loved it on drizzly days like today. Not as hot, less crowded, and the waters were choppy due to the winds. The sound of each pounding wave would slowly knock away whatever frustration tightened her muscles.

She'd walked a mile down the beach and was on her way back when her cell phone rang in her jacket pocket. She stopped and pulled it. One look at the screen and the tension that had just drained from her shoulders slowly started back.

"Hi, Mom," she said.

"Hello, Danielle, how are things going with my favorite daughter?" Adele Stewart asked in her cheery voice.

She was an only child, so the compliment didn't give Danielle any false sense of importance. "The board meeting was rough this morning. I'm out walking the beach now."

"Is this about the Clear Water expansion?"

"How did you know about that?"

"I read the board meeting agendas that you send me," Adele said, as if Danielle should have known that.

As little attention as her parents gave her, she was surprised to know that her mom read them. The young girl who still wanted their attention was the part of her that added them to the River Watchers mailing list in the vain hope that they'd at least find her work interesting.

"That's it, actually. I've got a board member who doesn't think we should ask the town to oppose the expansion before the permit is on notice. I disagree."

Adele sighed and Danielle pictured her mom shaking her head in disbelief. "I can't fathom why everyone doesn't understand the important role we play in making this world a better place."

"Not everyone thinks that way."

"They should. Don't worry, honey, good always triumphs over evil."

Danielle chuckled. "She's not evil. She just has her own self-interests."

"People who refuse to take responsibility for improving the world are a form of evil."

Words Danielle had heard most of her life. She loved her parents, but many times she'd wished they'd stopped trying so hard to save everyone else in the world and just focus on raising her.

"Where's Dad?"

"Oh, that's why I called. We're taking in another foster child—a boy, eight years old. His mother is in prison and the his father died last year."

"Another? You've already got two kids."

"I know, but I was so moved by his story when I went to the latest CASA meeting. Danielle, there are so many kids out there who need love. It's our duty to do what we can."

"I know, Mom, but you and Dad don't have to take in every child you come across. I thought you were coming to Ridgeport for the river cleanup this weekend. That'll be hard to do with a new kid in the house."

"Oh, Danielle, don't be selfish. We'll try to make it if we can."

Danielle bit her lower lip and dug the toe of her boot into the wet sand. Adele was an expert at hitting Danielle with the guilty stick. Danielle knew there were kids who needed love and affection. She knew that everyone wasn't blessed to have two parents like she did. But all her life her parents were busy with the causes they took up after they couldn't have another child.

"We don't need our own child. Not when there are so many out there we can shower with love."

Her dad has spoken those words to her mom when she'd cried after another failed pregnancy. Danielle had been nine when she overheard them. A few months later the various projects started. They'd built houses, feed the poor, championed animal rights, and now were taking in foster kids. They had taught her the importance of serving, but they'd also been too busy with their projects to give her any attention. From bad days at school, fights with her friends, or a choral recital they couldn't attend, their comments were always the same. There were people out there who had it worse than her.

Danielle used to wonder why they didn't want to shower their attention on her. Was she not good enough? Even though she was older, the feelings of not being enough for her parents hadn't gone away.

"I'm sorry, Mom," she said. "Bring him along. I've got to meet my new brother sooner or later."

"We'll see what the courts say," Adele said dismissively. "Even though his mother is in jail, they may grant visitation. You know I like to make sure the kids see their parents on weekends if they can."

She had her answer: her parents weren't coming.

Eventually, she'd stop caring when they missed something of hers because of another commitment. "Don't worry about it. As long as you guys make the gala in a few weeks that's all that matters. It's the inaugural event. I need to make an impression. It would mean a lot to me if you two were there."

"Of course, dear. Oh, your dad's home. We've got to go get a few things for your brother's room. I'll give you a call later, okay? Love you. Bye."

The call ended before Danielle could say anything more. Danielle stared at the phone for a few seconds, sighed, and then shoved it into her pocket.

"Good thing I don't crave my parents' attention," she said to the wind. "I would be constantly disappointed."

The sounds of excited conversation filtered from the house as Danielle trudged up the steps to the office's back door. She left her rain boots in the mudroom, slipped on her heels and followed the sounds of conversation toward the kitchen. Halfway there, the deeper sound of a man's familiar voice slowed her steps. Her pulse raced with anticipation and she carefully eased her way to the open door.

"Jacobe?" she said.

He stood next to the sink, a mug of coffee in his hand, surrounded by three of the interns. Blue-gray slacks covered his long legs and a crisp white shirt wrapped his muscles like the most desirable of Christmas presents. Unwrapping all of that toned, tight body would be something worth celebrating. He glanced up from the group and hit her with his devastating smile.

"Just the woman I was looking for."

He sounded happy to see her. Heat flooded her

cheeks. She looked away and pulled off the rain jacket. If she kept eye contact, she'd start grinning and stammering along with blushing.

"I was out walking the beach. From the looks of things, everyone here made you comfortable while you waited."

The interns all grinned and hurried to talk over one another about how they'd completed their morning fieldwork. Danielle lifted her hands. "You're fine. I'm not that much of an evil boss that I'm going to get angry about you being excited when a famous basketball player comes into the office."

"You have softened up," Jacobe said. "The Danielle I knew was always on task and never took a break."

She lifted her chin and met his eye. "That was the Danielle I allowed you to know."

"I think I got a glimpse of the more laid-back Danielle once." The corner of his mouth lifted in a smile full of the sinful secrets of that more laid-back Danielle.

She ignored the butterflies crashing around her stomach like drunken seagulls. "You said you wanted to see me—well, I'm here. Let's go to my office." She looked at everyone in the room. "You all can get back to work."

Jacobe grinned and strolled over to her. "That's the Danielle I know and love."

She snorted. "Love had nothing to do with our relationship." She spun away and marched from the kitchen. One of the interns winked at her as Danielle passed. She could only imagine the thoughts going through her mind.

She made her way down the hall to the last door on the right. Jacobe's footsteps followed.

"You're wrong," Jacobe said. "There were a lot of things I loved about you."

"What, my badgering you to come to our study sessions on time, or my endless lectures about what you could be contributing to make the world a better place?"

She stepped over the threshold into her office, but a tug on the back of her sweater kept her from taking another step. She faltered, then quickly turned. Jacobe let go.

"These little sweaters you wear. I loved those."

Danielle looked down at her rather unremarkable outfit: gray slacks, a black-and-yellow polka-dot blouse and a bright yellow cardigan, then back up at him. "My cardigans?"

"Yes, you're just as sexy in those now as you were then." He lifted a hand and reached for her face. Danielle jerked back before he touched her. He grinned. "I was only going to compliment you on the glasses. I like these better than the ones you used to wear." When he reached forward this time, she didn't pull away. Jacobe ran a finger over the hinges and lightly brushed her face. "Between the glasses and the sweaters you've got the sexy, good-girl vibe going on. I always knew there was passion in you for more than just class work."

Her body went up in flames. Taking a step back, Danielle inhaled a deep, shaky breath. "If you're here to repeat your request from Saturday night, then you've wasted your time."

She wished her office was big enough to stalk to the other side and put a decent enough space between them. Instead, there was little extra space in the small room. Between her desk, file cabinets and plastic tubs filled with materials they used for various functions, she barely had a clear path from the door to her seat behind the desk.

Jacobe followed her farther into the office. His huge, muscled form soaked up all the remaining space in the room. He pushed the door closed. When he faced her again, thankfully, he didn't step closer and leaned against the door, instead.

"That's not why I'm here. One of the reasons I came by is to apologize for the other night."

She'd opened her mouth in preparation for a rebuff. She snapped it closed. "Come again? You're apologizing?"

"Don't sound so surprised. I am capable of admitting when I'm wrong. You remember that much about me."

She did, actually. He may have given her a hard time when she fussed about him keeping her waiting and always had a reason for why he was late, but he never tried to blame his inability to keep to their schedule on anyone but himself. She would have had a much easier time not lusting after him if he'd blamed others for his problems.

"I do."

"I am sorry about approaching you like that. I had a bad game, as you saw. When I spotted you, nothing but good memories of that night popped up. I can't lie. I wanted you again."

Her knees went weak. She sat on the edge of her desk to hide the effect. "Oh. Well, good memories or not, I wasn't there to relive that one night."

"I guessed as much when you stalked out mad as hell. I still want you, but I'm willing to earn my way into your bed. Not assume you'll automatically let me there."

Awareness—no, anticipation buzzed through her body. "You're here to let me know you're planning to seduce me?"

He straightened from the door and shook his head. "I do think you should know that I'm perfectly willing to pick up where we left off, but that's not why I'm here. The other reason for this visit is because I need a favor that involves the River Watchers."

Her brain fought to keep up. He wanted a repeat of that night? That shouldn't make her so giddy. Pushing the giddiness firmly aside, she focused on the second statement. "A favor? Really?"

"Really."

"What kind of favor?"

He rubbed his hands together and examined the various framed awards and news clippings on her office wall. "I'd like to volunteer, do some things to improve my image by helping the environment." He focused back on her.

"Why?" She crossed her arms and studied him.

"Out of the goodness of my heart."

She shook her head. "Not buying it. Try again."

He grinned, completely unperturbed by her reply. "You're still a hard-ass."

"I still know when you're avoiding getting to the point. Why do you suddenly want to help an organization you hadn't heard of before Saturday?"

"I've got a five-game suspension. It's going to be announced later today. I need something to boost my image in my free time." He said "free time" as if it were a bad word. For him, she guessed it was. She could imagine how frustrated she'd be if someone took her work away from her.

"What do you have in mind?"

"I checked your website and saw that you have a few things coming up. A cleanup and silent auction. I'll come help, invite the media, and show everyone that I'm more than just a distraction for the team."

"You've got it all figured out."

"Those were just my thoughts. You're the head of this thing. You tell me where you need me to be and I'll be there."

She frowned, not sure if she liked the idea. The part of her that needed ticket sales for the gala knew having the star of the Gators attend her events would bring much needed attention, ticket sales and donations the River Watchers desperately needed.

The skeptical part thought this was an offer too good to be true. In her memory, those types of situations always ended with her left behind and forgotten.

"I can tell you're not convinced," he said. "I know having me around might cause a headache for you guys. I don't want to cause you too much trouble. If you'd like, we can go out to dinner and discuss the arrangements."

Skeptical, Danielle smirked. "We don't need to go to dinner to discuss you volunteering here."

"I know that. The dinner is my way of getting you out on a date." He held up two fingers. "Two birds with one stone."

Danielle stood and placed her hands on her hips. "Volunteering isn't how you earn your way into my bed."

Jacobe stepped away from the door. With one long stride, he stood before her in the pitifully small office. "Volunteering is only about my basketball image. I came here straight from a meeting with my agent, coach, PR and one of the owners. My suspension right before playoffs is making them question resigning me next year."

Danielle doubted the Gators would turn away a talent like Jacobe just because of one disciplinary action. But he had been traded because of his outbursts. His point might be valid, but the look in his eyes said something else was on the line.

"What's really at stake? This isn't just about re-signing with the Gators."

His head tilted to the side and surprise filled his gaze. "Why do you think it's something else?"

"Just a feeling."

He was quiet for a few seconds before speaking up. "Are you in the habit of turning down people who want to volunteer?"

Fine. He could keep his secrets. As long as he understood she wasn't going to fall at his feet just because he was bringing publicity to the River Watchers.

"We can discuss volunteer opportunities right here in the office. It doesn't have to be over dinner."

"If it'll make you feel better, we can do that. I still want to take you out tonight." He tugged on the edge of her sweater, right above her breasts. "Consider a date as the second half of my apology."

"The first half was more than enough."

"Then consider it two old friends catching up."

"We were hardly friends."

"Then accept the fact that I just want to spend a little time with you. No expectations and no strings attached." He took her hand in his and threaded their fingers together. "Believe it or not, I've thought of you a few times over the years and my thoughts weren't always about that night. I really do want to go out with you tonight."

His eyes never left hers. There was nothing sly or mocking in his gaze. The look, his smile and the delicious heat from his body delivered a sensual knockout that nearly stole her voice.

"Jacobe, we shouldn't blur the lines."

"Danielle, even if I found another organization to volunteer for I'd still be here asking you out." He pulled slightly on her hand until she shifted closer to him. "One date. That's all. Okay?"

His thumb brushed lazily across the inside of her palm. The light touch sent delicious shivers over her body. His gaze grabbed hers and held it hostage. Danielle was lost in the brown depths and lulled by the slow play of his hands on her. Jacobe's gaze lowered to her lips. Danielle felt every excited beat of her heart throughout her body.

She nodded. "One date."

His eyes heated to delicious pools of melted chocolate. He leaned closer. He was going to kiss her. Danielle's heart jackhammered.

She jumped back. He immediately let go. Her arm hit a small stack of papers on her desk. The sheets flew to the floor. Turning away from him, she quickly bent to pick them up. "Um…as for volunteering, I'll let you talk with Debra. She helps coordinate volunteers." She slapped the papers on her desk. He stood in the middle of the small path to the door. She tried to quickly scoot past him without touching.

Her breasts brushed his chest. White-hot desire slammed into her. Her nipples tightened. Danielle jerked forward and almost tripped. When he reached out to help her, she held her hand away and righted herself.

"No worries, I'm good." She glanced at his face. He was watching her, smiling. Danielle looked away and opened the door. "I'll get Debra." She hurried out of the room before she turned into even more of a stuttering ninny.

Chapter 4

"What's really going on between you and Jacobe?" Debra asked as she and Danielle skimmed a row of party dresses in Revelry Dress Shop.

The second she'd agreed to a date with Jacobe, Danielle realized she had nothing to wear for a date with a NBA superstar. Her dating life of the past few years had been filled with other men from the conservation field. Hiking, biking, and kayaking with the occasional dinner at Applebees. Jacobe hadn't said where he was taking her, only that he'd text with the details.

"Nothing. It's just two friends catching up." She picked up a pink sequined scrap of material she assumed was supposed to be a dress. "What's this? Why did you bring me here? I said I needed help picking an outfit for a date, not prom."

Debra laughed and pushed back several other dresses

on the rack in front of her. "You said you didn't have anything to wear."

"I thought we'd just go to the mall."

Debra leaned close. "You're going out with Jacobe Jenkins." Her voice was low as if conveying a big secret. "He'll probably take you to a nightclub. Do you have a nightclub dress?"

"No." She eyed Debra's Supernatural T-shirt and gray earrings in the shape of a skeletal hand. "Do you?"

"No, but if I needed one this is where I'd go. Now look." Debra pointed to the dresses.

Danielle sighed and looked through the dresses. "This isn't necessary. I just needed a simple dress and a new sweater. This isn't going to be a big deal."

"You don't know that. He came all the way downtown to apologize for whatever he did to piss you off after the game."

Danielle hadn't told Debra exactly what Jacobe said. Doing so would require revealing they'd slept together in college. She'd just said he'd been the same jerk she remembered.

"He's volunteering to help us," Debra said.

"To help his image."

"But it still helps us. And he asked you out. For once don't be so doubtful and just have a little fun."

"I'm not being doubtful, I'm being realistic. In what world does the professional basketball star fall for the conservation girl?"

"I don't know. Yours maybe."

"Look, I've been here before. Professional athletes have an unlimited access to money and women. Long term relationships aren't on their agenda."

"Hold up. Wait a minute." Debra turned to face Danielle and leaned one arm on top of the dress rack. "You've been here? I need the, who, what, when and where?"

Danielle nearly swore. She didn't like talking about what happened with her ex-boyfriend. She'd never mentioned him to Debra. She straightened her glasses and turned back to the dresses. "It's a figure of speech."

"Spill it, Danielle. Come on, I thought we were friends."

"We are."

"Then tell me the story. You hear all of my baggage. Spill yours."

Danielle stopped searching to glance at Debra. She had the determined look that said she wasn't going to let the subject die. Why not tell her? Maybe then she'd realize this *date* with Jacobe meant nothing.

"I dated Luke Kinard in college," Danielle kind of mumbled.

Debra's jaw dropped. "Luke Kinard? Like, professional football player, Luke Kinard?"

Danielle tried to give a no-big-deal shrug. This is why she didn't talk about Luke much. People got overly excited about a disappointing time in her life. "Yeah. We met at an Earth Day clean up my sophomore year and hit it off. We dated through college. I knew he wanted to go pro, but we both never really thought he would. He wasn't drafted, but he decided to try to be a walk on in Philadelphia. He said if he made it, we'd move to Philly and get married."

A line of confusion formed between Debra's brows. "He made it. He's one of their biggest defensive linemen."

"After he go the offer, he told me about the women who throw themselves at rookies. How much time he'll have to spend at practices and learning the play book.

He didn't break up with me. I don't think he wanted to, but I could tell he didn't want to miss out on all the *perks* of being in the league. So, I broke up with him. Took the job with the River Watchers and moved on."

"That sucks."

"No, it's reality."

"But weren't you upset?"

She had been upset. Hurt. She and Luke had talked about marriage. They both had similar interests. She'd loved him, and she believed he had loved her. He would have tried to make their relationship work. She hadn't wanted them to end up hating each other because of the pressures from being in the league.

"It was better that way. We're still friends. I meet up with him for lunch whenever he's in town."

"Wait? The friend Luke you meet up with every so often is Luke Kinard? Geez, Danielle, I can't believe you didn't tell me Luke was *Luke Kinard!*" Debra sounded a little hurt by the revelation.

"Only because I didn't want to sound like I was bragging. We're just friends now."

"Friends or not, that's important background information. Dang, first you know Jacobe Jenkins now you're Luke Kinard's ex-girlfriend. What next, is Halle Berry your cousin?"

Danielle laughed. "No. There are no other celebrities in my background."

Danielle's phone chimed with the text message alert. She pulled the phone from her purse. "It's from Jacobe." She read the message. "He wants to go bowling. He's asking if I mind."

"Bowling?"

Danielle grinned. "Yes! Thank goodness." She put

the pink monstrosity back on the rack. "I really didn't want to wear a sequined party dress and go to a night-club." She texted back that bowling was cool. "Let's get out of here."

"Bowling?" Debra said again and followed Danielle to the door. "That's not very romantic."

"Exactly. What did I tell you? We're just two friends catching up with each other. There's nothing that's going to come of this."

"I swore there were sparks between you two."

Sparks, flames, knee melting electric energy. All of that flowed through Danielle whenever Jacobe was near. She'd been burned by that flame before. She wasn't about to get burned again.

Danielle pushed open the door of the dress shop and marched out to the warm spring air. "Forget sparks. All I want, and need, from Jacobe is his help selling tickets to the gala to save the River Watchers."

Jacobe chose bowling for several reasons. One, he liked to bowl. He'd bought the bowling alley after the owner wanted to let it go a year ago. He frequented the place enough to not be mobbed by fans. Guaranteeing a little bit of privacy for him and Danielle without being too intimate. He also remembered seeing Danielle at the bowling alley in college a few times and hoped she still enjoyed playing.

"I hope you don't mind bowling?" he asked as he opened one of the double glass doors to let her in. In his other hand he carried the bag that held his bowling ball and shoes.

The sounds of music along with the crack of bowling balls against pins filled the air. She wore a pair of sexy black jeans that hugged her hips, a ruffled white top and a cute black cardigan with a flower on the breast. She wasn't wearing heels and he could look down at the top of her head, making him infinitely aware of how small and feminine she was.

"I don't mind," she said. "I haven't bowled in a while. This might be fun. Don't you own this place?"

The smell of her light flowery perfume drifted around him as she passed. He took a deep breath to take in more of her. "You know I own this place?"

"You're a local celebrity. I saw something on a news report once."

"I sponsor most of the leagues that play here. When the previous owner started to shut it down, I stepped in so they wouldn't have to find a new place to play or quit all together."

She glanced up at him as they made their way to get bowling shoes. "Wow, that's a lot of investment."

"I like bowling."

"I do, too, but not enough to buy a bowling alley. Why do you love bowling so much?" Her big brown eyes were filled with curiosity.

"I said I like bowling. Not that I love it," he deflected.

"To buy this place so the teams could keep playing says you love it. Why?"

He shrugged. "Just do. I played a lot as a kid." He turned away from her curious gaze to look at the guy behind the shoe-exchange counter. "What's up, Dennis. I brought a friend in for a few rounds."

Danielle turned around to greet Dennis. Usually, when asked why he'd bought a bowling alley, he answered because he liked bowling. At that response, people just moved on. He didn't get into why he liked bowling. After his dad was killed, his grandfather would take Jacobe bowling on Wednesday nights. They'd kept up the routine for years until his grandfather passed away. Those Wednesday night bowling sessions had kept Jacobe sane after the craziness of his dad's passing. But to tell Danielle that meant he had to reveal too much of himself.

"I hope you have a good arm," Dennis was saying to Danielle. He pointed to Jacobe. "This guy is serious about bowling."

Danielle handed over her flats and took the shoes Dennis held out to her. "I'm decent. I think I can hold my own against him."

"I wish you luck then." Dennis looked at Jacobe. "You got your shoes, or you need a pair?"

Jacobe held up the shoes in his hand. "Brought mine."

"You have your own shoes?" Danielle said as they walked toward the first alley. It was against the far wall, with two empty alleys between them and the other people out bowling. Jacobe smiled and nodded at the regulars he recognized.

"Yeah."

"But you just *like* bowling. I think there's more to the story."

She smiled at him, and it was so cute he couldn't help but smile back. "Maybe there is, but I'm not ready to tell the story." Her brows drew together and he knew she was about to go digging again. He leaned down and lowered his voice. "We've got to save something for pillow talk."

She waved a hand as if his words were ridiculous, but he caught the spark of interest that had briefly lit up her eyes. "Stop that. I thought we were just here as old friends."

"You said we were hardly friends."

"I had to say that. I wasn't sure if you meant what you said about volunteering or not. But after listening to you and Debra set up your volunteer schedule, I figured you are serious."

"Very serious. I need some good press."

"Because of the suspension?" She walked away to check out the balls on the rack near their alley.

"That and I've got plans. I don't need people thinking that all I am is a bad temper and partying." Jacobe sat behind the controls to set up the automatic scoring for the game.

Danielle came over and sat next to him. "What type of plans? Hey, I bowl first."

"Excuse me," he teased. He deleted his name and put in hers first.

"So, what are your plans?"

"To be considered one of the best players in the league."

Danielle turned in her seat to face him. "That's a wish, not a plan."

"What do you mean?"

"I want to be considered a leader in my field, but just because I want that doesn't mean it'll happen. Not without a plan with real goals to get there."

"Okay, Professor Stewart, what are your goals?"

"First is showing genuine enthusiasm for what I do. I want to make a difference. Not just here but on a larger scale. I pick projects that will have a measurable impact when they're done, like shutting down Clear Water."

"Clear Water?" Jacobe leaned down to pull off his shoes and slip on his bowling shoes.

Danielle's brows rose to her hairline, and her eyes were wide. "Do you live under a rock?"

He shrugged. "Apparently so. Tell me what it is."

"They're a sewer provider who can't properly treat the sewage coming to their plant. They dumped tons of bacteria-laden water into the creeks for years. I fought to get their permit enforced. Major fines were levied and they have to put together a corrective plan to either tie into a better system or shut down."

"Wow. You did that?" He was impressed.

She leaned back and straightened her glasses. She looked embarrassed by his praise. "Well, not just me."

"They're shutting down?"

"They're trying to expand. They want to dump into Springfield Creek!"

She looked at him like he should be outraged. He shook his head. "You need to school me again, Professor."

She did. For the next few rounds of bowling, she updated him on her efforts to prevent Clear Water from expanding and dumping into the creek. Jacobe was amazed that all of this was happening right here, and that more people weren't talking about it.

She obviously was an advocate for her work. Her passion to make things right in the world hadn't changed. What, or who, else was she passionate about? He'd experienced the heat of her fire during their one night together. He didn't for a moment think she was seeing someone else. Danielle wasn't the type to hang out with him if she had a man, but there had to be something else that excited her. If not, he'd be more than willing to bring fun into her life.

"You know," Jacobe said, after he'd bowled a spare

and was coming back to where Danielle was picking up her ball to bowl. "Back in college I knew you were into this stuff, but I thought—I don't know—that you were just being a Goody Two-shoes."

Her laugh was incredulous. "What?"

"I mean, I didn't realize that you really cared about this. Not just because it seemed like the right thing to do or that everyone else was doing it. You're kind of impressive."

She fiddled with her glasses again and glanced away. "I'm not impressive. I'm just a hard worker. You're the one people think of as being impressive. Famous basketball star and all that. People listen when you talk just because you're a celebrity." She met his gaze. "I know you don't want to tell me your ultimate plan and that you're only volunteering to help your image, but thank you anyway. You'll get us the attention we need. That'll go a long way to help me."

She walked to the head of the aisle to bowl. Jacobe sat in the plastic chair behind the controls to watch her. Danielle was far more impressive than he. He wanted the recognition for being the best; she wanted to make sure people had clean water. He cared about boys who didn't know what direction to take. After his spiral when his dad died, and later discovering he wasn't the father of Christy's son, he recognized the need for more male mentors out there. He funded programs for that, but he wasn't as driven to that cause as Danielle was to hers. He'd had nothing but basketball and anger. If he lost basketball, did he really just want to be left with anger?

Danielle rolled a strike and jumped up and down. Jacobe clapped and smiled at her. That was the first strike she'd bowled all night. The bounce of her luscious breasts while she jumped distracted him. His clapping slowed.

A quick vision of her on top of the dresser in a long-ago college room, her dress pulled down and her soft breasts in his hands while his mouth kissed and sucked on nipples as sweet as candy flashed through his mind. That night had been too fast, too rushed and hurried. Next time he'd be sure to take his time and kiss every inch of her body.

Jacobe looked away and forced the memory out of his head. His brain cleared, but his body didn't follow suit. His blood heated and his dick swelled just enough to let him know that if he didn't control his thoughts he'd have a full on erection in no time. He didn't want her tonight.

Yes, you do.

Okay, he wouldn't turn her down tonight, but that wasn't the point of this date. He'd tasted Danielle, then walked away without a backward glance after Christy tricked him. He wouldn't let her think that he cared only about sex when it came to her.

What the hell, Jacobe? You want a relationship, now? No, that answer was clear. Women like Danielle wanted commitments. He no longer did commitments.

"Hey, you okay?" Danielle said.

Jacobe had lowered his head, his eyes closed as first the memory, then the scary thought of a relationship entered his mind. He opened his eyes and slowly lifted his head. He tried to give her a smile but feared it looked as force as he felt.

"Yeah, I'm good."

Her answering smile was open and excited, so he assumed his didn't look as bad as he thought. "Did you see my strike?"

"I did. Still not enough to catch up with me." He pointed to the score.

Danielle rolled her eyes and hit him on the shoulder. "We're only halfway through the game. And this ain't the basketball court. I'm only a few points behind. Game time, baby."

True. If she hit a few more, they'd be neck and neck.

Jacobe had stood and picked up his ball when a thought struck him. He turned back to Danielle. "Do you hate me?"

"What?"

"Do you hate me for not calling you?"

Her smile slowly melted away. Her shoulders straightened and she sat up in the seat. When she met his gaze her eyes were serious. "I don't know what I expected after that night. Everything happened so quickly. I came to show you I wasn't afraid of the spark between us. Next thing I know we're…you know. It was great, but I didn't think anything too serious would happen afterward. Certainly no expectations for a relationship."

She sounded so calm. So over it. How could it not have bothered her when it had bothered him occasionally over the years?

He took a step toward her. "If I would have called and asked you to date me, would you have considered it?"

She shrugged and looked at the control board. "I don't know."

He had a feeling she was lying. "I'm sorry I never called."

"Don't be. I moved on. I wasn't sitting around campus pining for you."

"I didn't think you were."

She nodded. "Good."

"Did you start seeing someone else?" Why in the world was he torturing himself with that question?

Her gaze met his. "I did."

He tried to remember if there'd been a particular guy sniffing around her that year, but came up a blank. "Who?"

She raised a brow. "Does it really matter?"

No, it didn't, not really. He didn't want to know her past any more than he wanted her digging into his. "You're right."

"Besides, I saw you with Christy afterward and assumed you two were together."

His shoulders stiffened and he gripped the ball in his hands. "We weren't that night. I wouldn't have had sex with you if I'd still been with her."

The rigid set to Danielle's posture relaxed and she nodded. "I know."

That surprised him. "I wouldn't have believed you thought so highly of me."

"I did. I was around you enough to know how many women tried to sleep with you, and how you turned each of them down. It was an admirable trait."

"Just one admirable trait. Are you sure there weren't others?"

"You had a few, but that's the one that really struck me as odd. As popular as you were, and as conceited as you were." He opened his mouth to argue and she held up a finger. "Don't interrupt, you were."

Jacobe closed his mouth and motioned with his hand for her to continue. Who was he kidding? He had enough confidence in his game to be considered conceited.

"I expected you to take up every willing female that

came your way. Especially since it seemed like every other day you and Christy were arguing."

That was true. People used to ask him why he stayed with Christy. He'd never felt the need to say anything other than she had his back. He never talked about how his dad's death was proof cheating wasn't worth it, or that Christy had been the girl he'd fallen in love with in the middle of his grief. Right before he really became good at ball and women who'd once ignored him were suddenly offering him sex left and right. Danielle deserved more than that simple explanation.

"Christy looked out for me back in high school before I'd really blown up. I was a good player, but after my dad died, I started skipping school, being a smart-ass in class and playing pranks just to frustrate the teachers. One day one of my pranks went too far."

"What did you do?"

"Stupid, really. My English teacher gave an assignment. Write a paper on the great contributors of American literature. I didn't like anything we read that year, so my paper was on why English literature was better."

"That wasn't the topic."

"I know. Anyway, he threatened to fail me. I got mad because if I failed I couldn't play ball. I put some fireworks in his desk and set them off right before class. There was smoke and the fire department was called."

Danielle's hand was over her mouth as she laughed. "No."

He nodded. "Yeah. It was bad. I would have been suspended, maybe expelled." His laughter died. "Christy said she did it. Took the suspension and everything. When I asked why, she said because she knew I needed another chance before I screwed up my future. I did.

After my dad died, I hid the hurt behind smiles, jokes and basketball. Everyone viewed me as this star player or this screw up in class. Christy was the first person to call me on my crap. If she hadn't said that, I would have ruined my chances. That was the year I really got on the radar of college recruiters. If I'd been expelled, that wouldn't have happened."

Dozens of questions swam in her chocolate eyes. He'd revealed too much about himself in that story. Stuff that he didn't want others to know. He hadn't even told Christy why he'd stayed with her for so long.

"Why did you come to the party that night?" he asked, before she could start a line of questions he didn't want to answer.

She shrugged and looked away, but tugged on the front of her sweater. "You made it seem like I didn't know how to party. That annoyed me. I came to show you I could have fun."

"You came in a dress that made me want nothing more than to see you out of it. It was a pleasant surprise."

The memory of that night flooded his mind. Danielle in a sleeveless black dress that hugged every one of her curves. *"You wore that dress for me?"*

"I wore this dress for myself."

"Will you take it off for me later?"

Damn that line had been cocky, and corny. She'd rolled her eyes before grinning and walking away. He'd followed her like a dope for the rest of the night.

His eyes met hers. The tip of her tongue ran across her full bottom lip. Her breasts rose as she took a deep breath. He licked his own lips and remembered the sweet taste of her.

"Are you sure you didn't wear that dress for me?"

Danielle stood abruptly. "Want some nachos?"

He wanted to say no and continue their conversation, but he didn't want to push. "Sure. Get a pizza, too. Or whatever you want to eat. Tell them you're with me. It'll be on the house."

She nodded then turned toward the concession. Jacobe turned to bowl.

"Jacobe," she called. He turned to face her. Her full lips were raised in a teasing grin. "I guess you learned I could handle you after all." She spun away and hurried to the concession.

Jacobe grinned and turned back to bowl. Danielle Stewart was full of surprises.

He didn't like talking about himself. Danielle realized that about halfway through their date. Most people would respect that he didn't share much and move on. Most people hadn't known him in college and remembered that he'd been cocky and fun loving, but also open and straightforward. Now he was closed off. Still charming, but guarded. The need to get to the bottom of a situation was one of her strongest traits and biggest flaws. Trying to unravel the secrets of a guy like Jacobe could result in her becoming too involved with a man who'd proved he could easily walk away from her.

"I had fun tonight," Danielle said as they walked to his car. She hadn't known what to expect before going out with him. She had known she would need to limit the opportunities for him to suck her into his web of temptation as he'd done earlier that day in her office. Bowling had been perfect. Minimal chances to touch or get lost staring into his eyes.

"Then I'll have to take you bowling again."

She turned to walk backward and face him. "I offered one date. No expectations and no strings attached."

Jacobe took her hand in his and pulled her closer. She was so startled by the movement that she didn't pull back. "What do I have to do to get you to go out with me again?"

He was so tempting. She'd get wrapped up in Jacobe and lose her heart. It had been easier in college when he'd left because they hadn't been together long enough for her to fall in love with him. That didn't mean she didn't know how much it hurt to have someone she loved leave her behind. She wasn't going through that again.

"I don't view first dates as an interview for marriage, but it is a chance for me to decide if I want another date and possibly a serious relationship. I'm looking for a commitment one day. What are you looking for?"

She would not normally be so candid on a first date, but she had to with Jacobe. He might be more guarded, but his flirtatious side hadn't gone anywhere. She could only imagine the number of women he went out with. He needed to realize she wasn't interested in being his short-term bedroom playmate.

Jacobe stopped and let go of her hand. "I'm not looking for anything serious right now."

She wasn't surprised, but that didn't stop the small tickle of disappointment in her chest. "That's cool. I just need you to understand what I'm looking for. If you're not interested in the same, fine. I'm happy to work with you at the River Watchers, but that has to be it. If my position means you'd rather work for another organization I understand."

His brows drew together. "I told you helping the River Watchers is about my image, not a sneaky way to get you in bed. Volunteering will show critics I'm not spending my five-game suspension sitting around sulking or starting fights like everyone expects me to."

The need to know more perked up. "Why do you start fights? In college you were always the life of the party, not a fighter."

"When you're really pissed off, it's easy to take your anger out on other people."

"About your son?"

His body tensed. "He's not my son." Jacobe spit out the words in a hard and tight tone.

Danielle flinched and crossed her arms over her chest. Her cheeks burned with embarrassment. She never should have brought that up.

Jacobe stepped closer and used his finger to lift her chin. "I'm sorry. I don't like talking about that situation."

"I won't bring it up again."

He nodded and dropped his hand. "Right now my goal is to convince people in the league that I'm not the hothead I used to be. I went through some stuff and it overshadowed my game. I can't let that happen anymore. I've got plans. This suspension could hurt those plans."

"Plans with the Gators?"

"I'm happy to play for the Gators. What we've done is phenomenal, but if I get the chance to play for an even better team I won't turn it down. I'll do whatever I can to take my career to the next level. If the Gators don't believe in me anymore, I don't need other teams to be afraid to sign me. You can understand that much."

She could. As a Gators fan, she didn't want him to leave. He was an asset to the team—no one could deny that. As someone who yearned to find someplace where she felt like she belonged, she could understand his ambition to leave. She'd loved her work with the River Watchers until Liberty got on the board and began threatening her job. Not having the full backing of your organization left you feeling lost.

She turned and walked toward his car. Jacobe fell into step beside her, following her to the passenger side. Instead of opening the door, he leaned a hand against the roof and turned to her.

"As for what you said earlier, about wanting a relationship. I hear you." He reached out to fiddle with the chiffon petals of the flower on her cardigan. "I brought you bowling because I want to get to know Danielle, the woman, instead of just going off the memories of the Danielle who tutored me in biology."

"You can get to know me as a friend and colleague."

The corner of his mouth lifted. He stared at his fingers on the flower at her chest. "I'm always open to a friends-with-benefits arrangement."

He met her eye, slid a few inches closer. For a spit second she was tempted to say yes. Reality and common sense prevailed. "I'm not good at separating sex and feelings."

His body instantly stilled and his lips pressed into a faint frown. He dropped his hand from her flower and leaned back. "That night, were you…"

She shook her head. "No. I meant what I said about not being mad about the outcome, but our night together did teach me that I'm not good at the love 'em and leave 'em philosophy when it comes to relationships. I'm also not good at having one-night stands."

His retreat bolstered her confidence. She needed to see this. Needed to be reminded that Jacobe was looking for fun and nothing more. Better to be disappointed now than heartbroken later.

Danielle reached for the door handle. "It's getting late."

He stepped back and opened the door. "You're right. I should get you home."

Jacobe didn't say much on the drive to her place. She was dying to know what was going through his head. Was he angry that he'd wasted a date with a woman he wouldn't easily get into bed? Did he even care enough to be disappointed? An online search quickly revealed he had no shortage of women interested in him and that he was rarely photographed twice with the same woman. Her rejection might be just a minimal blip on his radar when it came to women.

When they arrived at her place, a small ranch-style home that she'd purchased the year before, he came around and opened the door for her. His hand was warm and solid when he placed it on her lower back to walk her to her front door. The porch light flickered, casting the porch in shadows. She'd been meaning to change that bulb.

"Thanks again," she said, getting her keys out of her purse.

Jacobe took her elbow in his hand and turned her to face him. He stood so close that she had to tilt her head back even farther to meet his gaze. In the unsteady light of the porch, she couldn't make out the expression in his eyes.

"I respect your honesty, Danielle." His other hand came up to brush across her chin. "Don't think this kiss means otherwise."

Her heart fluttered and anticipation tingled every inch of skin on her body. "Who said you could kiss me?"

His dark eyes met hers and the corner of his mouth tilted up in a smile that would make a nun drop her panties. "Tell me I can't and I won't."

The air crackled around them. Sparks of heat filled her chest. Her eyes lowered to his lips. Full and soft. Based on the smoldering heat in his eyes, desperately wanting to touch hers. A kiss wasn't sex. It was just a kiss.

"One kiss," she whispered.

"Good."

His lips brushed hers before he slowly pulled her lower lip between his. The kiss was a slow tasting. Not one long press of the lips, but several small sexy touches and pulls of his mouth on hers. With each sweep her body heated and tightened with need. Danielle shifted forward, closing the distance between them. Finally, his tongue slipped across her lower lip. Desire pulsed through her midsection. Jacobe's strong arm slipped around her waist and drew her flush against the hardness of his body.

He was so much taller. She automatically went onto her toes, parting her lips so he could deepen the kiss. The arm around her waist tightened, and a second later Jacobe lifted her off her feet. Her breasts pressed into the firmness of his chest, her arms wrapped around his neck. She shifted and her body rubbed against the growing bulk of his erection. Memories of the full length of him filling her completely flooded her mind. Heat pooled low in her midsection and between her legs.

Jacobe sucked in a breath and broke the kiss. His breathing was just as harsh and heavy as hers in the quiet darkness of her porch. She could feel him pulsing, growing between them. She bit her lower lip to keep from moaning and begging for more.

He slowly lowered her back to her feet and took one determined step backward. He cupped her chin and ran his thumb over her sensitive lower lip. "One kiss," he said. "I keep my word." He leaned down and pressed another quick kiss to her lips. When he pulled back, she couldn't stop herself from leaning forward to prolong the touch.

"Good night, Danielle."

Jacobe turned, jumped the three steps from her porch to the ground and strode purposefully back to his car. Danielle stood on her porch and watched him drive away until the taillights disappeared.

She pressed a hand to her pounding heart. "Don't ever kiss him again if you want to keep your sanity," she whispered.

Chapter 5

"How are you handling the suspension?" Isaiah asked Jacobe.

He, Kevin and Will, were all seated outside next to the full court in the backyard of Jacobe's riverfront home. Jacobe's suspension prevented him from going to the stadium, attending practices and doing anything related to the team. He'd expected to be completely ignored by his teammates. To his surprise, Kevin, Will and Isaiah had shown up on their off day to give him an update on what had happened at practice and the plans for their next game.

"I'm going to volunteer with the River Watchers." He palmed the basketball in his hands. They'd played one game shortly after the guys had arrived. Jacobe and Isaiah had won against Kevin and Will. "And beat Kevin in pickup games."

Kevin smirked "I'm just trying to make you feel better."

Isaiah laughed. "If that's what you've got to tell yourself."

Kevin laughed along with Will before he looked back at Jacobe. "Why the River Watchers?"

"I'm going to volunteer with them. Do some good stuff for the environment, try to show I'm more than a troublemaker."

Will frowned and ran a hand over the full beard covering the lower half of his face. "Don't you think you'd get more brownie points showing up at the place that you give money to for mentoring?"

Jacobe shrugged. "Maybe, but what can I say to a group of boys? Hold on to your tempers and act like gentlemen? I can't even do that myself. This will give me a new angle, and it's a local thing. If I can get the locals to care, then the management will, too."

"River Watchers," Isaiah said suspiciously. "Isn't that the group the woman you tried to hook up with the other night works for?"

"Yeah."

Kevin nodded his head and gave Jacobe a sly look. "Now I get it. You're trying to get in good with her because she turned you down."

"Nah, it's not like that."

Will's eyes turned skeptical. "You're not trying to hook up with her?"

Jacobe thought about the kiss and how he'd had to call on every ounce of gentlemanly behavior he'd ever picked up not to press to get inside Danielle's house and in her bed. Danielle wanted a commitment. He didn't do commitments. He wasn't opening himself up to a woman like that again.

"That's not why I'm volunteering. She'd see through

that, anyway," he said. "Me and her knew each other back in college. I wouldn't mind hooking up with her, but she made it very clear she's looking for forever. I stepped back."

Isaiah stood and held up his hands for Jacobe to toss him the ball. "Figures."

Jacobe threw him the ball, then frowned. "What's that supposed to mean?"

"You aren't ready to settle down. Figures you'd step back," Isaiah said, dribbling the ball.

Will sat forward. "But you're still going to work with her?"

"Why not? Her organization does good things—we can help each other out."

Kevin shook his head. "It's never a good idea to work with a woman you want to sleep with. That never turns out well for me."

Isaiah laughed and passed the ball to Kevin. "That's because you don't know how to say no to a beautiful woman."

Kevin stood, dribbled and threw the ball back. "Why should I?"

Jacobe shifted in his seat so he could better watch Kevin and Isaiah. "Just because it never worked for you doesn't mean it won't for me. I can handle working with Danielle."

Kevin raised a brow. "And if she just happens to forget she's looking for a commitment and you two end up in bed together? What then?"

"He's right, man," Will said. "It's never a good idea to mix business and pleasure, especially for a guy like you."

"A guy like me?"

"Yeah, you." Isaiah dribbled the ball between his legs,

then jumped to shoot for the basket. It went through with a swoosh. "You're so anti-relationship and up-front about not wanting to settle down that women try even harder to change your mind. She'll end up falling in love with you."

Jacobe laughed. "Doubtful. I don't think I'm the type of guy she'd want to be with long-term."

He was relieved she hadn't hated him all these years, but what had she meant when she said their time had taught her she wasn't into one-night stands anymore? Had she had others? The thought made him tense with jealousy. She'd mentioned moving on after he left. If she hadn't done the one-night stands, was there a serious boyfriend in her past? More than one serious relationship? If so, what had happened with those guys?

Isaiah had run to get the ball and jogged back over to them. "You make women fall in love with you without even trying. Believe me, she's going to fall. You always have the ones who want forever coming on to you. Me, I always end up with the crazy women who aren't about anything."

Kevin snorted and slapped the ball out of Isaiah's hand. "That's because you're trying too hard to find this perfect woman to marry. I'm telling you, she ain't out there."

"I want kids one day."

"You don't need a wife to have kids," Kevin said. "Take one of mine."

They all laughed. Kevin had four kids, two with his ex-wife and two from a woman he'd dated after his divorce. He took care of them all but had made it clear he didn't want more, going so far as to get a vasectomy in the off-season.

"I'd rather have my own kids than bum one of yours."

Jacobe held up his hands. "Can we stop talking about kids? You're making my nuts uncomfortable. I'm not trying to make Danielle fall in love with me, marry me, or have any kids. I'm not looking for that at all."

Isaiah studied him closely. "I think you'll change your mind one day."

Jacobe shook his head. "Hell no, I'm not changing my mind. I'm not setting myself up to get played for a fool again, and you know just as well as I do how hard it is to find a woman who's for real in this business. I'm only worrying about making the suits happy until my suspension is lifted. That's it. There will be no love or long-term commitments happening here."

Kevin looked at Isaiah and Will. "Five hundred says he's going to fall for this woman."

The guys glanced at Jacobe, then back at Kevin. Will shook his head. "Nah, I'd rather keep my money."

Isaiah held out his hand. "I'll take that bet. He won't fall, but she will and he's going to drive her away."

Jacobe shook his head and shoved up from the seat. He held out his hand to Kevin. "Make it a thousand. I'm not falling for anyone."

Kevin laughed and slapped hands with Jacobe. "I'll want my money the day after you propose to her."

Danielle returned from her walk on the beach to find Debra standing on the back porch holding two cups from their favorite smoothie place in her hands. Danielle smiled and skipped up the stairs. Debra handed her one of the cups. Danielle took a sip and the delicious flavor of strawberries, blueberries and banana filled her mouth.

"What's bothering you now?" Debra asked.

"Nothing's bothering me. I just needed to get up and move around."

"It's the date with Jacobe, isn't it?"

Debra never let her pretend there wasn't anything wrong. "Why does this have to be about him?"

"Just tell me."

Danielle leaned against the railing of the back porch and took another sip. A breeze ruffled Debra's ponytail, but neither of them made a move toward the back door. The interns were working in the office today. Danielle didn't want them to overhear her silly confusion over her date. That kiss.

"He says he's only volunteering to help his image."

"Which is great. Having him at the gala will bring in tons of money, and possibly even our odds in the upcoming fight with Clear Water, especially if you can convince him to speak up to the council."

"I know, but…"

Debra's brows rose. "But what?"

"I can't really refuse his offer to volunteer. I wouldn't turn anyone away who wants to help. But I just don't want him to think that I'll be so grateful for his help that I'm willing to sleep with him."

"Did he hint around that that's the reason he's helping?"

"No. If anything he made it very clear that his volunteering and his interest in me were two different things."

"And what did you say?"

"That I'm looking for a relationship and not interested in doing the colleagues-with-benefits thing."

"That's a perfect way to make a man run." Debra took a sip of her smoothie. "Did he run away immediately?"

Danielle shifted from one foot to the other. "He kissed me."

Debra almost dropped her smoothie. She caught it

and eyed Danielle. "Well, that's different. So, what, is he interested in you for more than a hookup? I'd think that's what it meant if he kissed you after you said that."

"I have no idea."

"Just think," Debra said, her face bright with excitement. "You could see Jacobe Jenkins in all his tall, muscled glory in your bed."

A vision of naked, glorious Jacobe lying on the flowered sheets in her bed filled her head. Followed by an image of him flicking her lace pillowcases and frowning. She giggled. "It would be a sight to see." She shook her head to clear it of the vision. "I can't go there with him. Making money at the gala and stopping Clear Water are the most important things. As the executive director, I can't turn away having someone as high profile as him bringing attention to our cause. As a woman, I can't afford to sleep with him just because I think he might eventually be interested in a relationship. I've been in love and had the guy leave for bigger and better things."

Debra held the smoothie between her hands and peered at Danielle as if she were analyzing her. Debra's brow raised and her unwavering gaze stayed with Danielle's. "What happened with Luke shouldn't color your future relationships. Don't let fear of not being enough prevent you from trusting your feelings for Jacobe."

"Are you a therapist now?" Danielle groused.

"I'm no therapist, but I have had a lot of therapy. Enough to tell me you want to get closer to him."

Danielle paced back and forth on the porch. "I don't want to get closer to him. I'm curious about him. Something is different about Jacobe. He's still a charmer, still as confident and sexy as ever, but he's holding back. He's not as open anymore. He's been hurt."

"And you can't resist a project."

Danielle's gaze snapped to Debra. "What's that supposed to mean?"

"You like to fix things. That's why you're great at this job." Debra shook her head. "You can't fix a man. Normally, I'd say don't get sucked into trying to figure out what makes him tick and just have a little fun, but that look on your face means if you sleep with him you won't be able to help yourself. Jacobe is sexy, but unless you can really sleep with him without getting your heart involved, stay away. Let him volunteer and help the River Watchers, but send him home alone at the end of the night."

"Is that your professional recommendation?"

Debra nodded. "It is."

Exactly the recommendation Danielle's sensible side gave her. The side that had sent her to a party in college with the hope that Jacobe might be interested said something completely opposite. She'd survived and moved on with just a bruised ego but no major damage to her heart. Could she do the same again?

One night is a lot different from multiple liaisons, the sensible side whispered.

"You're right. I'm going to forget about that kiss and only focus on getting him to help us raise money and beat Clear Water."

"Good," Debra said, pumping her fist in solidarity. "And if you do dabble into the Jacobe pool of temptation, I sincerely hope you prove me wrong."

Danielle hoped the same.

Chapter 6

The auditorium where the Department of Environmental Protection was holding the public hearing on Clear Water's new permit was woefully empty. Danielle scanned the room and caught the familiar faces of the leaders of a few other environmental organizations there, including her River Rat friends, to oppose the new permit and only a few residents of the Crescent Acres community. Public hearings at ten on a Wednesday morning, when most people worked, typically were sparsely attended. Between the staff of Clear Water, the environmental groups and the residents, there were barely twenty people there.

Danielle gritted her teeth. This was one of the most disheartening things about her work. Fighting every day to protect something that people enjoyed using, but getting little to no attention for the cause.

Danielle walked over to the people who'd become the

closest thing she had to family in the area. "Hey, guys," Danielle said to the two ladies and one man.

Mason Kelly lightly bumped her shoulder with his. "Hey, Danielle." His light brown eyes were friendly and he gave her a welcoming smile. He represented the local kayakers in the area. He wore his typical brown hat with a kayak paddle logo over his sandy brown hair, along with cargo shorts and sandals. "Ready to fight today?"

"I can't believe we have to fight this again," Danielle replied.

India Graham nodded. She wore her natural hair in a tapered style that complemented her oval face. "How do you think I feel? I work for Environmental Protection. This is why I need to be in charge of permits. I'd shut these idiots down."

India worked in the monitoring section of the DEP. A section that was slowly getting their resources cut as funding went to other projects. Even though DEP's hesitancy to shut down Clear Water annoyed Danielle, she was thankful there were people who cared like India in the organization.

"Then you better go for a position in permitting when it comes up," Danielle said.

India pointed at Danielle. "Oh, believe me, I am."

Patricia Taylor, the leader of a group who focused specifically on Springfield Creek, sighed. Her curly dark hair was cut short around her plump face and her already tan skin was darker thanks to days working outside. "Depending on how this goes, we may all need to try to work for DEP."

They all nodded. Clear Water had ties to the legislature, who in turn pressured DEP to get their permits approved. Another political battle that they all realized would never end.

"How about drinks later," Danielle said. "Either to celebrate or to drown our sorrows?"

The frown on India's face cleared. "Girl, you just say when and where and I'll be there."

Patricia and Mason agreed. They decided to meet later that day at their favorite bar before taking their seats. India in front with the rest of the DEP staff while she, Mason and Patricia sat on one of the middle rows. Danielle would tell Debra and their group would be set.

The head of the DEP's permit division went to the podium and tapped the microphone. "Thank you for coming. We'll start with a brief overview of the new permit conditions and then we'll ask each person who signed up to speak to come forward. Starting with those in favor of the new permit followed by those against it."

He started going over the main points of the permit. Danielle was already familiar with each one. She looked down at her notes to go over all of her arguments against the department approving the permit.

The man at the microphone stuttered. Danielle glanced up from her notes. The department director was staring at the back of the room, eyes wide. She and the rest of the people turned toward the rear of the auditorium.

"What the hell," Mason muttered to her right.

Danielle's heart fluttered when Jacobe's gaze met hers. He grinned and strolled down the aisle between the rows of metal chairs in her direction, looking confident and casual in a brown button-up and dark pants that flattered his tall body.

The public hearing was more of a regulatory thing,

with little possibility of the media showing up, so she hadn't called him to be there on behalf of the River Watchers. Seeing him made her want to bounce with excitement. When he reached her row, he managed to look cool and suave doing the awkward side walk between the chairs to reach her.

"What are you doing here?" she whispered.

He sat next to her, all masculine heat and intoxicating cologne. He leaned in close and studied her with those hot chocolate eyes. "Looking for you."

Mason lightly elbowed her. "You know him?"

"He's volunteering with the River Watchers."

Mason's eyes widened. He turned to Patricia, and they both nodded their heads before looking at Danielle with an *alright now* respect in their eyes. Danielle sat a little taller. Having Jacobe on the River Waters' side was pretty impressive.

The room was still silent as the rest of the occupants, including the director, who was supposed to be moving the hearing along, stared at them wide eyed.

"You're disturbing the peace," she said to Jacobe.

"This is a public hearing. I came to hear what's going on." He glanced at the department director and nodded. "Go ahead."

The director blinked and cleared his throat. "Um… yes, so, as I was saying." He shuffled through his papers and started droning on again.

Danielle glanced around at the sparse crowd now more interested in Jacobe being there than the status of the permit. "You're distracting everyone from the issue," she said so that only he could hear. Well aware Mason was leaning a little closer to eavesdrop.

"I'm curious about the issue, too," he said just as quietly.

"Since when?"

"Since finding out you were here. Debra told me," he said before she could ask.

"Why were you looking for me?"

Knowing that he'd sought her out sent little bubbles of happiness through her chest. "Debra mentioned a cleanup over the weekend. I had a question for you about that."

"She can answer any questions you have."

"Maybe I prefer talking to you." He shifted to spread his long legs as much as he could, which wasn't far into the aisle, and stretched his arms out over the backs of her chair. She became very aware of his arm pressed across the back of her shoulders, and of the curious gazes of her friends on her.

Danielle straightened her glasses and sat forward in the chair. "We're not supposed to be flirting."

Jacobe leaned closer. "I'm not flirting. I'm reaching out to my friend and colleague."

"That's all we are and are going to be," she said, more for her benefit than his.

"That kiss said otherwise."

"A kiss is just that—a kiss. Not a promise for more."

"I understand and respect your decision."

She nodded. He moved his hand over to run his fingers across her upper arm. The barrier of her sweater did nothing to stop the sparks that flew through her body from the soft touch. "That doesn't stop me from thinking about a lot more kisses with you."

Heat spread up her face. She swore she heard Patricia make an *uh oh* sound, but she didn't turn to verify.

Instead she swatted his hand away and perched closer to the edge of her seat. "Stop that."

She adjusted her glasses and tried to focus on the front of the room. The director had asked for the proponents of the permit to speak. Danielle tried not to think about Jacobe thinking about kissing her again. She needed to pay attention to this. The residents affected by this fight deserved her full attention to bring their needs to light. Not for her to spend the entire meeting flirting with Jacobe.

Thankfully, Jacobe didn't say any more and listened to the Clear Water representative speaking at the microphone. The proponents gave the usual argument. Expanding would allow them to handle the excess flow. They were planning massive upgrades to improve treatment. They even pulled out a report by an independent researcher they'd hired who'd said the stream could handle the excess flows they would be discharging—complete with the assurance that only a minimal amount of pollutants, well within the allowance of their permit, would enter the river.

Danielle snorted loud enough to garner some looks with those comments. Patricia and Mason echoed her disbelief. A little pollution from a lot of places added up, and she'd bet money their independent researcher was the same one who'd doctored the numbers in an attempt to show they'd met their permit levels before. Her leg shook with her efforts at restraint—biting her lip instead of calling the representative a liar with each one of his statements.

"And now the opponents," the director said. He glanced at his paper, then looked straight at Danielle.

"We'll start with Danielle Stewart, executive director of the St. Johns River Watchers."

Danielle jumped up. Jacobe stood to make it easier for her to slide past him. His body was a strong wall of warm muscle that she couldn't prevent from brushing against as she moved past. Tingles ran through every nerve ending, tingles she forced herself to ignore as she walked to the podium to make her points.

Tingly feelings for Jacobe notwithstanding, she was able to make her argument against allowing the new permit. Her voice rose with her fervor. Fueled by her annoyance at Clear Water's we-aren't-hurting-anyone speech.

"We cannot allow them to pollute Springfield Creek." Danielle slammed her hand on the podium. "Clear Water has failed to eliminate their exceedances for years, and *now* we're supposed to believe they suddenly care. I've brought my own monitoring results that are backed up by the monitoring results made by DEP." She glanced at India, who nodded. "Along with the volunteer monitoring of residents in Crescent Acres. Compare the numbers and you'll find that Clear Water has lied to us again."

She slapped the papers with her monitoring results on the podium. The end of her speech was met with agreements, head nods, and applause from the few people from Crescent Acres who'd attended. The Clear Water representative cringed. Danielle held her chin high and glared at the Clear Water representatives before marching back to her seat.

"You haven't lost that spark," Jacobe said when she was seated again.

"This is important. Other people should realize that." She kept her voice low as the next opponent, a Crescent Acres resident, gave his own impassioned speech.

"You look so sweet and innocent. Then you get up there and rip out their spleens with a few words." He leaned over. "That's incredible sexy." His lips brushed her ear.

Danielle's nipples beaded. She shifted in her chair and tugged on the front of her pink cardigan. Admittedly, people underestimated her zeal and ability to win an argument. She considered that the ace in her pocket. Never a source of sex appeal.

"I don't do it to be sexy."

"Which makes you even sexier." He turned toward the front and listened to the other arguments.

Danielle tried to do the same, but her gaze and attention kept floating back to Jacobe next to her. He watched each of the opponents intently and even nodded his head in agreement with a few of their points. His apparent interest added to his own sex appeal. Debra's warning grew fainter.

"That's the end of the list of people who signed up to speak for or against," the DEP director said. "Thank you all for coming. The comments will be taken into consideration and also posted on the website. The last day for written comments is in four weeks."

The hearing ended. Jacobe placed his hand on Danielle's arm. "Can you send me some of the points you made? I'm thinking of sending in written comments."

"Are you serious?"

"Why do you sound so surprised?"

"You never care about these issues."

"I live on the river a few miles down from this new industry. I had no idea they were dumping upstream from me. I'm going to look into what they're asking for and then decide."

"Oh…sure. I'll send over what I said."

Mason and Patricia hovered at the end of the aisle. The Clear Water proponents watched them with interest. They had to be curious about why Jacobe was there with her.

"Why didn't they do this hearing in the afternoon when more people could come and hear what's happening?"

Danielle shrugged. "That's a question for the state."

He nodded and looked at the department director at the front of the room. "I'll ask them about that. Call me with the details of the cleanup this weekend. I think I'd like to do the one along Springfield Creek." He stood and was so tall her neck strained to keep eye contact. She stood, too, but with flats on he towered over her.

He'd actually looked at the different locations for the cleanups? "You want Springfield Creek?"

"Yeah, it'll get the most publicity if I'm there. I think that makes sense, don't you?"

She'd planned to send him to Springfield Creek for that reason. She wondered if he wanted that location just to help his image or because of what he'd heard today. "I do."

He reached up to brush his fingers across her cheek. "Good." He glanced at her friends. "Introduce me to your friends before I go talk to the director."

Surprisingly, she wanted to say no. Every one of them had seen Jacobe's quick caress of her cheek. They wouldn't say much in front of him, but she'd be grilled at drinks that tonight. "Sure."

He followed her down the aisle to where India, Mason and Patricia stood. She gave quick introductions, which included where they worked. Jacobe smiled and effortlessly charmed her group.

"I really appreciate you all making those comments today," Jacobe said after the conversation lulled. "It gave me a lot to think about. Keep up the good work." He placed a hand on Danielle's lower back. "I'm going to talk to the director now. I'll speak with you soon."

He grinned, then worked his way down the row toward the department director. The Clear Water representatives headed in that way, as well.

Mason placed a hand on her elbow. "How did you get Jacobe Jenkins to volunteer for the River Watchers?"

Danielle shrugged. She wasn't going to admit that he was there because he needed the good publicity. "He just came in asking to help. I couldn't say no."

"You would have been crazy to say no," Patricia said. "Your gala sales will go through the roof."

Exactly what she needed with Liberty breathing down her neck. "I'm just happy to have him participate."

The three kept gushing about how lucky she was to have Jacobe on her team as they walked toward the door. Danielle participated, but her mind kept wandering back to Jacobe. She tried not to think about the meaning behind his touches. He was a flirt. He probably did that without even thinking about it, not because he had any type of feelings for her. She glanced over her shoulder before walking out. Jacobe was watching her, he winked and lifted his chin. Danielle turned away, and pressed her lips together to keep from smiling.

Jacobe had a phone call with his agent, which made him thirty minutes late for the River Watchers cleanup. The call had been worth the extra time. Eric called to give an update on the preliminary talks he'd had with the management of the Phoenix team to gauge their thoughts on Jacobe after the five-game suspension. The talk had gone better than expected. Phoenix would still consider him for their all-star team as long as Jacobe didn't have any more problems this season, which made today's cleanup and the subsequent media attention that much more important.

Groups of people in orange vests were already spread out, picking up litter along the road and in the creek. Danielle stood with a few other volunteers next to a van in the parking lot for the neighborhood's community center, which he guessed was the center of operations.

He'd thought she was sexy earlier that week in the pink sweater that clung to her breasts better than cotton candy on wet fingers. She managed to heat his blood just as much in the khaki pants and dark green shirt she wore today. Her hair was pulled back into a ponytail, and instead of her cute gold glasses she wore a pair of simple black frames. She looked like she was ready to go into battle. Today's battle might be against discarded plastic bottles and trash, but that didn't diminish her fervor.

Jacobe parked in a free space in the parking lot and strolled over to Danielle. "I'm here."

Debra and two of the interns who worked in Danielle's office were the people he'd taken for volunteers when he'd first driven up.

Debra's eyes lit up and she waved. "Jacobe. Great you made it."

He hugged Debra and the two interns. When he turned to hug Danielle, she crossed her arms over her chest and gave him a glower worthy of any five-star general. "You're late."

"I'm sorry. I was on the phone—"

"It's fine." She cut in, waving his words away with her hand. "At least you made it."

"Was there any doubt?"

She cocked a brow, then looked down at the clipboard in her hand. Guess there had been doubt that he'd show up.

He glanced at Debra, who did give him a reassuring glance. "Thanks again for coming out to help."

"I'm happy to," he said. "Where do you want me?"

"Well." Debra glanced at the watch on her wrist. "I've already broken everyone up into teams and they're out. I'm going with the interns. How about you partner up with Danielle?"

He was more than down with that suggestion. Danielle glared at Debra. Had him being late put her in such a foul mood? She probably thought he was just as inconsiderate of her time now as he had been back in college. True, he was mainly out here to try to improve his image, but after the hearing earlier that week, he did want to know more about the people living around the area. Based on Danielle's impassioned speech, there was a big potential for harm if Clear Water was allowed to discharge into the creek that went through the neighborhood. He wanted to see what was at stake firsthand.

"Sounds like a great plan to me," Jacobe said.

"Fine," Danielle bit out. She slapped the clipboard into Debra's outstretched hand, then turned to grab trash bags and long trash grabbers out of the back of a Jeep. "Let's go pick up at the bridge down there." She pointed in a direction away from most of the volunteers.

"Why down there? You want to be alone with me," he teased, and wiggled his brows.

She didn't smile. "I don't want to distract all the volunteers and take them away from what they're doing by having you nearby. When we meet up back here in about an hour, then they can talk and beg you for an autograph to their heart's content."

"Whatever you think is best."

She spun on her heel and marched toward the bridge. Jacobe looked at Debra, who shrugged. "She's been in a mood all morning."

"What's wrong?"

"I don't know." Debra looked away. Jacobe got the feeling that Debra knew what was bugging Danielle, but he respected that she didn't eagerly divulge her friend's secrets. He'd rather find out from Danielle herself.

He hurried to catch up with Danielle. She didn't even glance his way when he fell into step beside her.

"I wasn't brushing you off or trying to be a jerk when I got here late. My agent called. He had good news for me. I got caught up in that and didn't realize we were on the phone for so long."

"I understand. It's no biggie, really."

She shoved a plastic bag and a stick into his hand and then jerked her head toward the bridge. "Let's go."

"If you were banned from the public hearing earlier this week and one of your board members called to tell you about whether you still had a future with the organization, is there a chance you would have lost track of time?"

She glared at him over her shoulder. "I wouldn't have been banned from a public hearing."

"Humor me, Danielle."

She stopped at the edge of the bridge. The bridge on the two-lane road crossed a small stream that went into the larger creek the rest of the volunteers were cleaning. Even though the bridge was small he eyed the underbrush warily. The vegetation beneath and along the creek bank was thick. The weather was warm. One word crossed his mind: snakes.

Danielle sighed and stabbed at an empty potato chip bag. "I would have listened."

He let go of his concern with snakes to meet her eyes. She'd actually agreed with him. "Since you're the river general I'm sure you would have taken the extra time to talk to your coworker."

One cute arched brow rose. "River general?"

"You lead your troops into battle to protect the river. Sounds right?"

She rolled her eyes but smiled. "That sounds rigid."

"You are rigid."

Her shoulders stiffened. "Not all the time."

Thoughts of her body melting into his when they'd kissed filtered into his brain, warming his insides. "No, not all the time." His voice held whispers of the desire he'd felt that night.

She adjusted her glasses and looked away. "I guess I understand why you were late. I'm sorry for being kind of bitchy when you arrived."

"You know I'm always late."

"Which is so endearing?" She said, sarcasm dripping from every word. She turned and stalked directly into the tall grasses next to the bridge.

"Hey!" He grabbed her arm.

She spun to look at him with wide eyes. "What?"

"You're just going to walk into the grass like that?"

"Um…yeah." She turned to walk, but he didn't let go of her arm.

"Aren't you worried about snakes?"

"Not really," she said, then jerked her arm from his hand. She used the stick to knock the grass out of the way and strolled just as happy as she pleased toward the creek beneath.

Jacobe pushed back a frustrated sigh. Well, if she went down there then he had to go, too. He followed her, his eyes scanning left and right constantly on the lookout for something slithering in the grass. He needed to get his mind off of what might be lurking and focus back on the conversation.

"What was bothering you?" He used his grabber to pick up some of the trash along the way. Danielle moved directly to the water with the single-minded focus of a general.

"I'd hoped we would get some media coverage for this." She made it to the creek bank and began picking up discarded trash with her grabber. "Last year we had two stations show up before the cleanup. No one has shown up this year."

He joined her on the creek bank without coming across any reptiles, but his eyes continued the constant scan for movement. "Did you put in your press release that I was coming?"

"Could you be more conceited?" she asked, elbowing him in the side.

Jacobe laughed and rubbed the spot, though her elbow hadn't hurt. "I'm just saying. Knowing I'm here would do a lot to get attention."

"I appreciate you offering to help out, but I wasn't sure if you'd really show. Getting attention isn't really hard for us for things like this. I figured if they came and you were here it would be a surprise for the media.

Plus, I didn't want a bunch of extra *volunteers*," she said, making air quotes with her fingers. "Showing up just to get your autograph instead of actually helping."

Danielle walked closer to the underpass of the bridge. Jacobe once again took a hold of her arm. "Are you sure it's safe to go under there?"

She looked at him like he was crazy. "Do you see the spray paint? Kids hang out under here." She pointed to the graffiti on the cement underpass. "Are you still worried about snakes?"

"I'm trying to figure out why you aren't."

"Running across a snake is common when you work around water. The key is to not panic."

"Who, you or the snakes?"

She laughed, then strolled on beneath the underpass. He should let her go and deal with any snakes she ran across—Ms. Running across a Snake Is Common. He couldn't. If she got hurt when he was around he wouldn't forgive himself. He didn't like getting up close and personal with snakes, but he'd take a bite to protect Danielle.

You've officially lost your mind. What are you now—Tarzan?

He pushed the thought aside. "Why no media?" he asked.

Danielle let out a frustrated sigh and imploded a plastic cup with her grabber. "Council decided to hold a carnival today. That got all the media attention. Normally, I wouldn't care, but one of our board members is on council and I know she pushed to have the carnival on the same day."

"Why would she do that if she's on your board?"

"Because she's only on the board to prove we're keeping the interests of the business sector in mind. I got a lot of attention from council with my campaign against Clear Water last year. She mentioned that the River Watchers is having too much influence in politics that's one-sided. She's not there because she supports our cause."

"Sometimes the businesses have a legitimate argument," he said, sticking close to her as they picked up the litter beneath the bridge. "They can't all be bad."

"I'm not saying they're all bad, but they can try a little harder to protect our natural resources."

Her voice took on the same militant tone she'd used at the public hearing. A tone he'd gotten familiar with in college, which meant she was about to start in on a passionate speech. He didn't mind when Danielle's passion came out. He just preferred to have her passion surface in his bed rather than beneath a bridge.

"So the media was a no-show," he said before she could start. "I get that's annoying, but they might still send someone out. It seemed like there was a little more to your funk than that?"

"My...funk?" She grinned at him.

"You know you act funky when you're in a mood. Wrinkling up your cute little nose like you've smelled something bad."

She touched her nose. He had a strong urge to push her hand aside and kiss her. But, again, kisses were for better places than snake-hiding bridges.

"What's bothering you?"

She dropped her hand. Turning away from him, she sighed and grabbed more trash for her bag. Her bag was halfway full, and so was his. Jacobe took in all the litter in the small section of creek near the bridge. Driving over this road, he never would have realized there was that much trash out here.

"My parents were supposed to come to the cleanup today." Danielle wasn't looking at him.

"Do they typically come?"

"No. They typically promise to attend one of my events and not show up." Her tone rang with the false cheerfulness of someone who'd been let down often but didn't want to admit their feelings were hurt.

"I'm sorry."

"Don't be. If I'm a general, then my parents are admirals in the fight against social injustice. They've got more important things to worry about."

The hurt in her voice tugged at something inside of him. Something that made him want to pull her into his arms until the hurt went away. "More important than supporting their daughter?"

"I shouldn't expect to come first when there are so many people in the world that deserve attention more than me."

The words sounded rehearsed. He had a feeling she'd repeated the phrase hundreds of times. Whether to convince herself or others was what he wanted the answer to.

"Has anyone ever put you first?"

Her lips and the corners of her eyes tightened. "I put myself first."

"Do you? You're always fighting other battles."

"I fight important battles. I bring attention to things that affect people who would otherwise be ignored. No one deserves to be ignored or left behind. What battles do you fight?"

Her words pierced him. The anger in her voice made him freeze. He'd left her behind.

She walked toward a plastic bag near the other side of the bridge. Jacobe knew it wasn't his imagination. There was definitely something long, dark and snake-like beneath that bag.

"Danielle, wait!" He rushed over and jerked her behind him. In one quick swoop, he pushed the bag aside and used his grabber to fling the snake into the water.

"What are you doing?" she asked.

He spun to face her. "Saving you from a snakebite." Now that the moment was over he realized what he'd done. He hated snakes. They were the one thing he was afraid of, and he'd pushed her aside to face it himself. A surge of masculine pride puffed up his chest.

Tarzan, huh?

He looked at Danielle. Ready to soak in her awe and feminine gratitude for him coming to her rescue. Danielle's eyes sparkled with laughter and her hand covered her mouth.

"What? Did you see what I just did?"

She pointed to the water. "You saved me from a piece of inner tube."

He glanced in the direction she pointed. Sure enough, a piece of inner tube floated downstream. No sign of a snake anywhere.

"Well, damn," he said, and glanced at her. He joined in her laughter.

"I appreciate the attempt, though." Her smile softened. "And I'm sorry about that earlier comment. My parents not showing is kind of a touchy subject for me. I shouldn't have taken it out on you."

"I may not have called you, but I never forgot you. Don't ever forget that."

The humor and apology in her eyes shifted into something else. Something warm and inviting that had him taking a step toward her. To hell with the thought that kissing beneath a bridge was a bad idea. He was about to thoroughly kiss Danielle Stewart.

He reached out for her, his hand grazing her waist. She didn't pull back. A crackling noise interrupted the moment. Jacobe frowned and looked around.

Danielle stepped back and reached for the walkie-talkie on her hip. "Go ahead, Debra." Her voice trembled slightly.

"There's a reporter here who wants to conduct an interview and get more information about the cleanup."

Danielle's grin brought sunshine to the dark space they were in. "I'll be right there."

"See," Jacobe said. "I told you the news would show up."

Her eyes narrowed in on him suspiciously. "Did you have anything to do with this?"

"I may have asked my agent to call a few stations when I was on my way out here. I am here to show people I'm cleaning up my act." Though he now wished he'd asked Eric to call just to make Danielle smile like that.

They backtracked back to the Jeep, where the interns and Debra were. Many of the other volunteers were around and the buzz of excitement grew when they recognized him. Jacobe was happy to greet the volunteers, many of them teenagers and families who lived in the area. He snapped selfies that he knew would hit social media and spread the word faster than any interview the reporter completed.

"Do you want to talk to the reporter?" Danielle asked while the journalist set up his camera on a tripod.

"This is your event. You talk first."

He watched Danielle handle with ease the questions the reporter threw her way. She used the same confident tone, and he was learning to love that about her.

One of the teens volunteering came over. "I just want to thank you."

Jacobe shook the young man's hand. "I'm happy to come out and help. I care about our waterways."

"Not that," the kid said. "I'm in the Big Brother program. My mentor told me that you're a big sponsor. I just want you to know that I appreciate that. It's helped me a lot."

"I don't do that for the attention," Jacobe said. "But I'm glad it's helping someone. Do you live out here?"

"Yeah. It's why I volunteered. Me and my little brother used to play in this creek a lot when we were kids. My granddad used to fish out here. Gotta take care of your home, ya know."

Jacobe thought about what would happen if Clear Water's permit went through. Would it be safe for kids to play in the water, for families to fish? *"I bring attention to things that affect people who would otherwise be ignored."*

Jacobe patted the boy on his back. "You do. Keep up the good work?"

"I'll try."

Danielle called him over then. Jacobe patted the teen on the shoulder and went to do his interview. Two other stations showed up and also interviewed him, Danielle and the various volunteers. Jacobe had planned to give a canned response about doing his part and showing that he cared. Instead, he talked about the importance of protecting Springfield Creek for the kids who played in it every day. He didn't speak out directly against Clear Water—he needed more information before doing that—but he was no longer sure he could remain neutral in this publicity stunt.

The look of feminine adoration on Danielle's face that he'd expected when going up against the innertube snake was there after his interview. It sent a twist through his chest that made him want to come back next weekend and do the same.

The reporters went off to get a few shots of the volunteers picking up litter and the mountains of bags they collected.

"Thank you for that," Danielle said. "I didn't think you would sound so sincere in your efforts."

"Neither did I. I guess you're rubbing off on me just a little."

She laughed. "Doubtful."

"How are we going to celebrate a successful cleanup?"

"Debra and I usually take some of the volunteers out for lunch afterward. On Monday, I'll crunch the numbers and then when I get the weight of the trash from the landfill I'll send out word to the volunteers and our board."

He shook his head. "No, we've got to do something a lot more fun than that."

Debra came over and wrapped an arm around Danielle's shoulders. "Did I hear the word *fun*?"

"You did," Jacobe said. "I was just telling Danielle that we need to celebrate a successful cleanup."

"Beers over lunch is good," Danielle said.

"Shush, woman," Debra said. "A handsome and successful professional basketball player is offering to throw us a party. Don't ruin it."

Jacobe laughed. "I was thinking more along the lines of taking you guys out on my yacht. You're doing so much to protect the waterways, why not enjoy it."

The thought had just popped into his mind. He wanted another date with Danielle but knew she would find an excuse to say no. A trip on the water with her key staff would allow him to talk to her more and give them a treat for the good work they were always doing.

"You've got a yacht?"

"Not a big one, but yes, I do. Me and the guys go out deep-sea fishing every once in a while. I'll take you and the staff out. You can invite a board member or two, as well." He put emphasis on the words *board member*. He wanted to meet this person trying to snatch his general's stars.

"Yes!" Debra answered.

Danielle didn't look quite as convinced. He grinned at her. "Come on, Danielle. Even generals have to relax every now and then."

She studied first Debra, then him. He could see the yes in her eyes before she said, "Okay, fine. We'll treat the staff to a trip."

Chapter 7

Jacobe checked and double-checked the weather forecast the following Wednesday, when he'd agreed to take Danielle and the rest of the crew from the River Watchers out on his yacht. Today, the meteorologist had given a dead-on forecast. The day was sunny and beautiful seventy-six degrees with only a few clouds in the sky. All morning images of Danielle on deck in a skimpy bikini had danced in his head.

When she, Debra and four of the River Watchers interns arrived at the marina his hopes were dashed. Danielle wore a loose pair of jeans rolled up around her slim ankles and a dark blue crew-neck T-shirt. A thick blue-and-cream-striped sweater hung over her arm. She was covered from head to toe, but that didn't diminish how happy he was to see her.

"Right on time," he said to her and Debra.

Debra and the interns were equally covered in T-shirts, jeans or khakis, but he could see the straps of swimsuits beneath their shirts. He peeked at Danielle's neckline, but didn't see a bathing-suit strap around her neck.

"We always are," Danielle said. She glanced around. "I thought you lived on the river. You don't keep your boat at your home?"

"I keep her stored here for the winter and most of the year. This is the first time I've taken her out this year. When the season's over, I'll bring her to my personal dock if I know I'll go out a lot more." He glanced at Debra. "You all can go on up. My girl is the *Freedom*. I hope you don't mind, but I invited Kevin and Isaiah. Will couldn't make it. They're already on board."

A murmur of excitement went through the interns. Debra's eyes lit up. "We don't mind at all."

Debra and the interns headed down the pier to where his boat was anchored. Danielle had stuck behind, as he'd hoped. He wanted a few minutes alone with her.

"Anyone else coming?" he asked.

"I invited the board president and vice president. They've agreed."

"Is one of them the council member?"

Her hair was held back by a dark blue headband and hung to just below her chin. The breeze had blown a few strands into her eyes. He fought the urge to reach out and push them away.

"Yes, the vice chair of council and president of my board is Liberty Myers. I also invited Mr. Springfield."

"Springfield? Is the creek named after him?"

"Not him, his family. The Springfield family owned much of the land around the creek for decades. Clear

Water's discharge, if the permit is approved, will go through his land, too. He has an interest in preventing the permit, as well."

She shifted on her feet and tugged at her bra strap beneath her shirt. Maybe it wasn't a bra strap? Hope that he would still get to see her in a bikini sprang in his chest. "Do you think she knows that she's invited so I can change her mind?"

Danielle shook her head. Her arms crossed beneath her breasts, pushing them up. Jacobe's eyes dipped. He forced them back up. He wasn't an adolescent. He wouldn't stare at her like he couldn't wait to see what was beneath her T-shirt.

"As board president, it makes sense for me to invite her on a trip set up as a reward for the River Watchers. I wouldn't come on too strong, though."

"I like coming on strong." He took a step toward her. Jacobe ran his finger along the edge of her glasses.

"You're also very persistent. Jacobe, I meant what I said on our date."

Those were words that should have made him take a step back. Words that should remind him that Danielle wanted a relationship. Relationships required trust, and he wasn't ready to trust anyone again.

"I know what you want, Danielle." He ran his fingers down her cheek and neck, stopping at the rapid beat of her pulse at the base of her throat. "I also want you."

A line formed between her brows. Dozens of questions floated in her warm brown eyes. "What does that mean?"

"Exactly what I said. I want you."

Voices and footsteps drew nearer. Jacobe dropped his hand and took a step back. He looked in the direction of the noise and saw a man and woman approach. The woman appeared to be in her early forties. Her dark brown hair was pulled back into a ponytail and she wore shorts and a T-shirt. The man was older, fifties, if Jacobe guessed, with graying hair. He too was dressed casually for a day on the water.

They spotted Danielle and Jacobe. The woman smiled and waved before they both walked toward him and Danielle.

"Hello, Danielle. Jacobe Jenkins," the woman said, holding out her hand. "I'm Liberty Meyer and this is Jeff Springfield. It is a pleasure to meet you."

Jacobe shook her hand. "Pleasure meeting you, as well. Danielle has told me how much the board has supported her efforts as the director of the River Watchers. I insisted that we invite you to show our appreciation."

Liberty's eyes shifted to Danielle, then back to him. "We?"

"Danielle and I are good friends. We've known each other since college. I've always been impressed by her passion for bringing attention to causes that are easily ignored."

Jeff nodded in agreement. "Danielle is the perfect person for the job. She is very dedicated."

Danielle adjusted her glasses. "I just try to do what's right."

Jacobe rubbed her back. She stiffened slightly but didn't pull away. She was lucky rubbing her back was all he'd done. He wanted to pull her against him as if they really were a couple. "Not many people are willing to fight for what they believe in. Come on aboard. I'll let the captain know we're ready."

They went aboard and Jacobe left Danielle with her

people and his teammates to give the captain the instructions. Not long after they were heading to sea. He turned on music. He preferred old-school hip-hop, but with the mixed crowd he opted for the new music his friend Dante Wilson was putting out. A fusion blend of classical, hip-hop and jazz. He'd been skeptical of the idea of the fusion mix when he'd first learned about it, but after hearing the music Dante and his group, Strings A Flame, were making, Jacobe had become a fan.

He'd ordered food for the daytime excursion since they planned to be out for most of the day. They stopped about twenty miles offshore and dropped the anchor. That's when Kevin and Isaiah mentioned Jet Skis and swimming. The group congregated on the back deck. Debra and the interns and even Liberty and Jeff quickly stripped down to bathing suits and life jackets, and jumped on the Jet Skis.

Danielle opted out of getting in the water and sat in one of the leather seats and watched. Jacobe chose to stay with her while everyone else played. She had stealthily avoided him while they were heading out to sea, talking with his teammates, Debra, the interns or board members. He guessed she was trying to figure out what he'd meant. He was trying to figure that out, too. He wanted her, but how much was he willing to surrender himself to in order to have her.

When he sat beside her close enough for their legs to brush, she quickly scooted away. "Not going out with the rest of them?" he asked.

"Okay, don't laugh, but I'm afraid of getting on a Jet Ski."

He drew back with exaggerated shock. "The river general is afraid of a Jet Ski. You go under snake-infested bridges without batting an eye, but you're afraid of a Jet Ski?"

She laughed and hit his arm. "The bridge wasn't snake infested. It was inner-tube infested."

"They look the same."

"No, they don't."

He shifted closer. "We'll agree to disagree. Why don't you do Jet Skis?"

"I fell off a Jet Ski once in college and haven't gotten on another since."

"How did that happen?"

She shrugged. "Went to the lake with some friends. My boyfriend took off before I was ready and—splash, I fell off, and he zoomed on."

Jacobe's ears perked up at the mention of a boyfriend. His anger rose, too, with the thought of the guy leaving her behind. "Sounds like a jerk."

She shook her head. "Not at all. That was nothing but a lack of communication. He immediately turned around and scooped me out of the water. I was fine, but a bit frightened. Neither of us got back on the Jet Ski and spent the rest of the day chilling on the beach."

The nostalgic smile on her face, full of sweet remembrance of a fond memory, made his stomach clench in knots. Jealousy? Really?

"You liked that guy?" He hoped she didn't say the ex-boyfriend's name. Without a name, he didn't seem quite real.

"I did." Her brows drew together, then she looked out over the water at the group cheering and playing.

He wondered what that frown was about, but he wasn't interested in hearing any more stories about an ex-boyfriend. "Come on the Jet Ski with me."

"No, thank you. I'd rather not find myself plunged into the middle of the ocean."

He laughed. "You won't. If you prefer, I'll get behind you and hold on. You can plunge *me* into the middle of the ocean if you prefer."

"You can be annoying," she said with a grin. "But I don't want you to fly off the back of a Jet Ski."

"It'll be fun. Come on, let's try."

She watched the others and bit her lip. "Give me a second to think about it, okay?"

"Sure." He slid closer to her on the seat. She didn't notice and didn't move away. "That time in college— was it the first time you'd ridden one?"

"No. After Hurricane Fabian in 2003, my parents and I traveled to Bermuda to help with efforts to restore the coastline. My dad took me out on one once during that vacation."

"Sounds like a fun vacation," he said, not bothering to hide his sarcasm.

"Actually, it was fun. It was the first time I'd gone anywhere with just me and my parents that I can remember."

"You traveled with others a lot?"

"There were always other people around my parents. I'm an only child, but my parents always busy with other things. There are so many people who need help in the world, it's only right that they answer the call."

Her words had that rehearsed sound he'd heard before when she'd tried to hide that she was upset they hadn't come to the cleanup. The sound of someone used to being forgotten.

"When the opportunity to help after the hurricane came up, Dad signed us up to go. We helped rebuild the coastline and even worked on a few houses during the day. Sometimes, we got the chance to just hang out, but there was so much work to be done. Dad rented a Jet Ski and took me out. We had so much fun, laughing and going fast. Mama nearly had a heart attack."

"That docs sound fun." No sarcasm. "Did you go out a lot on the Jet Ski?"

"No. It was just that afternoon. There were too many other things to be done. The best vacations are ones where you're giving back."

He stretched out his legs and rested his arm behind her. The position allowed him to brush his thumb across her shoulder. He liked touching her. "To me, the best vacations are the ones where you do nothing but relax and have sex."

Her eyes snapped to his and she sucked in a breath. "What?"

"Exactly what I said."

She frowned. "That's not the point of a mission trip."

"Maybe not, but I'd find the time. I'd also make sure I planned vacations that are about nothing but having fun. If you spend all of your free time giving to others without doing something for yourself eventually you run out of things to give."

She looked away and sat up so he couldn't touch her. "That's a selfish thought."

"No, it's a true statement. We all have to relax and recharge. The world won't end if you take a second to just enjoy it."

"I was raised to believe it's the responsibility of every person on this planet to do what they can to make it a better place."

The general's voice again. "Really, so what's your dream vacation, then?"

She looked sheepish. "You're going to think I'm crazy, but there's this group that provides water-purification systems and builds wells for people who don't have access to clean drinking water around the world. I'd love to volunteer and go with them one year."

Jacobe sat up straight and pulled back his hand. Not because he disliked her idea but because her dream vacation was so noble. So damn honorable that it reminded him that he should walk away and stop pursuing her. She deserved better than the friend-with-benefits relationship he was able to give.

"You think I'm crazy, don't you?"

Jacobe took her hand in his and squeezed gently. "No. I actually think you're amazing." He looked into her eyes. "I admire your passion, and your compassion. But, can we at least agree that it's also the right of every person to take care of themselves, as well? Having a little fun, without guilt, isn't the end of the world. You know that. You've done that before."

A low blow. He didn't care. Right now he wanted the little bit daring, little bit wild Danielle who'd come to a party that night in college to come out for a little while.

"That night was…"

"A mistake?" He really hoped that wasn't what she was going to say.

She shook her head: "No. It was the only time I did something truly reckless and just because I wanted it. Because I wanted you."

"The world didn't end, and as you said, you moved on."

"Not easily, but I did." She whispered the words, then pulled her lip between her teeth.

He squeezed her hand again, fought the urge to pull her in close and kiss her. There were too many people on the boat. Too many people who had no reason to not tell the world that he'd kissed her. He normally didn't care who knew about the women he slept with, but he wanted whatever happened between him and Danielle to be between the two of them. Just like their night in college had been. Their own sweet secret.

"Ride the Jet Ski with me?" he asked. He needed something to do besides sit there and try not to kiss her.

She glanced at the group on the water, then back at him. "Okay. Let's do it."

Danielle had avoided getting on a Jet Ski ever since Luke dropped her into the lake back in college, but fear of falling off wasn't what caused her insides to flutter as she settled into the seat. The searing heat in Jacobe's eyes when she'd stripped of her jeans and shirt was the reason. Appreciation followed by the thorough inspection he'd given as she removed her outer layers made her feel like she was wearing the sexiest of bikinis instead of the sporty blue-and-black two-piece.

Before she could get a good grip on the gears, Jacobe sat down behind her, and wrapped her with the heat from his body. The inside of his legs pressed tightly against hers. The firm muscles of his chest were flush against her back, and his oh-so-long and strong arms wrapped snugly around her waist.

There was no way she should feel his body heat between two layers of life jackets, yet he seemed to burn into her flesh. Her mind had to be playing tricks on her.

He leaned forward. "You good?" His lips brushed her ear.

She tensed and gripped the handles. Jacobe ran one hand up and down her arm while the other squeezed her in what she guessed was a hug from behind. "It's okay, I won't let you fall."

Falling was not where her head was at right now. She cleared her throat and nodded. "I'm good. Just getting comfortable."

"Am I holding you too tight?"

He could hold her a lot tighter and she'd be cool. "Uh...nah. You're fine. You sure you don't mind being behind me?"

His hands gripped her waist and he pulled her farther into the crook of his legs. Heat shot through Danielle's body, and she fought not to twist backward in his embrace. "I'm loving this position."

His voice sounded thicker. She didn't dare glance over her shoulder to see if the look in his eye matched. His sexy voice and hot looks were all well and good when they were on the boat, not so much when his hands could singe into the bare skin of her hips and thighs and his very essence surrounded her.

"You ready?" he asked.

She nodded. The sooner she started the sooner this ended. "Let's do this."

Debra clapped from the back of the boat. "Have fun, Danielle."

Danielle shot her friend a glare, then laughed when Debra wiggled her eyebrows.

"Hold on." She twisted the controls and they shot forward.

Why had she told him to hold on? One hand stayed on her hip, and the other wrapped around her waist. He moved with her in perfect harmony. His body melding to hers as she zipped and streamed through the water. The Jet Ski hummed beneath her, but that was nothing compared to the vibrations going through her body. Despite the mist of water that hit them, she felt overheated, burning with a need to get closer to Jacobe.

Jacobe moved his arms from around her waist. One hand clasped her shoulder, and the other pressed against her upper thigh. His fingers trailed up to her hip then back down where he squeezed. Danielle's grip jerked and the Jet Ski lurched forward. His arm shot around her waist and he held her tighter than before.

"All right?" he asked.

Her heart thudded. "Yeah, I'm going back in now." She yelled over her shoulder and made her way back toward the yacht.

When they returned, she quickly took Kevin's outstretched hand and hurried off the Jet Ski. She didn't wait for Jacobe to get off as she hurried onto the deck.

A few seconds later, Jacobe lightly touched her arm. "Are you okay?"

She spun around and stepped out of his reach. Concern filled his eyes and he moved closer to her.

"Yeah, maybe it was all the jostling around, but I feel a little light-headed." A lame excuse, but she needed a second to compose herself.

Liberty walked over. For the first time in a long time, Danielle was happy when the woman interrupted her.

"You two sure looked like you had a good time," Liberty said. She held a small plate of shrimp cocktail in her hand.

Jacobe glanced at Danielle. "I always have fun hanging with Danielle."

Sharp curiosity filled Liberty's gaze. "Do you two hang out a lot?"

Danielle shook her head, but Jacobe spoke. "More so recently with the proposed permit for Clear Water. I live on the river and some of the boys in the mentoring program I sponsor live in Crescent Acres. We'll all be affected if their permit goes through."

Danielle had to give him props. He'd eased the conversation to the permit easily. But, then again, Jacobe had always been smooth.

"You're following the Clear Water situation?" Liberty sounded surprised.

"I am. Closely. Not just the situation with the possible pollution, but can the creek even handle the excess flows? I mean, it's a decent size, but will the extra water cause flooding of properties along the bank in larger rains?"

Danielle's and Liberty's jaws dropped. Liberty was too busy watching Jacobe to notice Danielle's shock, which gave Danielle the chance to snap her mouth shut. For him to bring that up meant he had to have done more research on his own. The point had been minor in her speech during the public hearing. She got a giddy, glowing feeling in the pit of her stomach, along with a tightening of her skin and an overwhelming urge to grin uncontrollably. There could only be one reason.

She was starting to like Jacobe. Not just like him as a sponsor and ally, but *like* like him. Like him as she would a guy she wanted to date.

Because you do want him. You want him bad.

Danielle swayed slightly, the thought an unwanted shock to her system. She did not need to fall for a man who clearly said he wasn't looking for a serious relationship.

He instantly looked her way and put a hand on her arm. "Are you okay?"

She nodded, but couldn't meet his eyes. The giddy, I-could-fall-for-this-guy feeling hadn't gone away. "I'm going to sit for a second. I think it's a combination of the ride and being on the water for so long. You two keep talking."

He didn't let her arm go. "Do you need to lie down?"

"No. Just a few seconds to settle my brain." She met his dark sexy eyes. Heat flooded her face.

Jacobe frowned. Maybe he saw that she was on the verge of losing it. "Come with me. Excuse us, Liberty."

He took her hand and led her into the cabin, then down into the bowel of the ship.

"Seriously, I'm fine."

"Just trust me. It's much quieter down here. Besides, you look as if you're about to pass out."

They went down a wood-paneled hall and into another room.

Danielle took one look at the queen-sized bed and her heart jumped in her chest. She did not need to be alone in a bedroom with Jacobe. "What are you doing?"

"Lie down for a few minutes. Take as long as you need. I'll go back up." He released her hand and went over to the bed, where he moved the covers. "The bathroom's in there. I think there's some antinausea medicine in there and something for a headache. Don't worry about falling asleep, I'll check on you in about thirty minutes if you're not back up."

He returned to stand in front of her. His concerned gaze studied her. She was a sucker for a man who cared.

He made a move toward the door. Danielle grabbed his arm. "You're really concerned about me?"

"I shouldn't have insisted that you ride the Jet Ski. I didn't think about you not feeling okay after you got off."

"I'm someone who doesn't like to be blindsided, and you're doing that to me."

He frowned. "I don't understand."

"You're being thoughtful and considerate. Not to mention talking to Liberty as if you really care."

"I do care." He sounded a little annoyed that she'd implied otherwise.

The fluttery feeling, the one she needed to ignore, intensified. "I'm...impressed. I didn't know what to think when you brought me down here."

He shifted back and eyed her warily. "You didn't think I would bring you down here for something else if you're not feeling well."

Danielle shook her head and waved a hand. "No. I just didn't realize you could be so sweet."

"Don't let the word get out. Some people take sweetness for weakness." A hint of cynicism entered his voice.

"Is that what Christy did?"

His body went rigid. "Something like that. Look, I'll leave you alone."

He tried to move away and again she held on to his arm. "I'm sorry. I said I wouldn't bring that situation up again."

"I know your intent isn't malicious."

"I'm sorry that she hurt you."

"Finding out that the child I thought was mine really wasn't came with a bit of pain." His face and voice were impassive, but she felt the hurt that accompanied the rigid tension of his body.

Danielle took a step forward and placed her hand on his chest. His heart beat wildly beneath the wall of muscle. "She sounds like a bitch."

Jacobe's eyes widened. The tension in his body evaporated. "Did the river general really just call another woman a bitch?"

"I'm sorry, but for her to treat you that way, to lie to you like that. There's no other word for it."

Jacobe shifted close until only her hand separated their bodies from touching. She was tempted to pull it away. "Danielle, let me apologize right now."

"For what?"

"I'm about to be anything but sweet." He gripped her hips and lifted her off her feet. Danielle gasped and grabbed onto his shoulders. He wrapped an arm around her waist to hold her against him.

"Just because I called her that?"

"That, and a little bit because of your bikini."

"It's sporty, not sexy."

He shifted her higher, nudging her forward with the movement. "Everything you wear is sexy." He kissed her.

She went with instinct. Her arms wrapped around his neck, and her legs circled his torso. Kissing would not help her get over the crazy feeling that she wanted to take a risk and be with Jacobe, yet there was no way she would stop.

In two swift steps, he had her across the room. A second later, her back met the cool sheets on the bed. Danielle opened to him. His large body pressed her deep into the soft mattress. The smell of the ocean, clean sheets and Jacobe drugged her. The heat of his skin over the play of firm muscles ignited her even more. Her short nails dug into his shoulders.

Jacobe gripped her hips and settled his firmly between hers. The insistent press of his erection pushed against the flimsy material of her bathing suit. The thick length rubbed enticingly against her dampening core. He rocked his hips. The ridge of his cock slid against the most sensitive spot on her body.

Danielle gasped and her head pressed back. Pleasure slipped over her body like silk. Jacobe pulled her lower lip between his, before deepening the kiss. She grabbed his shoulders. Pulled him closer. Jacobe's achingly thorough kiss was a sweet, intimate caress that slowly intensified her desire. One hand gripped the hair on his head, holding him tight. The other ran across the strength of his back. His hips continued to slowly push back and forth, winding her body tighter and tighter, pressure building in her midsection with each movement.

He broke the kiss to lick and suck along her chin, neck and torso. One of his hands cupped her breast. His fingers playing with the hard nub of her nipple.

"Damn, Danielle, you smell so good." He groaned into her neck. The tip of his tongue flicked against her neck. "Taste so damn good." His hips rotated again.

Danielle bucked, her fingers clinging to his head as he tasted her. "Jacobe," she moaned.

"If we were alone on this boat I'd strip this damn bikini off of you and taste every part of you. I still remember what you tasted like. Do you remember the way I licked you?" His tongue leisurely explored across her neck.

Did she remember? Was the ocean salty? He'd spread her legs wide that night so long ago. Spread her open and savored her for what felt like hours even though it was only a few rushed minutes. She hadn't lasted long. Had climaxed almost immediately around his expert tongue. Then he'd kissed her, and she'd been helpless to do anything but tear his shirt open and push his pants down in a frenzy to get more of him.

"Oh, you remember." The male satisfaction in his voice only melted her bones more.

Danielle pulled his head back up for another kiss. Memories of that night fused with the delicious imprint of his body on top of hers. She wanted more, needed more.

He reached down, rearranged himself until the full ridge of his erection pushed firmly against her swollen nub. His hips moved in deliberate, firm thrusts. The movement was both delicious and maddening. She wanted her bottoms off, his swim trunks gone and his body thick and deep inside of her. The image of him was so clear, the memory of their time together so real, that her body tightened. Her mouth opened to beg for more when her world exploded. Pleasure burst through every filament of her being. Her legs clenched around his waist.

Her shout was cut off by his mouth over hers. He kissed her deeply, slowly, as she eased back to reality. All too soon the reality of what had just happened set in. Her cheeks burned and embarrassment slammed through her.

"Oh, my God, I can't believe we just did that," she said between pants. She felt his gaze but kept her eyes firmly closed. She could only imagine what he thought. How uneventful her love life had to be for her to orgasm so easily. "We shouldn't have done that. We're just supposed to be working together. We're—"

He cut her off with a quick brush of his lips across

hers. "Worry about what we just did tomorrow, okay. Today is about having fun."

"I know, but we shouldn't have—"

"Danielle, I'm still between your legs with a pretty uncomfortable hard-on, and you're already telling me this was a mistake."

"Oh. I'm sorry. Do you want me to do something?" All the eagerness she'd felt earlier was gone, replaced with mortification and regret.

He shook his head. "No, you can stay. I'll need a few minutes to get…myself straight. If you know what I mean."

"What does this mean?"

"Let's not analyze that right now. Okay?"

Not exactly what she wanted to hear, though not a surprise, either. He'd already said he wasn't ready for a committed relationship. Of course, he wouldn't want to analyze getting her off with just a slow grind. More heat flushed her cheeks. "You're right. I'm sorry. You stay. I'll go back up."

"If that's what you want."

They stared at each other. His erection was not decreasing an inch. "You need to get off me."

"Yeah. Right." He pushed away from her in a rush. His gaze roamed over her on the bed before his lips pressed together in a thin line. He rearranged the bulge in his shorts and turned away. "I'll be up in a minute."

Danielle jumped off the bed and scurried to the door. "Take your time. You know, finishing—"

"Goodbye, Danielle." His voice was strained, almost angry. She hurried out and back up to the deck.

Debra came over immediately. "What's wrong? Liberty said you were sick. Where's Jacobe? Did he give you something?"

Danielle gripped Debra's arm. "Not now, Debra. I'm good."

Debra's gaze sharpened. A second later her jaw dropped and she leaned in. "Did you?"

Danielle shook her head. "No!" she said in a harsh whisper. "Not. Now."

Debra waved a hand. "Fine. Not now, but later." Her eyes sparked with interest.

Danielle's face burned so hot she was surprised smoke didn't rise from her cheeks. There was no way she could tell the story of how humiliating it was to get off from a fully clothed, slow grind.

Chapter 8

Leading the Gators to a twenty-point win in New York was the pièce de résistance at the end of Jacobe's five-game suspension. He leaned back and stretched his arms over the back of the leather couches in Mahogany, the swank uptown nightclub owned by Calvin Rush, a connection Jacobe had made through his friend, movie star Irvin Freeman. Isaiah sat on the leather chair to Jacobe's right, and buckets of champagne and empty glasses covered the marble table in front of him in the VIP section.

He normally enjoyed clubbing after a game but was having a hard time finding his groove tonight. If he didn't let off some steam he was likely to burst. His gaze roamed the crowded club, taking in all the beautiful ladies. Any one of them could help release the pressure building inside. Ever since Danielle had walked away last Saturday, he'd had a semi hard-on that only seemed to disappear when he played ball.

Frustration pounded through him with every beat of his heart. Not because she'd walked away—he'd never push her into anything she didn't want to do—but because she'd immediately regretted what happened the second after she'd climaxed.

And her climax had been something to behold. The way her small hands clutched his shoulders while her slim legs wrapped around his hips. The way her dark eyes had gone out of focus and rolled to the back of her head. The sexy sweep of her tongue over her lower lip. Her body jerking and bucking beneath him.

Jacobe groaned and reached for the glass of champagne on the table. Damn, he had to get her out of his mind. He'd been in a one-sided relationship before. If her first thought when they were in that position was that they'd made a mistake, then obviously she was still unsure about moving forward with him. That should be good. He knew he wasn't ready for anything serious. That didn't mean he wanted her to regret it if their relationship naturally progressed physically.

He needed to move on. He wouldn't get caught up in a woman who wasn't ready to acknowledge the heat simmering between them. Tonight, he was going to celebrate being back on the court and the team's win with one of the beautiful women in the place.

Kevin walked up with three beauties surrounding him. It was divine intervention telling Jacobe he was on the right path.

"Ladies, let me introduce you to my teammates. Jacobe and Isaiah. Fellas, these beautiful ladies are Teresa, Nicole and Davina," Kevin said, pointing to each of the women as he introduced them.

Davina, a sexy brunette with tan skin and attractive

green eyes sat next to Jacobe. The edges of her tight black dress rode up her toned thighs and the light scent of her perfume surrounded him. "Congratulations on your win." Her voice was like warm honey.

"Thank you," Jacobe said. He shifted away to give her more room on the couch, but she followed his movement, plastering her curvaceous body against his side. "Are you a fan?"

"Of basketball, no. Of you, most definitely." Her hand played along his thigh.

Jacobe waited for the arousal that had nagged him from the moment he'd left Danielle to take over his body. His body said yes. This is what he needed. This was what he should be doing. On a physical level he was fully capable of accepting what Davina had to offer. His brain on the other hand was hesitant. He could take Davina back to his hotel room, but he wouldn't be satisfied. The desire pushing at him from the inside wouldn't go away. Davina wasn't the woman that had caused the buildup.

"Excuse me, I'm going to get a drink." He pushed Davina's hand off his thigh and stood. Ignoring her gasp of surprise and Kevin's knowing smirk, Jacobe left the VIP section and headed to the bar.

Calvin stood at the edge of the bar talking to one of the bartenders. Calvin was quiet and mostly kept to himself, but Jacobe liked him. Calvin always found a table for Jacobe when he popped in, and he had let him leave through a secret exit once when Jacobe had wanted to avoid the paparazzi.

"Calvin, what are you doing hanging out at the bar?" Jacobe and Calvin clasped hands.

Calvin moved to the side to give Jacobe more room at the bar. "I like to come out and check on things every once in a while. I don't spend the entire night in my office."

"You really aren't enjoying all the perks of owning one of the hottest clubs in New York. If you let these women know who you were you'd have most of them trying to take you home tonight."

Calvin chuckled but shook his head. "Not interested in taking anyone here home. Too much of a chance they'd come back angry when things didn't work out. Speaking of which, why did you leave a beautiful woman to come hang out at the bar?"

Jacobe shook his head and motioned for the bartender to come back. "Crown and Coke," he ordered, before turning back to Calvin. "I'm not interested."

A knowing expression covered Calvin's face. "Really. Who's the woman?"

"Who said there's a woman?"

"Whenever a man is uninterested in a beautiful and willing woman it's usually because there's another woman he doesn't want to answer to."

The bartender returned with Jacobe's drink. He took a sip and shook his head. "Not the case here. I'm still single."

"Single and pining, from the looks of it," Calvin said with a grin.

A hand slapped him on the shoulder. Jacobe turned to Isaiah. "Sorry to interrupt, but I think it's time to go."

Jacobe looked at his watch. "We just got here."

"Believe me, it's time to go." Isaiah emphasized the last words.

Calvin straightened. "What's wrong? Is someone giving you any trouble? I can get rid of them."

"Not yet," Isaiah said.

"What do you…" Jacobe's words trailed off. Christy strolled up behind Isaiah. Her new man, some actor she'd started dating after she'd split with Jacobe's former roommate, best friend and teammate. The real father of her child.

"Hi, Jacobe. Good game tonight," she said in a sweet but hesitant voice. She looked good. Honey-toned skin, curved to perfection, long silky hair. She wore a tight red dress that was high on her thighs and low on the cleavage.

She met his eye boldly. The question that was always in her light brown gaze when they ran into each other still there: *Are we cool now?* Hell, no, they weren't cool. Never would be. Not after what she'd done to him.

He looked to Isaiah. "You know what, it is time to go."

Christy held up her hands. "Don't be that way, Jacobe. There's no reason for you to leave just because I'm here."

He glared at her, too pissed to talk. The way she was so blasé about the entire situation grated on his nerves. Her disregard for the way she'd betrayed him was a slap in his face.

He brushed past Christy without a word. More than ready to get the hell out of there.

"Hey, man, you heard my woman talking to you," the not-quite-B-grade actor she was dating said. "I can't let you disrespect her like that."

Jacobe's rage stiffened his spine and he spun back to the guy. "This ain't your fight, man. Stay out of it."

"It's my fight when you disrespect my woman."

"Your woman doesn't deserve my respect." He cut a glance at Christy.

Christy raised her chin. "It's been four years, Jacobe. Can't we get over it?"

The comment was so stupid he almost laughed and

would have if he wasn't so pissed that she'd asked him that. "Get over it?" He ran a hand across his face and took a deep breath. She wasn't worth the fight. "You know what, you ain't even worth it."

Christy's lip twisted. "You always were emotional and soft. You don't know how to let things go. What happened with Jake wasn't all my fault," she said referring to their…no, her son. "You've got to accept your part."

The word was on the tip of his tongue. The same word that Danielle had used just the other day. He could taste it, feel it with the boiling hot rage searing through his veins. He bit it back. He hated her but wouldn't call her that in public.

"To hell with this, and you."

The actor threw a punch. Jacobe dodged, but the edge of the guy's fist grazed his chin. Jacobe threw a body shot that knocked the wind out of the guy, followed by a swift upper cut that had him sprawled on the floor. He glared down at Christy's date, then at her and shook his hand out.

"But I'm soft," he said with a sneer.

Ignoring the flash of camera phones, Jacobe threw an apologetic look at Calvin, who only shrugged, then turned his back on Christy. Davina stood nearby. He was jittery, jacked up on anger, frustration, need. He could continue to pine for Danielle. Her voice rang through his head: *This was a mistake.*

Or he could move on. He took Davina's hand. Her smile was eager and willing. "Let's go." He led her out of the club.

Danielle stomped across the hall into Debra's office. Debra wasn't there. Grunting, Danielle spun around and marched to the kitchen. Debra was leaning against the counter, sipping from a cup of coffee and reading a trade magazine.

"Did you see that email?" Danielle asked, annoyance in her voice.

Debra slowly lowered the magazine and frowned. "What email?"

"The lead singer for the band we hired to play at the gala next week just found out he has to have surgery. They've got to cancel."

Debra shrugged and went back to scanning the magazine. "Then we'll hire a DJ, instead."

Danielle tapped her foot on the floor. "How are we supposed to find someone on such short notice?"

"I'm not saying finding a replacement will be easy, but it is possible. One of the interns mentioned knowing a DJ. If that doesn't work out, my gynecologist plays drums for a band. He's mentioned giving them a call if we ever need someone to step in."

"Any good band or DJ will be booked already."

"Really? I didn't realize mid-April was prime band season."

Danielle narrowed her eyes, but her foot stopped the incessant tapping. "Don't be annoying."

Debra slapped the magazine on the side of her leg. "You stop freaking out. Is this about that report on Jacobe over the weekend?"

"Why would that report have anything to do with us needing a band for next Friday?"

"The fact that you didn't ask what report means you know what I'm talking about and you are pissed off about it."

More like angry, jealous and confused. "Don't be ridiculous."

"What's ridiculous is you acting like you don't care about what happened with Jacobe over the weekend when you two are dating."

Danielle held up a finger. "We are not dating."

"That long disappearance on the boat the other day says you are."

Heavy footsteps stopped at the door behind Danielle. "That long disappearance was a mistake. At least, that's what Danielle says." Jacobe's deep voice.

Danielle sucked in a breath and spun around. A few days' worth of beard covered his square jaw. Black Nike training pants and a matching shirt made her very aware of every muscled inch of him.

He looked directly at Danielle. "Can we talk?"

She nodded. "Sure. I need to speak to you, too." Throwing a glance at Debra, Danielle ignored her friend's *told you so* look. She led Jacobe toward her office.

"Actually, can we talk outside?"

"Sure." The suggestion was appreciated. She didn't want to be cramped in a room with him when he looked sexy, smelled divine, and memories of the way he'd brought her pleasure in the cabin of his yacht floated through her head.

Danielle traded her heels for a pair of sneakers she kept in the mudroom, and then they walked toward the beach. Lots of clouds blocked the sun. The air was still warm, but when a breeze blew over them Danielle pulled her cardigan tight and crossed her arms.

"What did you want to talk to me about?" he asked.

"I wasn't sure if you still wanted to come to our gala

next Friday. I didn't want to put your name on the reminder emails if the plans had changed."

"Why do you sound like you've changed your mind?"

"I wasn't sure what the thought process was after your fight this weekend."

She wanted to ask about the woman he'd been photographed with leaving the New York club, but didn't. They weren't together. No matter how much jealousy carved away at her insides, who he slept with shouldn't play into his work with the River Watchers. Even if it did play with her personal emotions.

He stopped walking and turned toward her, his face a mask of hard stone. "My thought process? Look, Danielle, if you have something to say, then say it."

"I thought you were changing your image."

"Christy was there. Her new guy threw a punch at me. I'm not going to let a guy try to hit me and just ignore it."

"She was there?"

"Yeah." He ran his hand over his face. "We run into each other every so often. Each time we do she tries to act like we're friends. Like I should be over what happened."

"You're not over it."

"Four years have passed since I found out. I know he's not my son. I get that. But the betrayal—no, the pain of what she did... That is harder to let go. I never really realized how much I liked having a kid until he was taken away from me."

His voice was hollow, hurt. Danielle rested her hand on his tense arm. He covered hers with his. She didn't know what to say, knew he hated bringing this situation up, but she knew he needed to get this out.

"He was nine months old when we found out he had

hemophilia. We knew we'd have to be careful as he got older. Watch out to make sure he didn't hurt himself. He kept getting strep throat. Finally, the doctor recommended removing his tonsils before he got much older. They wanted blood on hand, ya know. Just in case things got iffy during surgery because of his hemophilia." A raw, pained laugh. "Christy didn't even bat an eye when the doctors brought up testing me to see if I was a match. She wasn't too surprised when the results came back either. She'd been cheating on me for years."

Pain shot through Danielle's heart. She couldn't imagine the pain, the betrayal he'd felt. "You had no idea?"

"Not really. We argued more as we got older, but I never suspected she'd step out on me. Mostly because I wouldn't step out on her. She'd been there for me for years. When we had Jake, I knew I wouldn't leave her and break up my family the way my dad broke ours. I thought I could trust Christy."

That was the first time he'd brought up his dad around her. She ignored her curiosity about this family and focused on the current conversation. "Do you know who Jake's father is?" she asked quietly.

"Martin is the father."

Danielle sucked in a breath. His roommate? The guy who'd been drafted onto the same team with Jacobe the next year. His best friend. "Martin?"

She remembered the reports of the locker-room fights and disagreements before Jacobe was traded. "That's why you two started fighting so much."

"That's why I was traded." Dark eyes met hers. "I've learned the hard way to be careful about the people I let into my inner circle. I know I can't allow him or old teammates get to me on the court. I try very hard to ignore Christy when I see her. But I *will not* let one of the guys she's sleeping with try to take their insecurities out on me. If they start a fight, I'm ending it."

"I wouldn't expect you not to."

His brows shot up. "I didn't expect you to say that."

"Everyone has the right to defend themselves. If that's what really happened and how things went down, then I'm sorry for what I implied." She lowered her eyes and readjusted the glasses. That explained one thing. "Were you able to calm down after you left the club?"

He lifted her chin so their eyes could meet. "I left with her, but nothing happened."

She pulled away from his touch. "You don't owe me an explanation."

"No, I don't," he said bluntly. When she would have turned away, he stopped her with a hand on her arm. "But I'm giving it to you anyway. Nothing happened because she isn't the woman I'm thinking about when I lie in bed at night. She isn't the woman I want."

The look in his eye said very clearly she was that woman. She bit her lower lip to keep from grinning. That still wasn't a declaration he wanted them to date, but it didn't stop the happiness welling in her chest. She wanted him, too.

"Now that you know the truth about what happened in New York, do you still want me to come? Even though other people besides Debra may think we're together?"

"Of course I want you to come. I'm not worried about what people think. We both know we're just friends, right?"

"Keep saying that." His smile said they were much more. Jacobe turned to stroll down the beach.

Danielle watched him for a few seconds before following, confused and a little thrilled by his response. Maybe if she gave in to this, they could turn into something.

Chapter 9

The crowd filling the country club for the River Watchers silent auction surprised Jacobe. Women in cocktail dresses and men in suits mingled around tables covered with the various items for sale while soft music played in the background. He didn't plan on buying anything. His attendance at the cleanup and the public hearing had already brought attention to the Clear Water permit and had put his name in a good light for wanting to protect the creek and river. Being here tonight should add to that positive chatter. The thought of seeing Danielle increased his interest in attending.

"Jacobe, you made it," Debra said when she checked his name at the door.

The blue dress she wore matched new blue highlights on the tips of her dark hair.

"I promised I'd be here." He looked over her shoulder. "You've got a big crowd."

"Thanks to you. The last blast we sent out that mentioned you would be making an appearance upped the number of ticket sales."

"I'm glad my name could help."

"I appreciate you offering to lend your star power to our cause. Danielle is, too, even though she won't gush over it the way I will. If we hadn't reached our goal in ticket sales, there was a real possibility we all would have been out of a job."

Debra turned and asked one of the people checking names to handle things for a second and escorted him into the main room.

Jacobe followed her and asked. "What do you mean about your jobs being on the line?"

"Danielle's done a great job increasing our revenue, but fund-raising isn't her favorite thing. She'd rather be in the trenches. Some people on the board know that and they made bringing in more donations a big goal for this year."

He had a good idea the person on the board was Liberty. He'd make a donation to the River Watchers tonight.

"Danielle never mentioned her job being on the line depending on the success of this."

"That's Danielle. She connected to the community here. To her, the work is about making a difference not about raising the funds. If she were worried, she wouldn't let us know."

Jacobe glanced around the room. "Speaking of Danielle…"

Debra grinned. "I knew you were waiting to ask about her."

"That obvious?"

"That, plus your eyes are scanning the room. Don't worry, she likes you, too."

"We're just friends." Though he was beginning to think he was breaking through that label and they'd soon be lovers.

"You two can save that lie for someone else. I warned her against getting involved if she thought she'd get attached. Danielle loves a challenge."

"I'm a challenge?"

"Every guy is some type of challenge. You're the hardest type to resist. A sexy basketball superstar with a love-'em-and-leave-'em dating history. She'll get close to you and fall hard. So, don't push for more unless, you know, you really want more. Don't start something knowing one day you'll walk away from her. She's been through that once."

"I didn't leave her. I declared for the draft," he said quickly. Immediately thinking Debra referred to him leaving Danielle in college.

"I'm not talking about you." Interest sparked in her eyes. "Why would you think I was?"

Someone walked over to speak to Debra before he could ask for more of an explanation. Greeting that person led to an introduction to Jacobe, which then opened the floodgates for the people at the auction. He spent what felt like a millennium shaking hands, smiling and taking selfies. Claiming a dry throat and the need for a drink allowed him to break away from the crowd and make his way toward one of the bars set up in the back of the room.

The entire time he'd been greeted he hadn't seen Danielle once. She had to know he was there—his arrival had made too much of a show for her not to. Did that mean she was avoiding him? Debra's words rushed back into his head. Don't start something knowing he'll walk away.

He hadn't exactly walked away from her. They'd known that night was spontaneous, and, yeah, he had meant to call her, but the mistake that was Christy and his good intentions had stepped in the way. Plus, she hadn't seemed hurt by that. Not that she'd show it if she were. Based on what he knew of Danielle, he doubted she'd spent the last few years pining for him based on a one-night stand.

If not him, then who else? She mentioned her parents always having more important things to do than show up for her events. Had they skipped out on this? There was also the boyfriend she'd mentioned but hadn't gone into detail about. She didn't seem angry when she spoke of him, but again, she wasn't the bitter type. Had another guy walked out on her before?

He ordered a Crown and Coke, tipped the bartender, then turned to face the room. He gave tight smiles to the few people who glanced at him with eager expressions, which meant the tide of happy fans was about to descend upon him again. Jacobe sucked in a deep breath to prepare himself. The air stuck in his lungs.

Danielle entered through the double doors that led out to the terrace with Mason and India. She wore a simple black dress that stopped above the knee and cut straight across her luscious breasts. A short-sleeved black cardigan with some type of sparkly stuff along the neckline covered her upper arms, and high heels brought out the curve of her sleek legs. Her hair was pulled back into a smooth ponytail. The glasses were missing. With her back straight and her shoulders back, she surveyed the room both critically and with pride while her companions talked. Just like a general examining the battlefield.

Damn, she was sexy. Prim, proper and perfect. Warmth and anticipation slowly spread through his midsection and then the rest of his body. Maybe he was a challenge she didn't want to deal with. He was also pretty sure he wouldn't be able to give her everything she wanted or deserved: marriage, a house and kids. But at that moment, he knew that he wanted her and every other man in the room to know that she was his.

His feet were moving before he realized what he was doing. Her head turned, and their gazes collided. She didn't look surprised to see him, which meant she knew about his arrival. Knew and still avoided coming to him.

"I heard you were here," she said when he reached her side. "What do you think?"

"Great crowd." He glanced at the man and woman. "Mason and India, right?"

Mason held out his hand. "That's right. Good to see you again, Jacobe. Great job in the game last week."

Jacobe shook his hand. "Thank you. It feels great to be back on the court."

India shook his hand also. "We were just telling Danielle she's putting the rest of us river rats to shame with this gala."

Jacobe glanced between them confused. "River rats?"

Danielle soft laughter washed over him. "It's what we call our little group after a reporter used the term to describe us. He said we 'scurry around the river looking for problems' like rats. Well, we kinda do. Except when we find them, we fix them." Danielle finished with a snap of her fingers that made India and Mason laugh and agree.

"Although with the success of this gala," Mason said, sliding closer to Danielle until their shoulders touched, "we may have to find a better nickname for you."

Jacobe's stomach tightened when Mason touched Danielle. There didn't seem to be anything sexual, or romantic between the two. That didn't make seeing another man in close contact with Danielle any easier.

"No way," Danielle said, waving a hand dismissively. "I still prefer scrambling in the river to putting on galas." She glanced at Jacobe. "Besides, our newest volunteer is one of the reasons for this success."

Her eyes softened with appreciation and he wanted nothing more than to kiss her. "How is the auction going?" he asked instead.

Danielle glanced at her watch. "It doesn't close until nine. I was just about to walk around and check out the bids. Want to walk with me?"

He wanted to take her out of there and peel that sparkly cardigan and dress off her body. Instead, he held out his arm. "I'd love to."

She hesitated and reached for her glasses, which weren't there, then dropped her hand. "Okay, sure. I'll catch up with you guys later."

She slipped her arm through his. Jacobe have a quick hand wave and led Danielle away. Even with the heels, she was small next to him that her head barely reached his shoulders. He wouldn't have to bend as far to kiss her. He glanced at her lips, shiny with a red lip gloss that made him want to nibble on them like ripe cherries.

They strolled toward the first table. Many people stopped to talk to her and be introduced to him. Their trip around the room took longer because of that.

"Are your parents here?" he asked when they left a

group of people to head toward another table. To his pleasant surprise, she hadn't pulled her arm away from his while they walked and talked.

Her hand squeezed his arm and her body stiffened. "No, they couldn't make it."

"I'm sorry."

"It's no big deal. Their work is important."

"So is yours."

She glanced up at him and smiled. "Thank you." She took a deep breath and the tension left her body. "I didn't grow up here, but this is where I ended up after college. I got involved with the community, kayaked the creeks and streams as part of my work, made friendships with the other river rats, and fell in love with the place. I finally feel like I belong somewhere. What I do seems like an uphill battle sometimes, but I love doing it. I make a difference, right here where I live. That is important."

His admiration for her grew even more. Danielle didn't fight for causes just because, she fought because she was connected to them. He hadn't felt connected to anything in a while. Sure, he enjoyed playing for the Gators and believed they'd make the play-offs, but he was ultimately trying to do that to snag a chance at moving to Phoenix. Even that wasn't because he was connected. He hadn't felt like he was a part of something great since his dad died. The feeling compounded when he'd discovered Jake wasn't his.

She stopped to check the items on another table that mostly held jewelry. Her hands lingered over one of the sheets for a simple, sapphire teardrop necklace. Her lips quirked up in a small smile when she looked at it.

"Are you bidding on that?" he asked.

Danielle pulled her hand back. "No. I don't bid on the items here. I leave that for the guests."

"But you like that?"

"It looks like a water drop. I work with water." She stepped back and slid her arm through his again. "Come on, let's go talk to the board members about Clear Water."

They did, and Jacobe did his part to promote the importance of stopping the Clear Water permit.

"Liberty, I know that as a River Watchers board member you care about stopping the permit," Jacobe said. "I hope you take the importance of doing so back to you fellow council members."

Liberty's surprised gaze darted from him to the other people standing around their group. "Of course, but we also have to consider the needs of industry."

"Along with the health and safety of the many kids who play in that creek. That's more important, don't you think." He didn't smile or try to be charming.

Liberty nodded. "Of course."

Danielle's eyes widened and she stared at him after his comments. He had researched the issue. He didn't like of the permit getting issued.

"You're against the permit now?" she leaned in and whispered when the group turned to welcome another person into the conversation.

"Not when it puts at risk the health of those kids I met at the clean up," he replied.

Danielle was pulled away a few minutes later. Jacobe took that as his time to leave the group, but he continued to mingle, sign autographs, take pictures and make his stand on Clear Water known. When asked why he was there he mentioned that he lived on the river and wanted to support its protection. The statements weren't just about improving his image. Somewhere along the way he had started to care.

He decided to bid on a few items. He didn't care much if he won, but hoped that by bidding he'd encourage others to spend more. He didn't get to be alone with Danielle again, and when nine o'clock came she and Debra closed the bidding and went through the bid sheets the interns had gathered up.

He actually won a few things—a new pair of designer sunglasses and a kayak, which meant he'd have to learn to kayak. The only thing he'd really wanted to win— and made sure he had the highest bid on—was one of the last things they announced.

When Danielle and Debra saw the final bid, their eyes widened. Both of their heads jerked up and they looked his way.

"You can't be serious," Danielle said into the microphone.

He shrugged and grinned. The people in the room looked between the two of them.

Danielle shifted and cleared her throat. "The sapphire necklace goes to Jacobe Jenkins."

He winked and raised his glass to her. Debra gave him a look that said she hoped he knew what he was doing. He did—what he didn't know was if he should have.

The party broke up soon after. He pulled out his checkbook to settle for his items.

"Congratulations on your wins," Danielle said.

Jacobe slipped the sunglass case into his pocket and eyed the kayak. "I don't know if that'll fit in my car." He was a tall guy, but he liked his luxury sports sedan.

She chuckled. "No, I doubt it will."

He looked at her. "You've got those boat racks on the top of your Jeep. If I strap it on, can I follow you home?"

"I'll be here a lot longer. We've got to break down and everything."

His disappointment was short-lived when the next thought hit him. "I can wait. I've got a game tomorrow. How about I swing by your place to pick it up before or after the game?"

A beat of hesitation. "Sure." She eyed the necklace box. "What are you doing with the necklace?"

"I'm giving it to the woman in my life."

Danielle frowned. "I didn't know you had a girl-friend."

He leaned in to whisper in her ear. "We've gone on a date, I've entertained your friends, and I've made you come. I'd like to think that makes you the woman in my life."

He saw the spark of desire light up her eyes before uncertainty dimmed them. "Jacobe, I meant what I said. We haven't talked about any of this."

"There's nothing to talk about. We both want this. That's all that matters." Debra and a few other people were heading in their direction. "I'll come by tomorrow." It wasn't a question. He ran his finger across her cheek. Her small smile and quick head nod sent fireworks through his chest. Just the boost he needed before leaving.

Danielle cleaned, grocery shopped, washed clothes and even planted roses on the side of her house, and still she wasn't able to lessen the hum of expectancy strumming through her body as she waited for Jacobe to pick up the kayak.

"We both want this. That's all that matters."

Those words had trailed her all day. She did want him. Was nearly convinced being with him wouldn't be so bad. He was doing great with the Gators. If they made the play-offs, she doubted the team would let him go, despite the suspension. That meant he'd be around for a while. No leaving her behind for an opportunity elsewhere. She wouldn't let herself think this was the start of the rest of their lives together, but she also wasn't ready to completely deny the possibility of some type of relationship with him.

Eventually she gave up trying to distract herself and watched the Gators game. The game went into overtime and didn't end until after ten. The Gators won. Considering the postgame interviews, and the team possibly going out to celebrate the win, she didn't expect Jacobe to be able to leave the place until nearly midnight.

The expectation rushed out of her in a disappointing huff. He'd just won a game that pushed them closer to the play-offs. Of course, he wasn't coming to her house for a kayak.

Her body was still tense from a day of anxiously waiting. There was no way she'd get to sleep like this. If she didn't relax she'd be pacing the house. Or, worse, texting Jacobe like a stalker to see if he was still coming by.

Fifteen minutes later she had a bubble bath prepared, candles lit around the bathroom, a glass of wine and a book. She connected her cell phone to the Bluetooth speaker she'd mounted in a corner, and soon the soft sounds of piano music played in the background.

A long, appreciative sigh escaped her when she finally slipped down into the warm sudsy water. After a few minutes, the edginess in her ebbed and she was thoroughly engrossed in the book. Then, even though the story was great, her mind began to wander as it had with every other activity she'd tried to distract herself with that day. Thoughts of Jacobe slipped over her mind just as warm and silky as her bubble bath. The thoughts poured into every nook and cranny of her brain, filling her head with the memories of the way he'd kissed her, the hardness of his erection rubbing against her, the sudden, unexpected pleasure that had exploded through her body when she'd climaxed. The heat of embarrassment she'd felt that day was replaced with the intense fire of need to experience the sensation again.

The chime of her text message alerts interrupted the music. *Jacobe?* Danielle shot up in the tub. Sudsy water splashed over the side. She tossed the book to the floor, hoped it didn't land in a puddle and snatched her phone resting on the window ledge above her tub.

I'm outside. R u up?

"What the…" she stuttered. "He's outside? Now?"

Danielle jumped out of the tub. Water splashed everywhere. The cover of her book was doused and she cringed. Better a paperback than her e-reader. Her fingers flew over the screen with a quick response.

Yes. Give me a sec.

She hurried out of the bathroom and grabbed a T-shirt and a pair of pajama pants from her drawer and slipped them on. She slid on her glasses as she hurried to the front door. Her heart pounded. All the tension she'd tried to relax away in the bath returned in full force.

She gave a quick look through the peephole. Jacobe stood on the other side, looking tall, sexy and way too tempting.

She swung open the door. "Hey, um, the kayak is in the garage. I'll let the door up and you can pull it out."

"You aren't going to invite me in?"

He had no idea how badly she wanted to invite him in. "It's late, and I was in the tub."

His dark gaze swept over her body, then heated. "I see."

A breeze swept through the door, and the wet material of her T-shirt and pants cooled against her skin. Danielle's nipples crystalized to hard tips. Jacobe's eyes lowered, and his tongue did a quick sweep of his lower lip. Danielle glanced down, then bit back a groan. In her haste, she'd grabbed an old white T-shirt. Combined with her wet, mad dash from the tub, the thin material could have clung better only if she were in a wet T-shirt contest. The thin pants of her pink pajama bottoms were no better, sticking to her legs and somewhat transparent in the light from her porch.

He jerked his eyes away, twisted his head to the side and tugged on the waistband of his Gators training pants. Of course her eyes dropped to his crotch. He wasn't rock hard, but he was definitely not flaccid. She pulled her lower lip between her teeth.

"You've got to stop staring at me like that," Jacobe said in a thick voice.

Danielle's gaze snapped up to his. "Like what?"

"Like you want me to peel those wet clothes off your body, carry you to the bedroom and finish what we started on the boat."

She did. "I do." *Oh, hell, I said that out loud.*

He took a step forward and braced his hands on either side of her door. "Don't play with me, Danielle. If I come in this house I'm going to do just that. No long conversations about you being the woman in my life."

"Will I be the only woman in your life?"

He leaned in. "You already are. Now tell me I'm the man in yours."

Her brain wanted to analyze the words. Dig down to find out the meaning. Discover if this meant a relationship or just friends with benefits. Her body and the seductive invitation in Jacobe's eyes made the decision. "You are."

Chapter 10

Danielle's simple declaration filled Jacobe with more excitement than any game win ever had. His hands were on her waist, and a second later he lifted her off her feet. He pressed her soft body into his and covered her mouth in a hot, impatient kiss.

"Bedroom?"

"Down the hall, last door on your right."

He kicked the door closed and took a step forward.

Danielle tapped him on the shoulder. "Lock the door."

He chuckled. "Always practical." He teased, but did lock the door, holding her up and against his body with one arm.

The practical business of keeping out intruders handled, Jacobe carried her quickly down the hall and into her bedroom. Her bedside lamps were on and the glow of candles from the open door of her connected bathroom cast a soft light in the room. Jacobe glanced toward the bathroom.

"Your tub is too small for me, but I will have to get you in my bathtub one day."

A sweet, feminine moan accompanied a slight shiver across her body. He gently set her back on her feet, then slowly unwrapped every inch of her silky skin from the wet T-shirt and pajamas. Back in college, their night together had been rushed. Though he remembered every exquisite detail from then, tonight he wanted to savor his time with her. Starting by taking in how absolutely beautiful her naked body was.

She reached for her glasses and slowly pulled them off. Then she pulled her hair from the haphazard knot at the back of her head. He ran his hands through the thick strands. Bracing her head between his palms, he slowly pulled her forward and lowered his head to kiss her. The tips of her breasts brushed his chest as she rose onto her toes to kiss him. Jacobe lifted her up. Only breaking the kiss when he gently laid her on the bed with her legs still hanging over the side.

He used his legs to nudge her knees apart and stood between her parted thighs. Leaving her body open and on display for his enjoyment. He ran his hands across the soft skin of her thighs. Her muscles danced beneath the tips of his fingers. Her wide dark eyes watched him from beneath heavy lids. The rise and fall of her breasts mesmerized him.

"Can I take my time tonight?"

Her smile was seductive. "Take all the time you want."

Running his hands up her thighs, his thumbs brushed the wet curls between her legs. He wanted to play there.

Part her folds and slide his fingers through her delicious warmth. Later. Now was time to savor.

He ran his hands over her round hips, the perfect curve of her sides and the outer swell of her breasts. Danielle's ragged breaths and soft sighs told him she wanted more. He wanted more. Wanted to be buried deep in her silky heat. Leaning over her, but not quite touching her, he ran his fingers from the fluttering pulse in her neck to trace across her parted lips. The tip of her tongue darted out to play with his fingers. The fleeting touch sent shock waves through his body.

Jacobe lowered himself and pressed his lips to hers. He savored her kiss. Tasting her sweetness. Indulging in her soft sighs, sweet moans and the seductive arch of her body against his. He needed to feel her skin on his. He lifted just enough to snatch off his shirt, then kissed her again. The pleasure that burst through him when her skin pressed against his was something he wasn't sure he'd ever get tired of feeling.

His hand completely covered a soft breast. He gently squeezed. Her back arched. He had to taste her.

Danielle's body was on fire. Hotter than the candle flames flickering in her bathroom. Jacobe was the lighter fluid, driving her to lava-like levels. His hands delivered a slow kind of seductive torture as they played over her body. When his tongue slowly ran across the hard tip of her breast she cried out her pleasure.

"Jacobe, yes!"

He tasted her breasts. Teasing, nipping and licking the hard tips. She squirmed beneath him. Her hands clutched his head, holding him in place as her body begged for more. One strong hand ran up her thigh.

"Open for me," he whispered against her breast before drawing her nipple into the welcome warmth of his mouth.

Danielle gasped and her legs flew open. Jacobe ran his finger over the seam that barely hid the swollen bundle of nerves there.

"Are you wet for me?" His lips played against her nipple.

Danielle nodded. "Yes."

"How wet?" His finger made a lazy circle over her clit then dipped to press against the opening of her core. "Almost wet enough."

Danielle would explode if he didn't push into her. Her hands stopped clutching his hair. Pushing one between them, she palmed his cock. "Show me how hard you are."

Jacobe shuddered. His finger pushed into her. Found the sweet spot that sent another wave of need rushing through her.

"That's my general," he said, his lips wrapping around the tip of her breast, his finger pleasuring her with steady strokes.

Danielle's hand slipped past the elastic waistband of his pants. Hot skin over rigid flesh filled her hand.

"No underwear." She didn't want to wait any longer. "Now, Jacobe."

He shook his head. "Not yet."

Strong hands gripped her waist. In a swift movement, he pulled her farther up on the bed. His body lowered until his shoulders could push her thighs apart, and he gave her the most intimate of kisses. The sweet pleasure of the kiss shot through every nerve. She bucked and lifted onto her elbows. His confident gaze held hers as he slowly devoured her.

Her head fell back, the sensations almost too much to handle, definitely too much to feel and watch. Just before she exploded he pulled back.

"No, don't stop," she pleaded.

He dug into the pocket of his pants and pulled out a condom, then pushed them down and kicked them off the side. "Now you're ready."

He quickly covered himself. Slowly he brought the full length of his body over hers. Taking his length in his hand he slowly eased into her, not once breaking eye contact.

Danielle gasped, and her nails dug into the hard muscles of his shoulders. She remembered this. The stretch to accept every thick inch of him. The fullness no one else could match. Except tonight was infinitely better. Then he'd driven her to new heights quickly. Hard and fast and over much too soon. Tonight his strokes were slow. Measured.

"Harder, Jacobe," she begged. "Harder."

He pushed deeper, pulling her legs up so he could fill her more. Her eyes rolled to the back of her head.

"Look at me." The deep command washed over her, leaving no room for argument, and she complied. "Who's in you? Who's making you feel this?"

As if she would ever forget. "You, Jacobe. Oh, my God, you feel so good inside of me."

Her legs tightened around his waist. Her hips lifted to meet each one of his thrusts. He groaned, buried his face in her neck and took her to a place of pleasure she didn't think anyone else would ever carry her to again.

Chapter 11

He didn't stay.

Something about early practice and preparation for the final games before the play-offs. He left her place at two in the morning with a quick kiss and the promise to call her later that day. She understood. A small corner of her mind realized he did have practice and his reasons for leaving were legitimate. The majority of her brain remembered the last time he'd said he would call and she wondered if she was about to be left behind again.

She buried herself in work and even went out to collect samples with the interns instead of sitting in the office doing work that wouldn't keep her mind occupied enough to not think of Jacobe. When Debra asked her out for drinks after work, she said yes and tried not to think about Jacobe not calling. She must have done a decent-enough job of hiding her fears because Debra didn't ask about Jacobe and Danielle didn't bring him up.

When she pulled up to her house after happy hour and saw Jacobe standing on her porch with his cell phone in his hand, she admitted she was way too happy and relieved to see him.

He looked up and smiled at her when she parked beside his sports car.

"Waiting on me?"

"I was just about to call you."

She had an overwhelming urge to hug him when she walked up to him. Was that something they did now? This was why she didn't do the casual hookup. She hated the freak-out over the boundaries when she'd already seen the guy naked.

Jacobe solved her inner debate by wrapping an arm around her shoulders and pulling her against the heat of his body. Her arms wrapped around his waist, and when he kissed the top of her head she had to suppress a huge grin.

"You're here to get the kayak, right?" she said after she drew back.

"To hell with the kayak." He pulled her back into his arms and kissed her.

She let her worries about him not staying and the questions about what they were to each other rest. She liked their current space.

"You taste fruity," he said against her lips.

"Strawberry daiquiri," she said.

"Hmm." He kissed her again. "Strawberry-flavored Danielle. I like it," he whispered in her ear. His lips tugged at the delicate lobe, then he groaned and pulled back. "I don't like these earrings. They're in my way."

She lifted her hand to the earrings. "Hey, don't insult

my jewelry. It's not the earrings' fault you're trying to nibble on my ear on my front porch."

She turned to pull out her keys and unlock the door.

"I'm going to toss out all long, dangly earrings that keep me from doing just that," he said.

She stepped through the threshold. Jacobe wrapped an arm around her waist and pulled her back against him. He kissed her neck. When he touched her ear, she slapped his hand. "No throwing away my earrings."

"What if I keep replacing them with things like this?" he said, motioning with his other hand. She recognized the box that held the necklace he'd bought at the auction.

"You shouldn't have gotten me that."

"You want me to give it to someone else." He pulled his hand back.

Danielle grabbed his wrist. "I said you shouldn't have. That doesn't mean I don't want it." She'd fallen in love with that necklace the second she'd seen it.

"Hold your hair up."

She smiled and pulled her hair off her neck for him to fasten it. When he finished he flicked her earring with his finger. "The blue does kind of match your earrings."

The earrings were made of copper wire with small blue pearls. "They were a gift, too." She turned to face him.

His brows rose. "Who gave them to you?"

"This guy I dated."

She could feel the sudden tension take over his body. "Must have been serious for him to give you jewelry."

"You've already given me jewelry that's much more expensive than these earrings. Are we serious?"

"Was this the college boyfriend? The one you got over me with?"

Her head jerked back. "What? I didn't *get over you* with him. We started dating the year after you left and stayed together until after graduation. I didn't need a rebound after our one-night stand."

"So then it was serious. You two were together for three years."

"That was years ago."

"Then why do you still have the earrings he gave you?"

She touched the earrings. "Because I like them."

"Or because you still care."

"Oh, my God, are you seriously going to be that guy?" She pushed around him and marched into her living area.

His footsteps followed. "What are you talking about?"

She dropped her purse on the couch and spun to glare at him. "Are you going to be jealous because I still have earrings from a guy I dated *years* ago?"

She crossed her arms and raised her chin. They were just earrings, and she didn't even think about her ex when she wore them. Only when people asked her where she got them from did she bring up that they were a gift. His history with Christy was completely screwed up, but that didn't mean she would pay for that woman's mistakes. If they were in this, he'd have to trust her.

What if he never does?

The tension left his body. Not in a quick rush, but what appeared to be a slow and deliberate manner. "No. I'm not that guy."

She nodded, but the tightness of his voice didn't really reinforce the words. Changing the subject to something else was their best bet. "I was going to heat up a frozen meal for dinner, but I can order something, instead. If you planned to stick around. Unless you're too pissed at me now?"

This time when he relaxed it looked natural. He crossed the room, put his hands on her hips and easily lifted her. "I want to kiss you, not argue."

He kissed her, and she wrapped her arms around his neck. All her frustration melted away and the smallest glimmer of optimism filled her again. But when he put her down, his gaze strayed to the earrings again.

Lying in bed naked with Danielle running her fingers across his chest, Jacobe felt he could stay there indefinitely. He'd felt that way a few times hanging with her in college, even when they'd bickered. He'd sometimes think they needed to get past the bull and just admit they wanted each other.

Except he hadn't because he'd been with Christy. He thought about the earrings and the guy who'd given them to her.

He squeezed her shoulder and she tilted her head back to look into his eyes. "Are you still in love with him?"

Her brows drew together and her fingers froze on his chest. "Who?"

"The ex that gave you the earrings."

She sighed and tried to sit up. "Are you still on that?"

He stopped her from leaving his embrace. "It's a fair question."

"What Christy did was reprehensible, but I'm not her."

"I know that. Believe me I do, but I won't get involved with you if you still have feelings for someone else. You two were together for three years. I know it's been a while since you broke up, but I just want to know if anything is still there."

Danielle flipped over until her chest rested on top of his. He dropped his hand to cup her backside, then tried to focus on the conversation and not how tempting she was.

"We were together a long time. Yes, at the time, we thought we were in love."

"What happened?"

"He was offered an amazing opportunity in another state. We tried for a little bit, but things didn't work out."

"If his opportunity was so amazing, why didn't you go with him?"

Danielle dropped her eyes to his chest. "The original plan was for me to go, but, like I said, it didn't work out."

"He left you behind." Debra's warning stuck in his head.

"I wouldn't view it like that. We wanted different things. Even if he'd asked I doubt we would have made it. Too many demands on his end to expect him to have the time for a relationship."

He didn't need to be in her bed right now, but he was. He should be at home resting for tomorrow's practice. "When you really want to be with someone you find the time to make it work."

She smiled and her eyes sparkled like chocolate diamonds. "I appreciate that. But you have a demanding career, too. You should understand."

"Does he play sports?"

She nodded. "He does."

"Professionally?"

"Yeah." His body stiffened. She must have sensed his

thoughts because she shook her head. "Not basketball. He's a football player."

"Who?"

"Does it matter? You two probably don't know each other."

"The world of professional sports is small. I probably do know him. I could guess if I think of the guys who were drafted from our school."

"Luke Kinard," she said.

He did know Luke. He was a friend of Isaiah's and would probably come to a few games if they made the play-offs. Definitely any parties. He wished he hated the guy, but he didn't. It was hard to dislike Luke. He was one of those all-around good guys, and he was very passionate when it came to being eco-friendly. Just the type of guy Danielle would be with.

"He's a nice guy," he said simply.

"He is."

He had a dozen other questions. Questions that would make him sound paranoid. He was done playing paranoid in relationships. Danielle wasn't Christy. He would have to try to trust her.

"Was there anyone else after Christy?" she asked softly.

He snorted and rubbed his forehead. How could he explain to her that he'd thoroughly enjoyed his love-'em-and-leave-'em life after breaking up with Christy without sounding like a pig? He couldn't.

"No."

She was silent for a few seconds. "How did your parents take the situation?"

"My dad died when I was thirteen. Killed by his husband's lover."

Danielle sucked in a breath. "I'm sorry to hear that."

"I thought he was this great guy. He had been great to us. That's one of the reasons I never cheated on Christy. I saw firsthand the trouble that could come from cheating." He ran a hand over his face. Danielle was quiet while he let the hurt and anger from that time die down before speaking again. "My mom took what Christy did hard. When I had Jake she said he was the best thing to come from me. When we found out he wasn't mine, she blamed me for not checking his paternity sooner. We don't talk much. The only other person who would have cared about how I felt was my granddad, but he'd died the year before. I really wished he would have been there then."

"Why?"

"After my dad died, my granddad would take me bowling every Wednesday night. After a couple of sodas, a basket of cheese fries, and a game or two he'd ask me how I was doing, say I could always come to him, but never pushed me to talk. He knew I was spiraling. Those bowling nights reminded me I had someone who cared. My mom was so angry after my dad was killed, she couldn't deal with me. I couldn't understand her anger until after Christy cheated."

Though he never would have taken his anger out on Jake. He wouldn't let any kid of his think they were a burden. If he ever had kids again.

He glanced at Danielle. The empathy in her eyes was more comforting than any words she could speak. There was nothing anyone could say that would make what happened in his past any easier. Talking to Danielle about it was easier than he'd imagined.

Her small hand rested on his chest right over his heart.

"You're the man in my life now. If a part of me wanted anyone else I wouldn't have let you in last night. I promise you my fidelity while we're together. If you promise me the same."

He ran the back of his hand across her cheek. "You've already got that. I've turned down every woman that's approached me here and on the road since reconnecting with you."

Her brow rose and her lip twisted. "Is that supposed to make me feel better?"

"Actually, it is. I haven't found a woman that I wanted to trust enough to be monogamous with. I'm willing to do that while we're together."

The twist to her lips softened to a small smile. He pulled her up by her waist until her body was completely on top of his. "Now kiss me before I have to get up and go."

"You're not staying the night?"

He was tempted, but even if he didn't have practice tomorrow, he wasn't ready to jump into a relationship with overnight stays. "Practice early."

Her smile wavered. He flipped her over onto her back. She giggled, the second of sadness erased from her face. Her laugh and smile made his stomach tighten. He hoped he was right to trust her. He liked her too much to handle being lied to again, which meant he couldn't let Danielle know how much of his heart she already had in her hands.

Chapter 12

Jacobe faked left, and the player guarding him fell for it. Stepping back, he shot the basketball toward the goal from the three-point line. Time slowed to an earthworm crawl as he watched the ball travel. It swooshed through the hoop a millisecond before the game-ending buzzer sounded.

Several seconds passed before the rush of adrenaline and excitement infiltrated his bloodstream. Jacobe jumped up and pumped his fist. His teammates hurried over and the crowd in the stadium went crazy with cheers. With that shot, he'd just secured the Gators' place in the play-offs.

He looked over the heads of the people celebrating around him on the court to the seats behind the bench. Danielle and Debra were both there, jumping up and down and clapping. A month in and he automatically looked for her behind the bench. The high rushing through his system couldn't be topped. They won, were going to the play-offs, and his girl was there watching.

He moved with the wave to the side of the court. More hugs and hand slaps with Kevin, Isaiah and the rest of the team. Coach Simpson came over and slapped Jacobe on the back.

"That's how you do it!" Coach screamed.

Jacobe went through the quick interviews with the reporters on the side of the court before going back into the locker room. Champagne popped, and people laughed and talked big about how they were going to go all the way in the play-offs.

"We're here, but that doesn't mean we're guaranteed the championship," Coach Simpson said. "We've built a championship-level team here, let's keep up the momentum and bring that trophy home." He looked at Jacobe. "Then come back next year and do it again."

Brian and a few other owners had come into the locker room. Brian came over and held out his hand to Jacobe, who was too stoked not to take it.

"I didn't think you were committed to the Gators," Brian said. "I didn't think you wanted to be in Jacksonville. But the work you're doing with the River Watchers and how you're leading this team to the play-offs is changing my mind. If you want to come back I won't oppose your re-signing."

"I appreciate that, Brian. We'll worry about next season when we get through the play-offs."

"Fair enough." Brian shook his hand again, then went on to talk to the other members of the team.

Looked like the team owners were over their concerns about his behavior.

He glanced around the locker room at his teammates.

Even though the Gators had been able to win during his suspension, when he'd returned to play he'd increased their shot percentage and the point spread of their wins. Between that and the extra press he got for his endeavors to improve the community, he had no doubts they would want him to re-sign next year. The work they'd done to build up the team and win games filled him with pride. He'd always dreamed big. Would always be proud of what they accomplished.

Isaiah, Will and Kevin walked over. They were showered and dressed for the postgame interviews, Isaiah in his signature bow tie, Will in a designer T-shirt and jeans, and Kevin in a tailored suit that allowed his arm and neck tattoos to peek out.

Kevin watched him suspiciously. "What's up with that look?"

Jacobe stood. He too was dressed and ready for the interviews. "What look?"

"The look I haven't seen since the last game of high school or college. The 'I'll miss this' look."

"Nah, man, I don't know what you're talking about." Jacobe hid his guilt behind a grin. Those were where his thoughts were going. A year ago he wouldn't have cared if his teammates knew he was looking to sign elsewhere. A year ago he hadn't cared much about what the guys thought. Now he did, and he didn't want to give them a reason to doubt his commitment before the play-offs.

He'd texted Danielle earlier and asked her to hang around to wait for him. He pulled out his phone to text her again.

Shower done. Now postgame interviews. Can you still stick around?

A few seconds later, his phone chimed.

If you want me to I will.

You know I want you to. I'll make it quick.

J

The smiley face she sent back made his lips curve upward. That was the other good thing about being in Jacksonville: having Danielle at the games. If he did make that move, what would she say? He'd left her once and she'd understood the reasons. Would she understand this, or would she just compare him to Luke? Both thoughts felt wrong.

The postgame interviews were full of the expected questions: "How do you feel?" and "Congratulations on making that shot." The effort he took to not look at his watch and hurry things along was staggering. He wanted to get out of there with Danielle.

"Jacobe, not only are you conquering the court," one reporter said, "but you're also trying to conquer the environment. Are you turning into a tree hugger?"

Jacobe laughed and shook his head. "I've recently had my eyes opened to a lot of the challenges threatening the river. I live and work here. All I'm trying to do is make the world a better place where I can."

"Does this have anything to do with Danielle Stewart? Are the reports that you two are dating true?"

His relationship with Danielle didn't have a damn thing to do with the results of tonight's game or the play-offs. He didn't comment on his personal life and wouldn't start now. "Danielle and I are cool. I've known and respected her for years. I'm just happy to work with her to protect the river."

Another reporter caught his attention. "You're a free agent next year. After leading the Gators to the play-offs, a lot of teams are going to be interested in you. There are rumors of the creation of a superteam in Phoenix and that you're on the short list of possible recruits. Do you want to confirm or deny?"

His agent must be doing a good job talking him up to Phoenix. From the comments Jacobe had gotten tonight, the word was getting out that he was considering leaving. "Hey, man, I'm just trying to get through this season. I'll worry about what happens in the off-season after we win the championship."

His prediction earned few laughs. Many in the crowd didn't look convinced. Let them wonder. Until he got through this season and thought things out, he wasn't making any hard decisions.

The interviews finally ended and Jacobe hurried out of the pressroom and back to the court, where Danielle would be waiting for him. She didn't like hanging out near the locker room, which he could understand. She also preferred to stay away from the media, which made him more comfortable, especially since the press were starting to ask questions about their relationship. His cell phone rang. One glance at his agent's number and he stopped to take the call.

"Eric, what's up?"

"What's up is that you're the number-one trend on Twitter right now." Eric's voice was excited.

"I don't care about that."

"You should. There are so many people sharing that final shot that I'm afraid the internet will implode, which is good for you and here's why. I just got off the phone with the Phoenix front office."

"I thought we were keeping that quiet. I'm getting asked questions about it. Questions I don't need right now. I'm trying to get to the finals here."

"As you should, but are you telling me you don't want to hear what they have to say?"

He couldn't say that. "What did they say?"

"They want you. Bad. They realize you've got to get through this season, but they've already secured Warren Hackley and Charles Johnson."

"Shit, for real?" Warren and Charles were two of the best players in the league. Combined with himself, the league might as well give them the trophy every year.

"Would I call you with this if I were lying? Listen, they know you can't promise anything yet, but they're already throwing out offers."

"How much?" Eric told him and Jacobe had to cock his head to the side and ask him to repeat. He'd been in the league for years and made his share of millions, but even this was an offer damn near impossible to refuse.

"Now, do you want me to tell them to shove off?"

"No. Tell them I'm interested. If that's their offer and they're willing to wait until this season is over, then we'll talk more. I owe all of my focus to the Gators right now."

"Of course. You're a good man, but also a smart man. I'll let you know if anything changes, okay."

"Okay."

"And good game."

He thanked Eric and ended the call. The remainder of the walk to meet Danielle was a blur. He liked what he had here, but, damn, you didn't just say no to millions of dollars because you liked an area. He'd have to put the offer out of his mind until the play-offs were over. But if they actually won the finals, Phoenix might want him even more, which would only make contract negotiations easier. He was finally getting what he wanted—to be recognized as an elite player on an elite team.

Danielle was sitting in an aisle seat right near the entrance into the stadium. She was scrolling through her phone with one hand and toying with the end of her hair with the other. No cute cardigan, but she was still sexy in her Gators T-shirt and tight jeans. She looked up when he came in. She jumped up from the chair and hurried over. He gripped her waist and hoisted her up for a kiss.

"You played awesome tonight. Congratulations on the game-winning shot."

Her chocolate eyes shining like diamonds behind her glasses, warm delicious curves in his arms and the smile on her face made him never want to let her go. A crazy thought popped into his head. "Would you ever move away with me?"

Her smile changed into a look of confusion. Then she shook her head and grinned. "Stop playing."

"What if I wasn't? What if I wanted to move to Canada tomorrow? Would you go with me?"

"What if I wanted to move to Mexico tomorrow? Would you go with me?"

No. The answer was immediate. He wanted her in his life, but things were going the way he wanted. If Danielle left and asked him to uproot everything, he wouldn't be able to leave this behind.

"Forget I brought it up." He lowered her back to her feet and took her hand in his. Questions filled her eyes. She looked like she was going to question him more, then shook her head and smiled.

"Let's go celebrate you making it to the play-offs."
She squeezed his hand.

"That sounds great."

Danielle rushed from her office to the copy machine.
There were no sounds of paper sliding from the machine.
She swore silently. The board meeting was less than
thirty minutes away and they were supposed to vote on
the written comments Danielle had prepared concerning the Clear Water permit to submit to the county. They
were similar to the ones she'd submitted to the state, but
since Liberty was on council, she needed to make sure
there weren't any potential problems. She had made copies for each member to approve—or would have if the
machine was working.

Lights flashed and something beeped. She pulled out
the paper tray on the front, but it was full. Frowning, she
looked at the warning.

Out of toner. Seriously? She checked the shelf next
to the machine. The toner shelf was empty. Danielle
marched down the hall to the receptionist.

"Do we have any more toner?"

She shook her head. "Sorry, we're out. I just sent one
of the interns down to the office-supply store for more."

"Crap. I need to make copies."

"You can try the printer in the interns' office. It might
work today."

"*Might* is the important word."

She spun on her heels and marched toward her office.
She pressed all the buttons to send the document to the
printer in the interns' office.

"What are you frowning about?" Debra asked from
the door.

"The printer is out of toner and I'm sending this document to the interns' printer."

"Don't bother," Debra said. "It jammed earlier and there was the faintest of burning smells. That's why I'm here—to get you to sign off on the purchase of a new one."

"Damn! Does anything work around here?"

"Whoa, what's all this?" She came farther into Danielle's office and pushed the door shut. "What gives?"

Danielle let out a long breath and plopped down into the chair behind her desk. "I think I missed a hint or something with Jacobe."

"How?"

Danielle gave Debra a brief rundown of Jacobe's question about her moving away with him and her response.

Debra played with the blue-tipped end of her plait and considered Danielle's story. "Do you think he was serious?"

"I didn't at the time. I listened to the entire postgame interview later. A reporter asked about him going to Phoenix. Jacobe mentioned when we first reconnected about the opportunity to play for a better team. What if that's really in the works? What if he asked me that because he wants me to go to Phoenix with him if he relocates?"

"Is this the same interview where he said you two were *cool*?" Debra made air quotes.

Danielle fought not to flinch. She readjusted her glasses and frowned. "You're right. I'm reading too much into things."

She barely saw Jacobe off the court or out of the bedroom. She had expected his schedule to be busy after his suspension ended and even more so when he made the play-offs. What she hadn't expected was the feeling that she really was in a friends-with-benefits situation instead of a true relationship. He never stayed the night, never asked her to stay with him. She came to the games and cheered for him, but then he told the media that they're *cool*. She was falling in love and he thought they were…cool?

"I think your response was perfect. You're guarding your heart, which is smart with a guy like him. Don't let him think you'll drop everything and follow him if he's not willing to do the same."

"I wouldn't drop everything and move away with him. I don't really expect him to do the same."

"Then what's the problem?"

"I don't know. I think he was hinting around at that, but I'm frustrated he would even consider that when he just told the world that we're *cool*. He's still guarded with me."

"I don't think the issue is if he asked you to move or not. The real issue is how Jacobe feels about you. I like Jacobe a lot, but you've got to look out for yourself first. Don't let him have more of your heart than he deserves."

Debra was right. Danielle had been in this situation before. She'd thought she and Luke were serious, but when he'd gotten the offer to play in Denver he'd taken it. She didn't begrudge him for doing so, but it had stung to discover that he hadn't believed they're relationship would have survived the move. If Jacobe had hinted around at her going to Phoenix, why? Was it because he cared for her? She needed answers to that before making any decision.

Her desk phone rang before she could reply. Debra reached for the door handle. "Think about what I said."

Danielle nodded, but didn't answer. She picked up the phone. "Danielle Stewart, how may I help you?"

"Danielle," her mom said. "Is it true? Are you dating that Jacobe Jenkins?"

Jacobe may have hedged with the media, but she wouldn't with her mom. "Yes, I am."

"Why?" her mom asked. Sounding as disgusted and disbelieving as she would if Danielle had said she didn't give a damn about doing community service. "He's not the right guy for you."

"How do you know that?"

"I'm no sports reporter, but I follow them enough to know he's a troublemaker in the league. Getting in fights and sleeping around with various women. You can't trust a guy like that. Plus, what good does he do in the community? You know he's only interested in the environment because he's trying to butter you up."

"Actually, he gives back a lot." She started to go into the various charities and organizations he donated do, but her mom cut her off.

"Tax write-offs, nothing more. Now, why don't you call up that sweet guy you dated in college? He was a pillar in the community and much better for you."

"Mom, you and Dad haven't come to Jacksonville to see me in over a year. Every time you say you're going to visit, something more important comes up. When I try to get you to pick a good weekend for me to visit, you're doing something else and the timing isn't right. I doubt you know who or what is good for me."

Her mom sputtered. "Danielle, that's not fair. We love you."

"I know you do, but that doesn't mean I'm a priority for you, either. So please don't comment on my personal life." She glanced at the clock. Ten minutes until the board meeting. "I've got to go. I'll call you later. I love you."

She hung up without waiting for an answer. Already the guilt for talking to her mother that way crept up her throat. She hadn't been disrespectful, not really, but she'd never been so blunt with her mom before. She'd hear more about that later.

Her cell phone dinged with a new email. Danielle rubbed the bridge of her nose and sighed. She should ignore it—the way this day was going any email was probably bad news. It could also be something important.

She stood and grabbed the items she needed for the meeting. She had emailed the comments to the board earlier so they didn't really need hard copies. She picked up her phone and opened the email while walking to the door. She froze right before exiting.

Speak of the devil and the devil will rise, she thought.

An email from Luke. He still did a lot of work in the community and occasionally would toss leads for new donors or projects her way. They had moved on. The romantic feelings from college were gone.

Danielle,

I just finished the details for a trip to Malawi with the Water for Kids Foundation. Me and a few other athletes are going as part of their initiative to install wells and water filters to some of the remote villages. They mentioned having a few environmental activists come along with us. When asked who to invite, I immediately thought of you. I know you've always admired their work.

Trip is in early summer. Late May or early June. Check your calendar.

Luke

PS: I'll send the list of athletes later. I know you want to know who's going.

She scanned the email again, and then a third time. The trip of a lifetime. The Water for Kids Foundation was the same group she'd told Jacobe about that day on the boat. Not only would the trip give her the opportunity to do something she'd always wanted to do, it would probably be highly publicized and would bring greater attention, and donors, to the River Watchers.

Her heart jumped with excitement. But concern made her chew her bottom lip. Leaving the country on a trip with Luke probably wouldn't go over well with Jacobe.

Maybe Jacobe will want to go.

Luke did say athletes were going. There might be room for one more.

Except Jacobe hadn't liked the idea of a service trip when they discussed it that day on his yacht.

The office door swung open. Danielle quickly stepped back to avoid being hit.

"Oops, sorry," Debra said. "We're ready to start. Wait, what's wrong now?"

"I don't have time to say," she said, meeting Debra's eyes, "but believe me we will need to be seated, at a bar, with drinks when I tell you."

Chapter 13

The conversation with Debra was the only thing on Danielle's mind when Jacobe called and asked if she'd like to have dinner at his house that evening. For her own sanity she needed to find out where they stood. She hated to be in this situation. She'd hoped they were on the road to seriously dating until she'd seen the interview.

She parked her Jeep right outside of the garage of his two-story brick home. His house was surrounded by palm trees and lush greenery. She couldn't see the river from the front, but combined with the wooded surroundings, his place was a perfect escape from the bustle of the city.

Jacobe met her at the door wearing a blue gingham shirt and gray chinos. "Right on time."

He took her hand and led her through the house. Soft jazz played in the background and candles were lit throughout the house.

"What's all this for?"

"All what?" He glanced over his shoulder at her with a teasing smile.

On the back terrace overlooking the river, there was a table set with a white tablecloth, candles and silver-covered platters. Jacobe let go of her hand and crossed to a bottle of champagne chilling next to the table.

Danielle crossed her arms and narrowed her eyes. "Okay, what's going on?"

He twisted out the cork in the champagne. "It's all an effort to bribe you."

"Bribe me to do what?"

"Come with me to all the away games during the play-offs and, hopefully, the semi-finals and finals." He poured champagne into two flutes and handed one to Danielle.

Danielle barely kept her jaw from dropping. "What?"

"I want you with me throughout the play-offs. I like having you at the games. I like hearing you cheer for me, and I really like seeing you after all the press stuff is over. I know you have work, and the Clear Water permit stuff going on, but I'm willing to cover the costs of airfare, hotel and whatever Debra needs to let you go with me."

"I'm surprised you want me to go."

Jacobe froze in the middle of taking a sip of the champagne. "Why would you think that?"

"I don't know—maybe because at your press conference you said we were cool. What does that mean?"

"Oh, that." He turned to put the champagne on the table.

Danielle scowled. "Yes, that."

"I don't talk about my personal life with the media.

They already knew the answer, so asking was just to try and get more out of me. If I'd said anything else about us then it's a new headline. There's a new woman in Jacobe Jenkins's life. Now everyone wants to know about you. The paparazzi come out, the bloggers start tearing you apart, and people start digging into your personal life."

She slowly walked over to him at the table. "I guess I can understand that, but did you start to think about how that would sound to me?"

"No," he said as if it were obvious that he wouldn't. "You know where we stand."

"Actually, I don't."

He took her hands in his and stared her in the eye. "I trust you, Danielle. More than I've trusted another woman in years. When you first mentioned wanting a relationship, my first thought was to step back and leave you alone. That's what I've done for years. Except, I couldn't."

So much anticipation swelled up inside of her, and it mingled with a bit of hope that the declaration meant what she wanted it to. That his feelings were just as strong as hers. "Why?"

"Because I walked away from you years ago. I wasn't going to do that again."

Her heart beat so hard against her ribs she wondered if it would bruise. She took a step closer to Jacobe. The swell of emotions filling her threatened to explode like a shaken bottle of champagne.

"Jacobe, I—"

"Shhh," he cut her off with a kiss.

Thank God he had. They were way too early in their relationship for her to blurt out what she was about to say. She was scared that the words had nearly bubbled out of her mouth without forethought simply because he wanted her with him during the play-offs. He pulled back just enough to trace soft kisses across her lips, over her chin and back.

Danielle accepted the distraction. She wrapped her arms around his neck and pressed her body against the hard heat of his. Her breasts grew heavy and languid heat took over her bloodstream.

"You keep kissing me like this," Jacobe said, between kisses, "and I'm going to forget about dinner."

Danielle rose higher on her toes and pulled his lower lip between her teeth. "You kissed me first."

Jacobe lifted his head. "Are you very hungry right now?"

Danielle shook her head. "I'm far from starving."

He swept her up into his arms. "Good."

He quickly took her back through the house and ultimately to his master bathroom. Candles were lit in there already. He set her on her feet, then moved away to turn on the water in his tub.

"You want to take a bath?"

"I want to make love to you in the tub. This was for after dinner." He picked up a jar of oil and poured some into the rising water. "I've thought about you in the tub ever since that first night at your house." Next he opened bubble bath and put a generous amount into the water.

Danielle's body heated as she watched him. "The food will get cold."

He pulled off his shirt and tossed it to the side on the floor. Her breath caught in her chest and her gaze slid over every wonderful inch of his chiseled perfection. "Then let's eat."

He moved to walk past her to the door. Danielle

hooked her fingers in the belt loop of his pants and pulled him back to her.

"That's what I thought." His smile was cocky before he lifted her up for a kiss. Jacobe carried her over to his enormous tub.

He undressed her slowly. His warm lips and wicked tongue flicked over every inch of skin he revealed as he pulled off her cardigan, T-shirt, and knee-length skirt. By the time he removed her underwear, her hands were clutching his shoulders, her breaths shorts pants and her body nearly boneless with desire.

Jacobe held her in his arms again then lowered her into the tub. The tub was so large that the water barely covered her waist.

"It's not ready yet," she said.

He eased her backward until she rested against the warm ceramic of the tub. "Shh, just relax."

He reached for a thick washcloth. After dipping it into the water, he picked up the soaking cloth and let the warm drops trickle over her body. Jacobe repeated the movement, his eyes dark and intense in the candlelight as he teased her. The warm rivulets flowed over her in slow, erotic streams.

"Let me take care of you," he said in a low, seductive voice.

He used the cloth to gather the suds from the rising waters and grazed the soft material across her parted thighs, up her stomach and around her breasts. He bathed her with slow precision, each stroke increasing her desire. Her head fell back and her legs spread wide. His fingers replaced the cloth, tracing down her neck and chest, swirling around the hard tip of her breast and the sensitive skin of her midsection.

His hand brushed the curls between her legs. Pleasure zipped across her skin. Gasping, Danielle's eyes opened to slits and she watched him. The smile on his face was all masculine pride. He gently ran his fingers across her core. Teasing and tormenting her. Danielle's hands gripped the edges of the tub. Her eyes never left his.

One thick finger pushed into her. Her mouth fell open with a silent gasp. His lips curved higher. With deliberateness, he drove her to the brink, holding her captive with his intense gaze. With each wondrous slide of his hand in and out, her thoughts fled and all she wanted was more. To have Jacobe touch her like this and never stop. The erotic pressure built. She pulled her lower lip between her teeth. Her body tightened more and more with pleasure. She exploded with a wave of delicious sensation. Her cry echoed around the bathroom. Her vision blurred and her heart beat frantically in her chest.

Jacobe stood slowly and stopped the water. She watched through half-lowered lids as he quickly peeled off his clothes. He slid on a condom then lowered himself into the tub. He took her into his arms and Danielle met his kiss with renewed passion. He flipped their positions until her legs straddled his waist.

Danielle dropped her hands between them, took him into her hands and lowered herself onto his erection. Her body was overly sensitive from his earlier attentions and she moaned in exquisite pleasure with each filling inch. Jacobe took her face in his hands and brought her forward for a kiss, his hips pushing up with each of her downward slides.

He leaned back and stared at her, his gaze possessive. "You're so damn sexy, Danielle." His hands slid over her shoulders and down her arms before resting on her waist. "So sexy and all mine." His hips pushed up hard and deep. "Tell me you're mine."

Danielle gasped and clasped his arms. The pleasure was so intense she couldn't stop a grin from curving her lips. "Yours, Jacobe. Only yours."

Several minutes later, Danielle lay with her back against his chest in the tub. The water was still warm and silky, and her body felt just as fluid. She could stay there forever. In his arms, forever. Because she loved him.

"Will you come with me during the play-offs?" Jacobe asked.

The excitement that he wanted her with him was still there, but the concern of giving up so much of her life to follow him made her hesitate. He'd already said he wouldn't disrupt his life for her. Was she being unrealistic and foolish to consider doing it for him?

"That's a lot of time away," she answered.

"Which is why I want you to come."

She took a deep breath. "Jacobe, I don't know."

"Forget it," he said, and tried to sit up.

Danielle pushed back so he couldn't get out. "Stop. You can't get mad when I bring up a valid point."

"I'm not mad. I'm surprised you don't want to come."

"I didn't say I don't want to come. I'm telling you that it's a lot of time away from my job. A lot of time at a very important time."

"I get it. You can't leave right now."

She shifted sideways in his tub to meet his eye. "That, and you're asking me to disrupt my life, drop everything and follow you around the country. But you describe us as being *cool*."

"What are you asking, Danielle? What do you want me to say?"

She wanted him to say he loved her. That he wanted her there not just as a lover but as part of his emotional support. Someone that he could lean on if they lost and who would celebrate any victory with the same enthusiasm and pride he would feel. But Jacobe wasn't likely to lay out any of those emotions at her feet. Those were the wishes of a woman who wanted to be more to him than she probably was.

"Do you want a cheering section, or me?"

"You, Danielle." His dark eyes were filled with an intensity that made her heart flutter. An intensity that promised her that one day he would say those words. "Only you. I haven't had a woman in my life for years. Seeing you the night we made the play-offs. That did something to me."

The words were a warm, happy squeeze around her chest. There was little else he could say to make her feel any better.

"I can't make it to all the games, but I will come to as many as I can."

The tension seeped from his body. The arm around her waist tightened. "Cool."

Danielle laughed. "That's all I get? Cool? After all that sulking and pouting."

"Hey, I don't sulk," he said, and kissed her neck. Jacobe ran a hand up her arm and squeezed her shoulder. "Will you stay here tonight?"

It was the first time he'd brought up either of them spending the night. She wasn't going to Malawi. Wasn't even going to worry Jacobe with the idea of her going. She wasn't sure when he'd be comfortable enough to say he loved her, but she felt his feelings for her. They were more than just the feelings a man had for a woman he only considered a lover.

She turned in his arms and straddled his hips. "I'd love to." When she kissed him she did so with every ounce of love flowing through her.

Chapter 14

"Let's hear it for the Eastern Conference Champions!"

A roar of cheers went up from the crowd in the Suite, a downtown club where the Gators were celebrating winning the semifinals. Danielle lifted her hand and cheered with them. Jacobe wrapped an arm around her neck and pulled her in to kiss her cheek. They were at one of the tables in the VIP section. Kevin and Debra were also there. Jacobe had also suggested she invite the rest of the river rats, who were out on the dance floor enjoying the party.

"This party is amazing," Danielle said over the music and cheering.

Jacobe lowered his head to speak directly into her ear. "If we make the finals, then the next party will be even better. The Gators haven't made it to the semifinals in ten years. I'm proud to be a part of it."

He squeezed her closer against his tall, hard body.

The room full of people and the sounds of the music became a distant hum. Danielle snuggled back into him. She could barely hear his moan, but she felt the rumble of it through his body.

"You're making me want to sneak you out of here," he murmured against her ear.

She wanted him to sneak her out of there. In the weeks since he'd asked her to attend the games with him, things had been great. No more leaving in the middle of the night, or pretending like they were just "cool." He still hadn't said anything in the media about their relationship, which she was okay with, but everyone on the team knew she was Jacobe's woman.

"Will you two stop," Debra said, looking between Danielle and Jacobe. "I'd tell you to get a room, but I'm afraid that you'll actually leave me here with this one." She pointed to Kevin.

Kevin laughed and raised his glass to Debra. "You'd love to be alone with me."

"Oh no, my mama taught me why I never should be alone with a guy like you," Debra replied, waving a finger.

Danielle grinned at the exchange. Debra was a fan of Kevin, and he had flirted with her constantly since Danielle started hanging with the group, but Debra had told Danielle she wasn't ready to be the next woman to have Kevin's baby.

"Whatever," Kevin said. His sly gaze slipped to Jacobe. "I guess you'll be paying up pretty soon."

Jacobe's body stiffened. Danielle glanced at him. He shook his head at Kevin. "Not quite there yet."

"What's that about?" Danielle asked.

Jacobe smiled and kissed her forehead. "Nothing. Kevin just jumping to conclusions."

She had a feeling it was more than that but dropped it. Kevin sipped his drink and winked at Danielle. She got the feeling she was missing something.

"Hey, look who just got here," Isaiah interrupted.

Jacobe looked up and his arm around her tightened. She turned to face Isaiah and her stomach dropped.

"Luke?" she said with disbelief. Every time she saw him she was struck by how he seemed to always look like the nice boy next door. Bright smile, friendly gaze and stylish but conservative clothes.

Luke's smile widened. "Danielle, I didn't expect to see you here." He glanced at Jacobe, then back at her. "How are things?"

Jacobe pulled Danielle tighter against him. "Things are great."

Danielle's lips pressed together. She could answer herself and didn't need him to puff up just because Luke was there.

"Things are well. What are you doing here?"

"I'm here to celebrate the Gators' win. Isaiah and I are good friends. I tried to make it into town for the game, but the flight got delayed. I'll be in town up to the finals, then it'll be time for our trip to Malawi. I planned to get in touch with you while I was in town. You know we're really looking forward to having you on board."

Danielle broke into a cold sweat. She'd assumed Luke's plans had changed when he didn't email again. He must have assumed her silence was acquiescence.

Jacobe cleared his throat and shifted next to Danielle. "Going where?"

"Luke is working with Water for Kids on a trip to Malawi to dig wells and provide water filtration for remote villages. They're taking a few environmental activists to provide guidance on protecting the limited water resources. He asked me to go."

"That's great," Jacobe said. "You always wanted to go on a trip like that."

"You want me to go?"

"I remember you said you always wanted to work with them. Well, now's your chance. That's cool." He sounded like he was all for it, except he'd pulled away from her.

"It's settled," Luke said. "Danielle, I'll call you on Monday to talk about the details." He slapped Isaiah on the shoulder. "Come on, let's get a drink."

Isaiah threw an apologetic look at Jacobe. He didn't look at Danielle before he followed Luke.

Jacobe slid out of the booth. "I'm going to get another drink, too."

"I'll join you," Kevin said.

Debra turned wide eyes toward Danielle when they walked away. "You didn't tell him you were going?"

"I wasn't going. I decided not to go the night he asked me to come to the play-off games. I didn't think I needed to tell him about the invitation. How was I supposed to know Luke would out me?"

Debra took a deep breath. "What are you going to do?"

Danielle looked at Jacobe talking to Kevin at the end of the bar. He glanced back at her. She smiled. He turned away. A dull ache started in her chest. "I don't know."

Jacobe sipped from his beer and glanced toward the windows. Moonlight glistened off the river in the distance, but he didn't see it. His mind was focused on Danielle's lie. That she would plan to leave the country with her ex and not mention it to him at all. He saw her reflection in the glass as she walked up behind him.

"Are you mad at me for not mentioning the mission trip?

"I'm curious about why you kept the trip a secret."

In the reflection, he noticed her lips pressed together. She looked uneasy, which made him uncomfortable. Had he finally trusted a woman only to be fooled again?

"I wasn't keeping it a secret. I forgot to mention that he made the offer."

"That's a convenient excuse."

"It's not a convenient excuse. It's what happened. Luke emailed me weeks ago about the trip. I wasn't sure if I was going, but the night you asked me to come to the play-off games I knew I wasn't going."

He turned to face her. "You were considering it?"

"I was. I've always wanted to do something like this. Of course, I would consider going."

"You'd go out of the country with your ex-boyfriend even though you're dating me?"

"It's a working trip. It's not like I would be going on a vacation with Luke. There's nothing wrong with it."

"Well, it doesn't matter now. Because you're not going."

Her brows drew together. "Are you forbidding me?"

"You said yourself you weren't going, so that's the end of it."

He tried to walk past her. She grabbed his arm to stop him. Her eyes flashed with an anger so sharp he wouldn't have been surprised if her glasses shattered. "If I hadn't decided not to go, are you saying you would have told me not to go?"

He ran a hand over his face. Frustration crawled over every inch of his skin. "I shouldn't have to tell you not to go. You should know better than to take a trip out of the country with your ex-boyfriend."

As soon as the words left his mouth and he saw fury on her face, he knew he'd made a mistake.

"I should have known better?"

He reached for her hand. "Danielle, listen—"

She snatched her hand away and took a step back. "I should have *known* better. Even if I chose to go, that doesn't mean anything about our relationship. You said you trusted me."

"I trust you. I don't trust him."

"What's that supposed to mean?"

"No guy asks his ex to take any type of trip with him unless he has other intentions." He meant that with everything in him. "I saw the way Luke looked at you. The way he looked at us together. He didn't like it and he wants you back."

She threw up a hand and turned away. "Now you're being ridiculous. Luke and I are just friends."

"You can't be friends with an ex."

"Just because you hate Christy doesn't mean everyone who breaks up hates each other." She sucked in a breath and her mouth snapped shut.

Anger, frustration and jealousy seethed through every poor of his body. When she took a step toward him he moved backward.

"I'm sorry," Danielle said. "I should have brought her up."

"Don't be. You said what you meant. I meant what I said earlier. You shouldn't have even considered going out of town with him."

"I wanted you to come with me," she said. "Several athletes are going. That's why Luke is going. I would have asked you to come."

"When is this trip?"

"Early June."

"That's during the finals. Right after I'll be preparing to go to Phoenix."

Her eyes widened. "You are going to Phoenix?"

"The offer they made is hard to refuse." He shrugged. "I'm not sure what I'm going to do. If I go to Phoenix we'll be the team to beat. My chances of winning a championship not just next year but for several years go up. It's the chance of a lifetime."

"When were you going to tell me about Phoenix?"

"After the play-offs." When he was also going to ask her to go with him.

"So it was over when the play-offs ended. You asked me to support you only so you could leave the second you got what you wanted."

The words to deny her accusations sat heavily in his throat. He wanted to tell her the truth, that he wanted her with him wherever he went, that he was falling in love with her. But he wouldn't put his feelings out there when she was considering leaving. He wasn't going to start checking up on Danielle. He wasn't going to worry about her sleeping around or going back to her ex. He'd been in one of those paranoid situations before. If Luke was who she ultimately wanted, then she could have him. If she wanted to go to Malawi with him, let her go.

"If that's what you want to believe, then I can't change your mind," he said.

"And if you want to believe that me going on this trip means I'm going to betray you the way she did, then you do that." She grabbed her purse off the couch. "I think I'll spend the night at home tonight." Then she left.

Chapter 15

The town council chamber was filled to capacity. A hum of excitement filled the room from the multiple people waiting for the meeting to start. The waste-water provider was answering several tough questions the council posed to it based on the letter and comments submitted by the River Watchers before they gave any approvals for local permits.

"I think the council may deny this," Debra said after she and Danielle finished talking to a few of the residents of Crescent Acres. Since the council meeting was at six o'clock many of the residents had come out in support.

"I hope so. We've brought enough attention to the issue. There are a lot more people interested in protecting the river than there were before."

Thanks in a large part to Jacobe. The times he'd

brought up the River Watchers, their website and social media accounts received a huge jump in hits. He may not have actively campaigned against the permit, but his knowledge of the subject when asked helped. The full council chambers was proof of that.

Danielle scanned the room again though the effort was useless. She would know if Jacobe was there. The buzz of conversation would have increased by now. She hadn't spoken to him privately since the argument. She still went to the semifinal games that were local. As Debra said, "Why waste good tickets?" He acknowledged her presence at least, but he didn't ask her to wait for him and hadn't asked her to attend the away games. Pain and anger were a constant clash inside her. He had said he trusted her, trusted her to *know better*.

A man and woman entered the council chambers. Hot, uncomfortable tingles rushed across her skin. "I don't believe it."

Debra looked up. "What's wrong?"

"My parents are here." They spotted her a second later. With hesitant smiles, they walked from the door of the chambers and over to her and Debra. Her mom had cut her hair, and her dad had more gray at his temples than before. The changes were a reminder that she hadn't seen them in a year.

"Mom, Dad, what are you doing here?"

Adele's smile appeared confident, but her eyes were uncertain. "Tonight's a big night for you. We missed the cleanup and the gala. We decided to come to the council meeting to show our support."

Debra touched Danielle's elbow. "I'm going to go sit down." Her smile was encouraging before she walked away.

Danielle focused back on her parents, shock and happiness swirling in her like a whirlpool. "You didn't have to do that. I could have come home this weekend and let you know how things went."

Her dad nodded. "You can still come home this weekend, or next. It's come to our attention that we've been too busy for our own daughter. That's about to change."

Danielle stepped forward, and took her mom's hand in one of hers and her dad's hand in the other. "I'm sorry I said that. Mom called on a bad day and I overreacted. I understand the work you two do is important."

"You're right," Adele said. "Our work in the community is important, but so are you. What you said made both of us realize that we don't always act that way. You were always so self-assured, so confident, we didn't think you needed our extra attention."

"I'll always need my parents," she said softly.

Her dad squeezed her hand. "We'll always be there to give it to you."

The intensity of the hum in the chambers increased. Awareness prickled the back of Danielle's neck. Jacobe was there. The thought passed a second before she glanced to the back of the room. His eyes were already on her. She gasped. He hadn't come alone. Will, Isiah, Kevin and other members of the team were there as well, and signing the paper to speak against the permit.

Her parents swiveled to see what the commotion was about. Adele looked back at Danielle. "Are you and he still dating?"

"We're cool," Danielle answered.

Her dad's brows drew together. "What does that mean?"

If only she had the answer to that. "Nothing. We're still dating, but it's not serious." That was the only answer she could think of that wouldn't have her dad bucking up overprotectively and her mom scowling at Jacobe.

Even though Jacobe and the rest of the team smiled and stopped to greet fans, it was clear he was making his way to her. She glanced across the room to where Debra, Mason and Patricia were all wearing victory grins. Danielle felt similar. This had to help their end.

She looked back at Jacobe and committed everything about him to memory, sure that soon she wouldn't even be able to say they were dating but not serious. His shoulders seemed broader, more powerful beneath a dark V-necked T-shirt and black blazer, his legs impossibly longer in dark slacks.

"You came," she said, when he made his way to her side. The rest of the team found seats in the chambers. "And you brought company."

"Of course I came. I would only have missed this for a game." He pointed to the rest of his team. "They just followed me." He looked at her parents.

Danielle quickly did the introductions. Jacobe's eyes widened. "I'm happy to meet you. Danielle has told me about the work you do in the community. It's admirable."

Her parents looked both proud and sheepish. "We're hoping to get more involved with Danielle's work."

The council members entered the chamber. Danielle led her parents and Jacobe to the seats in the front that Debra had saved for them. The council members quickly noticed the members from the Gators and smiled and waved their greetings. Everyone around here was an even bigger Gator fan now that the team had done so well in the play-offs.

The council meeting progressed quickly through the opening pledge of allegiance and as resolutions passed from the various members of the community. To Danielle's surprise, the chairman requested a change in the agenda to move the vote on the Clear Water permit up in the agenda. Danielle shifted in her seat and glanced at the agenda. He moved it ahead of the opportunity for citizens to speak. She gave Debra a wary look.

"What's this?" she whispered.

Debra shrugged. "I don't know and I don't like it."

Neither did Danielle. The council approved the change and then went straight into the vote.

Liberty sat forward in her chair and tilted the microphone forward. "As we can see from the turnout here today, including that from the members of our championship Gators team, this is an important issue. The council members have already discussed the seriousness of the outcome and have taken into consideration the multitude of phone calls, emails, and messages left by the community. Pleasé remember that as we make our votes."

Danielle held her breath as she waited for each member to vote for or against the proposal. When the proposal passed unanimously to deny the local permit, even though Liberty's yes was less than enthusiastic, she nearly bounced out of her seat and yelped her joy. Not getting the local permit would go a long way to the ultimate denial of the state permit.

After the council meeting ended, there were a lot of congratulations and handshakes. The council members came over to Jacobe to thank him for bringing their attention to the issue.

"Great job, Danielle," her dad said when they were standing outside of the council chambers an hour later. It had taken that long for most of the crowd and residents to clear out.

"Thanks, but this is just the beginning. I've still got to work to make sure the state denies their permit. Clear Water needs to shut down, not put in patchworks that will do more harm than good. The state knows it."

Pride filled her mom's eyes and she hugged Danielle tight. "I love you, Danielle. And I'm so proud of you."

Tears burned the back of Danielle's eyes. She'd known her parents loved her, but hearing them say that and having them here was ten times better than having the feeling as a vague belief she kept telling herself.

Jacobe came over after her parents said goodbye and walked to their car. "Can I give you a ride home?"

"How do you know I need a ride?"

"Debra let it slip."

She'd have to remind Debra to butt out. They had ridden together to the council meeting. Danielle wanted to be petty and ask if he was sure he wanted to give her a ride, except her need to be alone with him again burned away any petty feelings she had. She missed him. "I'd like that."

"You're victorious," Jacobe said once they were seated in his car.

"Thanks to you."

"I'm only a part of it. I got the attention your way, but you're the one who did all of the talking to convince me, the council and the public to support the measure."

"Still, you got their attention. I appreciate that."

"Working with you all helped my reputation more than I expected. It's amazing how much people saw me as less the bad boy and more the good guy just because I helped out at your events."

Danielle had forgotten he was only helping out to improve his image and not because he had any real care for the environment. Jacobe gave back financially, but working with her was the only situation where he gave of his time. Obviously, he wouldn't have wanted to go with her on the Water for Kids trip. No wonder he'd scoffed when she'd mentioned she was going to ask him to go.

He shifted in his seat and glanced at her out of the corner of his eye. "I've done some thinking since the other night."

She clasped her hands in her lap and looked out of the window. "Oh, really? What have you come up with?"

"I was wrong, and I'm sorry."

Danielle's head whipped around. "What?"

"I'm sorry. I said I trusted you and I do. I think you should go to Malawi with Water for Kids."

"You want me to go?"

"If we weren't dating, would you have hesitated to say yes?"

She shook her head. "I wouldn't."

"I know. You should go. I know something like this will go a long way to bring attention to the River Watchers. Ultimately it'll help your goals here. Don't hold back your dreams because of me."

Words every woman wanted to hear from her man, but was he telling her not to hold back because he wasn't holding back his dream?

"If I go to Malawi, when I return will you be packing your bags for Phoenix?"

He shrugged. "I don't know, Danielle."

Pain tightened her chest. She faced the window again so he wouldn't see. His hand, warm and strong, covered hers on the armrest. "If I do go, that doesn't mean I want it to be the end of us, if that's what you're thinking. I can't ask you to drop everything in Jacksonville and move to another state. Well, I can, and I want to, but I won't pressure you into that decision."

He took his eyes off the road for a second to smile at her. "Not much anyway."

"Are you serious?"

"I am. I care about you, Danielle. I trust you. At the end of the summer, you'll be back and I'll know where I'm going to play next season. It'd be juvenile for us to break up now because of what might happen. Agreed?"

He cared about her. Not *love*, but again she knew that was a word he wouldn't throw out easily. Maybe they needed this. The heat between them had burned hot almost from the start, but heat didn't build a long-lasting relationship. Would absence make their heat burn hotter, or would she return to find he'd cooled off?

The thought pained her, but it was a very real possibility and one she'd rather face sooner rather than later. She didn't want to move to Phoenix, but maybe she would later. If they couldn't survive a summer apart, which was nothing in the scheme of things, how would she survive a long-distance relationship?

His hand squeezed hers. "What are you thinking about?"

"Everything you just said. Okay, I'll go. And I'll consider how we'll make things work when you move to Phoenix."

His nod was stiff. He lifted her hand to his lips and kissed the back. "Cool."

"Cool," she said. She was really starting to hate that word.

The atmosphere on the plane delivering the Jacksonville Gators back home after winning the last game of the semifinals and making their way to the finals was nothing less than exuberant. Singing, drinking, chanting and lively conversation filled first class and had spilled over into coach. Jacobe laughed and joined in with his teammates, but his heart wasn't really in it, and more than once he drifted away from the conversations to stare out the window.

"Jacobe," Isaiah called. "What are you doing when you get home?"

Jacobe turned away from the window to Isaiah in the seat next to him. Kevin sat in front of them and was currently on his knees facing backward to talk with them.

"I'm taking Danielle to the airport later." Surprisingly, he said that without any of the unsureness he felt inside.

Kevin shook his head. "You really want to send your girl off with her ex-boyfriend?"

"I'm not sending her off with her ex-boyfriend. She's going on a trip to bring water to those who need it."

"With her ex-boyfriend," Kevin said, raising an eyebrow. "You're not worried that he might try to cuddle up in her tent one night."

"No. Danielle isn't Christy." He kept telling himself this.

"She may not be like Christy, but that doesn't mean Luke won't push up on her."

Jacobe glanced at Isaiah next to him. "You think?"

Isaiah shrugged. "I'm not sure. I know he has a lot of good things to say about Danielle. I don't think he'll try and go there. He's all saved now, and breaking up relationships isn't his thing."

"He said that?" Jacobe asked.

Isaiah shrugged. "In so many words. I pressed him about his relationship with Danielle."

"Why did you do that?"

"Because you're my friend," Isaiah said without batting an eye. "I know Luke has been cool with us, but I don't work with him every day. I know that your history with Christy really messed with your head. If his plans were to get with Danielle I wanted to know so I could tell you."

Jacobe was struck speechless. He'd never really considered Isaiah and Kevin close friends. In a few sentences, Jacobe realized he'd been wrong not to. They had his back, were men he could trust. That felt nice. He hadn't understood how much he missed having friends he could count on. "I appreciate that, man."

"What did he say?" Kevin asked. "When you pressed him about Danielle?"

"Just that things didn't work out for them in college. In hindsight, he let them break up instead of trying to keep her. He doesn't blame her, and he's happy if she's happy. He wouldn't do anything to mess that up."

Jacobe raised a brow. "So he's not going to try to sneak into her tent, like Kevin says?"

Isaiah held up his hands and shrugged. "He said he'll see what happens. He's not trying to break up a relationship."

"But if she seemed *unhappy*, he'd step in to help make her happy."

Isaiah's look screamed, *Bull's-eye*. "I thought you needed to know that."

Kevin looked at Jacobe. "But you trust her?"

"I do." He did.

"Does she know you're in love with her?" Isaiah asked.

Kevin laughed. "In love? Normally, I'd say every man isn't ready to be saddled up like you are, Isaiah, but since I've got a G riding on this…" He looked at Jacobe. "Have you told her yet, so I can get my money?"

Jacobe slapped away Kevin's hand. "I care about her. And the bet was you got money if I proposed. I'm not there yet." Even though he had thought about being with Danielle forever.

"And you trust her," Isaiah said. "You don't trust women."

"Trusting and loving aren't the same," Jacobe argued.

Isaiah shrugged again. "I'm just saying, it wouldn't hurt to let her know how you feel before she gets on that plane."

Those words stuck with Jacobe for the rest of the flight and through his quick drive home to drop off his luggage before going to pick up Danielle. Not for the first time since she'd told him about her departure flight did he wish she wasn't leaving so soon after he got back in town. They'd barely have time to talk. Instead, he was sending her off on a trip where she did something great for the world and he stayed behind to play a game. For the first time ever, he wished they hadn't made the finals. If they hadn't, he would be able to go with her. Not send her on the plane with another guy.

Funny, for a guy whose game plan was "we'll see what happens."

He cared about her. He wanted to be with her. He didn't want any other guy to try to come between them. That wasn't the same as being in love with someone. If he was in love, he'd know it without any questions or hesitations.

He didn't trust Luke. Danielle knew Jacobe cared about her more than he had any other woman in years, but was that enough for her to tell Luke she was happy if he asked?

When he rang the doorbell, she swung the door open just a few seconds later. Her eyes were bright with excitement and a grin covered her beautiful face.

"Congratulations!" She jumped into his arms and kissed his cheeks. "You're going to the finals! Aren't you excited?"

"Yes. More so about you all up in my arms like this." He squeezed her tight and kissed her. Holding her again felt good. He'd hated not having her in his arms when they'd fought.

"I'm so happy for you. You guys are going to win the championship. I know it."

He put her down and she turned to go into the living area. He followed, watching the sexy sway of her hips. She had on a pair of jeans and a green tank top that matched the Gators colors.

"I hope so."

"I wish I could be here to see it." She pulled a gold cardigan off the couch and slipped her arms into it.

"Yeah, so do I," he mumbled below his breath.

She turned a questioning glance his way. "What?"

He shook his head. "Nothing. Let's get you to the airport."

She talked about all the things Water for Kids had planned. She'd sent him a copy of the itinerary and promised to call. Her excitement about going on the trip she'd always dreamed about was palpable. Her enthusiasm only tightened the guilt in his stomach. All he wanted to do was turn around and ask her to stay.

"I wish I could wait with you at your gate," he said, after they'd checked her bags and were standing right before the security point. He pulled her against him and lowered his head to kiss her.

"I wish you could, too." Her arms tightened around his neck.

"Be safe and have fun." He started to let her go, then stopped. "Are you happy with me?"

She stopped smiling, and her eyes were serious when they met his. "Jacobe, I love you."

His heart dribbled against this ribs like an eight-ton basketball. He felt hot and cold. Free and trapped. Happy and uncertain. She loved him.

"Danielle, I…"

She pulled his head down and kissed him softly. "Don't say it just because I did. I just wanted to tell you before I left." She kissed him again. "I'll call you when I can."

Then she was out of his arms. In a daze, he watched her go through the security checkpoint before getting lost in the crowd. Danielle loved him, and he'd let her go without saying anything back.

Chapter 16

They'd won.

Jacobe stood in the middle of the court staring at the final score and the 00:00 time on the scoreboard, but the victory hadn't sunk in. The Jacksonville Gators were the league champions!

A second after that thought took hold, he grinned and was swarmed by people. His teammates, the media, members of the other team—everyone—were in the middle of the court. Congratulations went around, hands were shaken and microphones were stuck in his face, followed by questions of how he planned to celebrate this victory. His eyes kept going to the seats behind the bench.

He was happy. Ecstatic! Not only had the team that hadn't been predicted to win won, but they'd swept the series entirely. He was at the height of his career. On top of the world.

Why wasn't he more…happy?

"You cool, man?" Isaiah asked after they'd finished postgame interviews and were heading to the Suite to celebrate.

Jacobe nodded. "Yeah, I'm good."

"All right, because we are about to get crazy tonight." Isaiah slapped him on the back.

"You're getting crazy? Mr. Calm, Cool and Collected?"

"Man, we just swept the finals. I'm getting crazy. This is a dream come true. I just hope we can do the same thing next year."

"Yeah, me too." He meant it.

As they were leaving the auditorium, they passed fans lucky enough to make it back to the locker rooms. They shook hands and took selfies on the way out. Right before the door, a woman and young kid were waiting. Jacobe's heart tightened in his chest. Christy and Jake.

"You can just ignore her," Isaiah said.

Jacobe shook his head. "I can ignore Christy, but not Jake."

He walked over to them. Christy's smile was hesitant. Jake's was big and excited. He'd grown so much since Jacobe had seen him last. The three-year-old toddler now a tall seven-year-old. Jacobe studied Jake from head to toe. Even though DNA tests didn't lie, he couldn't help himself. He looked for any sign that the kid was his. There were none. Jake looked exactly like Martin.

Jake held out a basketball and a marker. "Hi, Mr. Jenkins. Can I have your autograph?"

The "Mr. Jenkins" hit Jacobe in the chest with the force of a heavyweight blow. Jacobe looked at Christy.

Her lips were pressed in a thin line. "He's a big fan," she said.

Jacobe looked back at Jake. The kid didn't know. Why didn't he know? Even though Martin insisted Jacobe stay away after discovering Jake's true paternity, there were dozens of pictures of him with Jacobe when he was a baby? He had to have seen them and asked his mom why was Jacobe in them. Unless Christy had gotten rid of the evidence. It would make sense. Hide the situation until Jake was old enough to understand.

Jake was pulling the ball back. Jacobe snapped out of his thoughts and smiled. "Sure." He took the ball and the pen. "What's your name?" The words hurt. Pretending he hadn't helped name him hurt.

"Jake Livingston." Martin's last name.

Jacobe was proud his hand didn't jerk as he wrote his autograph. He hoped his smile was friendly as he handed the ball back to Jake. "Here you go, Jake. Thanks for the support."

Jake stared at the signature, then grinned up at Jacobe. "Thank you. My dad's a basketball player. I hope to grow up and play just like he does."

Jacobe nodded. He couldn't stop himself from reaching out and rubbing the back of Jake's head. "Oh, yeah? You do that."

He glanced back at Christy. For the first time in years, she didn't look at him as if they could just be friends again. "I'm sorry, Jacobe," she said in a rough rush of words. She looked at Jake then back at Jacobe. Regret filled her eyes. "For everything."

He couldn't say they were okay. Could never say they'd be friends, or that he'd forget the way she and

Martin had betrayed him. He couldn't continue to hold on to the anger or the hurt. "Apology accepted."

The encounter stayed on his mind as he drove to the Suite. None of the anger that typically consumed him when he thought about Christy and Jake filled him. He was ready to move on. He expected thoughts of Phoenix and future championships to fill his mind. It didn't.

His thoughts revolved around his friendship with Kevin, Isaiah, and Will. The pride of how their team had advanced to and swept the finals. He was considered an elite player here. The men on the team and Coach Simpson weren't just his colleagues—they were his family.

Then there was Danielle. She was here. That's why he couldn't be happier after the game. Danielle loved him, but she didn't want to move to Phoenix. She'd made her own connections here. She cared about the people and the places. She'd gotten him to do the same. Why on earth would he leave her? He loved her.

Why on earth had he sent her to Malawi without telling her?

Because you're a fool.

Jacobe swerved his car into an illegal U-turn at the next stoplight. Instead of going to the Suite he drove toward his home and pulled out his cell phone to call the airport. He had a flight to book.

Danielle sat in the passenger seat of a rugged Jeep while Luke drove them down a bumpy road to the next village. They'd mostly provided water filtration systems, but today, they were actually installing a well.

"I hear that the Gators won the finals," Luke said from the driver's seat.

Danielle turned to glance at him. "I know. I used the satellite computer at the last stop to check."

She'd talked to Jacobe a few days ago after they'd won the first two games in the series, but it was a quick call and he'd been tired after playing. She'd suspected then that they would win the series. They'd been doing so well she couldn't foresee how they couldn't win. She'd expected him to call and tell her.

"He didn't call to tell you?"

"I talked to him a few days ago."

"He doesn't call you every night."

"So?" she asked, her voice sharp.

Luke raised one of his hands. "Sorry, I didn't mean anything by that. I just noticed, that's all."

"Why would you notice something like that?"

"I would have called you every day."

Danielle sighed and turned back to the window. "We've been there before, Luke. You didn't call me every day."

"A mistake I've learned from."

"Are you calling your girlfriend every night then? I haven't paid attention to how often you get on the phone." A true statement. She'd spent most of her time here talking to the Water for Kids people. Her time with Luke had been limited.

"I'm not seeing anyone right now. If that's what you're asking."

"That's not what I'm asking."

"That's what it sounded like."

Danielle turned fully in her seat and narrowed her eyes on him. "Are you trying to make a point, Luke?"

"Are you happy with him?" He glanced at her again. "Seriously?"

"That's none of your business."

"Sounds like a no."

He sounded so sure her back went rigid. "Not only am I happy with him, I love him."

Luke's head swung around and he stared at her wide eyed. The Jeep swerved to the right. He jerked it back in line with the train of vehicles in their party.

"You love him?"

"I do, and I think he feels the same."

Luke's brows went up. "You think?"

"Leave it alone." She turned back to the window, her face hot with anger and embarrassment. She sounded stupid. *I think he loves me.*

"Danielle, if he hasn't said he loves you, then you don't know for sure that's how he feels. You could just be making this up in your head."

"I'm not." She held up her hand to stop him from talking anymore. "Luke, we're friends. If you want us to remain that way, then stop talking. Stay out of my personal life."

Luke didn't say anything else for the remainder of the drive. Danielle stared out of the window, a multitude of thoughts swirling through her brain. They arrived at the next location thirty minutes later. She and Luke joined the rest of the group gathering around their guide's Jeep at the front of the caravan. Their guide had gone into the main building of the small town to find out about lodging before they unpacked all of their items.

The guide returned with a questioning look on his face. "They say someone from our group is already here." His eyes scanned the group. "I counted us all and no one left early or got lost."

"Are they sure it's someone from our group?" Luke asked.

"That's what the leader says. He said this guy came in yesterday and said he was with us."

"That sounds suspicious to me," Luke said. "Our trip isn't exactly a secret. It could be any wacko who knew we were coming here and is trying to get close to us."

"Apparently, the guy is out at the old well site now," the guide said. "He went there this morning. The villagers have already begun working on the irrigation trenches and he volunteered to help."

"Let's go see who this so-called volunteer is."

"I'll go with you," Danielle said.

Luke looked at her with concern. "Danielle, I'd prefer if you stayed here. We don't know anything about this guy. If he is crazy and things get rough, I'd rather you be away from any danger."

Danielle laughed. "I doubt a man who's helping villagers dig a trench would be dangerous. You said yourself one or two other celebrities wanted to volunteer but couldn't make it. Maybe it's one of them."

Luke sighed. "Fine, but stay behind me."

Danielle rolled her eyes. "I'm not some damsel in distress. I'll be fine."

"We'll go with you two," said one of the other football players from Luke's team.

Ten of them made their way to the old well site. If the volunteer was some crazy person, then they had nearly a ton of defensive linemen to answer to. The group of villagers digging the trench stopped as they noticed them approaching. They began talking excitedly and pointed to the people digging in the trenches. One man stood straight and cocked his head toward the villagers talking.

Danielle's breath caught in her throat. His back was turned, but she'd recognize that tall body and wide shoulders anywhere. When he turned to look at her, her heart danced. She grinned and took off running. Jacobe braced his arms on the side of the waist-deep trench and hauled himself out. He sprinted and reached her a few seconds later.

Danielle flung herself into his arms. "What are you doing here?"

"I'm dirty, Danielle," he said at the same time.

He was dirty. Filthy, actually. Dust and grime clung to his handsome face. She guessed his T-shirt was supposed to be white but was, instead, a rust color that matched the dirt on his jeans. She recognized them as an expensive pair that had never been made to wear during manual labor. He smelled like sweat and dirt. Beneath that the delicious musk that was all him.

"I don't care that you're dirty," she said. "Why are you here?"

"I'm digging a trench, woman. Can't you see?" He used his head to nod toward the trench.

"Don't be stupid. You just won the finals. Aren't you supposed to be going to Disneyland or working out the details of your transfer to Phoenix?"

"That's the thing—I'm not going to Phoenix."

Her heart jumped with excitement. "You aren't?"

"No. Jacksonville is home. The guys, coach, the city that I'm helping clean up—it's where I belong. Everything I want is there."

"Everything?"

His sexy grin made her body tingle all over. "Everything, including you. I should have said this before you left. I love you, Danielle. I shouldn't have let you leave without telling you how I feel."

Danielle wrapped her arms around his neck and squeezed him tight. "I love you, too, Jacobe. Even if you were going to Phoenix I would have wanted to make this work. Don't feel like you have to turn down the opportunity because of me."

"This is because of me. I've been afraid to trust people and to make a home for myself after what Christy did. Not anymore. I'm ready to make a new home with you—if you're ready to be mine forever."

She was so happy she could have exploded into a million pieces of stardust and it wouldn't have been enough. "I'm already yours forever. Only yours."

Epilogue

The sound of the ocean, along with the gentle sway of the hammock, and Jacobe's body curled up behind her, nearly lulled Danielle to sleep. Even being mostly naked except for the sheet wrapped around her, on a balcony in a villa in the French Riviera wasn't enough to keep her eyes open. Moonlight created shadows around them, she was thoroughly sated, completely happy, and absolutely lazy.

After leaving Malawi, Jacobe surprised her with a quick weekend in a villa along the French coastline. Tonight was their last night. She looked forward to getting back to work. Debra had kept her abreast of what was happening, and her parents were excited to see her. Well, maybe looking forward to wasn't the right phrase. Didn't dread was more suitable.

Jacobe tightened his hold around her. "I told you there is a definite perk to a vacation where all you do is have sex." His deep voice washed over her in the quiet night.

She smiled and snuggled closer into his warmth. "I wish it could last longer."

"I thought you were ready to go home."

"I miss my parents, and my friends," she said. "At the same time I never want to leave."

He kissed the top of her head. "Why?"

"Because I never want to forget how happy I am here with you."

"You won't. I'll make sure of it."

"Oh, really," she said in a low, pleased voice. "How are you going to do that?"

"By giving you something that will always remind you of tonight."

Danielle's eyes opened. Curiosity bubbled up inside of her. "You got me a gift?"

"Wait. I've got to get up." He slid her out of his embrace and got out of the hammock.

Danielle tightened the sheet around her chest and frowned. "Why? I liked laying here with you."

Jacobe grinned at her and wrapped the other sheet around his waist. "Just wait."

She let out a fake groan of annoyance. He went over to where his pants were folded over a chair. Danielle begrudgingly got up from her comfortable position to sit and let her legs hang off the side. Even though she wished he hadn't moved, she did enjoy the view of his muscular body in nothing but a sheet and moonlight.

Jacobe returned with a hand behind his back. He awkwardly lowered to one knee. The sheet around his waist hindered his movements. Danielle's throat constricted, and her heart danced.

"Danielle, will you do me the honor of marrying me?"

He brought his hand from around his back and opened a small black box that held a beautiful diamond ring.

Danielle sucked in a breath. Tears stung her eyes and happiness burst in her chest. "Yes!"

Jacobe got up and came to her. He took her hand in his and stared into her eyes. "Are you sure? I mean, I know this may seem sudden, but I love you, Danielle. I don't want anyone else, and I know I never will. I've wanted you since that first study session in college and nothing's changed. After all these years, I only want you more."

Tears slid down Danielle's face, but her smile couldn't be suppressed. Jacobe slid the ring on her finger then wiped away her happy tears. "Are *you* sure?" she asked. "Really sure. I love you, too, Jacobe. There's no one else for me, but you're going to be on the road. You're going to be giving up a lifestyle most men dream ab—"

He kissed her softly. "I'm completely sure. I've lived that lifestyle. I don't want do to that anymore. I want you with me at as many away games as you can make. There's no other woman I need by my side. In fact—" He leaned down and got his cell phone off the table near the hammock. "Hold up your hand."

She did and he took a picture of her with her hand up. The flash temporarily blinded her. After several blinks she watched him do something on his phone.

"What are you doing?"

"This." He held up the phone so she could see the screen. Her jaw dropped. He'd posted the picture online, thankfully of just her hand—diamond ring shining—next to her smiling face, with the caption: *She just made me the happiest man alive!!!*

Danielle laughed and snatched the phone from him. "I can't believe you did that."

He cupped the side of her face in his hand. "Let the world know I'm officially off the market. I've hid from relationships for too long. I won't hide this. I want everyone to know we're together. That I'll never leave you behind. That I love you."

Her heart filled with so much emotion, she couldn't speak. Tears came again. Jacobe leaned forward and kissed them away. Instantly her body responded. The masculine strength of his body pressed against hers, and she eased back in the hammock. His cell phone buzzed in her hand.

Danielle broke the kiss and looked at his phone. A text from Kevin popped up. Without her glasses, she squinted and read the message.

You owe me a G!!

"Why do you owe Kevin a thousand dollars?"

Jacobe grinned and looked at the message on the screen. He took the phone from her, which was now chiming with tons of responses to the picture. He silenced it before tossing the phone to the side. "Kevin told me from the start I was going to fall in love with you. He bet me. I lost."

"I would say I'm sorry," Danielle said grinning. She wrapped her arms around his neck.

"Don't." Jacobe pulled at her sheet until her body was naked beneath him. "That's a bet I'm happy to lose."

* * * * *

*Wealthy Alaskan Cash Outlaw has inherited a ranch and
needs land owned by beautiful, determined
Brianna Banks. She'll sign it over under one condition:
Cash fathering the child she desperately wants. But he
won't be an absentee father and makes his own demand...*

Read on for a sneak peek at
The Marriage He Demands
by New York Times *bestselling author Brenda Jackson.*

"Are you really going to sell the Blazing Frontier without
even taking the time to look at it? It's a beautiful place."

"I'm sure it is, but I have no need of a ranch, dude or
otherwise."

"I think you're making a mistake, Cash."

Cash lifted a brow. Normally, he didn't care what any
person, man or woman, thought about any decision he made,
but for some reason what she thought mattered.

It shouldn't.

What he should do was thank her for joining him for
lunch, and tell her not to walk back to Cavanaugh's office
with him, although he knew both their cars were parked there.
In other words, he should put as much distance between them
as possible.

I can't.

Maybe it was the way her luscious mouth tightened when
she was not happy about something. He'd picked up on it
twice now. Lord help him but he didn't want to see it a third
time. He'd rather see her smile, lick an ice cream cone or...
lick him.

He quickly forced the last image from his mind, but not before a hum of lust shot through his veins. There had to be a reason he was so attracted to her. Maybe he could blame it on the Biggins deal Garth had closed just months before he'd gotten engaged to Regan. That had taken working endless days and nights, and for the past year Cash's social life had been practically nonexistent.

On the other hand, even without the Biggins deal as an excuse, there was strong sexual chemistry radiating between them. He felt it but honestly wasn't sure that even at twenty-seven she recognized it for what it was.

That was intriguing, to the point that he was tempted to hang around Black Crow another day. Besides, he was a businessman, and no businessman would sell or buy anything without checking it out first. He was letting his personal emotions around Ellen cloud what was usually a very sound business mind.

"You are right, Brianna. I would be making a mistake if I didn't at least see the ranch before selling it. Is now a good time?"

The huge smile that spread across her face was priceless… and mesmerizing. When was the last time a woman, any woman, had this kind of effect on him? When he felt spellbound? He concluded that never had a woman captivated him like Brianna Banks was doing.

Don't miss what happens next in
The Marriage He Demands
by Brenda Jackson, the next book in her
Westmoreland Legacy: The Outlaws series!

Available April 2021 wherever
Harlequin Desire books and ebooks are sold.

Harlequin.com

HDEXP0321

Love Harlequin romance?

DISCOVER.

Be the first to find out about promotions, news and exclusive content!

Facebook.com/HarlequinBooks

Twitter.com/HarlequinBooks

Instagram.com/HarlequinBooks

Pinterest.com/HarlequinBooks

YouTube.com/HarlequinBooks

ReaderService.com

EXPLORE.

Sign up for the Harlequin e-newsletter and download a free book from any series at **TryHarlequin.com**

CONNECT.

Join our Harlequin community to share your thoughts and connect with other romance readers!
Facebook.com/groups/HarlequinConnection

HARLEQUIN

HARLEQUIN

Heartfelt or thrilling, passionate or uplifting—Harlequin is more than just happily-ever-after.

With twelve different series to choose from and new books available every month, you are sure to find stories that will move you, uplift you, inspire and delight you.